Cul de Sac
By Liz Crowe

Cul-de-Sac

Liz Crowe

Published by Liz Crowe, 2024.

CUL-DE-SAC

First edition. June 11, 2024.

Copyright © 2024 Liz Crowe.

ISBN: 979-8224183470

Written by Liz Crowe.

Table of Contents

Chapter One..1

Chapter Two...12

Chapter Three...22

Chapter Four...32

Chapter Five..40

Chapter Six...53

Chapter Seven...62

Chapter Eight...72

Chapter Nine..81

Chapter Ten..87

Chapter Eleven...98

Chapter Twelve... 106

Chapter Thirteen.. 114

Chapter Fourteen.. 125

Chapter Fifteen... 133

Chapter Sixteen 140

Chapter Seventeen 147

Chapter Eighteen.. 156

Chapter Nineteen.. 164

Chapter Twenty... 178

Chapter Twenty-One 187

Chapter Twenty-Two... 201

Chapter Twenty-Three 208

Chapter Twenty-Four.. 213

Chapter Twenty-Five 219

Chapter Twenty-Six 225

Chapter Twenty-Seven 235

Chapter Twenty-Eight... 242

Chapter Twenty-Nine 253

Chapter Thirty 258

Chapter Thirty-One... 265

Chapter Thirty-Two.. 270

Chapter Thirty-Three.. 275

Chapter Thirty-Four 284
Chapter Thirty-Five 291

This one is for you, Crowetowski.

Love ya.

Chapter One

---

*W*elcome to the Neighborhood

• • • •

"AND SO, AS YOU CAN see..."

Amelia ignored the real estate agent's droning voice and stared around at the perfect white-cabinet-and-stainless-steel kitchen. She took in the Instagram-worthy family room, the warm, walnut wood floors, and the gorgeous artichoke greens and heather grays that graced the walls. Her throat closed up. Her vision went blurry, all of which she could blame on her hormones doing their haywire dance.

Well, that and the extreme stress that this whole house-buying project had become.

"Ma!"

She blinked when her son called for her from somewhere then sighed and pressed her hands to her boobs, willing herself not to stain the pretty red polo shirt she'd put on that morning.

"In the kitchen," she said, more to herself than anyone else. She ran her palm along the length of cold granite. It wasn't the typical spec-house special. It was unique—black with irregular flashes of blue and silver that set off the stark-white designer cabinets so perfectly it made her back teeth ache.

It was the perfect kitchen. Exactly what she'd dreamed about when she started her social media mood board called *The Ross Family Home*. The process of researching different styles—craftsman, mid-century modern, faux farmhouse, generic suburbia—had forced her to admit she was firmly in the Venn diagram spot between craftsman and suburbia. Modern embellishments like cathedral ceilings, second-floor laundries, and giant mudrooms that kept the clutter and dirt from the outdoors away from the living spaces, were all on her must-have list. As were charm, coziness, a large main bedroom suite, and a finish-able basement, all at a minimum of twenty-eight hundred square feet.

She was firm in her desire not to have to renovate a kitchen or bathrooms. The last three houses they'd bid on had been, in some way or another, compromises on these requirements. It was probably why she'd managed to torpedo every deal, either based on a marginal inspector's report or the fact that known pedophiles lived within a quarter mile. A hard no for her, regardless of anything else.

"Ames?"

The sound of her husband's deep voice dragged her back to the here and now. She'd been busy staring out the French doors that led from the high-ceilinged den onto the expansive wooden deck overlooking the perfectly sized swath of green that would serve as play space for her children. She put a hand to her neck, ran her fingers along the thin necklace she wore. It calmed her, as it usually did.

"I love it. I want it."

Michael, her beloved spouse of the past four-and-a-half years blinked and shifted their little boy to his other hip. "You haven't checked out the upst—"

"I don't care. I love it and I want it. I know I haven't seen the upstairs yet. But unless there's a ghost in the attic or the basement is covered in black mold, I'm not going to change my mind."

She whirled to face their agent, a woman who'd stuck with them through all three fall-throughs Amelia had initiated with her dogged insistence that everything about her family's future home be perfect. Not for the first time, Amelia acknowledged her respect for the woman's sleek, pencil-skirted, form-fitting-blouse good looks. She was forty if she was a day but took care of herself. Something Amelia always admired. Letting herself go once she had kids and was past her thirties was something she had zero intention of doing.

"Melissa, how fast can you get our offer in front of the seller?"

"Ma!" her son squawked again. She held up a hand to keep Michael from relinquishing him. The timing was crucial. This was going to be her damn house, and nothing and no person was going to keep her from it.

"Well, as you know, you're seeing it before anyone else does. I haven't put a sign in the yard yet or entered it into the multi-list system." The woman's business-like, elegant blondeness had intimidated Amelia a little at first, but she'd done her due diligence and knew that Melissa Murphy was the best when it came to residential real estate. Amelia always went for the best and got it, if it was within her power to do so. Now that they'd spent all these hours together, between showings, negotiations, and three different house inspections, Amelia felt pretty close to the woman, in an odd way.

"Good. What's the price?"

"Wait, Amelia..." Michael said from somewhere to her left. She kept her hand up.

"Four-twenty-five," Melissa said.

The air whooshed out of her lungs. The room went dim as if a thundercloud had passed over the two massive skylights centered above her future kitchen island. "Are you joking? On this street? In this condition? What's wrong with it? It's worth five-ninety-five, minimum."

Amelia understood house values. Thanks to Zillow and Realtor.com, plus a year's worth of input from Melissa, she fully grasped what was what and where in the college town where she'd chosen to raise her family. She'd gone to university here. Had met Michael Ross, the love of her life, at a fraternity-sorority mixer her sophomore year. They'd agreed to come back after he finished law school in Chicago.

Or rather, she'd said that would be the only way she'd agree to push her baby plan up a year—if they moved back to Ann Arbor once he was hired by Taylor Thompson, one of the largest corporate law firms in Southeast Michigan. Amelia Stanhope Ross was a planner, a list-maker, a checker-offer of tasks. She'd mapped out her personal life in minute detail from the time she was old enough to write in her first journal—a sweet little purple notebook with an attached, sparkly pencil her mother had given her on her tenth birthday.

She'd ticked off all the *before I'm twenty-five* bucket-list items one by one. She'd backpacked around Europe. Spent two weeks on a yoga retreat in India. Had sex with a woman. And graduated cum laude from the university with a degree in business, emphasis: marketing. In the interim, she'd served as president of her sorority, organized a massive fundraising event for a local homeless shelter at the business school that had garnered her a bit of local celebrity bona fides, and met her future husband.

It was all going to plan, for the most part. She'd told Michael from the beginning that she expected them to own a house or at least a condo right after they got married. Her father would provide both the down payment and the co-signature on a loan if it were required, which it had been, which was fine with her because she'd chosen wisely. Michael Ross had graduated alongside her from the U with a business degree and had been accepted to four excellent law schools, including the one they'd chosen together. He was going to be, as her father liked say, "an earner." He'd take care of her and their future two children without any trouble whatsoever.

When he'd been offered the job back in Michigan, she'd been beside-herself ecstatic. A return to the idyllic, beautiful town where they'd met and always said they'd like to live as nonstudents—another tick off her list.

They hit the first major snag of their young marriage right after that when Michael suggested that instead of Ann Arbor, they live in one of the random Detroit suburbs, or even—horrors—Detroit itself. She'd balked. Michael took a firm stance that the house prices in Ann Arbor were ridiculous to the point of hysterical. They'd get a lot more house in, say, Ferndale or Allendale, or perhaps someplace farther to the north. They'd get a hell of a place if she'd allow herself to consider one of Detroit's downtown neighborhoods, many of which were reviving so fast residents would go to sleep looking at blight only to wake and find a shiny condo building in its place the next day.

Well, not literally but almost.

She'd agreed to consider it. Northwestern had really been her choice for his law school since it had put her close to her parents and her childhood home in Lake Forest—all forty-five-hundred square feet, water-side mansion of it. He'd taken her father's down payment and co-signature on a loan, keeping her current on her "to do by thirty" list. Their condo within walking and biking distance of campus wasn't fancy, but it was classy and a lot nicer than what almost anyone else had in his graduating class. They'd lucked out when it came time to sell it, with a market devoid of anything decent within walking distance to campus. Her father had insisted they keep all the proceeds, as she knew he would.

But Detroit? Seriously. She couldn't even consider Grosse Pointe. Not if Ann Arbor were on the table. No way. Yes, his commute would be a pain. But that wasn't her problem and it definitely wasn't the point. Having a happy wife and family to come home to was.

Hence her life timeline adjustment—unbeknownst to him, of course—which involved her getting pregnant earlier than they'd planned.

Twenty-nine had been her target age for becoming a mother for the first time. It seemed respectable to her. Not too early, and yet not too late that she'd have to worry about dried-up eggs or birth defects or anything else that might put a kink in things. The night they'd had a serious blowout argument, both sides digging in heels on the location of the Ross family's future homestead. She'd slammed the bedroom door in his face and sobbed for an hour, after which she consulted with her mom, ever the calm, collected giver of marital wisdom.

Resolved, she took a long hot shower, put on one of her slinkiest nighties, walked through a cloud of Hermes 24 Faubourg perfume, tossed her diaphragm into the trash, and got herself knocked up within two weeks. It was no hardship. Michael Ross had her number, sexually speaking, and could dial it up to a fever pitch with a flash of his dark eyes, a click of the softly padded handcuffs around her wrists. Amelia was addicted to his body and what he did with it, like a junkie needing a pop to make it through the day.

Amelia sometimes felt sorry for all the women in the world who didn't have Michael as their lover. Because at night—or at various times during the day when he wasn't studying or writing papers or doing his never-ending law school group work—his mild, agreeable, ever-positive persona morphed into something that had taken her by surprise at first. Until she realized that it was exactly what her high-strung, borderline obsessive/compulsive, control freak personality required in order to get off.

What had been a buzz that first time, in the dark, candlelit gloom of his somewhat damp-smelling apartment in college, had become something that transformed her into a walking horndog. He'd been the first man to ever satisfy her despite her ongoing efforts with several boyfriends and random hookups through college. Amelia had gone most of her adult life without knowing how an orgasm actually felt, until she'd met Michael.

That one time with the woman in the Dutch hostel didn't count.

It was a nice arrangement all the way around. A well-balanced relationship and marriage that kept some things under her control; like their social life, shopping, and meals, daily bill paying, vacation planning. While other things including lawn care, long-term financial stuff and taxes, and their sex life, well within his. Of course, she got pregnant and became a mother to Tyler a full two years earlier than she'd wanted. But it had gotten her to Ann Arbor, exactly as she had planned.

She'd bent on her resolve never to live in rented housing again since the whole sell-the-condo, move-for-the-job, and have-a-baby thing had tumbled down over them in a rush. The past year had been pleasant enough. She'd found a sweet older house to rent in Burns Park from a professor couple on sabbatical. It was a gentrified neighborhood near the university and downtown. She'd been fine to bring her baby home to that house, with its mix of new money and student neighbors.

But now, it was time to get real about where she'd raise her family. She touched the white gold necklace again—a piece of jewelry Michael had given her years ago—for strength to shove this thing past everyone's seeming reluctance.

Melissa's bright-blue gaze flicked over Amelia's shoulder, meeting Michael's, she assumed. "What?" She turned and glared at her husband. His expression was pensive. Tyler, their sixteen-month-old, was sound asleep against her shoulder, thumb lodged in his mouth. She reached over and pulled it out with a soft *pop*. Michael sighed. He was always after her to let the boy gnaw on his own fingers. "What's wrong with the house, Michael?" She used her *I'm dead serious* voice, knowing he would understand the gravity it imparted.

He blinked. "Nothing. I mean, nothing that I know of. Right, Melissa?"

Amelia could tell he was hiding something, but for some reason, at that moment, with the sun beaming down through the skylights and glancing off the giant six-burner Wolf stovetop, she didn't care. She shut her eyes, reopened them, and ran her fingertips down the spotless Sub-Zero stainless fridge door. Something that resembled a thrill of erotic energy ran down her spine, giving her full-body chills.

"Great. Let's offer four fifty."

"What?"

She didn't blame him for being shocked. She was a notorious underbidder. But as far as she was concerned, up to this point, she'd been dealing with inferior houses. This house was worth every penny of that and more. They were preapproved for well over six hundred thousand, thanks to the possibility of her father's co-signature and their condo sale proceeds as down payment plus their stellar credit scores. She did a quick mental calculation of what that translated to in terms of monthly principal, interest, taxes, and insurance, and realized it would be tight. But Michael was due for his first raise in another month. He was moving up the ranks with the exact speed she knew he would. All would be fine.

"Unless you think we should offer more?" She raised one eyebrow at her husband. He shook his head. "I want this one, honey. Real bad."

"Well, I'm all for making this happen. For real, this time." He shot her a pointed look. She smiled serenely. This was her bailiwick. She'd handle it. He was happy to surrender it to her.

Tyler yelped and threw his head back. She knew that face. He wanted to eat. "Here, give him to me." She was determined to breastfeed until he was twenty-four months and, besides, she enjoyed it. It gave her quality, one-on-one time with her baby. It was something only she could do for him, and she wasn't eager to stop, even though he was big for his age, and sometimes she felt self-conscious doing it in public. Not to mention it sapped every ounce of sexual energy out of her body, leaving her lying around like an empty wineskin, drained and useless. Even when Michael would come to her at night, eager to resume their formerly rambunctious state of affairs.

All the books and her obstetrician had supported her decision about her son's nutritional needs, however. Once she'd dumped the pediatrician who'd tried to convince her to put Tyler on rice cereal six months ago and found one who agreed with her about the gut-biome-building qualities of breast milk, she'd had all the professionals in her corner on it. And Michael claimed he didn't mind. His mother on the other hand...

Amelia shook her head, dismissing any negativity.

She had found her dream house.

And she was going to have it.

"Can we sign now, electronically?" She took a seat on the home stager's couch. She'd seen enough real furniture versus this fake stuff in the past year and half to know what she was looking at. She turned away from Melissa, lifted her shirt, shifted her bra aside. Tyler latched on with gusto, making her wince. "Honey? Michael, please?" She let a note of desperation creep into her voice, knowing the effect it would have on him, god bless him.

"Sure," Melissa said. "I actually thought you might feel this way, Amelia. I have everything ready to go right here. Michael, go ahead and sign for you both. You know the drill by now I think."

Amelia stared down at her son's face. She touched his cheek. His hand reached up as if to bat her away then rested on the top of her breast, the contrast between their skin hues breathtaking in a way that she'd adored from the first moment she'd laid eyes on Michael Ross, across the room from her having a beer with his fraternity brothers.

"We got our house, baby boy," she said, leaning down to touch her lips to his furrowed forehead.

Her life was perfect. Even though, sometimes, she'd had to deviate from her plans to get what she wanted. Once both sets of their parents had been informed of the engagement and the desired summer outdoor wedding, no amount of BS from either side would change their minds. The fact the Ross and Stanhope families would never participate in warm, multigenerational, Hallmark-channel-quality Thanksgivings or Christmases together was one regret. But she'd made her peace with it.

Besides, she'd already mapped out their holiday visiting plans, splitting them between the two families, who only lived twenty miles apart from each other after all, into the next ten years. No sweat. Planning was her thing.

She felt Michael's hand on her shoulder. She smiled up at him. Her life was right on track. And now she was about to get her dream house.

"Thanks, honey," she said, leaning against Michael's arm. Tyler disengaged and smiled up at his father, his full lips wet and split in a semi-toothy grin. "Da!" he blurted and scrambled off her lap and started messing with the house stager's display of fake fruit on the ottoman in front of them.

"Nope, Ty, not that," Michael said, scooping the boy up and onto his shoulders.

Amelia tucked herself away and stood, smoothing the wrinkle-free fabric of her khaki shorts over her flat stomach. She couldn't wait to move their stuff in, to fill these rooms with her tasteful things. She'd already ordered three rooms' worth of furniture, thanks to her father's housewarming gift of several thousand dollars. Michael had chafed for about three seconds then succumbed to the logic of it. Pretty house equaled happy wife. Happy wife equaled drama-free evenings and weekends. And maybe a return to their former sex life.

"Will we hear back from the seller tonight?" She watched her husband head for the front door—a classy, dark-wood style with arts-and-crafts glass sidelights—and tried not to scream at Melissa to get their offer in front of the seller now, not an *hour* from now.

"Yes, you will. She—the seller—is a friend of mine." Melissa paused, her wall of coolness melting a bit. "In the interest of full disclosure, my house is over there." She pointed through the front window at a house of similar vintage and style directly across the cul-de-sac.

This wasn't a fancy neighborhood. But Amelia understood the cache of living on this street, in an area of town with large lots and a variety of styles and vintages, where understated wealth didn't need to show off with obnoxious, overbuilt McMansions. There were chain-link fences around some of the yards, for heaven's sake. Talk about pedestrian. But never in a million years had she imagined they could afford to live here now. It was like...fate.

That cool, semi-sexual shiver of anticipation shot up Amelia's spine again. She swallowed and watched Michael bend over to grab Tyler, admiring the curve of his jeans-clad ass. Yes. She'd get this sorted, get Tyler into his own bedroom and off the breast soon so she'd be ready for her man to come back to her at night.

"Well then, we'll be neighbors."

"Yes." Melissa paused. "These people, the sellers, were good friends of ours. My husband's construction company did all the upgrades including the family room and deck addition last year. He did a full reno on the upstairs. You know, in the, um...main suite. Tom, the...husband, was an accountant. He handled my husband's company's books."

Amelia waited, sensing that a shoe was about to drop. "I see. So...were they transferred for his work, or something?"

"No," Melissa said, meeting her gaze with an expression that was part enthusiasm for a well-earned sale and part...pity. "No. Actually, and you should know this before we go any further."

Amelia rested her hand on her new granite countertop and tried not to scream. She waited a count of five then said, "I should know what, exactly?"

"Tom, the husband, he was an accountant, like I said. Had his own company. His wife, Laura, was a middle-school teacher and ESL tutor."

Amelia thought she saw the other woman's eyes glisten with the onset of tears. She clenched her jaw. "And?"

"Tom killed himself, here, in the house. In the master bedroom tub."

Amelia's blood froze. She curled her fingers into a fist, keeping it on the cold, comforting stone surface. "I see."

"So, if you want to think about it for a night…" Melissa closed her laptop. "I would totally understand. I mean, Ryan, that's my husband, he and his team demolished the entire suite and rebuilt it. It's not even the same floor plan up there, much less the same, ah… you know, tub." She paused. "I'm sorry. I'm babbling."

"That's why it's underpriced," Amelia said. She felt clammy and weak even as that odd sensation of wanting—needing—this house so badly continued to thrum up and down her spinal column.

"Yes." Melissa tucked her laptop into her Coach bag. "Seriously Amelia, I would love to have you as neighbors." Her gaze flicked out onto the lawn where Michael was running around with Tyler. A shiver of something else coated Amelia's brain. Something not unlike the old-fashioned saying about a goose walking over your grave.

She shook her head. Utter nonsense. She was eager, anxious, and probably horny. All of which she planned to alleviate within the next few weeks, in her new house, her new bedroom, on her new walnut four-poster, with a California king sized Tempur-Pedic Cloud Supreme Breeze mattress she and her mother had picked out together.

"I want the house, Melissa. I'll skip the inspection at this point, if there are other offers."

Melissa smiled at her, the genuine relief pouring out of her nearly visible. "No need for that. I know it will pass. And if anything needs to be worked on, I sleep with the guy who can fix it." She winked. Amelia frowned at this. Melissa had been all business, rarely joked about anything, super serious from the start. But she guessed now that they'd be neighbors instead of in an agent-client relationship, things would change. She smiled.

"Great." She stuck out her hand. To Amelia's complete surprise, Melissa grabbed her and pulled her in for a tight hug. "Okay, then," she said, disentangling herself.

"I'm on it," Melissa said with yet another wink as she held the front door open for Amelia. When she gave Michael a similar, out-of-character, full-body hug, he raised an eyebrow at her over Melissa's shoulder. She shrugged. Things would change now, she supposed. And it would be nice to know someone on the cul-de-sac from the start.

Chapter Two

Who Is That?

* * * *

"DEAR LORD, IT'S HOT as blue blazes today." Janice Cooper pressed the sweating glass of iced tea to her forehead.

"It is," her neighbor Emily agreed. She'd brought over a curried tofu salad and some lemon bars for the afternoon Euchre game. Janice had provided the tea. The other two women who'd been playing, a couple of Janice's friends from the country club, had already left. The late-August afternoon was hot, but the breeze they caught from their perch on the wraparound porch cut through it enough to be pleasant.

A childish squeal of laughter followed by a lot of splashing filled the air. Janice smiled over at the pool where her two grandsons and their nanny were playing. Emily closed her eyes and let her mind wander. She'd not been sleeping well for the past week or two for reasons she absolutely refused to attribute to perimenopause. Sai, her husband, could tell something was off about her, but she'd managed to avoid the topic. Talking about it wasn't going to help. She figured it wouldn't last much longer. If she confessed it to him, he'd have her on some kind of hormone replacement therapy that would make it all that much worse.

She sighed at the memory of spending her thirties on every possible form of hormones, desperately seeking motherhood, only to be repeatedly denied by the gods, or karma, or maybe the devil himself. Emily had no desire to take them ever again, regardless of her body's failings. Oddly, or perhaps not, her libido had been stuck in high gear for about a month, which helped keep Sai off track. But Emily sensed herself fading from that state as well. She sighed again and stared down at her red-painted toenails peeking out from her practical flat sandals.

Janice patted her hand. Emily smiled at her friend, the woman who'd sat with her through a particularly difficult, late-term miscarriage while Sai had been away teaching new cardiothoracic surgeons his groundbreaking techniques. "You all right?"

Emily shrugged and sipped her tea. It was fresh lemon and mint infused. Delicious and perfect for the Michigan summer afternoon as it eased toward evening.

She wasn't okay. She was antsy and bored. Summers always did this to her. It was a recipe for disaster, really, her being bored and antsy. She ended up spending too much money on stupid things like hummingbird feeders, fancy smoothie makers that would end up gathering dust in a forgotten corner of a cabinet, more patio furniture, and organic jackfruit. That stuff was simply gross, and being a vegetarian was no excuse to have to eat it.

She had to stop herself from sighing again. Her legs felt restless. Her skin was crawling with something she couldn't quite name. She and Sai had had sex the night before—the slow, satisfying, long-lasting kind he was really great at. This morning, before he'd left for the hospital, he'd cornered her in their oversized shower for another go 'round, this one hard, fast, almost painful but somehow necessary as the showerheads sprayed them from above and two sides.

"Hell-oh, ladies," a male voice called to them from the patio surrounding the pool. Janice raised her hand to greet her husband. Emily lifted her chin, suddenly too exhausted to move any other part of her body. She felt mired in mud, weighed down as if by chains attached to rocks. This didn't stop her from admiring Janice's husband's rear view as he pointed a huge water gun at the boys cavorting around in the shallow end. He wore a pair of swim trunks emblazoned with the block M of the university where he'd once worked as a professor in the medical school and as a successful, sought-after plastic surgeon. His tanned back and broad shoulders gleamed in the late-afternoon sun. His biceps flexed as he worked the pump on the toy gun.

The boys ducked under the water and tried to swim away from him. He laughed and ran around to the other side of the pool. Hating herself but unable to stop, Emily stared at his muscular chest and washboard-flat abs for a few seconds longer before realizing that he was staring over at them, the water gun at his side.

"Allen, would you be a love and please bring out the tea pitcher?" Janice called over to him. He shot her a salute. As he jogged back around the pool and into the house, Emily tensed all over.

Janice patted her hand again. She flinched away from the other woman's touch. Rude, she knew. She ought to be grateful for Janice and Allen Cooper. She should be happy to have them as her neighbors. And she was. Most days.

"How's Sai doing?" Janice asked, breaking into Emily's onrushing urge to get up and follow Allen into the house. "Getting ready for a fresh crop of residents I guess?"

"What? Oh, um...yes. That's right. He is." Emily reminded herself that Janice would be familiar with the annual influx of newbie doctors at the U. Allen had been surgeon to plenty of celebrities who'd fly to their tiny little Midwestern town in their private jets for the privilege of his surgical attention. And he worked with poor children in far-flung countries. Not unlike her own husband, the short, wiry Doctor Sai Arya, overachieving favorite son of Indian immigrants and fellow doctor. Sai was a cardiothoracic genius, much published, well-compensated and traveled, thanks to his commitment to Doctors Without Borders.

Sai wasn't quite as much of a physical specimen as her neighbor's husband. But he wasn't hard to look at, and he knew his way around her body like any good husband of twenty-plus years should. He was only an inch taller than she, at five foot eleven, but he put in his time at the gym, swimming five days a week and lifting weights. He was the sort of soft-spoken hero any woman would feel honored to have as a spouse.

And she was comparing these men, why, exactly?

She sighed then stopped halfway through it, glanced over at Janice, and smiled. "Sorry. I'm lame. I hate summers."

Janice smiled and set her empty tea glass on the table in front of their rocking chairs. "I used to get the same way. Come August first, I was chomping at the bit to get the kids out from under my feet." She stretched her long, slim legs out in front of her.

They sat in companionable silence a few minutes. Allen appeared at the end of the porch and headed up the steps and toward them. He held the crystal pitcher of tea, a fresh glass overflowing with ice, and a bottle of Pimm's.

"Thought we might liven this evening up a touch. You ladies game?" He raised one eyebrow and met first his wife's then Emily's gazes.

"You need fruit for that drink, Allen," Janice said, her smile indulgent. Emily took in her perfect nose, lineless face, the slim neck that should by right have a bit of sag to it. But then again, if you're married to a renowned plastic surgeon, your level of aging is akin to drinking from the fountain of youth every morning. Emily put a hand to her stomach, which was softer than she liked it to be.

"I do know, lovely wife," Allen said as he set the pitcher, ice, and bottle on the table. "And I will return with the rest of the required ingredients." He winked at Emily. She blushed and moved her hand up to her neck that was, she knew, saggier than it ought to be. She'd been riding the weight-struggle bus for a long time. Her years in culinary school had translated to a twenty-pound gain, which she'd lost when she'd met and fallen for the charming Dr. Arya in France. After their wedding, when she'd thrown herself with gusto into the effort to get pregnant and had learned that it was a losing effort no matter what they did or how much money they spent, she'd ballooned by thirty pounds.

That had stuck around, which put her at a weight that made her unhappy, at least during the summer months when she didn't have spelling tests and other school nonsense to distract her. She loved the nonsense. The fall semester especially was her happy place. It allowed her to do what she adored—to be around children, to guide them through the perils of modern elementary school, to chatter and gossip with her fellow teachers in the break room. She loved the smell of pencils, cardboard, new backpacks—even the lunchroom that always held the slightest tinge of puke. Part and parcel of her work life. And she'd not change a thing about it.

Unless, of course, someone approached her about taking over the kitchen at a legit restaurant. But she had sworn off life-choice regrets. They dragged her down and made her want to eat nonstop.

She smoothed the batik fabric of her dress over her thighs. Her wardrobe mostly now consisted of shapeless maxi dresses like the one she had on now. It was an expensive, designer, shapeless maxi dress and she could afford it. But that didn't change the fact that right now, this minute, she felt as frumpy as someone's grandma wearing it.

When she taught, she transitioned to slightly more formal wear. But the past couple of years, she'd given up trying to wear designer clothes like she had when she'd gotten her first teaching job, as the split K-first-grade teacher for the school where she now taught fourth grade. It was too frustrating to find nice things in her size.

Sai claimed he loved her exactly the way she was. Never said a single word about her weight one way or another. He was one of the good ones. She loved him. She was lucky to have him. But her lack of ability to bear children sometimes made her scream at him, throw things then eat an entire bag of Doritos, drink a liter of sugary soda, and sleep for twelve hours in the guest room so she didn't have to look at him, to see disappointment in his dark, expressive eyes.

Her life.

But at least school was starting soon.

A hand on her shoulder made her flinch. "You look nice today, Emily," Allen said as he put a bowl of cut limes, oranges, and cucumbers down next to the tea. "I like that color on you. It brings out your eyes."

"Oh, you charmer," she said, feeling the blush creep up her neck to heat her face. If she were honest with herself, she didn't care about the extra weight anymore. She was soft, comfy, with a tendency to take care of anyone and everyone around her. It made her a great teacher. There was no need to be a size six or eight to do that, and she'd never been big on denying herself the things she liked.

She had a good life. A job she enjoyed, a beautiful home with great neighbors. A fabulous, loving doctor spouse and wonderful in-laws who adored her. She smiled at Allen who took a little longer than was polite to take his hand off her shoulder. And that was okay, too.

Janice put the drinks together. They clinked glasses. The Pimm's tea was delicious, tart, thanks to the fruit, with a nice bite from the gin that served as the base of the brown liqueur. It gave the tea a lemonade-like tang that made it go down way too easy. Emily had never been great with booze. She was an eternal lightweight. Sai rarely drank, and she'd had no reason to keep beer or wine in the house before they moved here. Of course, once they'd been enveloped by her new neighbors, alcohol had become a much bigger part of their lives.

She'd still get tipsy after one drink, and could find herself full-on drunk in a room full of people who were only getting started.

Today, she was determined to enjoy the Pimm's Cup on her friend's porch on a nice Michigan summer evening, with a mere week and a half before she got to resume her life as the most-sought-after fourth-grade teacher at the best school in town. Janice and Allen chatted, but the sound was buzzy, like locusts in the distance.

Emily sipped and let her gaze rest on the house next door. The Franks' house. Where Tom and Laura and their two kids—what in the hell were their names—had lived and participated in the various cul-de-sac parties and other activities. She'd had the oldest in her class a year before. What in the world was his name?

It was also where Sai had gone when Laura had shown up at their door, pounding on it, screaming, her face covered in tears and mascara, demanding that Sai come and help her husband.

It had been too late, of course.

Emily shivered and put her empty glass on the table. Allen held out the Pimm's bottle, his hazel eyes shining. She smiled and shook her head. He held it up higher. She giggled. Put a hand over her lips and nodded. She liked Allen. She always had. He had a way of making everyone in the room immediately comfortable, no matter what the situation. She giggled again. Better watch it, or she'd have to be carried across the street later.

The sound of a diesel engine made them all look up. Allen handed her a freshly charged glass. She took it and sipped and watched while a U-Haul pulled forward toward the Coopers' house then backed into the Franks' driveway.

"Melissa said she sold that place," Janice said.

"It'll be nice to have new neighbors. Did she say anything about them?" Allen's voice was neutral, but Emily thought she picked up on something between him and his wife. Something that flared and then faded, like fog on a sunny morning.

"Not really, but we haven't had a chance to talk much. She and Ryan have been up north for most of August with Danny. His girls joined them for the last couple of weeks."

Emily let their gossipy conversation about the comings and goings of Melissa and Ryan Murphy flow around her. She wondered who the new people would be. What they'd be like. If they'd fit in. If they'd become a part of the cul-de-sac social circle the way the Franks had been. In some ways, she almost wished they wouldn't. But Janice and Allen Cooper would play welcome wagon in that special way they had. And the new family would get absorbed, one way or another.

As she watched, a tall, muscular Black man climbed down from behind the steering wheel. Another man, not quite as tall but equally impressive looking, hopped down from the passenger side, walked around to the back, and lifted the door. They were talking, but she couldn't hear their words, thanks to the ceiling fans purring above her on the porch. She wanted to hold up a hand, to tell Janice and Allen to shush. But that would be rude.

She sipped some more and watched as the two men moved a couch, some small tables, and a ton of plastic bins, all carefully labeled, into the garage and then into the house. She knew the Franks' house as well as she knew her own. As well as she knew the Coopers', the Murphys', and the LeBlancs'. The houses that made up their cul-de-sac were more familiar to her than she'd ever thought neighbors' homes would be.

The men paused after emptying the rental truck. One of them pulled a cooler from the front seat and set it in the mostly empty garage. The other one, the taller one who was, Emily noted, a mere hairsbreadth from perfect-looking with a strong resemblance to that actor...who was he?

She sipped and watched as the men popped open two stadium chairs and sat, clinked a couple of beer bottles together then drank.

"Guess the new owners don't mind if their moving guys cop a squat in the garage, huh?" Allen sipped his drink and glanced out over his own lawn. It was the biggest one, the anchor house. Not the oldest—that one would be Barrett and Cassie LeBlanc's. But it was large, built in the early sixties, massively renovated and added onto over the years.

"Hmmm," Emily said, curious about them. They were, in a word, hot. Both of them, with their deep-brown skin, bright white teeth, close-cropped hair, and massive shoulders straining T-shirts. She was all tingly now, probably from the booze, of course, but the moving-man show next door wasn't helping.

Guess her libido was still going to let her enjoy some things in life after all. She'd figured it for a blip in her dysfunctional hormones. A bit of fun, but something that would fade, leaving her holding another empty bag of disgusting, fake-cheese-coated food in one hand, a wineglass in the other.

"Well, I will say, that one looks like a young Denzel Washington," Janice said in a whisper, her green eyes narrowed as she pretended not to stare as overtly as Emily was doing.

"You should go on over and introduce yourself, then," Allen said.

She frowned at him. "Stop it."

"Stop what? I know you prefer them young."

"*Stop* it, Allen."

He finished his second drink and put the empty glass on the table with a loud thunk. "Emily here would know, wouldn't you, hon?" He patted her thigh. She shifted out of his reach. The Coopers were the epitome of community pillars and conducted their private life well beneath the surface, speaking in modulated tones of euphemism and code. Something was most definitely going on between them. Likely a function of the fact that their complicated cul-de-sac, close-knit relationships had come to an abrupt halt six months earlier with the death of Tom Franks.

"Let us enjoy the eye candy for a second, would you please, Allen, without editorial commentary," Emily insisted, keeping her voice neutral. "I was thinking more Tyler James."

"Who?"

"You know, the one in that show, about teachers?"

Janice slid her sunglasses up to her hair and squinted at the moving men still sitting in the garage. "You know, you're right. But that other one is all Denzel, only younger."

The men got up, folded their chairs, and leaned them against one wall, still inside the garage. Emily heard a phone bleeping. The taller man tugged a phone from his jeans pocket and put it to his ear. He walked out to one side of the truck, which sent the sound of his voice lifting up and across to them.

"Okay, okay, I know. We took a minute to catch our breath and have a beer. Relax." He leaned against the giant picture of a wolf or some other doglike creature that was painted on the rental truck. He stayed silent a few seconds, as the person on the other end of the call obviously had a few things to say about that.

"Amelia," he said after a bit. "Would you please give it a rest? I know I'm going to be gone but...I'm trying to...what...I mean..." He closed his eyes, apparently frustrated.

Emily glanced at Janice who was staring at the guy on the phone, her lips slightly parted. She looked at Allen who was in the rocking chair between them, ankle crossed over the opposite knee. He was still in his block-M trunks but had pulled a soft-looking dark-gray T-shirt over his bare torso before joining them. For a half second, Emily wished he hadn't. Then a loud curse from the vicinity of the moving van distracted her again.

"Brother, you got yourself in deep with that one," the other man said, clapping the taller one on the shoulder. "I do not envy you. No, sir, I do not."

"Well, I told her I'd do this before I left. She's in charge of the rest of it, and it's making her a little..."

"Whacked? Psycho? And this is new?"

The taller man glared at his fellow mover. "She's my wife. Have some respect."

The other guy held up his hands, as if surrendering. "You have my respect, my brother. All of it. Always have."

"Good. Let's go. I need to get at least one more load of boxes done then I have to get some sleep. I gotta be at the airport at five in the morning."

The other man whistled. "Gotta make sure the missus gets a place like this, huh?"

"Get in the damn truck."

They climbed into the truck and pulled out onto the cul-de-sac. Allen rose and stretched, giving Emily a nice, up-close view of his abs when his shirt lifted just enough in front of her. He headed indoors, and, the next thing she knew, the strains of Simon and Garfunkel were wafting out of hidden speakers. He held a hand out for her. She shook her head. She needed to go home. Maybe take a cold shower.

He held out his hand for his wife. Janice smiled and rose to her feet, graceful as a ballerina. They were dancing on the porch when she left. "I'll get my dishes later," she called over her shoulder, eager to get home, to that shower, or perhaps to her vibrator.

She glanced back at the two of them before she headed across the minimal expanse of asphalt that separated her house from the Coopers'.

Janice had her head on her husband's shoulder. He had one hand on her ass, the other held her hand, their fingers threaded together. They were such an attractive couple, Emily mused. No wonder they could do what they did. And convince everyone else to join them.

A shiver ran down her spine. She could hear Laura Franks' screaming, sobbing hysteria as if it were happening again, right now. She stopped playing Peeping Tom with her neighbors as they started kissing on their front porch and took the last few steps to her own house at a near run.

Chapter Three

M *oving Guys*

• • • •

LATER THAT NIGHT, EMILY sat with a cup of hot tea, willing herself sober and knowing it for a losing cause when a loud rap at her sliding glass door made her jump and spill a bit of the hot liquid on her bare leg. With mild curse, she hobbled into the kitchen and grabbed a hand towel the cleaning lady had helpfully draped through the stove handle. After blotting the mess and deciding she didn't need any first aid for it, she opened the door, unsurprised by who she saw there.

"Hey, Cassie. What's up?"

The young woman held a plastic dish with a lid. "I made some of your favorite," she said with a big smile. Emily tried to smile back. Her stomach was feeling more than a little iffy after those drinks. She stepped back.

"Great! Thanks. Come on in."

The woman hauled herself into the eating nook, her belly poking out enough that her condition couldn't be politely ignored. It made Emily's head spin, watching her flaunt the damn thing. But, of course, she wasn't flaunting it.

Emily took the proffered plastic dish and pulled off the lid. Six uniformly created falafel patties sat in a nest of dark greens alongside a dish of tahini sauce. She grinned. These were her favorite. It was sweet of Cassie to bring them. She hadn't eaten since lunch. No wonder she felt sloshed after two drinks. "Thanks, hon," she said. She reached for the cabinet to get a couple of plates for them.

"None for me, thanks." Cassie rubbed her baby bump unselfconsciously. "I can't keep anything down."

"Still?" Emily asked around a bite of the delicious chickpea concoction. "Wow, these are good."

"Thanks." Cassie looked around. Emily noted that the hollows of her cheeks were more pronounced than ever, and the dark circles she'd developed under her huge brown eyes now resembled ugly bruises. "Is Sai home?"

Emily ignored the hopeful tone of the other woman's voice. Sai always catered to their neighbor's borderline hypochondria. And why not? She was a gorgeous example of a trophy wife. Or at least she had been at one point in time. Now she looked positively haunted, and way too thin to be healthily pregnant.

As hard as it was for Emily to look at her, she made herself do it. Her natural tendencies to mother everyone extended to Cassandra LeBlanc more than most, and she knew it.

"No, not yet. Won't be until after ten most likely."

"Oh okay." The young woman seemed to wilt. "Sorry." She swiped at her face.

Emily put the dish of falafel on the table and draped her arm around Cassie's bony shoulders. "It's all right. Want some tea?"

"Sure, thanks. Chamomile if you have it."

"I do. Have a seat. I'll be right back."

She snagged another patty on her way past the table, dunked it in the sauce, and popped it into her mouth. How Cassie managed to make the most boring vegan food interesting was something that always fascinated her. Sai was strict vegetarian but not vegan, thank heaven. If Emily had to give up eggs and cheese, she might not have stayed married to him. She'd learned how to cook traditional Indian foods from her mother- and grandmother-in-law. But Cassie had taught her how to turn what could be a boring round of salads interspersed with random curries and tofu biryanis into something that made her eager to research what she could do with grains, legumes, leafy greens, and spices.

She'd be the first to admit that she'd learned as much from the former-paralegal-turned-yoga-wellness instructor and wife to wealthy Barrett LeBlanc, as she had during her brief stint at culinary school. The LeBlancs had moved into the house next to hers not long after she and Sai had completed their renovations, and she'd had her second miscarriage. Emily had been enthralled by them at first—rich, older super-alpha-male attorney with the sweet, sweet, soft-spoken but almost painfully attractive younger woman. Emily and Cassie had bonded immediately over their love of cooking and the fact of their mutual late addition to the cul-de-sac. They'd moved in within about six months of each other, joining the well-established Cooper-Murphy-Franks' friend group.

Melissa and Ryan Murphy lived on Emily's other side. Close enough for her to experience the volatility of the successful Realtor and contractor's marriage a little too much for her comfort. "The Murphys are either fighting or fucking," Laura Franks had observed once.

Emily had no reason to argue that point. Melissa intimidated the hell out of Emily and always had. But she wasn't home much. Her successful real estate career kept her busy, and Ryan ran his own construction company, which meant he was gone almost as much as his wife. Emily felt closer to Melissa's mother, Anne, who'd been their primary babysitter when their boy, Danny, was small.

She put the kettle on the stove and flipped on the gas, found some of her favorite chamomile mix, and filled the tea diffuser with enough for two cups. She could hear Cassie flipping through the Netflix options, the distinctive "bloop bloop" sound it made a strange sort of comfort. She couldn't help but feel protective of the woman, after what had happened. Even before that, when she and Sai had been at one of the cul-de-sac's many social gatherings, she'd felt drawn to her, looking tiny and birdlike and intimidated next to her spouse.

As she was half remembering one of their evenings together back when Tom and Laura Franks had been around, she heard the distinct low rumble of a diesel truck again. She turned off the burner and poured the not-quite-boiling water into the diffuser to let it steep before rushing over to the front window. She flipped open the wooden blinds enough to confirm what she suspected. The U-Haul with the beautiful mover men was back.

"Cassie, c'mere." She motioned for the woman to join her in the dining room. "You have to see this."

The women watched as the men got out of the truck, opened the back, and hauled in more furniture and plastic tubs. By the time they were finished, it was almost full dark. The street lights in the cul-de-sac shone their environmentally correct pale-blue light, highlighting the men as they wrapped up the work, had a beer then stood by the truck, seemingly deep in conversation.

"Nice eye candy, Emily, thanks." Cassie elbowed her in the ribs. "You're practically panting. Do you need a cold shower?"

"Way ahead of you. Took one already. This is my second viewing tonight. They came earlier, while I was over at the Coopers'."

"Girl, you are bad." Cassie giggled. At that moment, she reminded Emily of the carefree, friendly woman she'd met when she and Barrett had moved in.

"Yes, well, it was pleasant." She shut the blinds.

It had been more than pleasant, she admitted. This second time around had revved her all the way up. She glanced at her phone, wishing it were closer to ten so her husband would be home. Granted, he'd reek of hospital, be exhausted, hungry, and grumpy as a bear. But she knew how to fix all of that. She'd made a gazpacho earlier, one of his favorites, and could offer up Cassie's delicious falafel as a side dish now.

That gave her pause.

Cassie as a side dish, indeed.

Ugh. She had to stop thinking like that. Continuously backsliding into memories didn't help her at all.

"I should go, I guess," Cassie said before flopping onto Emily's leather couch again. "I don't like being in that house alone, you know?"

"How long is Barrett gone for?" Emily poured their tea and brought the cups into the den. She set them on the large wooden trunk she used for a coffee table.

"Another week. Thanks. Smells yummy."

They sipped their tea in silence a few seconds. When she heard Sai's Audi pull into the garage, she smiled into her cup. He was early. Good. Now all she had to do is get rid of Cassie somehow without being rude or making herself feel shitty about it.

The door between the garage and the first-floor laundry-slash-mudroom opened with a jaunty jingle from the bell she kept on the doorknob. It was something she'd found while they'd been on one of their trips to India, at the gift shop of one of the more commercially savvy ashrams. Silly, she knew, on a lot of levels. But the sound soothed her and always had. It was now one of those sounds she associated with her home, her life, with the pleasant experience of her husband coming home from work.

"Hey, babe," she called from her perch in her favorite chair. Her reading chair, with its ergonomically correct lamp and well-positioned ottoman. "You're early."

"Yeah. Last surgery got canceled. Jesus, I am— Oh, hello, Cassie."

Sai stopped between the den and kitchen. He was dressed as he had been when he left that morning—in a dark-blue suit, white shirt, and silk tie. The only difference, the top button of his shirt was undone, and the tie hung loose. Well, that and his stubble. Emily had given up convincing him that it was sexy, thanks to the bearded doctors on popular TV shows. He shaved every morning without fail, and by this time every night, his jaw was dark again.

Emily looked closer, sensing something off about him. He looked tired, as he always did on days he did back-to-back surgeries. But there was something else. She rose and went to him, wrapped her arms around his neck and pressed her lips to his. His hand was warm on the small of her back but the embrace felt just this side of perfunctory.

She watched him glance over her shoulder toward the pouty pregnant girl/woman on their couch. A thrill of something a tad too close to jealousy hit the base of her brain. "I'm glad you're home," she said, trying to keep the aggravation out of her voice. "I made gazpacho."

"Huh?" He blinked fast, and, with what seemed to Emily like a massive effort, shifted his gaze from Cassie to her. She barely resisted the urge to shake him.

"Dinner? You know, food?" She could hear the edge in her tone. She swallowed and forced herself to smile. It was to be expected, she reminded herself. Considering.

"Right, yes, thanks." He put his leather backpack down and rubbed his eyes. "I'm sorry, Ems. I'm wrecked."

She patted his arm and headed for the fridge, leaving him to whatever was going on in his head about Cassie LeBlanc. It wasn't like she could do anything about it anyway. Might as well get some food into him, to avoid the hangries.

"How're you feeling, Cassie?" Sai asked, keeping his distance and using what Emily knew was his clinical office voice. "Nausea any better?"

"Not really."

"I'm sorry to hear it. You look a little run-down. Have you been sleeping well?"

"Not really," she repeated.

Emily clenched her jaw with the effort not to snap back at her, to remind Cassie how lucky she was to be pregnant, regardless of the circumstances. Everyone knew *her* sob story. She was sick of hearing it herself. It was time, as her practical husband liked to remind her, to move on with her life and stop letting infertility define her.

Blah. Blah. Blah.

She scooped a portion of the cold soup into a deep bowl and topped it with sour cream and fresh cilantro. After deciding that she would keep the falafel patties for herself, she pulled a container of cold, seasoned polenta from the fridge and warmed it in the microwave while Sai did a perfunctory, arm's-length exam of their sad-faced neighbor.

When Sai's long-fingered, brown-skinned hands touched Cassie's bump, Emily experienced a visceral, throat-clogging surge of raw fury.

Not that her husband was touching another woman.

Hardly that.

But that her husband's capable, loving hands were practically caressing another woman's pregnant belly. Something he would never do to her.

She turned away from the scene, biting back tears, or a scream, or both. When she set the bowl, spoon, cloth napkin, and dish of polenta on the table, Sai must have concluded his exam since Cassie was sitting and staring toward the steps. For something like the millionth time, Emily's regret at her past behaviors and choices filled her chest and throat.

What had they been thinking?

Well, they hadn't been, really. They'd been consumed by the scene, the options, by the way Janice and Allen orchestrated her and Sai's introduction to the neighbors—the Murphys and the Franks—and their odd closeness. By the time Cassie and her attractive spouse had moved in to the vacant house next door, with Melissa's assistance, the whole thing had felt natural.

Big mistake. Colossal. Gargantuan. One she didn't intend to allow herself to make again.

"I should go," Cassie said, hauling herself up from the couch. She arched her back, which forced Emily to stare at her bulging belly. "Thanks for the tea, Em." Cassie brushed Emily's cheek with her cold lips and headed for the sliding door.

"No need to rush off, Cassie," Sai said when he reappeared at the foot of the staircase in a pair of jeans and a T-shirt. Emily glared at him then forced her expression to soften. He was only being polite. He wanted her out of their space as badly as she did, and she damn well knew it. The young woman turned, her eyes watery and hopeful and pinned on Emily's handsome, if scruffy-looking, husband.

Cassie's husband, Barrett, was easily the hottest man Emily had personally ever laid eyes on. He was a full-on, larger than life, at six foot four with the sort of body you might think was photoshopped, especially after you found out that he was fifty-eight years old. His coal-black hair, bright-blue eyes, and full, expressive lips were, in a seriously clichéd word, mesmerizing. He was brash and funny, if a little rude, and loved his racy jokes, but managed to get away with it. And of course he was rich.

All of them were that—rich. The fact that Barrett chose to downplay his wealth by not living in a huge cookie-cutter mansion and instead inhabiting a tasteful, 1960s era, center-entry colonial on their deceptively modest street confused a lot of people. If you listened to him, he'd been there, done that with the mansions and whatnot with his first two wives. For this, his third attempt at marital bliss, he desired a more low-key lifestyle to match his more low-key wife choice. Cassie was perfectly happy with that, she'd claimed to Emily more than once. She was "concerned about their carbon footprint" and hated over-the-top houses and gas-guzzling cars. Hers was a zippy, bright-blue electric something-or-another, Emily could never recall.

Barrett owned places in South Carolina and Jackson Hole, as well as Charlevoix on Lake Michigan. He had three classic Mustangs, and a custom Harley Davidson. He didn't exactly go out of his way to hide any of this. He and Cassie used to split their summer time between here and up north and took skiing trips to Europe, bespoke cruises on the Med, the works. This summer of course, had been a different animal altogether.

The bottom line was that her Sai—with his much shorter stature, milder personality, willingness to stay well out of any social-gathering spotlight—was the polar opposite of Cassie's husband. But, for all of that, Cassie had been drawn to Sai from the start.

Sai stared at Cassie for a few seconds more before he met Emily's gaze, his eyes wide, his expression with a shade of desperation to it. Emily put her arm around Cassie's shoulders again and guided her to the door, opened it, and eased her out into the night. She couldn't recall what words she used to get rid of her, but they must have worked.

She turned and faced her husband, who'd dropped into a chair and was staring down at the gazpacho as if it might reveal the secrets to the universe. "Water?" she asked, determined to keep this night neutral, drama-and-deep-discussion free. She wasn't in the mood for it. What's done was, as they say, done. No need to cry over already spilt milk—or over the proverbial horse that had exited the proverbial barn before the proverbial door got slammed shut.

"We're getting new neighbors," she said, taking a seat across from Sai, her tea cup warming her palms. "I saw the moving guys today." She sipped and watched Sai make his methodical way through the soup and polenta, taking small sips of filtered water between each bite.

He was so handsome, she thought as she rested her chin in one hand. Exotic looking, without a doubt, with his huge dark eyes, distinctive square jaw, thick black hair. All of which had attracted her to him at first on a purely physical level. Once she'd really gotten to know him—his innate kindness and softhearted nature—she'd been a goner.

The fact that he made a lot of money was a pleasant side bonus. Emily sometimes wondered if she took full advantage of their financial capabilities. She still used coupons at the grocery and drugstore, got her hair trimmed three or four times a month at a mall chain salon, and painted her own toenails. They took long, expensive vacations to be sure, eating and drinking their way through cultures and countries and staying at five-star hotels or resorts. But that was really the extent of their lavishness. She drove an older, practical, immaculate, Volvo. His Audi was the small sedan version, nothing fancy.

They were a great fit. Neither of them flashy or loud. It sometimes amazed her that they got along with people like Janice and Allen Cooper, Barrett LeBlanc, and the volatile Murphys.

They'd chosen this neighborhood, and this street in particular, with careful consideration and the expert advice of their Realtor, Melissa Murphy.

The house was a good-sized, well-built, four-bed, two-bath, fifties bi-level. They'd added their personal touches by renovating the kitchen to accommodate her commercial-level stove and fridge/freezer. But it was unobtrusive, only twenty-three hundred square feet, the oldest house in the cul-de-sac. She'd decorated keeping with its era, using plenty of mid-century modern touches combined with her affinity for Indian art and colorful style.

They'd overpaid for it, but when they'd been looking, it had been a full-on seller's market. And she'd loved the slightly run-down, wall-to-wall-carpeted house the second after Melissa had unlocked the door and she'd taken in the huge windows that overlooked the backyard. At the time, of course, she'd been picturing the pool they'd install for their large family, the play structure, the patio. But while they'd been vetting landscape architect's plans, she'd had her first miscarriage. And now, all they had was a modest brick-paver patio that they did use in the spring and fall for small gatherings of neighbors or—rarely—her elementary school colleagues.

It worked for her, this understated way of life, even though they could easily afford a much showier one. She wanted to believe it did for Sai, too. Although sometimes, she worried that since she'd failed in her number one goal as a female human—to create more humans and nurture them into worthwhile adults—she was getting slack or lazy about not only her looks and her weight but about them as a couple. They were stuck in a rut again, now that they'd extracted themselves from the cul-de-sac's larger social events. Or rather, since the cul-de-sac's social directors had declared a hiatus, given various unfortunate circumstances.

Sai laid his arm on the table, reaching for her with his palm up. She put her hand in his. "I lost a patient on the table this afternoon," he said, his eyes darkening with emotion.

"Oh, honey, I'm sorry." She rose and pulled him up with her, held him close, grateful for any excuse to feel his familiar compactness next to her. They stood by the table, arms around each other for a few moments. When he shifted in her arms and pressed closer, she smiled. "Upstairs?" she whispered into his ear before biting his earlobe. She was ready. She'd been ready for hours.

"No," he replied, his voice hoarse. "Here."

"Works for me," she said as he tugged her loose sundress off and dropped it to the floor before she got him into a matching naked state. He shivered and pressed her back against the glass door, kissing her, loving her, and fulfilling her as he always did.

And yet, that night, as she lay next to him staring up at the rotating ceiling fan, listening to his sleep mutterings, she knew something deep in their relationship had shattered and would never be the same again, no matter how often they screwed each other's brains out during this hot, drama-filled summer.

Chapter Four

T*he Matriarchy*

• • • •

"YOU KNOW," JANICE SAID as she slathered hundred-dollar-an-ounce revitalizing cream down her neck and across the top of her chest. "I really worry about Emily sometimes." She put the lid back on the small jar and turned her head left then right to ensure that her profile was still in good shape. She touched her jawline, pulling it back a half a centimeter then let it go, frowning at her image in the mirror.

"You always have to be worrying about someone," Allen replied as he dragged a towel over his wet hair then down his torso. "It's one of the things I love about you."

"Liar," Janice declared as she mulled over the cornucopia of lotions and potions arrayed in front of her. She picked up one and tried to recall what it was for—cellulite on her thighs, maybe. "Would you wash those for me, hon?" She motioned toward the double sink vanity top where two of her glass sex toys lay on a towel.

"Sure thing." Allen ran them under hot water, used soap, rinsed then set them on a different clean towel. He took a few moments to flex his biceps, triceps, and latissimus dorsi in the large mirror behind her, which made her smile.

Men. They really were all horny little boys in grown-up bodies.

That suited her fine. She preferred him that way. Dr. Allen Joshua Cooper had been her man since college, exactly as she'd planned it. They'd met at a house party his roommates threw for the express purpose of meeting their fellow female college students. She'd known the moment she laid eyes on him that he would be hers.

He was on the football team, which was a big deal at their college. All his roommates were athletes of some sort or another. He was a junior, like her. She was studying to be a nurse, something she'd wanted to be her whole conscious life. He'd poured her a beer from their keg and brought it over to her without asking if she wanted it. She'd smiled up at him—a tall, handsome boy-next-door type with his close-cut blond hair, compelling hazel eyes, and shoulders out to there. And that had been all she wrote, as her mama liked to say.

Janice was from South Carolina and had ended up in Michigan because both her parents had gone there themselves and swore it was better than any other school she might attend in her home state. Allen had declared her accent "adorable," at first, and "sexy as hell," later in their relationship.

She'd kept a tight hold on her virginity for exactly one year into their courtship, not for lack of earnest effort on Allen's part, insisting that he produce an engagement ring before she'd pull her panties off for him, no matter how badly she'd wanted to do that very thing at various times. When she finally did, it was under her terms, in a hotel room she'd insisted he procure for them, with lit candles, flowers all around. The works.

"I'm not about to be letting you near my cherry in the basement of your stinky house with all those other boys listening to us," she'd said more than once. Allen, who'd been utterly taken with her from the get-go, had agreed. He was rich, which helped with the whole engagement-ring-and-hotel-room arrangements. He was a tad shy of spoiled, too, something she'd been determined to beat out of him—in a nice way, of course.

Her mama had been beside herself that Christmas when she'd brought him home with her to Charleston. "Handsome and tall and a football player *and* he's going to medical school? My heavens, Janney, you've caught yourself a live one. Well done."

Her father had shaken Allen's hand and handed him a healthy pour of bourbon. "You'll be needing this, son, if you're aiming to be a part of this family."

"Yes, sir," Allen had said, laughing as he followed her father out onto the large front porch.

At that moment, Janice knew she had her life on the right track.

It derailed within a mere week of her wedding—at an extravagant over-the-top, full-frontal Southern affair to be held on the lawn of her childhood home, with a reception at her parents' country club. Janice blinked fast at her image in the mirror, dispatching the memory of catching her "live one" former football player fiancé with his khakis down around his ankles, spluttering and apologizing and begging her not to call everything off while her future—soon-to-be-former—maid of honor yanked up her panties. In her very own mama's kitchen pantry. *During* the engagement party, no less.

When Allen's warm hand landed on her shoulder, she flinched. Then she patted it and shifted away to continue her evening beauty ritual.

"What's wrong?" Allen asked. He was standing next to her, naked, his penis level with her face in the mirror in front of her. She regarded this, what Allen considered his most valuable asset, for a few seconds. As a retired doctor, he had access to colleagues who kept him loaded up with all manner of concoctions to keep him young in body and mind, which had served them well in the past decade. He took shots of testosterone and other hormones that kept his skin smooth, his energy levels high, and his dick hard.

She could hardly judge. She'd been lifted, tucked, enhanced, smoothed, and hormonally aided plenty herself. She'd be knocking on the door of sixty-one soon and passed easily for forty-one in the right light, thanks to Allen's surgery partner's assistance over the years. She was currently pondering a butt lift, which was basically some stitching to tighten up her vagina, even though Allen had his doubts about its efficacy based on recent medical reports.

Of course, they'd gone ahead with the wedding. Janice was no fool. But she realized when she caught sight of Allen's dick standing at attention in that dim closet, that she would have to adjust her expectations both of him and of herself if she were to carry on with this relationship. She'd borne him the requisite two kids—one of each, boy and girl, in the proper order. He'd worked his tail off to become a sought-after plastic surgeon who donated his time to poor children with their cleft palates or other deformities. She'd served as his office manager for the first few years of his practice. All the better to keep him on his toes, to observe him in action, to keep herself abreast of the competition.

Her dream of nursing got shelved in favor of being Mrs. Doctor Allen Cooper, and she'd never regretted that decision.

In short, they'd fulfilled their marital roles. And, in between, well, she'd learned a thing or three about how to keep her wandering-eyed spouse close to home.

Not quite the lifestyle she'd ever imagined for herself, a nice Southern girl, member of the best country club in town, on the board of the hospital and plenty of other worthy nonprofits. They were quintessential community pillars. Sometimes she wondered why they risked it. And realized the risk was part of the buzz.

She gave Allen's firm-as-any-forty-year-old's ass a smack as she rose and headed for her walk-in closet, pondering how they might welcome the new neighbors. "How about a Labor Day barbeque?" she asked as Allen flopped onto his side of their king bed, still naked, his preferred way to sleep no matter the season.

"Well, of course, I mean, we always have one of those, don't we?" He reached for his glasses and iPad. "Although I wasn't sure if we'd do it this year, since...well, you know."

Janice rubbed a final bit of lotion on her feet then on her arms and hands before sliding between the cool, bamboo sheets. "And I mean, to welcome the new people in the Franks' house."

"Melissa is a miracle worker," he declared, apropos of nothing, best she could tell.

"She didn't do anything other than underprice the hell out of it," Janice sniffed. Melissa Murphy was one of Allen's favorite neighbors and something about that had gotten under Janice's skin lately. Which was ridiculous. She'd not been jealous of any woman since catching Allen with her soon-to-be-former friend at their engagement party. It was something she'd simply taught herself not to be. It was a waste of energy. She and Allen agreed on that and, for the most part, they'd kept their promises not to let jealousy spoil anything.

But his seeming obsession with Melissa and her real estate prowess, not to mention her classy, always-put-together looks was, without a doubt, tap dancing on her last nerve. She decided not to confront it for the time being. They all had enough on their minds. The summer had been a quiet one. Meant for reflection and solitude, devoid of their usual gatherings.

Labor Day was looming, though, and since someone had snapped up the Franks' house—and no wonder since it was practically being given away, which didn't please Janice one bit as to her own home's value, thank you very much, Melissa—it seemed like a good time to put things back in their proper order. Since she and Allen usually were the ones to manage the social life on the street, she was ready to take up her role.

"She said she'd been working with these buyers, a much younger couple who wouldn't normally be able to afford it, for a year. They were picky, she said. And had let three deals fall apart on them, thanks to various issues," Allen said, his eyes back on his tablet screen.

Janice's face heated up. She closed her eyes, reopened them, and stared up at the ceiling fan. "When did you talk to her?" She knew damn well that Melissa and Ryan and their messy blended family were up north for August, like they always were.

"I don't recall. Right before she listed the place, I think. Why?"

"No reason," Janice said. She took tiny sips of air in through her nose and blew them out slowly through her parted lips. She had zero reason to feel the way she was feeling right now. What was wrong with her? Maybe she needed a hormone cocktail adjustment.

A hot plume of anger coiled in her chest, worked its way up into her throat, ready to explode out of her mouth. She pressed her lips together, willing it back down where it belonged.

"What's wrong, babe?" Allen asked, still not looking at her.

"Why would anything be wrong?" Janice pulled the top sheet up over her breasts and smoothed it across her firm torso. She had an early morning Pilates class. She could work out her frustration there and forget this whole thing. Not that there was a "thing" she should be concerned with, after all. It wasn't as if she suspected he was cheating on her with Melissa. The thought of that made her have to hold back a giggle. "So, about the barbeque…"

"Sure. Let's do it." Allen put his tablet on the bedside table and dropped the glasses on top of it before turning to her. He ran his fingertip down her face, to her neck, and across her bare shoulder. She smiled at her body's automatic response to his touch.

They'd worked hard for this, for their life the way it was. She had two sweet grandbabies, both rambunctious boys to carry on the family name, and a son who ran his own business. Things were lovely, and she had no reason to worry about Melissa or the man who'd died in his tub next door.

Allen leaned in to kiss where his finger had touched. First her cheek then her jaw, her neck, her shoulder.

The hormones they took allowed them to be this way. She understood that as clearly as she understood most things in her well-ordered life. Why shouldn't they enjoy their sex life? Who cares if it took a bit of coaxing in the form of a few shots a week? They lived well—exercised daily, ate organic, healthy, if somewhat uninspired meals. They donated to plenty of worthy causes. She volunteered at the local school library twice a week, which needed her help, thanks to budget cuts and recent close-minded, political nonsense.

They kept their grandsons several weekends a month, to allow their son, A.J., to settle into his new marriage with his second wife. A woman A.J. had traded down for as far as Janice was concerned. But it wasn't her business, as Allen liked to remind her when she'd get going on the first wife, whom she had adored.

They were good people.

Good people who enjoyed sex.

What harm did it do anyone if they made sure it was something they would and could continue to enjoy well into their empty-nesting years? It was something else they'd worked at—finding ways to keep things interesting and engaged when it came to each other's libido.

Once Janice had accepted that about Allen, that he required this from her, she discovered a fair bit about her own sexual nature. It had taken years of experimentation, going to parties, meeting new people, curating their friends list carefully, to get where they were today. She'd earned this. And she was ready to ramp things up again, preferably with the people she'd come to know, trust, and, in some cases, love, who lived all around her.

Allen moved down her body, doing all the things he knew well would satisfy her. He was an expert at it, as he should be by now. He always claimed that her satisfaction came first and foremost, no matter what they were doing, and he'd rarely deviated from that mission.

She smiled, dug her bare heels into his back, threaded her fingers in his hair, and forced herself to stop worrying about things that didn't matter.

Afterward, she cleaned herself up and decided to head back downstairs, too revved to sleep. She had a party to plan anyway. There was no time like the present.

"Where you goin'?" Allen mumbled from the bed, still sprawled and spent. But she knew he was only being polite. He'd be asleep before her feet hit the top step.

"I think I'll read a bit," she said, returning the bed to touching his chest. He grabbed her hand, kissed it then rolled onto his side. She pulled the top sheet over him.

"Love you, Janney," he said with his eyes closed.

She patted his hip. "I know you do."

She sat staring out her front living room window at the house next door. The U-Haul had returned. She treated herself to a few moments of illicit fantasy about the two handsome young movers. They were both nice and tall. Their arms and shoulders muscular and firm.

"Stop that right now, Janice Cooper," she said under her breath before yanking the drapes closed and cutting off her view as the two men stood in deep conversation, their work done for the night. But she was tingling at the thought of it—of walking out her front door in her nightgown and tugging both of them into the empty house with her. She'd leave the lights on, to better see them working her over in tandem. The fantasy of this as much of a turn-on as anything she'd ever done. Which was saying something.

She shook her head and made herself a cup of herbal tea—something Emily had recommended from a local tea boutique store she'd discovered. She sipped it and made a list of the things she'd need to purchase. Since the summer had been devoid of their usual round of parties, she'd let her supplies dwindle. It was time to stock back up with a Costco run.

When she heard the truck's motor roar to life, she wandered back to the window, teacup warm in her hand, and watched it pull out into their cul-de-sac and head toward the main street of their neighborhood.

New neighbors will be nice, she thought. It was time to move on from this whole Franks fiasco. She wondered for a moment if the LeBlancs would accept their invitation. It was a crapshoot, she supposed, given their situation. But she didn't care. She hadn't done anything other than host a few parties, after all. What Barrett did about his wife was up to him.

That poor, silly girl. She'd made every mistake in the book, really, including letting Barrett LeBlanc seduce her, marry her, install her as his third trophy wife, and then...well, it really wasn't her business, now, was it?

She let the drapes fall shut. The past year had been such a disaster for so many of her neighbors, she wanted to make it right again. To put things back the way they had been before, when everyone was happy, enjoying each other's company, while adhering to the rules.

It was why they had rules, after all. Janice had done her research. She knew what was and was not done in these sorts of situations. Cassie LeBlanc had broken one. Or rather, she and...well, it was done now. And nothing more for it. Cassie and Barrett would have to sort it out between them. She'd invite them to her Labor Day barbeque and pool party to welcome their new neighbors. She'd see how things went after that.

"Janice!" Allen called from the bedroom, surprising her.

"Yes, my love?"

"Would you bring me a glass of water please?"

"Of course." She got his water, with two ice cubes the way he preferred it, and headed back up to her bedroom. It was important for a wife to understand her husband's preferences, his needs, in order to keep a marriage healthy. He did the same for her, in all aspects of their relationship. She ought to tell him about her no-doubt-unfounded issues with Melissa.

Maybe tomorrow. Or maybe she'd observe them during the party, determine if she had any real reason for concern. Yes, that's what she'd do. She'd done it before and been proven wrong.

The bedroom door was shut, which was odd. She opened it and gasped when a hand grabbed her wrist, took the glass then pinned her wrists over her head against the wall. "Allen, stop it," she said, not meaning it.

"I want more," he whispered as he pulled her nightgown up and off. "Turn around."

"You're such a bad boy," she said as she turned, propped her hands on one of the chairs at her window, and arched her back.

Yes, it was time to get back into their social groove, she thought. They were both more than ready. Before Allen distracted her with his fingers, she briefly wondered if the new people would fit in.

She closed her eyes and imagined the moving men again.

Chapter Five

L *ocation. Location. Location*

• • • •

MELISSA MURPHY HAD never pictured herself in sales. Her parents, both solid Midwesterners, had raised her to think differently, to consider herself artistic, musical, anything other than as a salesperson.

Never mind that her father had managed to support a family of five, selling office machinery and furniture. Her mother had worked part-time at a local dentist's office and, between her parents' incomes, Melissa and her two sisters had never gone hungry. Granted, they'd shopped at their fair share of thrift stores and never got to take any fancy family vacations. They camped in tents a lot. No one had ever complained.

When it came to their daughters, her parents did everything they could to push them in different directions. Her older sisters were nurses and lawyers, and she, well, she'd tried her hand at novel writing while she'd been a secretary and scheduler for a large construction contracting company. It was her first job right out of college. It paid her $25K a year, plus benefits. She'd been fine with it, figuring it for a day job, while, at night, she pounded out her best-selling novel that would change everything.

Those years post useless English degree had been fun. Even more fun than the years spent in school, since she'd had to work in cafeterias and various offices to earn tuition money and, when she wasn't doing that, she was waiting tables at a local pub. In her new job, she'd learned enough about house building and the housing market that when her boss suggested that she take the real estate licensing class to help him put together deals, she'd jumped at the opportunity.

"Oh no, not real estate," her father had bemoaned when she'd told him what she was doing. "Anything but that."

When one of the subs, a married electrician named Ryan, with a too-handsome face and charming way with words, had convinced her to meet him one night after work for a beer, she'd chalked it up to adulting, to learning as she went, to a bit of illicit excitement that wouldn't mean anything to either of them. They'd been engaging in low-level flirtation for a solid six months, ever since he'd been added to the contractors' list as the go-to guy for all things electric. She'd liked him. She'd had no idea he was married, at least at first. He was merely an attractive, older man who always knew the right thing to say to her to make her feel pretty and smart.

Who wouldn't have fallen for it?

"Here."

She looked up, interrupted in her journey down annoying memory lane and pondering her many mistakes to find herself face-to-face with a big one. Her giant whopper of a mistake.

She accepted the ice-choked glass of gin and tonic from her husband's hand and took a sip.

"You're welcome," Ryan said in answer to her non-response. He dropped into the wooden Adirondack chair next to her and stuck his feet up on the table in front of them, brown-bottled craft beer in hand. Melissa bit back the urge to shove his stupid flip-flops off the thing and gulped another long, invigorating helping of her drink instead. It was their last afternoon at their Michigan lakefront home in Manistee and she was determined it would be drama-free.

Of course, that was somewhat out of her hands. Ryan's two teenaged daughters from his first marriage were the ones firmly in control of the drama quotient. But Melissa had decided several years ago that she would not rise to their ongoing bait. It wasn't worth the emotional energy.

When her phone buzzed on the table between them, she grabbed it, eager for an excuse not to have to talk. She filed through her emails, most of them from her two assistants filling her in on the various deals she had going. Three weeks away from her successful real estate business had been one thing Ryan had insisted they take every year. By the time August rolled around, she needed it. She'd give him that much.

When they'd purchased the lot with its tiny fisherman's cottage on it for a song in the first year of their marriage, they'd decided it would be the place where they'd build their dream home. Where they'd come with their family three or four times a year. Where they'd fill their phone albums with photo memories of their perfect life.

It was a nice house, of course. Built mostly by Ryan himself, with the help of his most trusted subcontractors, decorated by her, maintained by a staff of three who kept it up while they weren't there. But it was hardly a dream. And wasn't even in the vicinity of perfect.

Frowning when she spotted an email detailing a problem with one of her listings, she hit redial from her last call yesterday and closed her eyes to gather her thoughts. "Hi, Melissa," assistant number one chirped. "Aren't you supposed to be enjoying your last day up north?"

"Yes, thanks." She got up, taking her drink with her, and wandered over to the deck railing. "Fill me in on the Hill Street house. And did Amelia Ross get her keys? I asked you that yesterday."

She stood and listened and leaned on the rail, her gaze pinned downward on the pristine sand of Lake Michigan where her son Danny was kicking a soccer ball around with his half-sisters and some friends. At one point, the tall-for-his-age six-year-old whiffed a ball and landed hard on his butt. Melissa froze, her breath stuck somewhere between her lungs and throat.

The boy sat a few seconds, rubbing his eyes with his fists. The other kids went on with their game, thank heaven, instead of hovering. Ryan's girls had picked up that much about how best to handle him. He couldn't stand to be the center of attention. In fact, if more than one person at a time looked straight at him, he'd freak all the way out.

"On the spectrum," the pediatrician had declared when they hadn't been able to coax Danny out from under his bed for an entire day after she and Ryan had argued in front of him.

"Annoying," Ryan had claimed.

"That's because you're an asshole," Melissa had stated, never more convinced of that fact.

They had the whole thing under control now, more or less. Thanks to the miracle of modern pharmacology. But it was still touch-and-go at times, especially when they'd take him out of his routine, like when they'd decamp up here for the better part of a month. He'd get adjusted to the new program in time to head home and gear up for the school year. Which would require a couple of weeks of uneasiness and stress in the house while he recalibrated.

The thought of that made exhaustion wash over her. She wished she could have another vacation, this time on her own.

As if, to coin a step-teenager's phrase.

She turned away from the beach once Danny got himself back up and was running after the other kids. "The Hill Street seller wants what? That's crazy. I hope you told her as much."

While assistant number one assured her that yes, she had been well trained and had handled the seller's ridiculous demand that she be allowed to stay in her house three weeks post-closing to "organize her move."

As she paced the large deck, paid for with her hard work, implemented thanks to Ryan's well-compensated staff, tension consumed Melissa like thick, poisonous smoke. She stopped at the far end of the carefully maintained wooden expanse and took a seat in one of the lounge chairs in an attempt to remain calm in the face of the reality onslaught slamming into her nerve endings.

She liked her work. Truly she did. But sometimes, like right now, for example, the ongoing confrontational nature of it made her stomach churn and her jaw clench. She had two well-earned commissions coming her way within ten days of her return, helping to ease the anxiety somewhat. She reminded herself of them during assistant number two's ongoing litany of crises. Afterward, she gave marching orders, had the assistant read them back to her to make sure they'd translated then signed off with a brief "thanks, see you day after tomorrow."

She wasn't the warmest boss. But she wasn't doing this to make friends. She made money. Damn good money. It took every ounce of her friendliness and patience stores to manage all the clients she dealt with. Assistants and colleagues got a bit of what was left over. By the time she'd get home, sometimes late at night, many times on Saturday or Sunday, she'd be depleted. It made it difficult to be a good mother, much less a good wife.

Ryan was no different. His job was stressful, with the added bonus of being fiscally responsible for a dozen employees. Something he took seriously, which she respected. He, in turn, respected the hell out of her work ethic, her capacity to manage chaos, her quick wit, and her ability to close almost any deal.

But Ryan was a hothead. He claimed he'd inherited his hair-trigger temper from both sides—an Italian mother and Irish father. That excuse had been cute for the first few months of wedded life.

A low-lying thrum of mistrust and unhappiness ran underneath their marriage, destabilizing and undermining it the way a slow drip of water, ignored either willfully or not, will destroy the foundation of a perfectly nice house. Melissa knew it. Ryan did, too. But neither of them had the energy to face it, to expose it to the air and figure out if sustaining the relationship was worth it anymore.

She leaned back and let the late-summer sun warm her face, arms, and legs, calling on the meditation skills she'd learned a few years ago at a yoga retreat.

Something heavy hit her lap, making her yelp and lurch forward, startled out of a light doze. "Jesus," she muttered as she stared down at a phone that wasn't hers, now resting on her bare thigh. "What is it?" She picked it up, irritated that Ryan had interrupted her last chance at peace and quiet.

"Seems as though our friendly neighborhood party-people are back at it," he said without looking at her. His eyes were hidden from view behind the classic Ray-Ban Aviators he always wore. But she knew the set of his shoulders, the tightness of his expression. He was here. But he wasn't. Nothing new, really. These last three weeks, he'd spent half his time back at his office, a solid three-and-a-half-hour drive from their lake house.

The real tell that something was seriously off in their relationship was the distinct lack of physical intimacy. They usually had great sex out here, in their private, third-floor suite, far from the kids and fueled by afternoon drinking and long, lazy hours in the sun.

This year? Zip. Zilch. Nada. And she was starting to get antsy about it. Wondering if he was scratching his ever-present itch back in town with some hottie. She really ought to ask him. If only she gave a shit.

She looked down at the phone and saw the clever little evite. There was likely one on her phone, too. But she'd set it on the table next to her with the volume down, all the better to relax, after all.

Welcome To the Neighborhood!

Join us this Labor Day @ 4 p.m. for a cul-de-sac BBQ to welcome our new neighbors, Amelia, Michael, and Tyler!

We'll have the meat, beer, booze, and dessert. Please bring a cold salad or side to pass, your swimsuit, and smiling, happy faces!

Live music courtesy of Allen with his guitar (depending how much beer he drinks).

Otherwise, it will be a great time.

We can't wait to see you all again!

Love,

Allen & Janice Cooper

5527 Connelly Court

Melissa stared at the cutesy font, the silly graphic of a fat guy lying on a pool float holding a beer, and the address Janice had added for reasons that escaped her. They all knew where the damn house was. And she doubted anyone outside their immediate friend circle was the recipient of this particular email.

The Coopers' invitation-only parties were carefully curated. No outsiders allowed, except, of course, for the hapless Ross family this time. Melissa smiled to herself and handed the phone back to Ryan who was sitting next to her, thrumming like a live wire. Amelia Ross had been the sort of client who used up more than her fair share of Melissa's deep well of patience and politeness. But she'd gotten them sorted, as she knew she would. The fact that she'd managed to transform the irritating, control-freaky helicopter mom into her neighbor sometimes gave her pause.

She and Janice had agreed on both the Aryas and LeBlancs. They'd been a good fit for the street already established by the existing families. She'd sold both houses with an eye toward how well the two couples would blend into their unique mix. With Amelia Ross, she'd been lax, eager to get the woman into something she'd love and get her off her list of buyers with decision-making disorders.

It had gotten them out of her hair—or rather, it had gotten Amelia out of her hair. Melissa had dealt with enough humanity at the height of a stressful moment like buying a house to realize that something was wrong with that girl. Her husband was something else altogether.

Melissa froze with her drink halfway to her lips, the memory of Michael Ross' chiseled face, long legs, and fine ass hitting her like an ice-cold smack to her face.

She picked up her phone, found the evite, and hit "reply" with a bunch of smiley faces, kissy lips, and her contribution to the potluck—a big bowl of fresh fruit. She wasn't big on fancy dishes and, anyway, between Emily and Cassie, there'd be plenty of toothsome veggie options.

Glad we're all getting back together. It's time to pick things up where we left off.

She frowned at her words, hit the delete button back to *together*, and added *We're looking forward to seeing you again!* instead. A bit less loaded. She put her phone on the table and drained her drink.

"So, we're back at it, huh?" Ryan asked. He'd taken off his Ray-Bans and was glaring at her, eyes full of accusation, or questions, or something else. Something she didn't want to deal with, now or quite possibly ever.

"It would seem so," she said, not letting him coax her into an argument. "Don't act like you don't want to go, Ryan. That's a little unbelievable, you know? Considering?"

"Don't be a bitch," he muttered. He leaned forward, elbows on his knees, head dropping low.

"Dad! Daddy!" a chorus of Murphy-spawn voices called from below on the beach.

He sighed, rose, and made his way to the railing.

"Come down here," one of the girls called.

"Please, Daddy. Let's take the boat out one more time. We want to ski," the other one yelled. "And it's time for more videos!"

"Yeah, Dad! Ski," Danny parroted. Melissa wished Danny would ski, but he did love to play spotter while Ryan zoomed around, taking too many risks with his daughters' safety, best she could tell. "And videos!"

"Hang on a sec, gang. I'll be down. Go ahead and open 'er up, Cam," he said, telling his older girl, Camille, to ready the boat. "Fill up the cooler for me, Hales," he said to Hailey, the younger girl who was the spitting image of her mother in looks and temperament. "You help the girls out, Dan," he said over his shoulder. "And I am not doing any more of those damn videos. You're putting me on the internet and people are laughing their asses off at me."

He was leaning back against the deck rail, staring at her, arms and ankles crossed. Melissa took him in from tousled chestnut hair down his firm, shirtless chest and washboard abs, slim hips, and muscular calves. He was a hot husband, she mused as she got to her feet. That wasn't the problem.

She wrapped her arms around his waist and pulled him close. "It'll be fine," she said against his lips. He smelled of sunscreen, beer, an illicit cigarette, and something else. Something primal, leathery, musky. It made her tingly the same way it had all those years ago, back when Ryan was the forbidden fruit, at the same moment he kissed her, shoving his tongue into her mouth the way she liked it before pulling away and giving the side of her left breast a caress on his way.

"Gotta go be a good dad, now," he said, adjusting his shorts. Melissa licked her lips, letting him know that as far as she was concerned, the kids could wait twenty minutes or so.

He paused and faced her, his hand on the tent in his swim trunks. "You want this, babe? I was beginning to think you were all done with me."

She took a few steps toward him. He held up a hand. "You're gonna have to wait." He grabbed her, pulled her to him, stuck his hand into her bikini bottoms. "Nice. Hold that thought, hot stuff." He kissed her again, his fingers tangled in her hair. She sighed when he stopped and moved back from her. "A party invitation has you this worked up? Maybe I should be looking forward to it, then."

He grinned, which sent her spinning backward in time, to the moment she'd decided she wanted more from the handsome, sexy, funny electrical subcontractor who'd been pursuing her with a relentlessness she'd never experienced before. "I...don't know," she said. "About the party, I mean."

"Well, that makes two of us. I'll be back," he said with a squint up at the sun. "Couple of hours, max. Get the grill going for me, and I'll make those last steaks for dinner."

"I love you, Ryan," she blurted out, shocking them both.

"Yeah, I guess you do. In your way." He shot her a jaunty salute then bounded down the steps to the beach, hollering at the kids to grab their asses and get ready for a bumpy boat ride.

• • • •

MUCH LATER, SATED IN a way she hadn't been in a while, likely thanks to the half a bottle of Belle Glos Pinot Noir consumed while Ryan had the kids out on the lake for the last afternoon of their vacation, Melissa sat on the deck in the full dark, smoking a cigarette. This was one of her illicit vices. One she hid from everyone except her husband who had the same addiction and the same aversion to owning up to it.

It was a habit she'd developed during their early courtship. "Courtship" being a too-polite word for it of course. They'd flirted for half a year, face-to-face at first then via some kind of phone chat program he'd convinced her to use. Something that couldn't ever be tracked. As if that were possible.

She'd honestly believed she'd gotten to know him, the real Ryan, before she finally succumbed to his relentless charm and tumbled into the sack with him. Again, "in the sack" being a total misnomer. Their first time had been dumb. A stupid drunken hookup behind a bar, in the rain. At the time, it had thrilled her. Look at this daring girl! Not caring who watched while her handsome Prince Charming held her up against the wall and fucked her—without allowing her the opportunity to orgasm, she might add.

Never mind the wall gave her splinters she was digging out for weeks. And the smell of putrid garbage lit the edges of her brutal hangover the next day, reminding her that they'd been right next to the bar's disgusting dumpster. Plus, he forgot a condom.

It got better later, when he'd come to her tiny apartment over a coffee shop and make love to her like a champ, repeatedly. They still laughed over that first fumbling, sloppy, booze-fueled hookup. Or at least they used to. When they still bothered to laugh together.

She sighed and sucked the cig down to the filter then flicked it over the railing onto the sand. When she sensed Ryan behind her, she turned to face him, leaning her elbows on the railing. He grinned and held out a joint. She frowned. "Where did you get that?"

"From Cam's stash, where else?" He held the lighter out. She put the thing to her lips and squinted into the small flame as he lit it. After taking a long drag and filling her lungs, she held it out to Ryan then turned to face the lake again before letting the smoke release out her nose. Ryan leaned next to her, arm touching hers. They passed the joint between them in silence.

"So, we jumping back into that, or what?" Ryan held out what was left. She finished then tossed what little remained down to join the collection of filters that she'd collect and throw away before they left for the season.

"I don't know, are we?" She laid her head on his shoulder, relishing the high. He kissed her hair. When she blinked, it was as if she were doing it slow motion. The air was as soft as a blanket against her skin. Summer smells—sunscreen, boat fuel, bonfires, and the lake itself filled her nose, curling around in her head, making her sleepy.

"Do you want to?"

She moved away from him, aggravated that he kept nattering at her about it. Mainly because she wasn't 100 percent sure she did.

"Maybe. You?"

She mirrored him, leaning on her elbows, weaving from the wine and pot, and the admittedly great sex they'd had earlier. He reached for her arm. She resisted, mainly to mess with him. He was such a complex tangle of personality. Charming to a fault. A door-opener, chair-puller-outer, garbage-bin-hauler type of husband. He could fix absolutely anything that went wrong in their house or in anyone else's. And his competency extended to the bedroom where, at least since that first awful time, he took it as a point of pride that she would climax several times before he'd allow himself the same pleasure.

The problems came when he'd get mad, which was often. His temper was legendary, both at home and on the job. He was impatient with his kids, hated anything resembling a mess in any room of the house. His OCD tendencies were helpful in some aspects of their life but a total hindrance in others. He'd completely lose his shit if anything in his man-cave garage was out of place, including the carefully ordered rows of beers, organized by style—not label color which made more sense to her—in the fridge.

Speaking of beer, Ryan had zero control when he drank. He'd guzzle, be it whiskey, wine, or his favorite IPA, and end up stupid drunk, convinced that he was "fine," while he managed to embarrass her at more than one social function. "The Irish in me," he'd claim.

"The loser, more like it," she'd think to herself as she tiptoed around him the next day, while he nursed a hangover and swore he had no clue where it came from.

The man was an unapologetic flirt. Which irritated the hell out of her at first until she had to accept that he wasn't about to stop doing it. It was something he couldn't control, this urge to conquer yet more women with his pretty face, twinkly eyes, light banter. When he'd stop short of doing anything more, since he was a married man after all, sometimes the women in question didn't appreciate it. She'd had at least two of them confront her, one in person, the other via screen grabs of a string of texts Ryan had exchanged with her while his company was renovating her McMansion in a nearby city.

She'd turned the confrontation around to him. He'd deflected, suggesting that she was overreacting. He'd not cheated on her. Not once. At least, not in a way that mattered.

The final straw was how he dealt with Danny's "issue" as he referred to it. The concept that any child of his perfect loins would be in any way defective, especially if it meant his own son wouldn't or couldn't be his father's type of social butterfly, was worse than if the kid had a physical defect. They'd fought loud and long over this one thing when Danny was four. She'd actually taken Danny and left Ryan for a solid two weeks, right after they'd gotten the autism diagnosis. She adored her boy, even if he was, at times, four or five handfuls. She was not about to let Ryan run him down.

Their reunion had been tearful, apologetic, and exactly what she'd needed from him. It had been right before they'd received their first, exclusive cul-de-sac party invite from the "anchor house," as they'd come to call it. The Coopers, a couple she'd admired, envied for their closeness and apparent marital bliss, had shown them exactly what it took for them to maintain such things. She and Ryan had eased right into it without forethought or any real discussion. Which had been one of the many errors of judgement they'd made, right from the get-go.

She let him tug her close. She put her arms around his waist. After ten years of marriage, one messy miscarriage plus Danny's harrowing birth and subsequent challenges, she was too exhausted to consider leaving him again. She loved him. Actually, she adored him. But, many times, she hated his damn guts for the way he'd treat the kids, or her. Which would usually force her to face her core weakness—that she should leave him for good, but she never would.

He wasn't physically or emotionally abusive. He loved her spirit and drive and earning capacity. But a man who'd cheat on his first wife with her with such energy, such dogged determination to get her in the sack and then continue to mess around with her for a solid year until she told him she was knocked up and he had to leave said first wife or she was getting an abortion, was not a good man. No matter how you sliced or diced it.

The way he'd not-so-subtly insinuate that, perhaps, Daniel wasn't his biological son because he had no defects of body or spirit whatsoever was both incomprehensible and stupid. The damn kid was a mirror image of his handsome father. But he did it a lot, usually in a fake-joking way in front of friends or colleagues at social events. Typically, when he was drunk. All of which made her want to shove him in front of one of his goddamned heavy pieces of Murphy Construction equipment.

But, of course, he was awfully good in bed. She glanced down at her wrist, her pot-fogged brain seizing on the gorgeous diamond tennis bracelet he'd given her earlier this year, right out of the blue. Something he did a lot. She touched it, ran her fingertip along its expensive length. He was giving, in his way. When he was in the right frame of mind, he was nothing but a charming, handsome husband who made her feel pretty, smart, good at her job, and with their son.

She felt the heat of him next to her at the same time that she thought this. She grinned and turned, letting her breasts, bare under her sleep shirt, brush his arm.

The pot continued to coat her nerves, leaving her loose-jointed and slippery. She slid her hand into his shorts. "I say we go. I mean, it's to meet the newbies. I'm sure it'll be fine."

"Hmph." Ryan moved his hand under her arm and cupped her breast. "I don't know, Mel. I mean...you know. All that fuckin' mess last year and everything."

"Oh, you mean the sweet young hottie one of you dumbasses knocked up?"

"Don't," he said, his voice tight. "Just, drop it, okay?"

She leaned over and pressed her nose into his shoulder. She was high as a damn kite, she thought, licking his warm skin, tasting salt and a whiff of her own cologne and stroking him until his dick was hard.

"Cut it out," he said, but his voice had shifted lower, gone rough in a way that turned her on all over again.

She pulled her hand out of his shorts, turned him to face her, and rested her hands on his bare shoulders. Ryan wasn't a gym rat, but he'd never carried a spare ounce on him. It made her crazy, considering he ate like a horse and didn't have to constantly slave on a treadmill or spinning bike or hot yoga room like she did. "Jerk," she said, as she licked her way up his neck, her body on fire the way it always got when they'd pilfer one of Cam's joints.

"What?" He unbuttoned her silky nightshirt and lowered his lips to one exposed breast.

"I said, you're a jerk and I hate you, some days."

"Yeah, well, it's mutual, babe." He lifted his face from her nipple, his grin white in the light thrown by their environmentally correct deck lamps. Her man. Her not-so-charming prince with his silly jokes, his surprise gifts, and his utterly aggravating manner. "Let's fuck," he said in that way he had as he picked her up and carried her over to one of the large lounge chairs and got down to business.

• • • •

AFTER, SHE LAY IN HIS arms, sweaty and smiling, afterward, his fingertips trailing up and down her arm. "Let's go to the Labor Day thing, okay?" she asked. Something about the prospect of leaping back into their former social life with their neighbors was both thrilling and terrifying at the same time. But she wanted it. If for no other reason than she and Ryan could get back on something like an even keel.

"Fine," he said, kissing her hair. "Bitch."

She grinned, pressed closer to him, and drifted a few minutes before he pulled her to her feet and they made their stumbling way back into the house.

Chapter Six

R*ule Breaker*

. . . .

WHEN THE INVITATION to Janice and Allen's Labor Day barbecue landed in her inbox, Cassandra LeBlanc was in the tub, scrolling through her Instagram feed, ignoring her email. It was something she did a lot lately, mainly to keep her mind off herself and the stupid predicament she was in. And to relax...*and* to not have to look at the way the skin of her stomach seemed to be getting thinner. She could already see blue veins making spider web patterns across the baby bump.

She sipped ginger ale, the one thing besides lemon-infused water that she could keep down at night, and touched the heart to like several of her friends' posts. The act made her die a little inside every time.

They were lucky. Living their carefree lives without a pissed-off husband glowering at her as if she were the only one who'd done something stupid. Without the bitchy stares from fat, old, whiny neighbor ladies. Without the sheer, mind-numbing boredom of her life trapped in this house, afraid to go out and face the judgy attitudes of everyone around her.

She sighed and kept scrolling and sipping as the hot, bubbly water cooled around her bare skin. After a half hour, she drained the giant tub and climbed out, trying but unable to avoid the mirror vision of her faded tan, her now-scrawny arms and legs, and that stupid, parasitic thing that had kept stretching her belly and making her sick as a kennel full of dogs day and night for the past five months.

She hated herself. And the choice she'd made when she'd let Barrett LeBlanc sweep her off feet, all in an attempt at that elusive fountain of youth.

Granted, she'd not exactly discouraged his attention. She'd spent plenty of time with her fellow admins and paralegals at lunch, gossiping about all the eligible attorneys in their high-powered practice. Barrett was at the top of every list. He was between wives and easily the most handsome older dude in the building.

It had only taken her six months of flirtatious compliments and offers of fresh coffee for him to turn his double take at her yoga-sexy ass, always highlighted by classy work trousers or slim skirts into something more serious. Barrett was a sucker for younger women. That much she knew. But it stretched the limits of his willingness to play down the roster with her. She was only twenty-eight; he was fifty-two at the time. Shocking. But that made it more interesting as far as she was concerned. And sexy. Feeding straight into her daddy complex as she well knew from reading psychology books and watching afternoon television on her days off.

Funny thing was, by the time they had their fancy Mackinac Island wedding with her five besties as maids of honor and a few of his fusty law partners standing with him so they wouldn't look unbalanced, she actually believed she loved him. He'd been brutally handsome in his tuxedo, his thick black hair, deep-blue eyes, and close-trimmed beard making him resemble one of her favorite romance novel heroes.

She sighed and turned to take in her rapidly devolving profile view. Her breasts were still firm and high, thank the lord, but that would change soon. She looked deformed. Positively repulsive with this growing belly contrasted with the rest of her, shrinking from lack of food.

It wasn't like she didn't want to eat. She did. But she couldn't hold anything down but ginger ale, lemon water, and extra-salty chips. She hadn't been able to since that first horrific morning when she'd jumped out of bed and run for the toilet before she puked her guts up on the sheets.

She'd never, ever forget the look in Barrett's eyes as he sat across from her at the high granite eating bar in their kitchen when he'd reminded her of one hard truth of their marriage. He was sterile, thanks to heavy doses of chemotherapy he'd had as a prepubescent boy. He'd been told he would never would be able to father a child and had proven that to be true through two previous marriages. And yet, here she was, bun in the oven.

His face had been vulnerable at that moment. She'd swear that he'd almost wept, right there in his striped pj's. And then, while she watched and sobbed and tried not to vomit all over her nice kitchen, his expression had changed, hardened, closed off to her. And it had been that way ever since. Not that she saw him much anymore. He took every opportunity to travel to visit clients or handle cases. His firm had plenty of corporations they dealt with, including all the major automotive ones, so, if he wanted an excuse to exit, stage left, he didn't have to look far.

She missed him. That was the thing, really. Barrett had managed their lives from top to bottom and she'd let him. She'd encouraged him, acting more airheaded that she actually was. Her daddy complex again. Not to mention the fact that she really and truly had had no sense of order, no purpose to her life before she'd decided to become the next Mrs. LeBlanc. And now, she was floundering without him.

She rested her hand on the bump and wished with everything she had to go back in time, to make better choices when faced with…well, anyway. She pulled on her thick robe and tugged her long black hair into a ponytail. Her stomach growled, which made her want to cry. She was hungry. It wasn't like she wanted to starve the damn kid and besides, based on her understanding, the kid wouldn't starve, she would. Her doctor had insisted that the nausea would ease after three months, but she was still miserable, approaching the six-month mark. If anything, it was worse. Hot tears slid down her face as she padded out into their big bedroom, past the bed she'd been happy to share with her handsome, rich, loving husband.

The whole what-was I-thinking mental-argument loop she kept up was getting old. She hadn't been thinking. That was the problem. None of them had been.

She sniffled her way down the steps to the kitchen, flipped on the lights, and found one of her many half-empty bags of chips—a type of processed, preservative-choked pseudo-food she never would have touched in her previous life. It was time for her vitamin, and she'd been keeping that down as long as she chased it with the chips and some lemon water. The weird part about it all was that familiar odors that used to make her happy—her yoga mat, lavender oil, her favorite candles, her wheat grass shots, kale—all only made her retch if she caught the slightest whiff of them.

And she'd been that way almost from the moment she'd figured out that her period was late, that she'd gone and done something stupid. Something that would probably end her marriage. Not that the inciting incident had been her damn idea. It had been Barrett's. She'd gone along with it to humor him. He'd confessed some of his fantasies to her. An opportunity or two—okay three or four of them—had materialized. They'd availed themselves.

She'd lost herself in it, discovering her inner exhibitionist as well as voyeur. But she'd broken a rule—along with the other rule breakers in the room at the time, mind you.

She swallowed the giant pill and jammed several chips into her mouth, washing the whole mess down with lemon-choked water. The tears kept falling. She kept eating, filling her empty belly. But she could only manage few more of the salty snacks before she felt sick again.

When she slid off the tall bar chair, the room spun. A loud humming filled her ears, making her head pound. Her heart started racing at the exact moment she broke out in a cold sweat. Something was wrong. But who cared, really? Not her husband. And who would blame him.

Of course, he'd hardly stood by and observed what went on. He had his fair share of fun, including watching her get literally screwed by all their neighbors, fulfilling that particular fantasy a lot.

Once she felt halfway normal again, she let go of the chair and headed for the couch, eager to stare at something brainless on TV until she fell asleep. After two steps, she was hit hard with a rush of sickening dizziness. She stumbled and dropped to her knees. The chips, vitamins, and lemon water surged up and out, hitting the dark hardwood in front of her with a nasty splat.

"Oh...shit," she cried out, on her hands and knees in her own mess. "Oh crap ... Barrett ..." But he wasn't here. She sat, no longer caring that her own sick was all over the place and pulled her phone out of her robe pocket. The screen swam in front of her face. She was fading. She was dying and taking this damn kid with her. That would show them—all of them and their judgmental bullshit. She'd keel the hell over in her vomit and croak.

When she realized that she'd dialed Emily's number, she put the thing to her ear, although her hands were shaking so badly she dropped it once onto her lap. Cursing, she picked it up, hearing her neighbor's tinny voice coming from the device. "Em? I...something's wrong. I'm dizzy and I...I fell down."

"We'll be right there, Cass," her sweet, fat, easygoing teacher neighbor said, soothing her instantly. "Don't move, okay? I'll call an ambulance."

"Yeah, okay, thanks." All of a sudden, the floor looked like the most comfortable place in the world to take a rest. "Gonna take a lil' nap. 'K?" She let the phone drop. The last thing she recalled for a while was how nice it felt to be lying down.

"Cassandra, honey. Can you hear me? Sweetheart?"

She opened one eye then closed it immediately when the harsh fluorescent lights hit her brain. "Ow," she moaned and covered her face with her hand. But it was tethered to something, not allowing for movement. Plus, she had to pee something awful. She tried to get up, but someone was pressing on her other arm, holding her in place.

"Not yet, dear. Let me get your vitals."

"I have to pee," she said. But nothing coherent came out of her mouth. She licked her lips, or at least tried to. "The baby," she whispered. "It's okay, right?"

"The doctor will be here in a few minutes." The woman's gaze flicked to someone on her other side. Someone Cassie hadn't yet acknowledged. "You and your husband are in good hands with Doctor Cole."

Cassie reached for Barrett, fear lighting the edges of her ever-present, soul-draining nausea. "What are you doing here?" Tears streamed down her face as she gripped onto him like a barnacle.

He looked drained, exhausted. But his eyes, his beautiful blue eyes, were kind for a change. "It's all right, Cassandra. You're going to be fine."

"The...the...b-b-b-"

"Shh," Barrett said, getting up off his chair and sitting next to her, pulling her into his arms. All the tension of the past six months came pouring out of her in torrents as she held onto the lapels of his suit jacket. "Hush now." He stroked her arms. Kissed her forehead and cheeks. She felt safe and loved and hopeful for the first time in ages.

The doctor came in trailing a bunch of residents, presented her case, did a quick perusal of her vitals, and made a cursory check of her bump. "A classic case of *hyperemesis gravidarum*, somewhat atypical in a *gravida* of this age." He put a hand on Cassie's calf. "Misdiagnosed. This young lady was dehydrated to the point of fainting. We're giving her a dose of promethazine[1] in her IV. She was one sick puppy, weren't you, dear? But her baby is fine. Strong heartbeat. Positive ultrasound."

Cassie tried to smile, but she felt awful, and she must look like death warmed twice over. She sensed herself drifting as she whispered to Barrett. "I need to pee. Can you help me up?" It was beyond embarrassing, but he

---

1.   https://www.healthline.com/health/promethazine-oral-tablet

kept his arm around her waist as she shuffled to the bathroom. He went in with her, helped her sit then got her back to the bed. It was sweet, especially considering he didn't really groove on bodily functions like pee or periods or other icky stuff.

She leaned into him, already feeling better while Barrett fussed around her making sure she was warm, asking if she needed anything, wanted food, any food; he'd go and find whatever she desired. She touched his cheek, loving the familiar sensation of the tight curls of his beard under her palm. She always used to joke that the gray curls in his beard were proof that he colored his hair to keep it black. He didn't. But it was their little joke. Or it used to be.

He took her hand and pressed it to his lips. "I'm sorry, Cass. This is much as my fault as it is yours. I won't, I mean, I'll be...here for you. Both of you."

He put a shaking hand on her bump. She put her cold hand over his. "Will you sit here with me? While I sleep?"

"Of course," he said, pulling his chair close, resting his arms on the bed next to her. "Don't ever scare me like that, okay? Please?" He put his head on his hands. Cassie smiled and touched his hair then drifted off, hoping that this might, please God, be a welcome reset of her former life.

On the way home the next day, he held her hand the entire way. While they waited at a stoplight near their neighborhood, he kissed her knuckles then let go of her and gripped the steering wheel. He was tense again, angry. She could tell.

"What's wrong?" she asked, touching his leg. She felt about a million times better, thanks to whatever miracle drug they'd given her. She'd been sent home with orders to rest as much as possible and use these little suppositories of the same medication on an as-needed basis. She planned to use them all, no matter she had to stick them up her butt. She was not going back to that horrible place where she wanted to die every stinking minute of the day ever again.

"The Coopers are having a party," he said, his voice tight.

She curled her hands into fists on her legs. "Oh?"

"Yeah." He glanced at her then back out at the windshield. "Labor Day. A barbecue for the new people."

"New people?" She was confused a half second. Part of her sometimes forgot—or refused to accept—that Tom and Laura Franks were gone. They'd once been her favorite neighbors, after Emily and Sai. And Tom...she bit her lip and tried to hold back the tears. But it was no use.

He patted her leg. "Yes. A younger couple, apparently. With a little boy. The woman and her son are moving in tomorrow. Her husband's on a business trip but will be back in time for the...party." His slight hesitation before the word "party" made her suck in a breath.

"Oh. Well, that will be nice." Her voice sounded as small as she felt. "Are we going?"

He glanced at her. She preferred it when he made the decisions. These past few months had left her needing him to make decisions for her, in more ways than one. Having him back in the driver's seat, literally and figuratively, gave her comfort. The thought of losing that again made her want to die.

"Perhaps. We'll see how you feel. It wouldn't be neighborly of us not to welcome the new family."

"Right. Okay. You let me know, okay, Barrett?" She leaned on his arm. He put his hand between her thighs and gave her leg a squeeze. To her surprise, she realized she was reacting to his touch in a way she'd thought she never would again. She shivered. He tightened his grip on her thigh. "We're going to be okay?" She made sure to frame it as a question. She looked up at him through her lashes, the way she knew he liked.

He glanced down at her, his expression unreadable. "We're going to try," he said. "But I need something from you, Cass. Do you think you can manage to...sleep with me tonight?"

"Yes," she said, keeping her voice soft.

"Good," Barrett said as he pulled into their garage. He helped her out and into the house then drew her a bath and bathed her himself, using care and a loving touch until it got sexy and sexier. When he eased her back on the soft carpet in their giant bathroom, it was nice, really nice. He kissed her all over, which wasn't really their dynamic, sexually speaking. He kept muttering things to her, calling her "sweetheart" and "my love," as he pushed all of her buttons, plus a few new ones.

When he came inside her with a low groan, Cassie put her hand to his bearded cheek and smiled. The satisfaction that oozed through her body was more than sexual. She'd wanted this man. Had gone after him carefully, groomed him for exactly what she'd gotten—a giant engagement ring, a fancy wedding, and a stable life for the first time ever. The thought that she'd gone and messed it all up over a spur of the moment's—okay, several moments'—action had almost killed her. But he'd come back to her. And she could see it in his eyes, He was once more firmly lodged on her hook.

"I love you, Cass," he gasped before he pulled out of her and rose gracefully to his feet. She stretched like a happy housecat on her fluffy bathroom rug. She knew he liked it when she did that after sex. His expression was soft and moony as he watched her. He held out his left hand. She stared at the thin platinum band he wore, denoting him as hers forever. "Come on, honey. Let's get you into the bed."

Chapter Seven

P*re-Party*

. . . .

"YOO-HOO...ANYONE HOME?"

Janice glanced up from her cutting board. She'd managed to get all the watermelons sliced and de-seeded—she didn't hold with those weird, seedless ones as they seemed artificial to her. But she needed to get going on the burgers. The task of shaping the 100 percent organic Wagyu beef into perfectly structured patties that wouldn't shrink or otherwise shrivel on the grill was an important one for a successful cookout. It was a small detail. But small details added up to successful social events. Janice knew this well.

The concept of an unexpected guest at her kitchen door irritated her. But she set the paper-wrapped packets from the butcher on the counter, washed her hands, took a deep breath, and smiled. Her mama had taught her that if you smile before you speak, it shows up in your voice. And one should always be polite, at least at first, when answering one's door.

It figured that it would be Melissa Murphy standing there, looking slim, trim, and perfect in her Lululemon-ed glory. Janice forced her smile wider and opened the French doors, letting her neighbor into her kitchen.

None of the people on this street were the type to be showy with their homes. And Melissa knew that better than most, considering it was her job to know houses and what people to place in them. Regardless of that fact, Janice always got a tiny thrill of pride whenever any one of her neighbors walked into her kitchen. It was a masterpiece of understated class and expense. She'd had it designed specifically with that goal in mind. It was their second renovation, this one with a bump-out expansion of the entire back side of the house to allow her to update her private bathroom, the second bath, and the guest room.

She and Allen had decamped to a hotel suite for the duration of the work, to stay out of the way and not be inconvenienced any more than was necessary. Allen had been winding down his practice by then, only taking office visits one day a week, surgeries twice a week—and those, ones he'd cherry-pick—often making the hapless individual wait eight months or more for their nip or tuck.

The result was a set of improvements well worth their expense and fuss, as far as she was concerned. Her low-profile, no-handle, natural cherry cabinets were perfectly highlighted by the streamlined double-wall oven, and six-burner cooktop with griddle, and massive fridge freezer, all Gaggenau brand, which fit the look she wanted to a tee. She'd gone with a Vetrazzo countertop material that featured recycled glass bottles in them instead of natural granite or other rock. She'd chosen the backsplash tiles and industrial-looking drop lights that resembled big, plain lightbulbs to match everything, giving the space a combination industrial, futuristic, clean-lined look that she loved every single day she walked into it.

Melissa Murphy knew exactly what all of this cost. Her appliance allowance alone had been a few bucks shy of sixty grand, something Ryan hadn't even blinked at when he'd quoted it—once he'd fully grasped the nature of what she was trying to accomplish. The bathrooms were designed along similar sleek, expensive lines. Her guest bathroom was now as nice as many homes' main ensuite bathrooms. But she entertained a lot, she and Allen had justified. The expense was well worth it. Their guests' comfort was as important as their own. And almost everyone who'd done it loved to soak in the guest bathtub.

"Would you like some juice, my dear? Allen made some before he left for the gym."

Melissa, who looked a tad more rattled than a woman who'd returned after three weeks on Lake Michigan should, handed Janice a massive plastic container of fresh-cut fruit. "No thanks. I'm headed there myself."

"Well, you two should've carpooled. Saved a bit of our ozone layer." Janice opened the container and admired the lovely collection of mangos, strawberries, blue, and raspberries. "Lovely. Did you cut all those mangos yourself? Such a fuss for such little result. But delicious." She snapped the lid back in place and put the container into her fridge, which, despite being enormous, was full to bursting. She'd gone a little overboard in her excitement about having her friends back at her home again. She let the cool air calm the heat rising in her face. Why did this woman have such an effect on her lately? She had no idea.

Or rather, she did. But she refused to acknowledge it.

"Maybe," Melissa said. Janice was shocked to note that the woman seemed, well, wigged out was the best description she could think of. She was gnawing on her lower lip, which looked chapped and red already. Her fingers were locked together in front of her, and she shifted from foot to foot like she had to pee.

"Why don't you have a seat," Janice said through her irritation at being distracted from her tight morning schedule. Parties don't throw themselves, after all. But Melissa was her neighbor—her friend, or at least she'd claimed as much. "Would you like some coffee? I made a fresh pot using those beans Emily recommended. It's delicious."

"No, thanks. I mean...sure." Melissa eased into one of the tall chairs at the counter.

Janice poured her a cup, added a splash of milk from her memory of how the woman took her coffee in the mornings, and placed it in front of her. She recharged her own cup but kept her distance, letting the counter and kitchen island form something of a barrier between them.

"Thanks," Melissa said, looking down into the mug with something like relief. The silence took on a life of its own. Janice felt it as a cool mist against her face, unpleasant yet soothing at the same time.

Janice waited. Melissa would spill whatever it was that was making her look like she needed a vacation from her vacation. She was incapable of doing otherwise. "Do you mind if I work while we chat?" she asked, setting her coffee aside and unwrapping one of the packages of ground beef.

"No, no, it's fine. I'm fine." Melissa put the mug down on the counter. Janice heard it rattle and knew the woman was lying. She pulled a hunk of the pinkish meat from the paper and began forming a perfect patty.

"I'll tell you, those fellows at Hanson's, you know, the butcher, down in Watertown? They sure are nice. I mean, they'd have to be, charging what they do. But I've gotten to where I don't trust any of the prepackaged stuff from the grocery. I've heard some stories." She glanced over at Melissa who was staring at her coffee mug, trancelike. "Anyway, they grind this up fresh. I know what I'm getting. No nasties in it. Worth every extra penny, I say." She was on the fifth patty when Melissa cleared her throat. Relieved and hopeful this would be short and sweet, she looked up, her meat-slimed palms resting on the stainless island countertop.

"So, this party..." Melissa began. Her face was beet red. Janice's inner almost-nurse worried for her blood pressure. "Um, well, are we...is it...oh shit. I hate this."

Janice raised an eyebrow at that. Last she checked, Melissa Murphy didn't hate the parties she and Allen used to host before the ridiculous mess that silly girl got everyone into. As a matter of fact, she was one of the more exuberant participants. Janice shook her head. She was getting caught up in some kind of petty jealousy thing that had no place in her life. She forced a smile back on her face and kept quiet. Melissa had come here to say something, obviously. Janice was going to wait until it got said.

The women locked eyes for a few seconds. This, Janice understood. If any woman was her match in the alpha matriarch department, it was this one. Which was likely the crux of her problem with Melissa. They were ever jockeying for first position within the tangles of their various relationships. She kept her expression as neutral as she could. Melissa blinked first. Janice felt herself relax to the point where she was willing to help the poor woman out, conversationally speaking.

"This is a party to welcome our new neighbors," she said, reaching for another chunk of meat. "Please bring Danny to swim. The grandboys will be here until about seven thirty."

"Oh," Melissa said, her shoulders slumping. "I didn't catch from the invite that..."

Janice looked up, her gaze sharp on purpose. "Melissa, you know as well as I do that my parties are always open to families. At least until it gets late, and it's time for the kids to head home." She was having way too much fun making the woman uncomfortable. She really ought not to be pleased to observe her neighbor squirming in her seat as much as she was.

A brief memory vision flashed across her brain—Melissa, Ryan, she, and Allen in her newly redone kitchen, toasting with some expensive Italian wine, and talking about something important to Janice and Allen. Something they wanted to do to enhance their friendship. At the time, Janice had been focused and sincere. She and Allen had had some experience outside of their immediate geographical location. But they were looking to keep things more, well, local. If they could manage it.

They both enjoyed the Murphys' company—their youthful energy, their obvious love yet aggravation with each other. Plus, they were both extraordinarily attractive, of course. Janice recalled how she'd been fixated on Ryan Murphy's lips. Full, tinged purple from the wine that night. Tempting, close, and full of potential.

She stopped patting out the meat and took a breath. "We've all been through a terrible time these past few months, Melissa. I'm not sure...well, I guess I'd like to see things go back to the way they were, but perhaps they never will. The Franks are gone, and they were such an integral part of our...unique friendship. And poor Cassie...well, anyway." She stopped, unsure what point she'd planned to make.

Melissa turned her mug around and around on the countertop, nervous as a cat in a room full of rocking chairs. That much was obvious.

"I think Ryan... Well, I'm pretty sure he and Cassie... Oh shit, Janice. I don't know anything anymore."

Janice sighed and got back to work on the hamburgers. "It's immaterial to me at this point. The silly girl and whomever did it to her broke a rule. That was the beginning of the end as far as I'm concerned. And I assure you that I place a lot of blame at her feet for ruining everything we all had together."

"Well, Ryan—or whomever—has to take half the responsibility."

Anger flared up Janice's spine. "I think it's clear who it was, Melissa. And he's dead, remember?" She gripped a hunk of meat tight, making it ooze between her fingers. She had to get control over herself, over all this chaos. But she wanted things back the way they were. It was part selfishness, part marriage survival. She knew Allen. Her husband was getting restless again. She recognized the signs.

She walked to the sink and washed her hands, staring at the small chunks of meat swirling down the garbage disposal. When she looked back over at Melissa, the woman's expression was slack, as if she were shocked. Janice frowned. "What? You don't know? The poor man killed himself because of what he did to Cassie."

"I...mean, I thought, I guess, we thought, but something in me suspected Ryan. He can be, um, impulsive."

"Yes, I know." She had to say it. Seriously, Melissa walked right into it. But the split second she did, and met the other woman's gaze, she regretted it. It was mean-spirited. Petty. All things she and Allen had sworn not to be, way back when they'd made some choices and decisions about how they would keep their marriage together.

For some reason, lately, Melissa was triggering her. It was a red flag. She knew she should steer clear of the Murphys for a while, if not forever. But Allen liked Melissa, and she wasn't in the business of denying her husband what he wanted.

You control this. You can tell him no. You have before, way back, before you decided to start this neighborhood thing.

Janice shook her head to clear it of the annoying nag. "I'm sorry. I didn't mean to be..."

"Bitchy?" Melissa was smiling. "It's okay, Janice. I know how you feel about my husband. It's fine. We agreed to it, remember?" She took a moment to tug the hair tie out and let her long, golden-blonde locks cascade around her shoulders.

Janice gritted her teeth. The damn woman was practically preening. What for? She wasn't into her and never had been.

And she had the nerve to turn this around on Janice? To imply that she was the one who couldn't go without Ryan's direct attention? This woman had a pair on her. Janice would give her that much.

"Hey, Allen," Melissa said. Janice flinched and managed to knock one of the unopened packages of meat onto the tiled floor. Melissa took a few more moments to gather up her hair and refasten it, shoving her chest out and making sure Allen noted it. Which he would. Because that was Allen. No extra effort necessary. "Nice to see you."

"Howdy, neighbor," he said, giving her a light peck on the cheek before coming around and retrieving the paper packet from the floor. "Here, babes. You all right?" Her husband touched her arm. "Janice?"

She blinked, smiled, and, with an epic effort, cleared her mind of the growing fury. This would never do. She needed to take some steps. Perhaps it was the six months they'd all spent avoiding each other, after the cul-de-sac had cleared of ambulances, cops, and, later, plain-clothes investigators snooping around the Franks' empty house, asking questions and generally being a nuisance. The poor man had taken a fistful of pills, gotten in the tub, and died. Pure and simple. Not to mention selfish, Janice thought. What if one of his kids had found him?

"Of course I am. I mean, I'm busy, you know. Doing too many things at once." She glanced over at Melissa, who was staring at Allen's ass. She cleared her throat. Melissa's gaze shifted to her, slowly and with purpose. "Melissa was keeping me company, weren't you, hon?"

"Yes, and thanks for the coffee." Melissa jumped down from her perch at the counter, stretched up then left and right, putting on quite the show. But Janice's head was clear. She had no time for this. And she controlled it after all. She did have plans for later tonight. But perhaps, now, they wouldn't include the Murphys.

"Looking good, Realtor lady," Allen said as he gave Janice her own cheek peck before wandering around the counter to smack Melissa on the ass. "Real good."

"Stop it," she said, her tone flirty. Janice smiled at the two of them, as if she were observing a couple of little kids acting out. But a plan was formulating for her. One that didn't involve Melissa. Which would be odd, considering that the Murphys were their first, special cul-de-sac friends. "I'm thinking I might need to go see one of your partners," Melissa said, making a cutesy pout. She touched her neck, which was flawless, and then cupped her breasts, which weren't huge but were firm and high, nipples poking through her fancy workout top like little pebbles.

Allen chuckled. "No need to spend the money on an office visit when I'm down the street. Let's get you into some better light." He took Melissa's elbow. "I can make my recommendations and I'd say have Simon do the work, wouldn't you, Janney?"

"Hmmm," Janice replied, rage boiling through her bloodstream like molten lava. Bitch knew what she was doing, didn't she?

Allen must have sensed something in her non-answer. He let go of Melissa's arm and turned to face her. She pretended to be too busy with the meat prep to notice anything. "Janice? Do we have a problem?"

"What?" She raised her gaze to meet his. "Oh no, of course not." She smiled again. "Go on, Doctor Cooper. Make recommendations then get your butt in here and help me. We have a party to throw, remember?"

Allen's grin was boyish and eager. It made her want to smash him in the nose.

Men. Simple creatures, remember, Janney? This is your scene. Tell him that him touching Melissa Murphy for any reason, including her fake need for a plastic surgery consult right here in the kitchen, makes you want to scratch the woman's eyeballs out.

She let her smile falter to let him know she was not good with it. Not at all. Allen took a few steps closer to her, reading her signals loud and clear, bless him. She held up a meat-smeared hand. "I'm fine, Allen. A bit flustered about all of this is all." She gestured around the kitchen, which resembled the back of the house at a restaurant at the moment. Piles of buns, stacks of compostable plates and napkins and utensils, condiments, bags of chips, ingredients for fresh salsa and guacamole, and, of course, all the booze and mixers covered every square inch of all the many inches of Vetrazzo countertop.

He patted her arm then gripped it and leaned into her ear. "I love you, you know. I'm not doing anything but giving a quick consult. Don't be..."

She jerked her arm out of his grip. "*Don't* tell me how to be, Allen." Her voice, lowered, was firm and packed with a message she expected him to hear.

He pulled back, crossed his arms, and glared at her. "You have a problem with Melissa. You always have. Don't think people haven't noticed it."

"Sh. For heaven's sake." Janice jerked her chin toward the den where Melissa had taken up residence on Janice's favorite reading chair. She was messing with her hair again, grooming herself, showing off. "I have a *problem* with you standing there not helping me. We have work to do. Get on with whatever you're doing with her, take a shower, and get back down here." She kept her voice at a whisper.

His Adam's apple bobbed up and down. He was confused by this. Was she actually giving him a short hall pass? Did telling him to "get on with whatever" he was doing meant could, indeed, do what he wanted to do to the hot-as-hell neighbor lady?

She frowned at him and shook her head once then again. The lightest of signals. But one they'd worked out years ago and both honored, regardless of how badly one might want to enjoy someone else's company. It was the only way to hold it together, given what they allowed into their marriage. Respect for the other when it came time to close the deal.

He swallowed hard. His face got redder. He was pissed but understood what she meant. Good. He would be well served to remember who was in charge of things. Especially the one thing, the unspoken thing, the thing she and Melissa Murphy and Laura Franks had, at one time, been happy to orchestrate together.

Back before Laura's stupid goddamned husband went and spoiled everything for everyone.

Oh, you were headed for a blowout with Allen over Melissa before that, Janney girl. Do not pretend otherwise. What you suspect about them is most likely reality, given how unhappy the woman is with her husband, combined with Allen's ever-eager dick. Damn man was harder to control than a pack of feral cats sometimes.

She sighed. Sometimes it didn't pay to be on the receiving end of all the gossip and inner-workings details of other people's marriages. Ryan liked to run his mouth too much, especially during afterglow. So, she knew a lot about Melissa. More than she wanted to know.

She silenced her inner nag, pinned a smile to her face, and stuck her hands back into the meat, squeezing it between her fingers again. The sensation was oddly satisfying. She'd deal with this later. This party was about welcoming the neighbors and sizing them up, deciding how best to proceed.

Allen held out a hand to touch her shoulder.

She moved pointedly out of his reach. "We'll discuss this later," she whispered. "Go on and do ... whatever. Then get her out of here."

Allen blinked fast in the face of her curse. She dropped an eff-bomb maybe twice or three times a year, usually after too much to drink. His expression hardened into stubborn lines. "Fine. But we will discuss this." He moved close before she could shift away, grabbed her arm, and put his lips to her ear. "Including how I feel about Ryan Murphy playing favorites with my wife. This shit runs both ways, Janney. Don't ever forget that."

She frowned. But a familiar, illicit thrill shot up her spine. She closed her eyes. Reopened them. Allen headed into the den, already talking to Melissa about the risks versus rewards of plastic surgery. He made sure to stay well within Janice's sight line as he examined her, only asking her to pull off her shirt at the very last moment, once he closed the blinds at the back windows. He kept it clinical, purely business. They didn't call him the most-sought-after neck-and-tits man for nothing. Allen had been an excellent surgeon, easily one of the best.

But when Melissa bounded back into the eating area between the den and kitchen, her face had a flush to it Janice recognized. "Okay, we'll be over later. Thanks for the coffee, Janice." She winked.

Winked.

Janice pressed her lips together. Allen watched the woman go, his face pensive. Absentmindedly stroking his stupid erection. "Take a shower," she said, keeping an edge to her voice. "I don't have time for this right now."

He turned and headed upstairs without another word. When Janice looked down, she noted that she'd ruined at least two of her perfectly formed patties by pressing down on them so hard the meat had squirted out from under her hands, leaving her pressing down on the cold countertop. "God damn it." She washed her hands, stared at them a few minutes then headed upstairs to join Allen in the shower.

Chapter Eight

Pre-Party. Take Two.

• • • •

"I DON'T WANT IT THERE, Allen. That corner of the patio gets too clogged up."

"All right. How about here?" He rolled their portable bar around to the opposite side of the pool. She was testing the full limits of his patience, and she knew it. "This work?"

Janice glanced around, taking in her party setup. She'd pulled out the round tables she'd bought from the rental company years ago and had Ryan repair for her. Four tall ones and four seated ones were covered in her decent—not best—cloths. She was going with a patriotic theme, since they'd skipped the Memorial Day event that was typically their biggest one. Janice had good cloth table covers in almost every color of the rainbow. She had them professionally washed and pressed after every use. The centerpieces of contrasting flowers—red on white, white on blue, etcetera—were surrounded by sprays of natural greens. She didn't hold with sparkly confetti or other gaudy nonsense. Fresh-cut flowers, greenery, appropriate-height candles, or the occasional string of tiny lights should the occasion demand it. That was her style.

She'd purchased white folding chairs from another rental company that was going out of business and had over a hundred of them altogether, stacked neatly in one corner of the large garage. She was expecting twenty people for this particular event, including all her neighbors. Her son, A.J., his boys, and his new wife were coming. As well as two other couples she and Allen played golf with, plus her euchre friends from the club with their spouses. One of them was bringing their granddaughter to swim since they'd been keeping her during the last two weeks of summer.

All in all, it would be a lovely mix of people who could mingle and chat and enjoy the food, drink, and ambiance. The pool was cleaned and ready. The bar prepared. The ribs already filling the backyard with mouth-watering aromas from the smoker. Janice checked her watch. It was only one thirty.

She had time for another shower, which she needed after bustling around for the past two hours setting everything up. Then she'd have her party-pre-tune gin and tonic with Allen.

They'd cleared the air between them in the shower. She was feeling much less fraught and looked forward to sitting with him, their feet in the pool, drinks in hand, before everything got started. A.J. would show up first, she knew. Any excuse to get the boys distracted. She had to get all this done by three thirty at the latest, including the drink, which she'd make a double, to tolerate her new daughter-in-law.

"Janice?"

She turned at the sound of Emily's voice. Not quite as irritated as she had been by Melissa's intrusion earlier, but no less annoyed by the fact of the interruption. The woman was holding two huge Tupperware bowls, one filled with something green; the other looked like rice or maybe quinoa. Her face was red and sweaty. She seemed flustered. Janice's mother-hen tendencies flared. Emily always brought that out in her.

"Let me take those. Have a seat before you fall down, Em." She put the dishes in the big, outdoor fridge, on the shelf above Allen's beer collection. She grabbed two cans of lemon La Croix and headed back to the patio. "Let's take a break," she said, as if this were on her agenda, which it most definitely was not.

"Oh thanks," Emily said, as if surprised at the courtesy. It was one of the things that annoyed Janice most about her. She took self-deprecation to a whole new level. She wondered how the woman managed to stand in front of a classroom full of little kids, all looking to her for the sort of role-model guidance kids these days seemed to crave.

Emily sipped then put the can on the glass-topped table next to her. "Listen, um...I need to ask you something."

"Okay." She had a feeling she knew what the question would be. She knew that Emily, easily the shyest of their group, would be unable to formulate it. She waited.

"Is this...um, party, today. Is it...uh...you know. Are we...well, I mean, Sai and I, we don't..."

Janice put a hand on Emily's, which was ice cold and trembling. Not for the first time, Janice wondered why in the world Melissa had placed these people in their midst. It wasn't that she didn't like them. Emily was such a sweetheart. Kind and thoughtful, unselfish to a fault. She didn't have a mean or vindictive bone in her body. Something new to Janice, when it came to women. She'd always operated under the assumption that men were cheaters and women couldn't be trusted. But the Aryas threw a kink into that philosophy.

Dr. Sai was an attractive man. Okay, that was an understatement. His deep-brown skin, thick hair, and huge, expressive eyes were only the surface of his many positive qualities. He was funny, for one thing. As good as Allen was at putting people at ease. Allen sometimes came across as too pushy, she knew. Sai was quietly confident in a way Allen never would be. And with good reason. He was a world-renowned cardiothoracic surgeon. He saved lives. While Allen and his cabal of well-trained physicians had made a living feeding people's insatiable egos.

It didn't hurt that Sai had the biggest cock she'd ever encountered. Again, this was saying something, considering the breadth and depth of her personal experience. Janice sometimes wondered if Emily appreciated the man the way he should be appreciated.

She patted Emily's hand. "It's okay, hon. I hear you." She sat back, sipping her fizzy water. "You know, I'm considering this truly a 'welcome to the neighborhood' event. I have some folks coming, other than…you know." She waved her arm, taking in the houses around them. "I'm not sure when we might resume our…activities." She winced. She hated using euphemisms. But one had to, didn't one? Especially with someone as skittish as Emily Arya. "Relax, my dear. Enjoy the day. Meet the new people. We're all friends here. It's my sincere desire to keep it that way."

Well, except for one of us, that is.

"I got a call last night. From Laura."

A gulp of fizzy water shot down Janice's windpipe. She spluttered and choked a few seconds. "Excuse me." She took a deep breath to settle her suddenly rattling nerves. "And how is Laura coping? She moved back near her parents, right? Over in Grand Rapids?"

"Yes," Emily said. She took a sip. Her deep-green eyes narrowed, startling Janice. Emily had never looked at her like that before. She wasn't sure she appreciated it, considering how generous and helpful she'd been.

Don't be bitchy. It doesn't help anything.

"And? How are Colin and Tyler?"

"They're okay, I guess." Emily took a deep breath. "Tom's parents have convinced her to open an investigation into his death."

"An investigation? Why ever for?"

"Because they don't believe he killed himself." Emily's tone was flat.

"That's ridiculous. I mean, you saw him. You and Sai." She and Allen had been away for the week it happened. After the Cassie news flash, they'd decided to decamp, collect themselves, and think about what to do next. They'd spent a lovely two weeks on the southern coast of Spain. Availed themselves of sun, the sea, plenty of great food and drink. Plus a few parties they had standing invitations to attend. Europeans were lovely. They lacked the baked-in puritanical DNA that Americans hauled around like sacks of rotten potatoes, spoiling everything it touched.

"Yes. We did." Emily stared at the deep-blue pool water, her eyes widening before she turned them on Janice. "It was chaotic. I mean, that day. Sai tried to revive him after we dragged him out of the tub. But it was obvious he'd been dead for a while. I don't know." A tear slipped down Emily's cheek. She swiped it away. "Shit."

"Indeed." Janice drained her can of water. "But of course, it has nothing to do with us. I can't imagine what Laura and her parents think happened. Allen said his system was full of opioids, he was dead well before he sank under the water. The poor man was obviously distraught. Getting that many drugs of that caliber is no mean feat. He put some thought and effort into it."

"Yes, Sai said the same thing. But..." She bit her lip. "I mean Tom, you know? I mean, he was the most easygoing, sweetest man. He adored his kids and his wife. We all knew how much he did. Right?" She pinned Janice once again with her glare.

"Yes, we did." Janice mused on that a few seconds. The Franks were a bit of a strange couple, though they'd formed the original cul-de-sac group with her, Allen, and the Murphys. They'd go through periods where only one of them would attend parties. The other staying home with the kids or whatever. They always claimed it had nothing to do with anyone else involved. It was merely how they were "handling themselves" at the moment.

Janice thought she'd understood. Sometimes it was difficult, watching and realizing that your spouse was enjoying themselves when perhaps your experience that night wasn't quite as great. It was part and parcel of the thing. She had no problem with how they handled it and had assumed they were okay with what they were doing.

"Well, anyway. We all know what happened. So, I guess Laura can do whatever she wishes. He was her husband, after all." She rose, unwilling to traverse any further down this conversational side road. She needed a shower. And an extra strong drink.

Allen appeared at the French doors, looking fit in a pair of flat-front khaki shorts and a light peach Polo shirt. His long, tanned legs seemed especially muscular and attractive to her at that moment. His blond hair was a bit tousled, but she could fix that. "Emily," he called out as he took the steps down to the patio. "Here already? What a lovely surprise."

Emily rose and let Allen envelop her in a bear hug. Janice watched, content with how nicely he treated her. The woman had such a massive low-self-esteem problem. Sure, she carried around a bit of extra weight, but she was tall enough that it wasn't unattractive. It made her soft where Janice herself could be sharp and angular. She was warm and friendly and always helpful. Never selfish about anything, up to and including her own husband's attention. Janice had always valued that, even if she felt that half her time was spent building up the woman's ever-deflated ego.

Miscarrying twice hadn't helped. She knew. The first one had happened right after moving onto Connelly Court, before she'd gotten to know them. Emily had spent several days away, and Janice had hardly noticed at the time. She'd been caught up in other things, with other friends.

The second one happened while Sai was gone overseas to lecture. Janice and Allen had helped her through it, gotten her to her doctor who'd admitted her to the hospital for overnight observation. Mainly because the poor thing hadn't been able to stop sobbing. They'd given her a walloping dose of Xanax, hydrated her, and left her alone. Janice had driven her home the day after and stayed with her all day, drinking tea and eating sympathetic, empty calories.

Emily had given up on hormone treatments and risky IVF after that, based on her obstetrician's advice. After that, Janice had decided she and Sai should join their closer-knit friend group. Something she had questioned, at times. But between Emily's innate shyness and her initial unwillingness to go very far into their party activities, Janice knew it had been something good for them, for Emily and Sai as a couple. It had gotten her out of herself, proven to her that sex was good for more than making babies.

Janice got to her feet and stretched out a kink in her lower back while Allen held onto Emily's arms and looked into her eyes. "You okay, Em?"

"Yes, I'm fine. I was telling Janice about Laura's investigation."

"Investigation into what?" He dropped her arms and flashed Janice a look.

Janice shrugged. "She seems to think Tom's death wasn't suicide."

"Huh. Well that's going to be a waste of a lot of time and money. But I guess she has plenty of both." He turned to look around at the party setup. "We good here, Janney? I thought I might have a beer and a sit-down. I mean, if you're done ordering my sorry ass around." He grinned at her then at Emily.

Emily seemed to shrink in the glare of his attention, as usual. "I brought my food over. They can both be served cold. I'll be back in a few hours. With Sai."

"Thanks, Emily." Janice held out her hand for the empty can.

"Do you think... I mean, what if Tom didn't—"

"Don't be silly," Janice snapped. Emily flinched. Janice tried hard not to yell at her to grow a dang spine. "We all know what happened to Tom Franks. And why. Now, let's get ourselves ready to meet the new people. I think it's high time we all moved on, don't you, Allen?"

"Sure do, honey." Allen opened the smoker lid. The odor of perfectly cooked pork ribs wafted out over the patio. "Emily, tell Sai to bring his bocce ball set. We are way overdue for a rematch."

"Okay, I will." Emily stood, staring at Janice then at Allen. Janice smiled, or tried to, while Emily gnawed on her lower lip not unlike Melissa had done earlier that day. A thrill of panic hit Janice's brain. But she brushed it away. She'd spent too many years feeling unhappy with her marriage. The steps she'd taken to save it—to keep Allen focused on her, on them, on their life together, and not on the hundreds of women who crossed his path, their quest for physical perfection driving them to pay thousands of dollars for him to cut them open, clouding their common sense—did not allow for useless worry.

"Laura said…" Emily's voice broke.

"You know what? I say we save this conversation for another day. A day that we aren't planning a party for the new people." She took Emily's elbow and guided her toward the side of the house. "We'll see you and Sai in a few hours."

Emily glanced over her shoulder, seeking Allen most likely. Janice blocked her view on purpose. She was done with this now. Emily needed to get her lumpy rear end home and keep the "Laura said" gossip to herself.

She watched until the woman had disappeared around the front of the house. Then she turned back to the patio, fury making her vision tunnel as she stomped over to Allen. He was futzing around with the ribs, turning them, slathering on more of her homemade barbecue sauce, whistling to himself. She stopped herself before she grabbed his arm. His broad shoulders, strong back, slim waist, all familiar and beloved, made her want to shove him into the pool. She took a long, shuddery breath. He turned at the sound of it, sensing her wanting something, like the well-trained husband he was.

"Janney? Baby? You all right?" He reached for her. She took one then two steps back, the thought of his hands on her making her want to peel off her own skin.

"I'm fine," she said, rubbing her arm. "I need a…shower. And a drink. A very strong drink."

Allen crossed his arms, narrowed his eyes, hardened his expression. "Janice, what's going on?

"I'm stressed about this for some reason. I don't know why." She was shocked to feel the onset of tears. She was no crier. When Allen tried to pull her into a hug, she whirled away from him and ran into the house, up the steps to her perfect, resort-level bathroom, and slammed the door behind her.

She allowed herself exactly five minutes of waterworks before she pulled it together. She had a party to host. As well-preserved as she was, her self-expectation for her looks took a bit of time. The showerheads came at her from every angle, reddening her skin with stinging jets. She raised both her arms and let it beat the sadness or whatever it was right out of her.

Revived, she stepped out onto a soft mat and wrapped herself in one of her oversized bath towels. She sat in front of her mirror and began putting on her face, after using eye drops to lessen the redness from her crying jag. Enough was enough. She'd let Melissa rile her up, and Emily had thrown her way off with the news about an investigation into poor Tom's death. Which meant one thing—her home, her cul-de-sac, her friends' homes, would soon be invaded all over again by policemen, detectives, all manner of people who had no business poking their noses into her business.

She closed her eyes, opened them, and finished her makeup ritual before blowing out her hair then tugging it up into a ponytail. Thanks to all the interruptions, she was too far behind to do anything more. The hour that she preferred to spend admiring all her careful preparations and relaxing with a stiff drink with her husband was already cut to forty-five minutes.

"Janney!" Allen's voice hit her ears like a physical blow. She frowned then forced herself not to. It caused too many wrinkles.

"Yes, dear?"

"Can you come down here please?" His voice sounded tight, pinched, like it did when he was stressed.

"Hells bells," she muttered under her breath. "What is with people today anyway?"

She tugged on her slim, navy capri pants and a sleeveless peach Polo shirt that highlighted her toned and tanned arms nicely and matched Allen's. "Hang on a second. I'll be right there." She grabbed up the fancy, silver flip-flops she preferred for her backyard parties, stopping at the top of the steps to find Allen staring up at her, his eyes wide and filled with something she didn't quite recognize at first. He moved aside, letting her see who else had come by to mess with her pre-party ritual.

"Well, hello, Cassie. What brings you over early?"

Janice took the steps down slowly, trying to order her thoughts about what in the world the silly, knocked-up girl could want with her.

"I want to know if this party is for sex. Or are we pretending we're all regular old friends and normal neighbors again?" Cassie demanded, her hand on the tiny bump of her stomach. Her huge eyes looked haunted, and she was still way too skinny to be almost six months pregnant.

"I'm sure I don't know what you mean," Janice said. "Let's sit down and have some iced tea." She steered the girl clear of Allen, who was standing in the middle of the floor, rubbing the back of his neck and looking like a teenager caught with his drawers down by some girl's parents.

Men. Sometimes, she truly hated them.

Chapter Nine

B*un in The Oven*

....

CASSIE WASN'T 100 PERCENT convinced she was in her right mind when she decided to abandon her kale-and-red-cabbage salad and march herself over to the Cooper's to confront Janice. No one, best she could tell, had ever dared do such a thing. To confront or question or otherwise undermine the woman's supreme alpha-female status on their street. And not just any confrontation, either. An in-her-face blunt question, using language she knew Janice didn't like.

But, at this point, Cassie figured she had little to lose. Sure, Barrett had returned to her side, more or less. But things were still weird, which wasn't surprising. The morning she'd woken up after that lovely night he'd brought her home from the hospital, he'd left for work already and hadn't returned until well past eight p.m., with nary a bit of communication in between. He'd made love to her again after a dinner of homemade tempeh burgers and quinoa broccoli salad. But there had been an edge of anger to it she didn't care for. She didn't like it rough—never had, and he knew it.

For all Barrett's bluster and braggadocio, there were still some things he wouldn't do. Oral sex, for one, which was something she liked. Oh, he would happily be on the receiving end but never, ever, for any reason, would return the favor. He'd gladly *watch* her receiving it, but he never got the message that she wanted it. That she'd like for *him* to do it to her.

Selfish bastard. He was that without a doubt. He was set in his ways, from how he wanted his shirts laundered and hung on wooden hangers with the top button done up, to the way he expected her to be the perfect corporate wife—throwing dinner parties, attending others, acting like the arm-candy airheads his partners were married to. Cassie was a lot of things. Flighty was not one of them. Although she knew enough to play that part when she needed to. She had deep thoughts about a lot of things, real issues like climate change, vaccinations, organic farming, and equal pay for women.

All her fellow trophies wanted to discuss was Botox, butt lifts, and Pilates classes.

Cassie took herself seriously. She took her health that way too, and had spent a lot of energy attempting to convince Barrett to try her wheat grass and all-natural-vitamin regimen. He wouldn't touch wheat grass but had become 90 percent vegetarian, thanks to her cooking skills. She kept salmon and trout on rotation, making them more pescatarian.

She knew her looks didn't lend themselves to her being taken seriously. Barrett had, at least once upon a time. But now, when she'd catch him staring at her when he thought she wasn't looking, she saw a mixture of disgust, pity, and a healthy dose of scorn.

Maybe she deserved it. Maybe it had been all her fault. But then again, it wasn't, now was it?

Something about this revelation had made her drop her fancy cutting knife mid-slice. She barely heard it clatter to the tile floor. Not knowing what was expected of them tonight, when once upon a time an invite to a party at the Coopers' meant one thing only was pissing her the hell off.

She hesitated before marching herself over to the Coopers' house, taking in her profile in the downstairs powder room mirror. Her bump was more pronounced, and she could no longer ignore the tiny flutters she felt more and more frequently.

The baby. Her baby. A baby. It was living inside her right now.

The medication she'd gotten in suppository form helped. She'd regained a smidgeon of her appetite and had made a point to eat nothing but dark-green leafy vegetables for the folic acid they supplied, along with peanut butter. Lots and lots and lots of peanut butter. She craved that nasty stuff day and night and would give in to the cravings, as her doctor had ordered her to do. She had a serious weight deficit to make up, if she expected her baby to be born healthy.

Her baby.

A baby whose father was a man who....

She forced herself to stop that line of thinking lest it make her scream.

It was official. Her life was a long, waking nightmare anymore.

She ran her hand down the bump, felt the little wiggles and jiggles under her hand, pondering how lucky she was that Barrett had come back to her, at least on the surface. She'd worked hard to get him where he was, with her, in this house, as her husband. The whole Cooper-initiated special party scene hadn't been something she wanted. But he had. He'd wanted to do it and had told her in no uncertain terms that they would be. If she didn't like it after they'd gone to one or two of the Coopers' events, they would reevaluate it together.

Thing was—she had liked it. Man, oh man, had she ever. Several of her neighbors blew her mind on a regular basis with their oral skills—and one of them wasn't a man. She'd enjoyed it enough that she and Barrett had hosted a couple of gatherings themselves, more intimate than the ones at the Coopers'. And therein was her core problem. She'd never experienced anything like it and, quite frankly, if she had to do it over, she'd get herself on the pill or something, despite her mistrust of Big Pharma and their happy hormones.

As she watched herself and thought about some of her more gratifying experiences, practicing the lifestyle they'd been invited to participate in and that her husband had insisted that she try, a deep-red flush crept up her neck to her cheeks at one memory in particular. She touched her face. It was hot, as if she had a high fever. Her skin prickled. Her scalp tingled. Her nipples hardened in an embarrassing way.

Cassie turned away from the mirror, tears making her eyes burn.

No more, Cassandra. You had a nice thing. And you messed it all up.

Without another conscious thought about the consequences, she slid her feet into flip-flops and marched over to the Coopers' house and said her piece, right in front of Allen.

Then she let Janice manhandle her over to the kitchen table. Took the glass of water. Drank it. Swiped at her lips with the back of her hand. Janice was sitting, looking perfectly put together as always. The jarring fact of her and Allen's matching preppy getups no longer made her want to laugh. The other woman's makeup was flawless. Her hair was tugged back in a youthful ponytail. Her eyes were bright. Her skin glowed with good health and plenty of time spent under a talented surgeon's knife.

Cassie swallowed hard. She still looked like lukewarm shit, and she knew it. While she wasn't as vain as Janice Cooper, she took pride in her looks. She had to, as the wife of a partner in one of the most powerful law firms in Southeast Michigan. It was her job to look good and to maintain their home in such a way that gave every outward appearance of successful happiness. For this, she was compensated handsomely, as plenty of people liked to remind her—either overtly or with a sort of snide disdain that she hated. Mainly because it made her feel worthless.

"So, about my question," she said. Janice wasn't going to wiggle out of this. It was a legit request for information. She had to know what she and Barrett were walking into here, in this house, where they had spent many pleasant hours since they'd moved onto the street. "I need to know…" She gulped. Tears were bubbling up in her yet again. One slipped down her cheek. She let it, knowing it might soften the woman up. Allen lurked nearby. She could sense him, smell his sandalwood soap, and other familiar odors that she'd come to associate with him.

Janice patted her hand. "Cassie, honey, this is a party to welcome our new neighbors. You know that. I've got some other nice folks stopping by, too. My grandboys will be here for the first few hours."

"I figured that much, Janice. Please don't use that condescending tone with me." She took a deep breath. "Plenty of your parties begin that way. You know this. I know this. He knows this." She looked at Allen who took a couple of steps back as if unwilling to acknowledge his part in any of it.

He was a selfish bastard. Not quite on the same level as her own beloved spouse but not far from it. The only truly nice men in their friends' group were Tom, who was dead now. And Sai, of course, bless him and his super-talented lips and tongue to heaven forever. Ryan Murphy was more confusing. But that made him an awful lot of fun. That and the fact that she always felt as though his wife, the classy blonde Melissa, didn't quite approve of any of it.

"What I want…what I need to know, is if we are all expected to gather later, after all the straights have gone home and all the kids have left. It's an honest question, Janice, and I need an answer. I've gone too far with this." She rested her hand on the bump—the baby, she had to start thinking about it as a baby. "To talk in euphemisms and secret goddamned code."

Janice's face flushed. "Cassandra, you know I don't care for that kind of language." She sounded like someone's virginal librarian, cat-lady aunt. Cassie threw her head back and laughed until her throat hurt. Janice's frown deepened.

Gasping, and barely able to contain the giggles, Cassie swiped at her streaming eyes and pointed at Janice. "You? You have the dirtiest fucking mouth of any of us...under the right circumstances. Don't deny it, Janice."

The woman blinked. She looked over at her husband then back at Cassie. Her ice-blue eyes were no longer twinkly and accommodating. They were frozen and sharp. Cassie believed she could feel them piercing her skin and drawing blood.

"I think that perhaps you and Barrett should skip today's event," she said, rising to her feet. Cassie matched her, put a hand on her arm, felt the warmth of her skin. It sent a shaft of something familiar up Cassie's spine.

She leaned into the party host's ear and whispered, "We're coming to the party, Janney. You can't cut us out of this now. I heard Tom's parents want to reopen the investigation into his death. We're all going to need to have our stories straight, won't we?" She allowed herself a tiny nip of earlobe. A slight brush of the side of Janice's breast with her fingers. She felt the corresponding response all the way down to her core.

Come to find out, Barrett and Allen had something in common, fantasy-wise, at least as related to their wives. She had obliged, mostly to humor him. What difference did it make who she kissed? Who went down on her? Turned out, fulfilling her husband's voyeuristic fantasies was the hottest damn thing Cassie had ever done. As a matter of fact, the show that she and Janice would put on suited a lot of their neighbors quite well. And it was the only way she and Barrett would remain in the same room with her—if she were doing the girl-on-girl bit with Janice.

The other woman's soft angles, lips, and light touch did something to her she never thought she'd enjoy. She'd gotten addicted to it by the time Tom Franks had come to her house in the smack middle of the afternoon and told her that she was the most beautiful woman he'd ever seen.

She sighed and let go of Janice's arm. Touched her cheek. Smiled. Janice was breathing heavily in a way Cassie knew very well. Her entire body yearned for a return to the good old days. She felt Allen's heavy hand on the small of her back, giving her a tiny push forward. She stumbled, more than she should have. Janice grabbed her to keep her from face-planting like a clumsy fool. Lips brushed her burning-hot cheek. Hands pushed her hair back from her face.

Someone helped her into a chair and put a fresh glass of water in front of her. "Cassie," Allen said. Janice shot him a look that Cassie believed could easily have killed the man then crouched in front of her, hands on her thighs. "It's all right, Cassandra. You and Barrett should come. We want you here. As for later, I'd say the answer to that is no." She pressed her palm against the bump—the baby. Cassie squeezed her eyes shut, a roil of fury, frustration, embarrassment, and visceral lust. She tasted it—like copper or blood—consuming her. She covered Janice's hand with hers. She'd broken more than one rule. Not only had she let a man other than her husband impregnate her, she'd gotten emotionally attached.

But not to anyone's husband.

Oh no. Leave it to her to discover her inner lesbian in the midst of all this crap.

Janice squeezed her knee and rose. "Drink."

Ever the good girl, the girl who did what she was told, Cassie took a sip, put the glass down, and wiped sweat off her face. Nausea teased around her edges. She was due for a dose of medication. She got to her feet again.

"I'm sorry," she whispered.

Janice's smile was the opposite of warm. "You don't owe me an apology."

Cassie stood, weaving, miserable, and ashamed and willing the woman to pull her into her arms and hold her. To tell her that everything would, indeed, be fine.

She didn't.

They parted ways with forced pleasantries, promises to see each in a few hours. Allen didn't glance at her as she made her way past the pool and to the side yard, on her way back to her own house.

Chapter Ten

P*arty Time*

• • • •

"COME *on*, Michael. You're going to make us late." Amelia glanced around her kitchen, satisfied that she could leave it in its current pristine state. She obsessed over cleanliness. Always had. But now that she and her family were in their very own home, she was determined to make everything shine, no matter what.

Tyler wandered in, thumb stuck in his mouth, ragged blankie clutched in his other hand. He'd been out of sorts since they'd moved in, but she'd been prepared for that. Her pediatrician had warned her. The books she trusted concurred. Her little man would take some time to adjust to his new house, the room she'd designed and outfitted for him, his fabulous new yard where a safe, modern, play structure would be done in another day or two.

"Hey, baby. C'mere. Give Mama a kiss." She crouched on the floor. It was important for children to not feel they were being spoken down to. "Come on, sugar." She held out her hand. He shook his head and backed around the cabinets that separated the kitchen from the den, hiding again.

Amelia repressed the urge to grab his arm and yank him to her. She took a long, calming breath and got up slowly. She'd been advised to ignore this sort of behavior. Not to give it any oxygen. The problem was, Michael had been in Illinois for depositions last week and she'd been unable to go anywhere, thanks to Tyler's inability to control himself.

She'd had groceries delivered, as it was a much better use of her time, and it allowed some other person to get paid to shop for her. But she wanted to explore her fitness center options, check out the local coffee shops, some of which had changed since she'd last lived here, visit the farmer's market for some fresher produce, that sort of thing. She hadn't done much of it while at their rental place. She'd been busy with a newborn, she'd told herself. And, for the last several months, finding and procuring the right house had been her main obsession.

When she'd called her mother, sobbing in frustration after a dismal twenty-four hours in the new place sans Michael and with a little boy who wouldn't stop crying, or screaming, refusing to eat, the woman had been in the car and on her way to them within an hour. Precisely what Amelia had known she'd do.

Theresa Stanhope's tendency to overemphasize Tyler's dark coloring, his full lips, his curly hair was irritating as all get out. She did it in an irritating fake-complimentary way that Amelia knew would cause conflict for them soon. But what she provided in the way of letting Amelia get the hell out of the house for an hour or two at a time was worth it for time being.

Besides, it wasn't like Michael's mother didn't do the same thing, only in the other direction. Annoying. But what could you do?

Her mother had left the morning Michael was due back. Which was best for all parties concerned. Amelia appreciated that much about her sense of timing.

At this moment, she sure did wish her mom were here again, scooping her son up and spiriting him off to his room, or to the bathtub, or down the road to a park she'd found. She was nervous about this silly block party thing or whatever it was. She'd sweated through two shirt options already. The thought of not having to drag him over there sounded like the best idea ever thought by anyone.

"Okay, we ready, guys?" Michael appeared in the kitchen. Tyler ran to his leg and gripped it, thumb still in his mouth, dark eyes pinned on hers. She sighed and picked up the glass of Merlot she'd poured herself. Or was she already on her second one? She couldn't recall. It didn't matter anyway. She drained it then headed into the powder room to brush her teeth.

"God damn it," she burst out as she stared at the dark stains under both arms. Ever since having Tyler, excess sweatiness had been a serious problem for her. Today it was a thousand times worse. "What the hell." She ran up the stairs to her room. "I'll be back in a sec, Michael."

"We're good," he said. She ignored the flare of anger over the fact that Tyler preferred his father over her lately. It was to be expected. Her pediatrician had warned her that her ongoing close proximity during the stress of moving could force the boy to turn to others, her mother, his father, as representative of something that didn't make him upset. She was okay with it. She and Michael were a team after all.

As she was staring at the options arrayed neatly on wooden hangers, her nipples tingled then began to ache. "Crap." She'd forgotten what time it was. She grabbed a sleeveless black linen top, figuring that when she got all sweaty, no one would notice. Why she hadn't thought of this before was anyone's guess. She ran back down the steps, leaving her blouse unbuttoned.

Tyler was starting to fuss, right on schedule. When he spotted her, he reached out, tiny fists making gimmie-gimmie motions. Michael handed him over then glanced at his phone screen. "I thought we had to be there by now." But his voice was calm. He knew this drill. She sat on her custom leather couch, cradling Tyler to her breast. This was her time with him. She never skipped it.

Ten minutes later to the second, he let go of her nipple and looked up at her, his expression a mix of confusion and adoration. She took his hand, kissed it, and pressed it to her heart. "I love you, baby boy," she said.

"Ma," he said with that big grin that turned her heart into mush every single time.

She smiled and touched his nose. "You want to go swimming, sweet boy? Our new neighbors have a pool."

His eyes brightened. He rolled off her lap to find his father. "Da!" he yelped. "Sim!" She buttoned her shirt while Tyler scrambled over to his father. "Sim! Sim!" It still amazed her that the boy's every utterance was exclamatory.

"All right, buddy. All right." Michael picked him up and kissed his cheek. "Do we have all the necessary stuff, Ames?"

"Of course," she said, irritated. How long had he known her? She was always prepared. "Bag's by the back door." They made their way as a unit toward the glass door out onto the deck. She grabbed Tyler's bag, which contained a complete set of fresh clothes, his adorable tiny swim trunks, a swim diaper, two regular diapers, her breast pump. All the essentials.

Michael smiled down at her. She slid her arm around his waist. They hadn't had a chance to christen their new bed yet. He'd only been back for a couple of days. But the time he'd been gone had thrown Tyler for such a massive loop, they'd been forced to let him sleep in their bed again.

Something she'd promised Michael would end for good once they'd gotten properly settled in the new house.

He'd been a good sport about it. It was hard not to be. Their poor sweet boy had been flexible. This move had simply been too much to ask of him. They'd fallen asleep as a group, their fingers entwined on Tyler's hip. His soft, sleepy breath blew the ends of her hair, filled her restless mind with confusing dreams.

The bottom line was, she and her fabulous husband were still in the negative column when it came to sex. Something her post-pregnancy mind and body was clamoring for all of a sudden. More importantly, she knew her man needed it from her.

The press of the side of his body against hers as he held Tyler in his other arm and she clutched the diaper bag, was driving her mad. What she *wanted* to do was to feed Tyler a few bites of her homemade baby food—she didn't trust that nasty processed crap—give him a bath, and tuck him into his new big-boy bed. This whole party thing was messing with his established schedule. It would be simple, really. She could wander over for a few minutes while Michael gave the boy his bath, send her regards, explain the problem—her toddler son and his rigidity was making everyone nuts. Michael was exhausted after his grueling travel and work schedule. That sort of thing.

Then she'd wander back over and meet Michael in their new bedroom. That was what she wanted right now. Not to meet a bunch of intimidating strangers.

"Sim!" Tyler yelped again. "Da! Ty sim! Want sim!" He had his father's face between his hands. Amelia felt a rush of pride at the fact that her son was speaking in short sentences already. It was the breast milk, she knew. And the way they communicated with him—in full, adult sentences, not baby talk.

"You know it, buddy," Michael said. He kissed Tyler's cheek then Amelia's hair. "This is gonna be awesome. Cool neighbors. One of them with a pool? We scored. Thanks to your Mommy, Ty."

"Ma!" Tyler reached over and patted her cheek. "Love Ma!"

"Yep. I love your ma, too, my man." Michael's hand dropped to her ass and gripped hard. "I miss her," he whispered into her hair.

"Not long now, Michael," she said, her lips pressed to his firm chest, meaning it more than she'd ever meant anything. This whole parenting gig wasn't quite what she'd imagined, at least when it came to her body and how it would remain hijacked well beyond giving birth.

"I love you, Ames," he said.

She looked up at him, met his gaze fully, ignoring Tyler's incessant clamoring for their mutual attention. "I love you, Michael. I adore you. And I'm going to make this up to you, soon."

"It's okay, honey," he said, pressing his lips to hers while Tyler wiggled and hollered about swimming and the pool. "I understand."

Her entire body filled with the sort of pleasant satisfaction she hadn't felt in a while. This was why she'd married him. He was, on many levels, such an amazing man. "I know you do. But I need you. I'm ready," she insisted.

She knew full well that getting him worked up before they headed into a social situation would make the party that much more interesting for them both. Role-playing was something else he'd introduced her to, something else she never in a zillion years thought she'd enjoy doing, sexually speaking. She went up on her tiptoes and bit his lower lip.

"Agreed," he said, his voice dipping lower in that way it did when he was turned on. It made her warm all over. "Short and sweet."

"Da!" Tyler tried to grab Michael's face again and tug it around to get his attention. "Sim!"

"Wait, Ty. Dad's busy right now." He grinned down at her, cupped her cheek with his hand. "Soon, baby."

"Yes." She nodded. "Very soon."

All right, son," Michael said, shifting Tyler higher on his hip. "You ready to meet some new friends?"

"Sim!" the kid hollered for the millionth time.

"Right. That," Michael said. "What about you, Amelia? You ready to meet our new neighbors?"

She squared her shoulders. Her parents had excellent relationships with their neighbors. The way everyone flowed from one house to the next, stopping by for coffee early, booze later, had made an impression on her. She wanted that same experience. To feel like her house was merely an extension of a bigger ecosystem—a block, a street, or in her case, this amazing cul-de-sac she'd lucked into.

"Yes. I am. Let's meet the neighbors."

They made their way the short distance between their house and the Coopers', who were hosting tonight's shindig. It was almost five thirty, a full hour and a half past the official start of the party. But that was all right. They were the guests of honor, she'd been told. They should come when it was convenient for them, given the baby and all.

Amelia hesitated about halfway over. Something about the scene in front of her eyes—the couples arrayed around the pool in varying stages of drinking, eating, laughing, talking—made her uncomfortable. She froze and tugged on Michael's arm, willing him to go back to their house, to their life, without all of this fuss.

"Amelia!"

She looked over to where the sound of her name had emerged from the din of partygoers. Janice, the hostess, and one of the three women including her real estate agent who'd shown up at her door this past week with cookies, brownies, and in the case of the pregnant one, gluten-free lemon bars. "We're happy you're here."

She'd been embarrassed that Tyler had refused to emerge from his room during these neighborly stopovers. But she hadn't forced him out. That would only make him more resentful. None of the women had minded when she'd said he was "napping." They'd be getting their fill of him soon enough.

Janice stopped dead in her tracks when she saw Michael. Amelia grinned to herself. It wasn't anything new. Her husband was striking at first glance and only got better looking the more you got to know him. Her grin faded when something about the way Janice took her husband in, the way her gaze raked him from head to toe seemed blatant, borderline rude.

Then her new neighbor rallied. She smiled. Reached for Michael's outstretched hand. Shook it. Touched Tyler's hair with a more genuine grin. "Do you like to swim, Tyler? We have some floaties, if you want them. My grandboys would love some company." She glanced back at Amelia, and something about that look made her feel as if she'd been forgotten in the last few seconds. It wasn't a pleasant sensation but one she chalked up to her nervousness and aggravation at having to be here, and not in bed with her husband.

Tyler wiggled out of Michael's arms and made a beeline for the patio. She started after him, terrified by the fact of the pool and of her little boy falling right in headfirst. Michael gripped her arm.

"It's okay, Ames, I see him."

She tensed under his touch. Janice's smile became something resembling benevolent. A sort of *Oh, how cute the adorable couple is feuding over helicoptering.*

Before Amelia could react, a tall, handsome, older man, slid inflatable bands onto Tyler's arms. She lurched forward when the man led her son to the edge of the pool. Michael held her back. "He's fine, Ames. Relax."

"But...he...he's not wearing his swimsuit." And like that, he was in the pool, wearing the borrowed floaties and in nothing but his diaper, laughing and splashing with the other kids. A youngish woman in a modest one-piece suit got in and stood next to him then waved over at them. "Oh." She forced herself to relax.

Janice took her elbow. "That's Suzanne. She's my grandsons' nanny. He's in good hands." Come on, honey. People are dying to meet y'all." Her soft Southern accent was out of place enough to be comical. Amelia stared at her, nerves shredded from the past days' worth of stress.

"Okay," she said, glancing back at her husband, her rock, her anchor. He smiled at her then turned to face an attractive blonde woman who'd appeared at his other side, her gaze as eager as Janice's had been.

It was all a bit too weird, or maybe the word was surreal. But Amelia let herself be carried along, passed from group to group, from one set of admiring eyes to the next. She ate ribs, kale salad, some kind of quinoa thing, and plenty of fresh fruit. Once she'd declared that she wanted wine, a glass was pressed into her hand and never allowed to empty.

At several points, she heard Tyler yelping, laughing, hollering. But he never seemed to need her.

At another point, she sought Michael's face. She could always locate it. But it seemed to get farther and farther away from her as the night went on and she got steadily drunker. Irresponsible, as a mother. She'd have to pump her breasts and dump out the poisoned milk. Give Tyler a sippy cup of thawed breast milk from the freezer.

But it was all right. These were the nicest people. Friendly, and eager to put her at ease.

She smiled at her host, Allen Cooper, who'd barely left her side all evening. "This is a great neighborhood," she said, hearing herself slur.

He grinned at her. She squinted through her increasing booze fog. Gosh, he sure was a good-looking older guy. At one point, she'd swear someone touched her ass, cupping it gently, making her glance over her shoulder, expecting to see Michael but seeing Allen instead. She'd gasped, flinched, and moved out of his reach. "Sorry," she said for some reason as a bolt of something like dread hit her brain. "I should go. We should go. I'm...I've had way too much to drink."

She needed Michael. Something was off about this whole thing and she wanted her husband by her side. Now.

"You all right, Amelia?" Janice appeared at her elbow with a bottle of water.

"I'm...yes. I'm fine." She grabbed the water and gulped it down. This had to be the oddest barbecue she'd ever attended. "I've had a bit too much to drink though."

Janice patted her arm. Handsome silver fox Allen was on her other side. She blinked fast. "Where's my husband? Where's Tyler?"

"They are right here, sweetie," Janice said, stepping aside to reveal them both. Tyler was sound asleep on Michael's shoulder, thumb in his mouth. Amelia exhaled in relief.

"Oh okay, thank you. Thank you both." She turned to smile at Allen then over at Janice. All of a sudden, she was surrounded by the people she either already knew or had met tonight. Melissa the real estate agent, and her handsome husband Ryan. The Aryas. The LeBlancs—the wife, Cassie, resting her hand on her baby bump and looking serene.

Exhaustion stole over her. Michael pulled her close. "This was amazing," he said to the gathered group, which at that moment resembled a den of wolves licking their chops at the sight of fresh meat. They were all...staring at her, at Michael, sizing them up. But why? For what?

She glanced up at her husband when he spoke again. Jesus, she was sloshed. For the first time since she'd gotten pregnant. "Thank you," Michael was saying. His body was relaxed. His smile legit. "This is going to be better than we ever thought it would be."

An odd thing to say. Suddenly, she wanted nothing more than to be away from this...this wolf pack. Wanted to be back in her house, their house. She slumped into him, trying and failing to ignore the way every single set of female eyes locked onto Michael as he spoke.

"Let's go," she said under her breath. "Michael," she said, louder.

"Better get my wife home," he said. "Good night, all. Thanks Janice and Allen, for hosting us." He tightened his grip on her arm.

It was the last thing her conscious brain retained for a while. That, and the way Michael had tucked her into their bed, kissing her softly on the lips. She dropped off, or, rather, passed out cold for a few hours, wakening when the pain in her swollen breasts wouldn't allow her another minute of sleep.

"Ow, crap." She sat, cupping them in both hands, their heat radiating down her arms. She let go of one and reached for him, but her hand met an empty pillow. "What the..." She turned, wincing at the pain. "Michael," she whispered into the pitch-black room.

No answer. She realized at that moment that he'd not been in here with her at all. She could tell. A good wife always could.

She swung her feet around and put them on the Turkish carpet she'd chosen for their bedroom. Pain in her boobs and her head made her dizzy for a few seconds. But aggravation at Michael's absence from their bed subsumed all of that. She rose, looked down at herself, and realized she was still in her clothes from the party, for heaven's sake. But there was no way she could take her bra off right now. She had to get her hands on the damn breast pump, and fast.

A quick limp down the hall, a peek into Tyler's room to reassure herself he was still alive and breathing then more limps down the steps to the kitchen. The moon sent a shaft of bright light onto the island from the skylight. She paused, admiring it a few seconds before the pain hit her in both her nipples and her head. "Shit. I need painkillers. Where is my...Michael!" She yelled this time, thanks to her frustration at his odd absence combined with the way her tits felt like someone had shoved bowling balls inside them that were trying to burst out of her body.

Keeping an ear out for Tyler who would no doubt wake up with all the noise she was making, she sighed and looked around for the diaper bag. After downing a couple of Advil, she stuck the suction cup onto her left breast and flipped the switch, exhaling in relief but still having to hold her right one to keep it from falling the hell off.

She heard something that sounded like it was coming from next door. Something like a loud burst of laughter. She got up, hobbled to the back door, and peered through the custom wooden vertical blinds. The Coopers' backyard and patio still had a few tiki torches lit, but, best she could tell, no one was out there. The noise hit her ears again. It was part laughter, part...something else.

She unlocked the door. Slid it open a fraction of an inch. The sound of night insects filled the air at first. Cursing under her breath, she ran back to the kitchen to dump the boozy breast milk down the sink then latched the thing onto her right breast for a few seconds then dumped that out, too. Thankful she could breathe now, she opened the door wide enough to slip through it.

Her deck and yard were full dark. The next-door patio was, indeed, empty. But people were making noises, talking, or something, still. Curious, she made her way to the corner of her deck, which was angled such that she could see lit windows on the back of the Cooper house.

One big one, upstairs, shone with light. Amelia leaned out over the railing. Curtains were drawn, but they weren't opaque enough to hide much. A couple of backlit figures walked in front of the window. They stopped, turned to each other, kissed. No biggie, she figured. Janice and Allen celebrating the end of a successful party. She drew back before she fell onto the grass below.

At that moment, another shadow seemed to cross the window then another. The new shadows joined Janice and Allen. Drew them apart. "What in the..."

"Ma! Ma!"

The sound of her son's cry made her pull back from the railing fast, stumbling over her own feet.

He was really crying, like he was scared, or in pain. "Maaaaaa..."

"Coming," she muttered under her breath, wondering if she could feed him or if her milk were still too wine-tinged. She looked back once more, confused by what she thought she'd seen at the Coopers' bedroom window. But the light was out now. All was dark but for the flickering torches around their pool. All quiet, but for their sound system which she could've sworn had been off when she'd come out here. Now, strains of Simon and Garfunkel trailed across the pool, the lawn, to her back deck.

Tyler howled again. Amelia headed inside, ran upstairs, scooped him up, and held him to her. He gripped her neck, obviously in the throes of a nightmare. Once he got awake enough to fumble around for her breasts, seeking comfort, she headed downstairs and held him, letting him suck on his thumb while she heated a container of stored breast milk.

"Ma," he sighed, as she stuck the bottle nipple into his mouth. Too tired to think straight, she headed upstairs, back to her room, settling Tyler into her side and letting him drain the bottle. The fact that Michael hadn't materialized hit her sleepy, still-drunk brain, but without enough force to keep her from dropping back under once she'd put the empty bottle on the bedside table and felt her boy snuggle into her side.

Chapter Eleven

I*n Hindsight*

• • • •

"YOU KNOW, THERE'S NOTHING quite like a well-made cup of coffee on a holiday Sunday morning."

"You speak the truth, my love."

Ryan looked up from his perusal of the morning news via iPad and smiled. None of the news was worth his time. It was all crap. The whole world was going to hell, sans handbaskets. But he read it nonetheless, seeking local nuggets he might put to use for his company. Murphy Construction Company had snagged at least two prime retail projects, thanks to him keeping his ear to the ground. They had projects scheduled well into the next eighteen months, but that made him nervous. He preferred to see his crews booked a solid twenty-four, or thirty-six months into the future. Given the inevitable screwups and fall-throughs, he'd be stupid to consider anything else acceptable.

And, while Ryan Murphy was a lot of things, stupid was not one of them.

"C'mere," he said, tugging his wife toward him and into his lap. She giggled when he cupped her breast under the silky nightie and buried his face in her neck. "Mmmm," he said when her nipple hardened under his fingers. She shifted to allow his hand to drop between her thighs. God, but he was horny, especially after last night. That was one of the things about this illicit shit they did together, he realized as he rose, taking Melissa with him.

"Upstairs," she whispered against his lips as she reached into his shorts. "Now."

"Your wish," Ryan said, taking her hand and double-stepping to the flight of stairs, tiptoeing past Danny's closed door, turned on beyond belief at the sight of Melissa's long, bare legs and bikini panties as she ducked into their bedroom. He shut the door behind him and pointed to the rumpled king-sized bed with its expensive sheets and mountain of pillows. "My command," he said, licking his lips.

98

The thing was, he mused later, watching her while she rode him like a rodeo queen, her body gripping him hard. The thing was...he groaned when she dropped over his body her long blonde hair framing their faces and ground down. The thing was...resuming their previous activities with the Coopers didn't deplete him the way he'd figured it would. Oh no. It had the opposite effect. Memories of last night, as fraught as it was, made him tense then sent him right over the edge.

"Jesus H., Mel," he said, trying to catch his breath.

"Yep, my thoughts exactly." She lifted up and off him and headed for the bathroom, her sweet bare ass swaying. She shook him awake. "Danny's calling for you," she said, brushing her lips over his. "I'm going to the gym."

"Okay. Got it. Dad time," he grunted as he sat, rubbing his eyes, discombobulated for a moment as to the time of day, much less the day. She tugged on those expensive leggings with the weird Greek letter logo. Shrugged into a matching bra with a zillion straps. Put on socks then her shoes then tugged her dark-blonde hair up into a messy ponytail. "I love you, Melissa."

She glanced over her shoulder at him, her eyes flashing before she headed into the bathroom again. "You love what I let you do," she called back to him. "I get that."

"Well, okay but still..." His limbs felt limp from all the action. His brain was fuzzing over, dragging him under for his preferred fifteen-minute post-orgasm snooze. Something about her comment was shitty. He knew that. But it was true. He did love it. What healthy, red-blooded, honest-with-himself man wouldn't? When they'd been at the Coopers' that first evening, eating perfect steaks, drinking expensive booze from the old-fashioneds to the red wine, he'd been clueless what was actually going on, Melissa had had to practically draw him a picture once they got home.

That was the thing, he mused once more as he heard Mel's footsteps on the stairs then the door to the garage slam shut. The very concept of what the Coopers had proposed to them that night—that he'd totally missed somehow—had turned her on to the point of ravenous. She'd fucked him the next morning, too, and again, later that day. It had been a pleasant change of scenery considering they'd been in one of their dry spells, mostly thanks to how much Danny drained them emotionally and physically.

"Dad?"

He jerked awake with a snort, dragging the sheet over his naked lower half. "Yeah, uh, hey buddy. Sorry. Dad's still tired." He sat, confused for a hot second as to what time of the day it was. His dick tingled, reminding him what had been going down for the last few hours. He grinned to himself.

Going down indeed.

Jesus, he was a sicko, thinking about sex while his fragile, handsome little boy stood right outside his bedroom door, rubbing the sleep out of his eyes. He stepped into his jockeys and found a pair of jeans on the floor. "Okay. I think it's a pancake morning. You?"

Danny eyed him for a moment before dropping his gaze to the floor, something that irritated Ryan to no end. His own father had been adamant about meeting people's eyes when you spoke to them when he'd been growing up. And he'd not hesitated to bestow a solid whap upside his kids' heads to make his point, either.

Ryan dragged a T-shirt over his head, relishing the soreness in his nipples. He washed his hands and face, brushed his teeth, ran fingers through his too-long dark-blond hair. Pancakes. And more coffee. That was what he needed.

"Can I stir the batter?"

Ryan blinked at his reflection in the mirror. He'd actually forgotten Danny was there. He did that a lot. He'd done it with the girls, too. It wasn't that he didn't love them. He adored them, all of them, but sometimes it was in the abstract. Like, yeah, his DNA had contributed to their existence. But someone else was responsible for the day-to-day well-being. That was the way of things. His first wife hadn't worked, other than volunteering at the girls' various schools.

Melissa, on the other hand...

He shook his head, refusing to admit that the very fact of Daniel Sean Murphy's existence was thanks to his own dogged desire to get between the sexy young woman's legs. While he was still married.

Jesus, he was an idiot.

"Dad?" The boy's soft voice made him close his eyes and deny that the sound of it was like fingernails down some kind of internal blackboard to him.

"Yeah, buddy. I'm ready. Let's go make breakfast."

. . . .

A COUPLE OF HOURS LATER, he was back combing through the boring local news, seeking more work for his company while Danny stared down at his iPad, intent on god only knew what. *Screen time* was a point of contention in the house, among other things Danny-related. Melissa said that they couldn't deny that Danny was really good at games and enjoyed his time on the tablet, or in front of the TV screen in his room. Ryan insisted he needed to get the hell outside, throw a ball, ride a bike, find some friends.

He stared at his son's profile as he finished his coffee, the smell of pancake syrup and bacon still clinging to the air around him. The boy was the spitting image of his mother—sharp nose, thin lips, huge green eyes. He was a good-looking kid. Everyone had always said so. But he had no interest in any of the things Ryan enjoyed, and probably never would. And his cringy, eyes-on-the-floor mannerisms, while an improvement over how he used to scream and hide under his damn bed for hours, confused and irritated Ryan to the point of fury at times.

He was a shithead about it. He knew that. He loved his boy, his one son. But damn him to hell and back, he didn't get this whole *on-the-spectrum* BS other than to accept that whatever drugs Melissa and the doctors had sorted out did help the kid manage better at school.

"Knock, knock!"

Ryan flinched in surprise at the sharp rap on the French doors behind him. When he confirmed who matched the voice, he motioned for the man to come on in, shoving the slight thrill of aggravation at the sight of Allen Cooper wearing his usual, happy-go-lucky smile.

"Morning," he said, holding up his Murphy Construction Company branded mug. "Can I pour you some?"

"Would love it," Allen said. He held up an empty plastic bowl. "Making the rounds with these."

"Set it there," Ryan said, motioning to the kitchen in general. It was messy, thanks to their breakfast. But he'd deal with it later. "Thanks." He got up and poured from his second pot. "How do you take it?"

"Straight up," Allen said, holding out his hand. "The darker the better."

The men sipped and eyed each other a few seconds. Allen turned to look at Danny, who'd retreated to a far chair and pulled a blanket over his head. Ryan could see the glow of the screen from underneath it. "How're you this morning, young man?" Allen boomed. Ryan tensed. The man knew loud voices made the kid twitchy. If Janice were here, he'd never have done that.

This guy, he thought, who had drilled Ryan's wife while he'd watched, mere hours before.

He shook his head, trying to get rid of the cobwebs. He hadn't wanted to resume the wife swap activities. But he and Melissa hadn't discussed it before they'd gone to the so-called welcome-to-the-neighborhood party. They should have. Somehow, any conversation they attempted lately—or at least since Tom Franks had pulled his stupid stunt—devolved into a fight.

He sighed. Allen turned back to face him, his expression neutral.

"Good party," Ryan said. "Thanks."

"Our pleasure." Allen sat in one of the bar-height chairs. "I'm beat."

"Yeah. Same."

Ryan really didn't care for the man's company. He was a blowhard, a show-off, a braggart who couldn't ever resist the opportunity to mention his son's successful business. It didn't escape Ryan's notice that he never mentioned his daughter. The woman apparently lived out West somewhere, Oregon maybe, or possibly Washington. They were, as Janice liked to say, "estranged."

Ryan grinned around the lip of his mug at the thought of Janice. Then he forced himself to neutralize his expression when Allen glanced over at him. He would be hard-pressed to consider Dr. Allen Cooper his friend. He'd written Ryan's company plenty of checks for expensive renovations, to be sure. Most of the people in the cul-de-sac had done the same. They had shared certain interests on one level. But he didn't like the guy. And he suspected the feeling was mutual.

Cooper had gone to medical school, done fancy fellowships or some shit, and had made a fortune doing boob jobs and whatnot. Ryan had barely made it out of high school with a diploma and had gone right to work as a licensed electrician. But he had plenty of money now, too, thank you very much. He'd earned it all himself. And with Tom Franks' help, he'd held onto plenty of it.

Stupid Franks. Why had he gone and done such a selfish thing as to off himself? And over what? Knocking up that scrawny trophy wife across the street? I mean, seriously. It could have been dealt with.

Allen cleared his throat, dragging Ryan back from his musings about how much money Tom had helped him save, and make, thanks to his accounting tricks and tips. Not to mention that one contract, the parking-garage gig that had cemented his company's rep to some out-of-town investors. "So. What do you think of the addition to our neighborhood?" He put the mug to his lips, keeping his ice-blue stare on Ryan.

Ryan shifted in his seat, recalling his initial response to the hot little number who had arrived on the arm of the tall, good-looking Black man. He'd sensed a shift in things the second the couple had made their appearance, mostly from the women who'd been unable to keep their eyes off of Michael Ross. Dude was a specimen; that much was a stone cold fact. Ryan had glanced at Allen then at Barrett, and finally at the amenable Dr. Sai. Each man was feeling the same thing right then, he'd sensed, in a burst of unfamiliar insight.

Intimidation had only been one of the words for it.

Luckily, Janice, the Supreme Hostess of All Things Party, had separated the couple, guiding Amy—was that her name? He couldn't recall right then—over to the men. She was a sweet-looking woman with a bright, full-lipped smile, a tangle of dark-brown hair, and a pert, small-waisted figure. He'd felt like a wolf sizing up the latest female addition to their pack. He'd sprung an embarrassing boner under his shorts, which had driven him inside for a few minutes to splash cold water on his face, thinking for a moment that Janice would follow him inside to give him a hand.

She hadn't. She had other duties.

"They seem nice," he said, not breaking the stare down. "What do you and Janice think?"

About their potential addition to the group, he thought, already wondering the same himself. The man, Michael, had fit right in, seemed completely comfortable with all the female attention he was getting. The woman, Amelia he recalled now, had been stiff for a while, until they got a couple of glasses of wine into her.

The whole thing had been surreal on a lot of levels. He and Melissa, along with the Coopers, were the founding couples, as it were. The ones who'd started this whole thing and had brought in the Franks first then the Aryas, and finally the LeBlancs. The ones who'd gone and screwed everything up, somehow. Cassie and her tight little ass, long yoga-toned legs, the way she refused to shave her underarms, which he'd thought would be a turn-off. But which wasn't.

The abrupt halt to their activities, thanks to the horror show at the Franks' house, had almost been a relief. Even if, sometimes he wondered why he was doing it. Why he enjoyed it as much as he did. How they, as a group of adults, could be normal neighbors ever again.

And now, thanks to the summoning of their alpha couple—the Coopers—they'd resumed their positions as it were. As if they'd never taken the break.

"We think they're wonderful," Allen declared, setting his empty mug on the granite counter and getting to his feet. "But..." He shrugged. Ryan felt a sudden kinship with the man. Michael Ross was almost too perfect. Maybe it would be better if they steered clear of the cul-de-sac's out-of-the-ordinary gatherings.

"Yeah, I hear you." Ryan rose and walked over to the sink, busying himself cleaning the breakfast clutter, hoping that Cooper would get the message and get the hell out of his house.

"Well, I should go," Allen said, pointing to a stack of plastic crap on the deck table outside. "Need to deliver the rest of these. Thanks for the coffee."

"Welcome," Ryan grunted, not turning to see Allen out. Being an asshole, he knew. But that was the other thing about this whole lifestyle, he thought as he swiped the plates and utensils with a brush before shoving them into the dishwasher. When it was happening, in the heat of the moment, he was okay with it. He got off on watching his wife enjoy herself with his neighbors. It turned him on more than anything he'd ever done, which was saying something.

But, in the days and weeks later, something about the presence of these men—the men who'd done things to his wife while he did things to theirs—made him furious enough that he had a tough time containing it.

His temper was nothing to trifle with. He knew that. Melissa knew it, too. None of these other overeducated rich assholes did though. At least, not yet.

A small, enlightened part of him understood it wasn't healthy. That they shouldn't have done it in the first place. Much less have leaped back into it the way they had last night. The room had been overwarm and the people in it overwrought, pent-up, energetic in a way he'd enjoyed. But that now made him want to puke or put both his fists through the drywall. He finished up the cleaning instead then dragged Danny outside to help him do some busywork in the yard for a few minutes before Melissa got home and relieved him.

Chapter Twelve

B*uyer's Remorse*

. . . .

THE SUN FELT OBSCENELY bright as Sai sat attempting to enjoy his morning tea. Attempting being the key word. The word of the day, he surmised as he jerked the blinds on the back wall of windows shut, sparing his retinas further abuse.

He set the mug of strong Darjeeling down on the counter and placed his hands on either side of it, bracing himself against the jet-black stone, as if readying for a particularly difficult surgery. His skin felt abraded, raw in places he knew made sense but at the same time, he didn't like to admit. His brain was at a sort of parade rest he associated with being sexually sated. But at the same time, it raced ahead, making assumptions and decisions about what he had done, what he planned to do, and what he wanted to stop doing.

He groaned and leaned forward, stretching out the tension between his shoulders that had woken him, driven him from the warm nest of silky sheets and the comforting sensation of Emily's body next to his. "Obscene" was a great word for this morning. The sunlight's invasion of his eyeballs was obscene. The way his body was simultaneously satisfied and revved was entirely obscene. His relief at their renewal of normal cul-de-sac activities was totally obscene.

He stood back up and rolled his neck around, trying to come to terms with how crappy and fantastic he felt all at the same time, regardless of how illogical it was. He loved Emily with every inch of his being. He had almost from the day he'd laid eyes on her covered in flour and crying on the bench outside the famous Parisian bakery. At first, she'd seemed vulnerable and sad, triggering his natural caretaker. He'd been in town for a conference—one of the first he'd been invited to as a surgeon—and was high on life, feeling as much like a master of the universe as he'd ever allowed himself.

But when he'd stopped in his tracks, watching the people ebb and flow around Emily on that busy sidewalk, something in him shifted. He'd never regretted stopping, sitting, offering his handkerchief, buying her a coffee, and, later, taking her out to dinner.

Not even when he'd accepted that she would never bear his child. Something he'd always wanted. Something his parents berated him for, for exactly twenty minutes before he informed them that if they ever said anything to Emily about it, he would cut them out of his life like a malignant tumor. They'd never mentioned anything about her "failing" as a woman ever again. For which he was grateful.

His brothers had huge families, none of whom were nearby, which was a blessing. Emily would go through stages of being utterly broken by her infertility, enough that he worried she'd never recover. But these episodes were lessening, thankfully. And he would have to credit the odd invitation they'd received within the first couple of months of moving into this house.

The Coopers' house more or less anchored the circle, sitting as it did at the end, being the largest home, with the best yard, pool, and various other amenities. Their first weekend, he and Emily had been the guests of honor at a cookout and pool party, at which they'd both admit they'd felt a little like they were auditioning for something. They understood what later, at the more formal, sit-down dinner with the Coopers, the Franks, and the Murphys.

He sighed and slid into a seat at the kitchen table. The damned sunshine forced its way in between the wooden slats. He glared at it, angry but unable to pinpoint why.

"Hey, you're up early on your day off."

He glanced up to see his wife tugging the belt of her robe around her waist. She looked disheveled in a way that both charmed and irritated him. Which was ridiculous. He took a deep breath. Smiled at her. Rose and held out his arms. She slid into them, burying her face in his neck. She always got this way on the mornings after. Shy. Embarrassed. Worried he'd be upset or angry or jealous.

As if he had room for any of that. He took another deep breath to calm his racing pulse. Felt her stiffen and pull away. He brushed a lock of her hair off her face and widened his smile, attempted to look like anger wasn't making him see red at the edges of his vision.

"You all right?" she asked.

"Of course I am." He turned away from her, jaw clenched with frustration at her ongoing inability to see her own value. She was an incredible teacher. All her kids adored her. And no one was her equal in the kitchen despite her having quit the culinary school shy of an actual degree.

He could sense her worrying behind his back. And the sensation—like warm, sweaty waves washing over him—only ramped up his aggravation level. There was no accounting for it. He should feel relaxed, considering. But he was the polar opposite. His nerves thrummed, pulled tight under his skin like violin strings on the verge of springing free. Possibly putting out someone's damned eye in the process.

He clenched his fists. Took a deep breath. Used all the meditation tricks he knew to keep from shaking his sweet wife until her expensively straightened teeth rattled in her head.

When she touched his shoulder, he jerked away from her with such force, he knocked his still-full teacup into the sink with a clatter. He cursed under his breath. When he turned to face her, Emily's dark eyes surprised him. "What?" she asked. "What did I do?"

Okay, now they were back on familiar ground. Unsure Emily. Insecure Emily. Emily always seeking validation at every turn. He sighed and slumped back against the counter. "You didn't do anything, Em," he said, his voice low. She moved closer to him. He tugged her close, pressing his slightly sore body against hers, his face buried in her hair. "We shouldn't have..."

She wrapped her arms around his waist. Nodded. "I know. But..." She pulled away from him, her eyes dry. Another surprise. "I had fun. You did, too. Don't deny it."

He looked down at the floor, embarrassed by the rush of memory that hit him, hard. He'd had a lot of fun. There wasn't any way he could deny it. He'd had way too much fun. That was the problem. "It's wrong, Emily. It's not...right. It's not how normal adults behave."

"Oh?" She crossed her arms, a movement that forced her breasts up, drawing his gaze to the line separating them. The robe was threadbare. He could see her nipples—large, and extraordinarily sensitive—poking through the fabric. He licked his lips, unable to rip his gaze away from her cleavage. His body rose to the occasion. Another surprise in a way, considering the workout he'd gotten the night before. But, then again, one of the things they'd discovered about this lifestyle thing they engaged in on a semi-regular basis was that it served as a kind of a vitamin shot to the libido. Not only for him, either.

Emily's face flushed. Her lips parted. He forced himself to remain still, not to reach out for her, yank her close, shove his tongue into her mouth—do anything but talk about this whole sordid mess. Her expression—a mix of remorse and needy proved to him that she wanted to do the same. That was holding herself back same as he was. He had to restrain the urge to groan.

"I'd say it is normal. More normal than pretending that you aren't horny for a hot neighbor."

Sai blinked, shocked by her bluntness. Not to mention the raw truth of her words. But something in him resisted it. His conventional, conservative Hindu upbringing. "I..." he began. But before he could concoct anything resembling a logical response, she'd shucked off the sorry excuse for a robe and stood, tall, full-hipped, firm breasts, lush as all hell. Sai's breath caught in his throat. He put a hand on the counter, as if it could hold him back. He wanted to make his point. He needed to say what he was thinking.

Or what he had been thinking, before Emily had decided to get naked in the kitchen in front of him. When he spotted the red, round spot on her skin at the point where her neck met her shoulder, that tore it. He made a low, guttural sound and yanked her to him, putting his mouth where someone else's had been to make that angry-looking hickey.

Sai went deaf, dumb, blind to anything but her skin, her hands, her hair. "Oh God, Sai," she said, as he walked her backward into the den and pulled her down onto the scratchy sisal rug.

· · · ·

THEY LAY WITH THEIR legs and arms entangled on the floor a few minutes later, both breathing heavily, neither of them able to conjure words. Finally, she rolled over to him, propped her head in her hand, and ran her fingers down his sweaty chest. "I love you," she said. Her voice was calm, neutral, without overt emotion. His relief at that one simple thing made him want to weep. He took her hand and pressed it to his lips.

"I adore you," he said, never meaning anything more. This thing they did—this weird relationship they'd developed with their dynamic, outgoing, at times overwhelming neighbors was, without a doubt, not something he'd ever thought he'd do. But, damn him, he liked it. A lot. And Emily did, too.

They always remained in the same room—one of the hard and fast rules they'd made after a bit of research. They had sex with other people, but never outside of each other's sight. Many times, they'd engage in foreplay together then turn to the other couple to finish. But always in the same room. They were the only couple in the group who had that rule. It was a rule more of his neighbors should adhere to, in his opinion.

He brushed her hair off her face, tucked it behind her ear. His body was still thrumming, his brain buzzing. He even felt like he could do it again—a phenomenon he'd been surprised by at first but something he'd gotten used to, now that they'd apparently resumed their activities as...what? Swingers? Wife swappers? Life stylers? Polyamorous fuck buddies?

"Stop over thinking," Emily said before pressing her lips to his. He sighed, closed his eyes, and let her work her magic on him.

As he emerged from the shower, Emily held out a towel with a smile and traded places with him. "Those ladies should consider themselves lucky," she said over her shoulder before she shut the glass door between them. They'd installed a Japanese-style bathroom, with a deep bathtub and half-open shower.

"How's that?" He dried off, wincing when the soft towel rubbed his abraded skin.

"They missed that," she said, looking right at his crotch. "I let them have it. They'd better be thanking me today."

He flushed then grinned. She was smiling. She was okay. She was relaxed. It was all good. She'd had her fair share of fun, too, with her favorite partner. It had been an odd configuration. Not the usual coupling off and disappearing into the various Cooper bedrooms. They'd all been in one room this time, not unlike their first time together. It had been an actual orgy. Straight up. No doubts and no denying it.

He flushed hot. And his body acted as if he could do it all again, like some kind of a hormonally overdosed teenager.

Emily hummed Beatles songs under the shower water, leaving him to watch the lather rolling down her breasts and stomach. He adored Emily the way she was. He didn't want her to change anything. He understood the pressure she put on herself to have a slimmer, more fit body. He never ventured an opinion about it. It would be like talking to a wall anyway.

Emily met his eyes, smiled, blew him a kiss. He caught it and pressed it to his heart.

All was good.

At least for now.

He hummed his way down the stairs.

"Good morning." The voice startled him and made him stumble. "Dropping off the Tupperware stuff." Allen Cooper stood at his back door, clutching Emily's two plastic containers, emptied and cleaned.

"Oh, right, great." He stood, looking at the tall, handsome, man. A fellow doctor—a plastic surgeon, of course. But still a doctor. And a sought-after one to be certain. "Come on in."

Allen hesitated. The man looked uncomfortable. For some reason, that made him smile. Dr. Cooper was the king of every room he entered. Seeing him squirm gave Sai no small measure of satisfaction.

"Can I get you something to drink?" Sai pulled a pitcher of fresh-squeezed orange juice from the fridge.

"Sure. Thanks."

Sai poured two glasses. Handed one to his neighbor. Held his up as if it were a glass of whiskey. Allen touched his to it. They sipped. Allen smacked his lips. "Damn. That is delicious." He finished his off. Sai held out the pitcher and refreshed it.

They drank in silence. Sai relished Allen's obvious discomfort way more than he should. Both men looked over at Emily when she walked into the kitchen rubbing her hair with a towel. She'd pulled on a pair of yoga pants and an oversized sweatshirt. Allen's gaze followed her to the fridge, to the cabinet then when she joined them with her glass of juice. "Cheers," she said with a grin.

Allen nodded. But his glass was empty. He put it on the counter with a clunk. "I brought your plastic dishes back." He pointed to them, as if to prove his point. Emily nodded.

"Thanks, Allen. Great party last night," she said. Sai admired the hell out of her equanimity. It was unlike her. She usually got all giggly and silly, blushing constantly if they'd run into Allen or Barrett or Ryan, or Tom, of course, in the days following one of their parties. Allen seemed thrown by it, too. He swallowed, opened his mouth as if to say something. Then closed it.

"Right. Yeah. Sure. It was, wasn't it." He ran a shaking hand through his hair.

Sai narrowed his eyes as the physician in him lurched into action.

"You all right, Allen?" He took the man's wrist. Felt the racing pulse. The man was pale, sweaty. "Why don't you sit a minute." He pulled a chair away from the table.

"No, no, I'm fine. Too much to drink, you know." He winked at Sai. Back to his old self. Good old blustery, boasting, show-offy Allen.

"Yes. I know." After the resumption of their usual activities, the men had shared an overpriced bottle of bourbon. He could still taste it on his tongue. They stared at each other a few seconds. Sai had zero problem with any of these men. The same way Emily claimed to have no issues with any of the women. It was how they were—happy, content together, yet enjoying this odd yet satisfying diversion.

The only one who had ever bothered him was Tom. Something about Tom Franks had captivated Emily in a way he thought he understood but didn't like very much. Tom. His now-dead neighbor. Former owner of the house currently occupied by a young couple who'd mesmerized everyone the night before, at the party before The Party. Who'd fluffed the whole group, he figured, in hindsight. As a matter of fact, Sai had caught himself fantasizing about Amelia at one point the night before. And he knew damn good and well that every woman in their hot, candlelit rooms had been thinking about Michael Ross at least once.

Sai lifted his chin. Allen did the same. Emily sighed and put her glass in the sink, shoving her way past the wordless chest beating. "I need to do some stuff in my classroom, Sai. I'll be home in a few hours."

He grabbed her arm when she tried to brush by him again on her way to the garage. He kissed her, hard, while Allen watched, perversely unwilling to leave the house. She broke away, smiled at him. Smiled at Allen. And left.

"Well, I guess I'll see you around, Dr. Sai. Got surgeries in the morning?"

"Yes," Sai said, as all the adrenaline in him whooshed out, leaving him limp and depleted. "I do."

"Have a good one." He held out his hand.

Sai stared at it, confused for a second before he put his in it, and they shook as if they'd concocted a transaction. "You do the same, Allen."

When the man finally left, Sai collapsed on the couch and dropped almost immediately into a long, dreamless nap.

Chapter Thirteen

T*he Player*

. . . .

BARRETT ROLLED OVER and sat on the side of the bed, trying to regain his equilibrium. The past few days, okay weeks, all right, months, had been, in a word, chaotic. His job was kicking his ass, for starters, thanks to the departure of one and the retirement of another of his law partners. Right in the middle of a long-running court battle on behalf of one of their more prominent clients.

He sighed and rolled his head around, working out the neck kink he seemed to wake up to every day, lately. It was like he couldn't fully relax in sleep. Like his jaw stayed clenched and his neck tight, no matter what he did to unwind before allowing himself the five hours of sleep he normally required.

He heard something behind him. Startled for a moment, he sucked in a breath when he realized it was only Cassie, making her usual sleep-talk noises.

Your wife, Barrett. Remember her? The third go-round you swore on a stack of law books you'd never, ever embark upon? The one who's knocked up and not by you because you can't knock anybody up, much less a wife? That one?

He muttered a string of curses, then rose to his feet, sensing every ache in every joint as the mantle of stress settled across his shoulders. Without looking back at his wife, because right at this particular moment it would piss him off, he headed for the bathroom. The bathroom he'd had renovated to suit himself after they'd bought the house in this weird, old-money neighborhood.

He pissed, washed his hands, brushed his teeth, and splashed cold water onto his face, hoping it would clear some of the cobwebs. It didn't work. He tried it again. Finally, he stared at himself in the huge mirror, forcing himself not to frown since it made him look old. Of course, everyone looks their worst after they first wake up. But damn it if he didn't look like he was sixty-five or something when he was only fifty-three.

He glared into his own eyes. Eyes that had seen too much, and still never seemed to change. They were an ice-blue, almost-gray color, with long lashes that used to get him noticed by girls in high school. His hair was still the same jet black with a few spots of gray creeping in, still nice and thick, thanks to expensive products he'd been using on it since he made partner in the firm and could fully justify and afford such vanities. The shots he got from a so-called "esthetician"—someone Cooper had recommended to him after they'd first moved onto the block—didn't hurt. He got some cocktail of hormones once a week that allowed him to feel young in various parts of his body, including his mostly wrinkle-free face, his well-honed legs, abs, and chest.

And, of course, his dick.

He glared down at that particular appendage. It was limp at the moment but, thanks to the shit surging through his system, it didn't take a hell of a lot to bring it to full attention. There it went now, with a mere thought about it. He sighed and looked back into his face.

What a mess. What a goddamned ridiculous, selfish, crazy mess he was in. And he had no one but himself to blame. Oh sure, he could blame Cassie. Cassandra—his sexy, sweet, crunchy-granola third wife—Little Miss I won't take chemical birth control. Given his reality, it hadn't mattered much when it had only been between them. But the rule about using condoms with her had flown straight out the window at some point, and someone not him had knocked her up.

Of course, he'd been the one to suggest it to her, this lifestyle thing the Coopers had laid on him within a week of them moving into their remodeled house. It'd sounded hot as hell. He wouldn't deceive anyone including himself about that fact. His reputation practically demanded he at least try it, as long as Cassie was amenable.

She'd been reluctant at first, which hadn't surprised him much. She was kind of the anti-trophy wife despite her shocking good looks. She wasn't demanding of his time or much of his dough for clothes and trinkets, as long as she got to teach her yoga classes and drink her kale-infused organic crap every morning from the five-hundred-dollar blender. Sometimes he wondered what in the hell had prompted her to go after him, back when she'd been one of the gaggle of paralegals and admins seeking to bag themselves a partner.

He sighed again, deeper this time. Exhaustion crept up and blanketed him, as if he'd never slept the night before. It was happening a lot lately. He'd have to ask the esthetician about it. Maybe they needed to adjust his cocktail.

At that moment, he missed Carolyn, his second wife who'd been his one shot at true love and he'd known it.

His first married life experience had been a whacky whirlwind with a petite, tight-bodied brunette fellow law-school graduate based on nothing but a ton of super-kinky sex, plenty of weed, and the buzz that came with graduating and being swooped into a high six-figure-salary job right off the bat. She'd lasted exactly five years. Three of which he spent screwing every paralegal and secretary at his firm, with an enthusiasm that had shocked everyone. He'd considered it his due, in a sort of throw-back Don-Draperish way.

Stupid. Selfish. But he'd not really liked wife number one anyway. She'd talked him into the whole marriage thing almost on a whim. The divorce had been amicable and, last he heard, she was living in Connecticut with the requisite two kids and a craftsman-style pile of a house while her stockbroker hubs brought in the dough.

Carolyn had been something else altogether. They'd met at a running club he'd joined for something to do to keep him from not exercising since he'd gotten bored with gyms and biking. She was a local TV personality, host of a daily morning talk show, and easily the most gorgeous redhead he'd ever met. She was practically Amazonian at five feet nine in her flat feet. Her talk-show heels made her a hair taller than he was. It was her aloof—borderline rude—attitude towards him when he'd sidled up to her at the club after perusing her rear view long enough to decide to make a move.

She'd read him like a book, crushed his alpha-male-player spirit, and he'd adored her. With every inch of his sorry ass being. They'd been happy for almost twelve years. Cheating on her had never entered his consciousness. She had him by the balls from the get-go, since the level of her hard-to-get was somewhere well north of expert. Later, she'd captured his wayward heart and held it in her long-fingered, well-manicured hands for a few years.

It was as if she understood him the moment she laid eyes on him and had determined that she'd tame him of his man-whore ways. But, once she'd done that, she got bored. Granted, they had some great times together, traveling all around the world, sometimes by private jet, getting her dream mansion built in one of the faceless Detroit suburbs, attending night after night of glitzy fundraising events where he'd drop thousands of bucks on whatever charity she told him to.

Sometimes, he'd lie awake and watch the woman sleep. Such a sap he'd been.

He wasn't sure when he figured it out but, by the time he did, she'd been screwing one of the new producers of a show she'd been working on. He'd gone into a serious downward spiral after divorce number two. Even though he'd given her whatever she'd asked for. Like the sap she'd turned him into.

Suffice it to say, he picked up the mantle of Man Whore and wore like a pro for a few years after that. Seriously, he could've given lessons in how to pick up a hot woman at a party and be between her thighs by midnight. By the time Cassie had her clutches in him, he'd been worn down by it all. Truly pining for Carolyn and their life together most days and nights didn't do much for the old libido. So, he'd focused on his real career instead. He'd won some huge cases for his corporate clients and had started to do a bit pro bono work through one of the many nonprofits he'd donated to.

Cassie was his type, or at least the type he'd developed a taste for in the years post-Carolyn. Younger than him by a lot—she was only twenty-eight when they'd married two years ago. Slim, blonde, attractive in a way that might seem unapproachable. It had put him off at first, seeing her around more and more in an obvious attempt to catch his famously wandering eye. She was a near-perfect female specimen, at least on the outside. When he'd finally decided to ask her out, she'd been shocked.

"I figured you'd want to fuck me first," she'd said in the blunt fashion that he'd come to appreciate. "Take a test drive, as it were."

He'd taken her out to dinner, amused by her seeming innocence blended with just enough savvy about humanity. And there was, indeed, plenty of sexual activity, but not until the eighth date—a solid two and a half months after their first, which was a bit of a slow burn for him. It had been spectacular, worth the wait. Younger women always turned him on, and she was no exception. But as he got to know her, he came to realize he might have hit the relationship jackpot a second time. Cassandra was beautiful and skinny and blonde, but that's where the trophy wife clichés ended. She was a health nut, always trying to turn him vegetarian—which he resisted mostly on principle.

She had him doing hot yoga and meditation within a month of their modest wedding, albeit on a beach in Maui—something she'd been dreaming of since she was a girl, she'd said. She loved to exercise, but she hated to shop, rarely got her hair or nails done. She didn't trust all the chemicals involved, she claimed. She could spend hours in a used bookstore or at a farmer's market or volunteering at the humane society but would forget to pick up his shirts at the laundry or to at least think about what they might eat for dinner that didn't involve tofu.

Mrs. Barrett LeBlanc Take Three was kind and nice and cared about other people more than herself. Something he could never say about versions one or two. She'd cry when a bird would hit one of their massive windows and die, twitching, on the grass below. The sight of a crop of mangy deer gnawing on their trees would make her rapturous. She owned a contraption meant for rescuing spiders and releasing them outdoors instead of squashing them like a normal human being.

She was smart, too. She'd challenge him on his to-the-right-of-center political leanings or offer opinions about current events both local and wider scoped, with a bit of a hippy-dippy outlook but having researched it and understood all the ramifications beforehand. She'd shocked him more than once by insisting they go to some play or concert or rally or something, and he'd find himself enjoying it.

It had been a good life.

And then they'd moved into this damn house in this stupid neighborhood.

She'd picked it out. He'd bought it with cash and told her his requirements for things like bathrooms, kitchens, and basements. She'd managed the renovations like a pro with the help of their neighbor's husband—a brusque Irish type who conveniently owned a contracting company. Ryan Murphy had irritated the shit out Barrett from the get-go with his *I know the real world get back in your ivory tower* swagger. But he'd left it all to Cassie, and everything had come in on time and, miraculously, only slightly over budget.

And then they'd accepted their first dinner invitation from Janice and Allen Cooper.

"Honey?"

Barrett flinched. The sound of Cassie's voice was like a fork dragging across an empty plate to him lately. Which wasn't fair, and he damn well knew it.

It was why, when Emily Arya had texted him with the news that Cassie was in the hospital being treated for severe malnutrition and dehydration, he'd surrendered. He'd gone straight to her, cutting short his trip to Chicago to meet with banker clients. He'd brought her home. Let her sleep in their bed again. Had sex with her plenty of times, despite the fact that the baby was starting to get in the way.

But he hadn't forgiven her. He couldn't, no matter how hard he tried to be a nice guy about it, to remind himself it was only partly her fault, that she hated taking birth control pills, claimed they were messing with her chakras or some shit. That it wasn't like she'd held a gun to someone's head and demanded they not use a condom. No matter how many hours he'd berate himself for keeping her at the sort of emotional arm's length that was wearing her down, he couldn't stop.

He turned and looked at her. She had a short, silky robe on over her usual sleeping nudity. Her face had filled out with the pregnancy, making her even more attractive. Her hair was too long—he'd remind her to go get it cut soon. Her face was flushed. Her lips slightly parted.

While he watched, the robe fell open, revealing her newly pregnancy plumped-up breasts. Without a word, he took her hand and pulled her to their rumpled bed.

• • • •

LATER, HE WOKE ALONE, the light at a distinctly different angle than it had been before. He grabbed his watch. He was old school about timepieces and refused to give them up in favor of checking time on his phone, or on a phone masquerading as a watch. It was almost ten thirty. His usual for a weekend after a week's worth of being up at four thirty a.m., working out for an hour at the gym, showering and donning the tailored suit, crisp shirt, designer shoes, and Rolex-du-jour, then working for ten to twelve hours straight.

The bedroom door opened, revealing Cassie in a pair of yoga pants and a straining T-shirt. She was carrying a tray of food. He sat and pulled the sheet up to his waist. "Thanks," was all he could manage, after a really great session that he would call lovemaking, instead of the screwing they'd been doing once she'd claimed she felt better. "Did you eat anything?" He eyed her, looking for signs of her earlier nausea and extreme thinness around the edges.

"Yes, but can I join you here?" She put the tray across his lap and crawled in next to him. She'd taken a shower, he noted as he picked up his perfectly brewed, imported fair-trade Ethiopian blend.

"Do whatever you want," he said, wishing he could loosen up, be nice. But he couldn't. She was here, wasn't she? Sporting that damned baby bump that wasn't his?

"Okay." She picked up a strawberry and held it to his lips as he put down the coffee. He tried to resist. Her bright blue eyes flashed up at him, pouting a bit as if to show him what she wanted him to do. He ate the strawberry. "Did you have fun last night?"

Barrett tensed. Oh right. Last night. Shit.

"I guess," he said. And that was the truth. He'd gotten off, sure. Had been the happy recipient of some pleasant attention from two of the women in their little group. Like he was some kind of a sex charity case. He ate the rest of the food without tasting it, even though he was certain it was delicious. Cassie was chef-level good in the kitchen when she remembered to cook. But the memory of the night before, the seeming resumption of activities as it were, made everything he put into his mouth taste like sawdust.

The uncomfortable silence in the room didn't help. But Jesus, what did she expect from him anyway? He was a rich, successful, sexually vibrant man. Doctors had warned his parents that the lifesaving chemotherapy he'd received as a ten-year-old might make him sterile, but he'd not given it any thought. Until Carolyn had told him she wanted a baby, and he'd had himself tested with less-than-stellar results.

"Your odds are about one in a thousand," the unhelpful doc had told him.

And here he was, crammed into this overpriced hunk of classy real estate, in love with his too-young, too-sweet, too-pretty third wife who was swelling up in front, thanks to some other asshole's lucky sperm.

Anger almost blinded him at that thought. He picked up the tray and headed out the bedroom door, down the short flight of steps, and into the kitchen. The sight of Allen Cooper himself at the back French doors made him do a double take. "Hang on a sec," he called out before putting the tray on the stainless-steel island counter and grabbing a pair of shorts he'd left on the floor the night before.

"What's up?" he asked, running a hand through his hair as he opened the door for his neighbor.

"I'm on a delivery run with all this stuff." Allen held up a couple of plastic containers Barrett didn't recognize. "It's what Cassie brought her food in last night."

"Oh right. Sure. Thanks." He took them and tossed them onto the counter next to the tray. He didn't want Allen Cooper in his space right now. He didn't want anyone in it. He wanted to go for a miles-long run and sweat and breathe heavy and forget the goddamned mess his life had become.

"So," Allen said, leaning against the bar-height chairs at their square table next to the deck doors. Barrett tried not to punch him. "What do you think about the new people?"

"If you're asking me if I'd hit that, the answer is yes. But if I didn't say something along those lines, you'd probably worry I had the hots for you or something."

A smile played around Allen's lips. As the two official alpha males in their group, Ryan Murphy acting as wanna-be, and Sai as a classic gamma who all the ladies respected and loved—well, him and his giant cock—he and Cooper butted heads a fair bit. They both wanted to get with Ryan's wife Melissa, the sweet-assed Realtor. And they'd almost come to blows once over Laura, the widow of the hapless Tom. But it was okay. It was mostly for show. It was their role, after all.

Thoughts of their one not-too-dearly departed friend made his blood boil. That kid growing in his wife's belly was likely Tom Franks'. Cassie had been enamored with him and his softspoken four-eyed, nerdy ways. Not that he hadn't been good-looking. He had been, but in a totally different way than the other men involved in their too-close group. Tom's hook had been way more subtle. Or, as Cassie had told him, *like that boy you were friends with all through middle school then discovered was really super cute in high school even though he was president of the chemistry club* or some shit like that. He'd definitely been popular amongst the ladies of Connelly Court, that much was certain.

"Not sure about Mr. Ross," Allen said, something like actual anxiety clouding his eyes for a second, interrupting Barrett's trip down Tom Franks' memory lane. A place he'd sworn off of the minute he'd seen the ambulance and cop cars surrounding his former neighbor's house.

He chuckled. "Why, Al? Because Janice was practically straddling his thigh all night?"

Allen sighed. Something about that made him want to tear the man's jugular out and spray his theoretical blood all over the kitchen this fine late-summer holiday morning. He crossed his arms over his bare chest. "I'm pretty sure that if you put the kibosh on it you're gonna have a battle on your hands. Never mind how hard you'd like to rattle Missus Ross' hot little cage."

Allen's face reddened. His lips pressed together in a tight line. A thrill hit Barrett's spine. He let his arms drop to his sides. His fingers curled into fists. Yes, hitting something would help. He readied himself.

"Go fuck yourself, LeBlanc."

"I'm all set there, thanks."

Thanks to your wife, and quite nicely, too.

But Allen knew that. He'd been in the room.

This was one messed-up life he was living right now. No doubt about it. He let himself recall Amelia Ross. How they'd gotten her tipsy then drunk, each of the men sizing her up like...like she was a slab of meat. While their wives did the same with the tall, dark, handsome man who was Amelia's husband.

Messed up. Fucked-up. All of the above. "I was about to go for a run," he said, by way of getting Allen the hell out of his face. A thin sliver of guilt hit him. Allen and Janice had done nothing but welcome them, albeit in an oddly intimate way. Allen had found him the lady with her syringes full of youthfulness that Barrett was now hooked on. Janice was...well, she was great at sex, and they were happy to share all of that.

But last night had been more than a little weird. Fraught with too much shit left unsaid. Cassie's baby belly stuck out there, obvious, mocking him, making everyone feel sorry for him in a way he didn't deserve or want.

They really shouldn't have participated. But the cookout had had its usual foreplay-like effect. And he'd been sucked into it—sucked being a good word for it. His hormonally enhanced penis stirred under his shorts. He and Allen did their traditional mental chest beating as they stared at each other for a few more seconds.

"Okay. But we're gonna have to make a decision about the Rosses," Allen said as he opened the door that led to the deck.

"I already have," Barrett said. A lie. He was more unsure about adding a pair of virtual strangers into their odd mix than he had been about anything in his recent life. The mess the Franks had left behind, the assumptions that Tom was Cassie's official sperm donor, thanks to his behavior, the way Laura Franks had instigated plenty of extracurricular action on the side with him and all the other men, it had been a sign.

They should stop.

But they hadn't. After resuming it in such a pleasant, and super-vigorous way the night before—hell, it had been a full-on orgy, almost, but for Cassie. She had a thing about watching him with someone else, as in she insisted that she never wanted to watch him do it. Which was fine. He was the same way. They were one the couple who went into separate rooms in order to accommodate their jealous tendencies.

"Fine," Allen said. "I figured as much."

"Like you haven't."

"I told you I don't know about...never mind."

Barrett shrugged. Allen left. Deciding to put the run off a bit longer in favor of relieving the distinct painful pressure under his shorts, Barrett headed upstairs, forcing his mind blank of anything but the need to get off, again. That was easy. It was all the rest of his life he didn't want to deal with right now.

He joined Cassie in the shower and surprised himself with his level of tenderness with her. When she came—and he knew she did for real because she had a distinct tell, a hitch in her voice and a corresponding jitter in her left leg that he adored—they were on the soft rug in front of the massive tub. She had tears in her eyes when he looked at her.

"Don't cry, Cass," he said, his voice rough, body zinging with satisfaction. "Please don't."

Chapter Fourteen

A*lpha Female*

• • • •

"ALLEN, HON, WOULD YOU mind?"

The sun felt great on his face, arms, and legs. He honestly believed he could sit here, in his overpriced outdoor lounge chair, by his pool behind his over-renovated home for the next few hours, hell, days, and be perfectly happy.

"Allen!"

And be perfectly happy for the rest of his life, without the sound of his wife's voice, yelling at him to do something.

"God damn it, Allen."

Allen opened one eye halfway, hoping he could feign sleep and she'd leave him alone. But, of course, she was glaring straight at him, arms crossed, lips pressed thin. Damn woman. She was always forgetting to get her collagen injections. After all these years of reminding her that the expensive, carefully implemented, body-care regimen steps had to be followed, or she'd be worse off than she'd been when his office partner had put her on them.

It's not that she wasn't attractive without them. She was. He never would have fallen for her otherwise. He'd swear he would never forget the moment he'd seen her at that college party. A tall, blonde, slim, cool goddess. Those ice-blue eyes piercing his chest, sending shock waves straight to his crotch.

She'd known what to do with that power, too. Oh yes. Janice Gallagher had been a rich Southern girl who knew how to work her assets. How to hook him then lure him then hold him hostage by his balls for almost a whole year before he got anywhere near second base.

Allen sighed, feeling the radioactive heat of her stare on him. That same stare he'd felt plenty the four, okay, five—well, okay, six—times she'd caught him red-handed, or red-dicked, however you wanted to look at it. Who would've blamed him really? Sure, he had a lovely fiancée, and, later, a wife. But he spent his days staring at and giving advice to perfectly lovely women with serious self-esteem issues. His extraordinarily well-paying job had been to convince these women to alter their breasts, noses, chins, thighs, and asses to suit some ephemeral concept of female perfection.

The last time he'd strayed, when A.J. was three, had been what tore it for Janice. He couldn't really blame her. He'd been banging that hot-as-shit but super sad-sack patient for a solid year by the time they got caught. And Janice had likely known about it the entire time.

Allen shifted in his seat, recalling that woman and how pliant and eager she'd been for him. All he had to do was tell her one nice thing about her body, hair, voice, and she'd have her toned legs spread for him where and whenever he wanted it.

It had been a challenging time in his life. Janice was struggling to recover from her pregnancy. A.J. had been a total pain in the rear end, best he could recall. The house had been a smelly mess of baby puke and shit. He'd had zero fatherly patience for the squalling baby, and, later, the tyrannical toddler.

He'd started staying late at work. Gone on important, long-weekend plastic surgery conferences. The last was where he'd met his longest-running and final girlfriend.

"I know you're not asleep," his lovely wife said, jarring him from his musings. Allen stretched, relishing the heat on his limbs, the way his overtaxed muscles sang out with enough soreness to make him happy with the reasons why.

He got an illicit charge out of pissing her off. He couldn't lie about that.

The warmth disappeared from his face and chest as if a cloud blocked the sun. He opened one eye wide. Janice loomed over him. It wasn't a great angle for her, truth be told. His practiced eye noted that gravity and the inevitable drag of chronology was not doing her carefully stretched neck and jaw any favors.

"Stop staring at my neck," she said. "Shove over." She slapped his thigh. The towel he had covering his crotch after swimming his naked laps slipped. Making him wince at the contact. Which made him smile wider at the memory of why he had to wince.

He shifted to make room for her. She dropped onto the lounge next to him with a loud sigh. He'd chosen this furniture for this reason. It accommodated more than one adult body at once. Or a bunch of grandkids. Or whatever.

The sensation of her cool hand on his upper thigh made him flinch. He really wanted—needed, it could be argued—a few more hours alone, in silence, in the sun. But he took a deep breath, forcing himself to be calm. He'd had a stressful morning, making all those stupid deliveries of clean, empty plastic ware. Having to be face-to-face with three of the men he'd hosted at his house into the wee hours last night. Janice knew damn good and well how he felt about that. He preferred to take at least a day, if not two or three, before encountering any of those assholes. Murphy especially. Jesus.

But no. Janice had roused him way too early from the sort of deep sleep he only ever really experienced after one of their cul-de-sac neighbor gatherings. On purpose. Of that, he had no doubt. She was becoming less and less sanguine about their complex relationships while becoming more obsessed about Melissa Murphy.

Fine. He should've known better. He'd been married to Janice long enough, had seen that look she'd get when she'd reached her jealousy limit enough times. And he'd noted it the last few days whenever Melissa's name came up, much less if she'd show up, like she had the day of the party.

Yeah. Okay. He should've steered clear of Melissa last night. Fine. Whatever. He hadn't. There was something about her he craved. And he'd missed it these past few months of pretending they were all regular old borrow-a -up-of-sugar-at-the-back-door neighbors. He chuckled at that thought.

Melissa Murphy was definitely a back-door kind of a neighbor. That was a truism. And how.

"Allen," his wife said, her lips next to his ear. She slipped her hand under the towel. He grunted then relaxed as she stroked him exactly the way that would get him off fast. She kept whispering to him, using flat-out filthy talk, biting his earlobe in between dirty words. There was something to be said for having the same sexual partner for a lot of years, he thought, right before his mind went all white noise and he leaned forward with the force of his climax.

Janice wiped her hand on the towel and leaned back on the seat as he attempted to recover normal breathing and pulse rate. That was getting harder to do lately. He should get his cholesterol checked. Maybe lay off some of the stuff he was injecting into himself every day.

"So, will we be extending an invitation to the Rosses for our next gathering? Allen?" She leaned on his name a little too hard.

He finally opened both eyes and turned to look at her. She had her Gucci sunglasses on. A baseball cap with the logo of the university that dominated their town. Her blonde hair was tugged through the back in a ponytail. Her skin was a soft, carefully tanned shade of bronze. Her nose and chin as close to perfect as his excellent former practice partner could make them.

He let his gaze shift downward, the plastic surgeon in him noting that her well-hydrated skin above her breasts was getting a tad crepey. But those tits. He smiled and reached over to cup one D-cup orb in one hand. They'd been using a state-of-the-art new material when she'd had her enhancement. And they were damn perfect.

"Get off me," she snapped, slapping his hand away. He shrugged and draped one arm over his eyes. "And answer my question."

"I'm guessing the answer is yes, right, my love? I mean, if the way you ladies were slobbering all over Michael."

"Not like you weren't doing the same over his wife, my love," she said, parroting him in a way that made his teeth hurt. Damn woman. There was that flip side of being together as long as they'd been. The aggravating yin to the pleasant yang. She could read him like a book. And a simple book at that. He hated her sometimes.

"Janney, I ...I don't know...he's...so..."

"Perfect? Gorgeous? Hot as absolute walking perfection?"

"Yes, well. I mean, his wife isn't exactly hard on the eyes."

"No. She's a tight little package. Maybe a little young. Look what happened the last time we let a high-assed sweet young thing into the group. It messed everything up."

"Yes," Allen agreed, shoving aside his compulsion to defend himself. By killing himself, Tom Franks had all but admitted he'd been that sperm donor. Thank Christ.

He resisted the urge to look at her and risk letting her see his expression when he thought about Cassandra LeBlanc. That asshole Barrett got what he deserved with that one.

He'd known Barrett LeBlanc, J.D. before he'd moved onto their street. They'd moved in similar philanthropic circles when the guy had been with his second wife. But that had been the extent of it. When he realized the man was now living in his inner circle, and with some crunchy granola hottie, he'd been flabbergasted. This was not a showy kind of a neighborhood. Not a Barrett LeBlanc-style place at all. But there he was. With Cassie. Damn him to hell and back, but he'd wanted that sweet piece of tail in on their parties, and that right quick.

"You're a pig," Janice had said. Back then, she'd been a lot more relaxed. Eager to expand their close friendship to another couple. Granted, Barrett was good-looking. And he had hooked the guy up with all kinds of potions and enhancements, administered by the very best pseudo-medical professionals money could buy.

"But I'm your pig, right?" he'd asked before chasing her up the steps, all while pretending he was doing it to Cassie. Something he'd do plenty of, later. Many times well outside the parameters of their hard-and-fast rules. But that was then. This is now. Allen was aces at letting go of guilt.

"Well?" Janice said, yanking him back to his present reality-based dilemma. "What are we going to do about them?"

"What I think is that you'll decide what you want to do about them, and you'll tell me. And the decision will be made."

He felt her tense. Something he knew she would do. But it was the truth. He would never in a zillion trillion years have suggested they embark upon this particular lifestyle. Once he'd sworn off girlfriends in the face of Janice's serious threat of divorce, he'd started staying home more. Long enough to knock her up again anyway. Once their daughter Alicia turned two, he'd been at the peak of his career, making an obnoxious amount of money. But Janice kept the house in near constant renovation mode, thanks to that dough.

The day he'd looked up from the clipboard to meet with his final patient on a long, boring Thursday—a day he'd been seriously flirting with one of the nurses at the hospital for something to do—and had come face-to-face with none other than Mrs. Allen J. Cooper, he'd realized something. That he was the luckiest damn son of a bitch on the planet with this woman for a wife.

She'd shut his office door and admitted to him that she was there to get a consult from his practice partner. But first, she wanted to propose something to him. Something outside the realm of what was considered appropriate in their Midwestern pillar-of-the-community, suburban life. Something that had made him grin at her, lock the door, and take her then and there on the exam table.

Their early forays into it had been far away from their home, on the West Coast, attending some high-class parties she'd found in her research and had gotten them into with a shit ton of money. It had been challenging, to say the least. They'd tiptoed around the edges of the scene, observing, trying to figure out if it would work for them. It had taken three trips out to the host's house in Orange County before they'd partaken of the riches.

To say they'd never had a problem with any of these encounters would be a lie. But they'd worked through it, after some loud, scary fights, typically culminating with some of the most intense sex he'd ever experienced—and he could honestly say he'd had plenty of experience. But after three years of out-of-town trips to partake in all manner of orgies, partner swapping, parties, and more-intimate two-couple dates, they had a good sense of what they liked and, more importantly, what they would each tolerate from the other.

They decided to stop traveling to find the sort of sexual outlet they'd both come to require, and to crave with the sort of intensity that caught them both by surprise. Mind you, he had them both hopped up on a ton of hormones by then, keeping their skin taut, their eyes bright, their muscles supple, and their libidos amped.

"I'm sure I don't know what you mean, Allen," Janice said now, in a voice that could slice metal. She had that way about her, his lovely wife. She was horny. She was aggressive. She was without a doubt, bisexual. He sometimes wondered if she'd rather have sex with women than men, even though she claimed it was a fifty-fifty thing.

She was a full-frontal alpha female. His alpha female. And he loved her. Although, lately, she was as annoying as all get-out. He was self-aware enough to acknowledge he wasn't that easy to live with at times, either but still, she was wearing him out and he could sense his patience with her waning.

He turned to face her, rolling all the way onto his side. She did the same. They lay with a few centimeters of space between them, their noses almost touching, fingers entwined, breathing each other's air. "I love you, Janney," he said, pecking the tip of her nose then each cheek then her lips.

"I know you do, Allen." She let go of his hand and rested her palm alongside his stubbly cheek. "I love you, too."

He smiled. She smiled. "I want them to join us, baby," she said. "I think they'll be a fine addition. Something about them is…I don't know…"

"Sexy?"

"No, it's more than that," she said. She ran her thumb over his lips. He bit it gently then sucked it into his mouth. She shivered. "They're already into something kinky. I can tell by watching them."

"Oh?" He hadn't picked up on it, but his Janney could sniff that kind of thing out like a predatory animal seeking prey.

"Yeah, probably some Master-slave play or something."

"Hmmm…" Allen could feel his body responding to that concept. He tugged Janice close, grinding against her like a damn teenager. "I like. Tell me more."

"Wait," she said, pulling away and staring into his eyes in that way she had. Reading him again like the simple book he was. "You have to promise me that you won't be…weird, you know, about Michael."

"I swear, I won't be." He nuzzled her neck, sucking in sweat, sunscreen, a whiff of soap. But he wasn't 100 percent sure about that claim. Not at all. Michael Ross intimidated the shit out of him for a lot of reasons, not the least of which was his youth, his firm ass, muscular legs, and the fact that he knew what was on his wife's bucket list with regard to the tall, movie-star handsome young Black man next door.

He owed it to her, he supposed. He'd gone off the rez with Cassie, plenty of times, having more than a little fun with the eager young woman on the afternoons when Janice was volunteering at the library or the hospital. None of those times with a condom. It had made the whole thing feel that much worse, and, hence, more of a turn-on.

God, but he was such a shit. He'd been 99 percent convinced he'd slammed that baby into her. Until Tom Franks had done them all a favor and copped to it by offing himself.

"Let's invite them," he said, tucking back a lock of hair that had escaped her ponytail and hat.

She smiled. And, at that moment, for the first time since they'd agreed to practice polyamory or wife-swapping or swinging or whatever the hell it was they'd been doing for the better part of the last fifteen years together, Allen wondered if this were the right thing to do. If he might be making a mistake.

But then she kissed him in that way she had, molding her body to his, and his mind went blank but for one thought, yet again. Playing like they had the night before always did this to him. Turned him into a full-on horn dog for a solid twenty-four hours afterward. He got up, letting the towel slide off, leaving him naked and ready for her. She grinned, got up, and pulled him into the house.

Chapter Fifteen

The New Guy

• • • •

MICHAEL COULD NEVER put his finger on the exact moment it happened.

Sometimes he wondered if he'd had any say in the matter.

Those times, when he felt railroaded into his current life situation—dream job at the right law firm, beautiful wife, perfect-so-far son, house on the right street in the right city—he'd chastise himself for it. He had no reason to complain about anything. Amelia had supported him and his desire to go to law school, granted with her wealthy family supporting them both. She'd gotten pregnant a solid year before her life plan had determined was right.

But there it was. The life plan.

The goddamned life plan Amelia, quite literally, had written down in one of those expensive Moleskine notebooks. She was old school that way. No Word doc for his woman, no, sir. "Because it would be too easy to change it. To deviate from it. To forget how important it is to adhere to carefully laid plans," she would say right now if he asked her.

But, of course, she wasn't here. She was back at their picture-perfect house on what she had declared a once-in-a-lifetime-opportunity cul-de-sac location, passed out drunker than a skunk on all the wine the men in said cul-de-sac had plied her with at their welcome-to-the-neighborhood cookout.

Which was one of the reasons he was out here in the dark, cool hour of four thirty a.m. on a holiday Sunday, his Nike Air Zoom Pegasus shoes slapping against the asphalt of the early morning empty roads of his barely explored neighborhood. He was only jogging. Being extra careful since he didn't know the roads well enough to run full-out yet. And being cautious was his nature, after all.

His parents had been solid blue collar middle class, and raised him to appreciate every dollar made, adamant that he and his siblings succeed at life. They'd instilled relentless drive, along with a sense of caution that many times seemed counterintuitive. It definitely confused him, this message of "never give up" but, at the same time, "don't get too big for your britches because everything you earn can, and likely will be taken from you at any moment."

A dog barked from somewhere as Michael continued on his slow journey through the picturesque tree-lined streets of his new neighborhood. The light was at that perfect moment, the one he loved to experience and had plenty, thanks to early morning study sessions, work prep, and of course, his beloved son, Tyler.

Mornings were without a doubt his favorite time of day. His parents were early risers by necessity. His mother had retired after thirty-five years with the United State Postal Service. His father had been a high school teacher then counselor in his later years, staying with the inner-city Chicago public school that he'd refused to send his own children to until he'd been eligible for retirement four years ago. Or rather had been forced into, thanks to a mild heart attack that had given his mother the impetus to insist he hang up his decades-old leather briefcase and lunchbox—two things that had been such familiar items of his boyhood mornings, he'd purchased his own versions of them when he'd been hired for his first job.

Growing up, coffee had been bubbling away in the percolator, eggs and bacon in the pan, and news on the radio without fail every single morning. Those sights, sounds, and odors had anchored his life as one of the token Black kids in the moderately decent but way-better-than-inner-city elementary, middle, and high schools. He'd been a straight-A, all-state in track and baseball student athlete. He'd dutifully taken his girlfriend to junior prom, only to be dumped by her the following summer. A heartbreak that he sometimes wondered had set him up for the moment his lovely wife had plucked him out of a crowd their first weekend at the university. The exact location of their first meeting mere blocks from their new house.

He'd spent his senior year trying not to let on how much he'd been hurt, his future at college already secured, thanks to his grades and top SAT scores. He'd qualified for plenty of free money, not to mention all the scholarships thrown at him for various reasons. His mother had taken on the task of getting him into this particular school and getting all four years paid for with a vengeance that had paid off. His siblings had been similarly indoctrinated. His brother Lawrence was currently a sophomore at Northwestern. His baby sister Candace was a junior in high school and entertaining both athletic and academic money offers, thanks to her status as a top soccer player.

Michael picked up his pace, determined to clear his head of the onslaught of interesting input from the past twelve hours. It had been the reason for this outing after all.

He slowed then paused at the intersection of five different streets, unable to work his way past the extreme oddness of that barbecue party at the Coopers'. As soon as they'd been assured that Tyler was in safe hands in the pool with floaties and a babysitter, he and Amelia had been separated, and kept that way for the bulk of the evening. It had taken him about forty-five minutes to realize that despite a few crossovers, he'd been predominantly surrounded by women, while Amelia had been the focus of the men.

Strange, he recalled thinking as he turned in a circle, taking in the neat homes, nothing obnoxious or over the top but all located in what he now understood to be the best possible neighborhoods.

It had been a strange gathering to be certain. Mainly because of the distinct undercurrent of...well...sex.

Michael shook his head. Surely he had imagined it. He was pent up, after all. He and Amelia still hadn't resumed their once-robust level of sexual relations since Tyler had been born. He understood. She'd been exhausted by the end of the pregnancy. Her labor had been protracted, terrifying, ending in an emergency C-section to save both her and their son's lives.

Like he said, he got it. And he'd been supportive—staying up with her through all the late-night seemingly nonstop nursing sessions before doing his part by changing diapers, rocking, walking the floors, and watching his son sleep while she attempted to rest between all the feedings.

Never mind he had to be at his office as junior-attorney-on-the-partnership-track by seven thirty every morning of the week, sometimes on Saturdays in order not to drop back in the pecking order. He'd wanted a baby, he reminded himself a lot in those early, mind-numbing mornings trying like hell to stay awake at his desk.

His mother-in-law had swooped in after the first three weeks, coming when Amelia had sobbed to him one afternoon as he was trying to take a deposition that she thought she was going to kill herself if Tyler wouldn't go to sleep. He'd called the woman himself, using a suitably humble tone of voice and biting back the need to hang up on her and her supremely passive-aggressive message that he'd obviously failed in his duties as husband and father, but perhaps that was to be expected, after all. At that point, he didn't give a shit what she said, as long as she would get her ass in her Beemer drive over to help them.

He picked up his pace as the light went from rosy to orange between the thick trees that made this neighborhood what it was—an oasis of nature in the center of a semi-busy college town. Summer mornings were the best, he mused as he hit his stride and let his brain shut down. His heart pumped, lungs and legs burned, and he was able to let go of the onrushing sense of weirdness that had hit him at the hour mark into the party.

Weirdness. And an increasing sense that if he asked, any one of the attractive suburban women gathered around him as he drank, and ate, laughed, and chatted would have dropped to their knees and sucked his dick on the spot and in front of a crowd of her jealous friends.

"Shit!" He stumbled on something invisible in the road. Dropping to one knee, he felt the asphalt tear into his skin. "God damn it." He stayed down, face pressed against the knee not currently getting road rash. "Fuck." With a sigh, he dropped onto his butt, brushing the tiny rocks off his skin and ignoring his sudden erection.

After making sure Tyler was tucked in and Amelia was the same, snoring away with wine fumes rising off her like visible waves, he'd poured himself the first of two bourbons while he sat in the big leather chair of his new home office for a couple of hours. He sat, and he pondered what he'd experienced in his next-door-neighbor's backyard.

At one point, restless and edgy in a way he understood was half him not getting properly laid in months and half the sensation of Janice Cooper's soft, cool palm, which always seemed to be on his arm, or his knee if they were seated. Or maybe the way the real estate agent who'd sold them this house would lean into him enough that he could see the dark tips of her nipples when he'd say something innocuous, while attempting and failing not to look down her shirt. Or perhaps the way the sweet-natured Emily, the teacher married to the good-looking Indian heart surgeon guy remained stuck to the side Janice wasn't on, her thigh pressed against his, the side of her breast brushing his other arm when she'd reach across to grab his empty beer bottle.

Jesus. What in the hell anyway?

He stared down at the crotch, gritting his teeth. He'd done his usual quick, take-into-his-own-hands action not an hour ago when he'd woken up with his neck cricked against the arm of the stiff leather sofa. He hated masturbating. It always felt teenager-ish, immature and clandestine and silly for a grown man with a wife who'd been eager for him and his preferred kink.

Thankfully, Amelia had been feeling better since they'd moved in here. She'd promised him they'd resume things soon. And he'd believed her. He could tell she was getting back to her old self. He had plans for a private room in their basement. She'd given that contractor guy who'd been practically cupping her ass the whole night before a check to get started on the project that included an over-the-top play-room-slash-secondary TV room for football games. Plus a room that would always remain locked.

All he'd asked for was four drywalled, insulated walls with extra soundproofing, decent hardwood floors, no windows, and a bathroom with top-of-the-line finishes. He'd told Ryan Murphy not to finish the ceiling. Simply to install two light fixtures and reinforce the overhead beams. He'd handle the rest of it.

Yeah, that helped him in the hard-dick department.

He stayed seated, trying to think about anything but the night before and his body's lack of the kind of sexual attention he required. But it wouldn't leave him, no matter how much he tried to shove it out of his damn head. The hands, thighs, nipples, lips, voices, shining eyes, flipped-back hair, the blatant, *would you like to have us, Michael? All of us? Right now? By the pool? Because that can and will be arranged for you* vibe that was being shoved down his throat, haunted him, grated on him, burned every inch of his skin even now, in the cool morning air.

He'd consumed his second bourbon on his deck, woozy from the earlier beers and the previous glass of brown liquor. Until something had caught his eye. Something about the light in what he assumed was the Coopers' bedroom. It hadn't been on when he'd come out here, he was pretty sure. But now it was. He'd eased back, trying to get a better angle on his view, confused by the mix of shadows that moved, ebbing and flowing in a bizarre mix of what was obviously more than one body.

He sipped, not terribly surprised by it on some level, fascinated by it on another. At one point, he put the glass on one of the tables Amelia had purchased when he'd been gone last week. Without realizing it, or maybe pretending he was doing it because he was drunk, he found himself on the patio next to the Coopers' pool, staring up at the erotic play of shadows in the large window, only partially hidden by a curtain.

At one point, the shadows parted, and he was certain there were at least four people in the room, maybe five or six. He took a few steps back, wanting to see more, recalling the dark tip of Melissa's nipple, the soft brush of Emily's thigh, the sensation of Janice's hand on his leg. A split second before he ended up in the damn pool, the light went off, leaving him standing there, breathing heavy, fascinated, repelled, and more turned on than he'd been in ages.

He'd stumbled back home and sat next to Amelia for almost an hour, brushing her arm, her hair, her thigh. But she'd been zonked. So, he'd made it as far as the couch in the living room.

And now, here he was. Sitting on his ass with yet another tent in his shorts, like some kind of hormonally addled teenager. If he wasn't careful, someone would call the cops on him for running or rather sitting while being black. He got up and limped home.

To his surprise, Amelia was up, sipping coffee and scrolling around on her iPad at the kitchen eating counter. To his pleasant further surprise, when she slid off the tall bar chair and walked toward him, her hips swaying, her lips parted, her eyes shining, she dropped the robe, under which she was naked.

"Thank God," he muttered, pulling her into his arms. "I need…I have to…I…"

"I know," she whispered into his lips as she slipped her hand into his shorts. "Let's go upstairs."

"No," he said, his voice choked. "Right here. Now. I mean it."

He felt her shiver in his arms and almost came right then and there.

"Yes, Sir," she said, her voice soft and pillowy, like her lips and breasts. "How would you like me this morning?"

She was stroking him, kissing his shoulder, sliding her other hand up his sweaty shirt. He took her hands and pinned them at her sides as he walked her backward toward the kitchen table. He kissed her, hard, the way she liked it, hiked her legs up and around his waist, and took her right on the table.

"More," she whispered. "I want more."

And something about those words made him understand that their lives were about to change.

Chapter Sixteen

L*adies Who Lunch*

• • • •

"ARE YOU SERIOUS?" MELISSA put the final touches on her makeup. It was Labor Day, but real estate recognized very few holidays, and she'd spent too many weeks out of pocket already. There was work to be done. Money to be made. "Hello? Emily? You there?"

"Yes, sorry. I had to…"

But Melissa didn't hear her. Not really. Most times, she was barely aware of Emily Arya. Emily was that kind of a female—the easily ignored kind. She was a good teacher. Melissa was sure enough of that to have ensured that Danny was in her class this fall. And Melissa admired anyone who actually enjoyed being around little kids all day.

But Emily had said something fairly shocking. Melissa blinked fast to dry her mascara then picked up the phone and took it back into the bedroom with her to look for the shoes she wanted. Pressing the Bluetooth earpiece farther into her ear canal, she surveyed the footwear options on the long shelf in the walk-in closet Ryan had designed for her. Once she located the wedge sandals with open toes she'd been thinking about, she slipped her feet into them and sat a moment on the leather chair near the bedroom window. "Well? Are you? Serious?"

"As a heart attack. And I'd know."

Melissa chuckled. Emily could be funny, in her wry, quiet way. "Well, I have to say, I'm surprised. I mean, we all know that Allen isn't keen on it. He's obviously intimidated by Michael."

"Or he's a racist."

"Of course he's a racist. Shit, Ryan's a racist mick if ever there was one. But he's pretty keen to have little miss pretty buns in on the fun. He'll have to get over it."

The was a beat of silence on the other end of the line. Melissa only noticed it when it stretched into a second minute. She was preoccupied, trying to gather all her crap together anyway. She passed by Danny, who was curled up on his usual end of the couch diddling away with his iPad. Of Ryan there was no sign, which irritated her. He knew she had appointments today. He'd said he'd stick around and hang out with Danny.

"Mama, do you have my Lunchables ready for tomorrow?"

Melissa sighed. Danny and his damn Lunchables. But getting mad didn't help. Besides, in a way, she was pretty damn obsessed with routines herself.

She knew better than to make what was wrong with Danny into something as routine as an exaggeration of her own simple compulsion to have a specific salad with a certain kind of dressing on the side every day at twelve thirty. She'd been warned by enough doctors not to do that. Danny's issues were deeper, more complex, and required way more patience. It was that, sometimes, her patience was stretched thin by recalcitrant sellers or needy buyers, and she had nothing left.

But there was no excuse to be bitchy this morning. She'd had three weeks of lake vacation, plus a reasonably pleasant return to the cul-de-sac status quo two nights ago.

A smile snuck across her face at the memory. It had been a real free-for-all. Something they'd never actually done in a group, or as a group, or whatever you wanted to call it. She'd enjoyed her time with Allen, as usual, but with the added bonus of Barrett, before she'd turned to find Sai watching from across the room. A shiver snuck down her spine.

Damn, but it had been wild.

And now they were going to add this couple, Amelia and Michael Ross? Really? She'd been ready to say no if it came to some kind of a vote. Then again, it wasn't a democracy. It was the Janice and Allen Show.

"Emily? I'm gonna have to get to..."

"I don't know if Sai and I...I mean, we..."

"I know, Emily. I feel that way sometimes, too. I mean, especially after this last...um...experience."

"Right. It was kind of crazy. I don't know. I mean, all this stuff with Laura. And you didn't see Tom in that tub. I did. It was horrible."

"I can only imagine." Melissa's pulse was racing. She needed this conversation to end. Now.

"I think that somehow, what we did, I mean, all those times we..."

Melissa rolled her eyes at the sound of Emily's voice breaking. "I have to get to work, Emily. But to recap: We're supposed to take Amelia out to lunch and ask her to, ah, join us in the, um, group?"

"That's what Janice told me over coffee. She asked me to call you. She had to go do her volunteering. I need to get over to my classroom now, so I'm calling you, but I don't know who's calling Cassie."

Melissa winced. Cassie had been as eager as any of them the other night, jumping right into the fray as it were, her baby bump sticking out like some kind of a bad omen. Of course, all she'd wanted was to mess around with Janice. Which suited everyone else, as a bit of a fluffer foreplay.

"So, we're on a phone tree now?" Melissa was pissed Janice hadn't told her first. She and Ryan had formed the original foursome after all. But Janice had something up her ass lately when it came to Allen and her. She needed to get over it. That didn't stop the immature thrill of female friendship jealousy hitting her brain, making her skin hot all over.

"I guess," Emily said. "I don't know anymore, Melissa. The time we took off, those months, it was kind of normalizing."

"And boring," Melissa said, sharply. Too sharply. She was sick of her neighbor's mealymouthed crap right now. Especially since she'd availed herself of Ryan's talents the other night. Ryan liked her "softness" as he put it. The way she was "pliant" and "sweet."

Stop it, Melissa. You're being childish.

"So, about this lunch..."

"Right. I'm going to call Amelia later today and invite her this coming Sunday to the country club for brunch. Just us girls, you know. Plenty of mimosas, gin and tonics, whatever. The guys are gonna take Michael golfing I think."

Melissa sighed again. She had her purse on her shoulder. Her leather briefcase was at her feet. She needed to get the hell out of here. To work. To put this behind her. She hadn't realized how much this past year had been spent normalizing, recalibrating, letting go of the things they did together with their neighbors. Things that were utterly sordid. Things that she had neatly compartmentalized, tucked away in the inner recesses of her brain during the days she woke, rose, fed her son and husband, and went to work making money. A lot of money. While Ryan did the same.

On the other hand, they were all consenting adults. They'd made this arrangement over a lovely steak dinner and too many bottles of expensive Cabernet. They'd consummated it that very night. A night that would go down in Melissa's memory as the most erotic, amazing, eye-opening experience of her life.

The Franks were the first to arrive. She'd met them, gotten a good feeling about them, introduced them to Janice then closed the deal on the house. Ryan's company had more or less gutted it and put it back together to Laura's specifications. Tom Franks was an accountant. They'd moved here when he got hired by a large firm in Detroit. But, after three years, he'd gone out on his own, opened an office in a restored building downtown. And seemed to be doing very well, considering.

It had always struck her and Ryan as odd that they had top-of-the-line new Audis every other year. They went on fancy vacations all over the world with their kids. Laura had had plenty of surgical help to keep herself looking fresh, thanks to Allen's practice. "I mean, seriously, how much can the guy make doing taxes for the yoga studios and restaurants?" Ryan asked her repeatedly, as if she would know.

They'd taken Tom up on his offer to take a look at their situation, which was triple complicated since Ryan had an LLC and she worked on 100 percent commission. Once he'd figured out what a genius Tom was with tax shelters and whatnot, Ryan had stopped complaining about him. And she'd forgotten about it altogether. As long as she didn't have to write a big-ass check in April to cover her tax bill, she was fine with whatever Tom and Ryan did with the money.

"Sunday brunch with the neighbor ladies, huh?" Melissa picked up her bag and glanced around, trying to figure out where in the hell Ryan was hiding himself. "All right, fine. I'm in."

"But what are we going to say to her?"

"Not sure. But I am sure we can follow Janice's lead. She's the boss lady in all of this after all."

"Right. Sure. Okay."

"You don't sound too convinced."

"I'm not. I told you already, Sai and I are probably going to, um, stop. You know."

"Well, it's a free country." Melissa would miss Sai. He had an amazing cock, truly. Even Ryan was impressed by it. They always paired off in the same room and had spent several pleasant hours with the Ayras. The one time she let Ryan play outside of her line of sight in the early days after they'd added the Franks into their mix, she'd been riddled with jealousy. She'd almost given the poor man a concussion later in a knock-down-drag-out fight that had ended with Ryan in the emergency room, telling the doctor that he'd fallen off the ladder, her in hysterical tears at his bedside while they kept him overnight for concussion observation. She'd not meant to hit him with the damn decorative vase. Or had she?

"I haven't made up my mind yet. Not really. I mean, don't you ever feel, I don't know, weird about all of this? Isn't it kind of...sick and wrong?"

"No, I don't ever think that, Emily," she lied. "I really have to go to work."

"Okay. Sorry."

Melissa felt guilty within a fraction of a second. "I'm sorry. I don't mean to snap or cut you off. I'm kind of busy. But I'm thrilled Danny's going to be in your classroom this year. He's a handful. As you already know."

"I love Danny. He's a wonderful boy." The sincerity in Emily's voice, which had switched into teacher mode, relieved Melissa. She looked over at her son, his nose close to the screen that lit his face up with a weird, sickly blue glow. "We're going to be fine."

"He has his educational plan already set. And gets therapy twice a week."

"I know. I'm ready for him. I'm really looking forward to it. You'll see. He's going to love school this year."

"God. I hope so. Listen, I'll call you later, okay?"

"Okay. Thanks."

• • • •

SHE MADE IT HOME BY five and walked into a hellscape of family dysfunction. Danny was screaming and rocking with the quilt pulled over his head. Ryan was standing over him, yelling his damn head off. She dropped her bag and purse in the hall and ran for them, yanking her husband away from her son, pulling Danny into a tight hug, still covered in the quilt.

She knew if he'd devolved to this state, it would be hours before he could communicate with her.

"God damn it, Ryan," she said. "What did you do to him?"

"I didn't do anything but try and get him to come outside for a while. To put that damned screen away."

"Mama, iPad is broke!"

She glanced around her and spotted the thousand-dollar device leaning against a wall, its screen shattered. "Seriously, Ryan? You did that? Way to set a mature example." She'd be the first to admit that she'd been close to doing that very thing. She shouldn't judge. But she wasn't about to give him any benefit of any doubt. Not with Danny in this condition the night before the start of the school year. Something Ryan knew was always a tough night without the extra drama.

Ryan threw his hands up and walked away. Melissa let him. It took a couple of hours, plus a warm bubble bath and a dish of day-glow orange Kraft mac and cheese before Danny stopped sniveling and mumbling about his iPad. She read him a chapter of *Captain Underpants*. He wanted *Harry Potter*, but she agreed with his therapist that it would upset him. They went through their ritual of kisses, hugs, reassurances that he'd love school. That Miz Arya would be his teacher this year. That he knew and loved Miz Arya.

By the time she emerged from his room, where a small lamp stayed lit the whole night, no matter what, she felt like she'd run a marathon. She leaned against the wall, closed her eyes, slid to the floor. When she opened them, Ryan was standing over her, looking contrite and holding out a glass of red wine. "Pinot?" she asked, taking it from him.

"What else?" He sat next to her, his arm around her shoulders. "I'm sorry, baby."

"Don't call me that." She leaned her head on his shoulder and let tears slide down her cheeks. "God, Ryan. Are we doing the right thing?"

"What? With him? I have no idea. You're the expert on that."

"No. With...the neighbors. You know."

Ryan sighed and held out his hand. She gave him the wine. He took a drink and handed it back to her. "I don't know, Mel. I almost feel like they're innocents. You know? Like we're luring them into some kind of..."

"Sickness?" She sipped. The rich, deep alcohol coated her tongue and slid down her throat.

"No. It's not...we aren't...shit. Are we?"

She stared at her bare feet next to Ryan's on the rug runner on the upper hallway walnut hardwood flooring. "I don't know anymore, Ryan. I really don't."

She finished the wine and took his outstretched hand after he got up. She slipped into his arms, let him kiss her then disentangled herself. "I need to fix lunches for tomorrow. I won't feel like it in the morning."

Ryan patted her butt. "I will tell you one thing," he said to her retreating back. "You are one sweet woman. And I love you. And for the record, I did not throw the iPad hard enough to break it. Our son did that."

She waved a hand as she headed down the stairs. She should answer. Tell him she loved him, too. That he was a wonderful man, a fabulous provider, if way too impatient with their son's issues. That she was sorry for blaming him about the stupid iPad.

But she didn't. She finished Danny's—a pepperoni pizza Lunchable and carefully sliced apple, and then hers, a spinach salad with tomatoes and feta and a small container of garlic and oil dressing. Realizing that she was bone tired, she headed straight for the couch. After about fifteen minutes of some random movie, she drifted.

"Come on, baby," Ryan said.

"Stop calling me baby," she mumbled into his neck as he carried her up to their bedroom and held her tight as she fell back asleep.

Chapter Seventeen

S*hort Game*

• • • •

"MICHAEL?" AMELIA CALLED over her shoulder. She was trying to follow the instructions to her new pasta-making machine and failing at it, which pissed her off. The sound of his phone buzzing its way across the kitchen island didn't help. She had about forty-five minutes of naptime left to get this done, and she was determined her first try at linguini be a success for tonight's dinner.

When he didn't answer, she wiped her floury hands on her apron and grabbed the phone before it landed on the floor. She didn't recognize the number, but that was nothing new these days. It was likely someone trying to sell them a home security system. But she didn't feel like answering it. "Michael!"

"Down here, Ames," she heard him answer from the basement. The phone stopped ringing and buzzed almost immediately with a text. They kept their screens locked but knew each other's passwords. She tapped his in *0625*, their anniversary date. The screen jiggled, indicating it wasn't the correct code. She wiped her fingers on her apron and entered *0625*. Again, she got the screen jiggle.

Complete transparency was a central tenet of their relationship and always had been. They had enough to battle without adding in secrecy between them. She leaned against the island counter and blew her hair out of her face. She must have entered it too quickly. And her fingers were still a little oily from the dough.

Carefully, she entered *0625* one final time.

Nothing but the jiggle.

"God damn it, Michael!" She slapped a hand over her mouth, praying that her tone and volume wouldn't rouse Tyler too early. He'd been a total beast all morning long. She couldn't wait to get him down for his nap.

"What?"

She looked up and spotted him standing at the top of the basement stairs, a wrench in one hand, a coil of soft cotton rope in the other. She bit her lip as her well-conditioned body reacted to that, before she crushed it under a healthy helping of indignation. "Your phone's password doesn't seem to be working for me anymore." She held it out to him.

He crossed over to her and took it. With one arm draped over her shoulder, he tapped out another set of numbers. "I'm sorry, babe. I had to change it since the firm put me on their account. It was that, or try and juggle two phones, and I'm not about to do that." He kissed the top of her head. "It's 0712 now. Another easy number to remember, right?" he said, making her feel guilty for being pissed off by using her birthday.

"Well, whatever. You have a text." She was only moderately satisfied with that answer. Something about it, combined with the events of the past few days, was making red flags flap around in her brain. He was classy enough not to make her feel like an idiot for getting polluted at the cookout, but he had his ways of reminding her that it had been less-than-stellar behavior on her part. His brow furrowed as he read the text. She turned away to pour him a glass of filtered water from the front of the fridge. He took it then put the phone down on the island.

"Thanks." He drained the glass and put it in the sink then picked up the rope he'd dropped onto the floor by the basement doorway. "Almost done down here."

Amelia was re-re-reading the instructions on the pasta maker, determined not to let him know how much him changing his damn phone password had thrown her. She was still jittery from the unaccustomed hangover, not to mention the actual events of that strange barbecue party. "Who was it?"

"Ryan Murphy. Wants to know if I have a decent golf game, and, if not, he's inviting me to play next weekend."

She looked at him, tall, handsome—okay, hot as shit—standing there in his running shorts and T-shirt, his dark-brown skin shining in the light from the window. God, but she loved him. She let her gaze drift to the rope, at his long, talented fingers wrapped around it. She smiled. "Sounds like fun. You tell him your actual handicap?" Michael was a total ringer on the links. He'd tried to get her interested in playing, but it bored her.

"Hell no. Thought I might take him for a few bucks first."

She'd opened her mouth to respond, thankful things seemed back on familiar ground, when a wail rose from upstairs. "Maaaah! Mama!"

"Crap. I need to finish this." She was pulling at her apron strings, angry but resigned, when Michael touched her shoulder, sending a shock of raw lust to the base of her brain. Their physical reunion the day before had been incredible, if short. And she knew well that it was a mere taste of the satisfaction to come.

"I've got him. Finish...this." He gestured vaguely to the ugly glop of dough she'd been trying to form into sheets to feed into the expensive device she'd bought from Williams Sonoma. "Whatever this all is." He grinned when she smacked his arm, grabbed her hand, and put it to his lips. His deep-brown eyes flashed, which didn't help her current state, simultaneously frustrated with pasta and horny as hell. "Date night tonight, my love," he whispered. "I'll have everything ready for us. Your mother's taking Ty, right?"

"Yes," she said. "She'll be here around five. I figured we'd sit out on the deck about an hour, have a glass of wine first."

"Sounds like a plan," he said, all business again. Tyler let out another howl, demanding her immediate presence and attention. "Got him. Carry on."

She gnawed her lip and admired her husband's spectacular rear view as he bounded up the steps, hollering back at their son to hold his horses, Dad was on the way. She heard the boy's delighted cry of "Da! Da!" before returning her focus to the confounded effort to do something as simple as turn some strips of dough into noodles. But it was a losing effort. Between her now strident need for Michael, her aggravation with her inability to do something as simple as the task in front of her, and her overarching uneasiness after the neighbor's gathering, she simply couldn't get it done.

Cursing under her breath, she dumped the uncooperative wad of dough into the garbage and rinsed off the dishes, keeping her finely tuned mom radar to the noises upstairs. Her men, she thought with a smile as she wiped down the black granite countertop. Acting like a couple of little boys. They were stomping around, hollering, running, the works. But she didn't care. She desperately wanted Michael to have a healthy relationship with their son. Enough that she overlooked his tendency to turn into a giant child whenever he was put in direct charge of the boy, which forced her to play bad cop. Which pissed her off.

Despite her best efforts, she had a sneaking suspicion her sweet little boy was turning into a tiny tyrant. When she heard a loud, scary thump above her then a beat of silence then a loud shriek of pain, she resisted the impulse to run upstairs. Whatever it was, let Michael handle it. He'd initiated the roughhousing. He could deal with the fallout.

She scrubbed the kitchen surfaces once more and sprayed window cleaner on the faucet to make it shine. Tyler screamed for a few more seconds then there was more silence. She patted herself on the back for not freaking out like she might have done a few weeks ago when it came to Tyler's well-being, and decided to reward herself with a beer. Michael had an impressive collection of local and nationally famous craft options in the drinks fridge. She studied them a minute then pulled two dark porters out, opened the bottles, and poured them into glasses.

By the time Michael appeared with a snotty-nosed Tyler clutching him, his thumb stuck in his mouth, she'd finished half of hers. "We messed up, Mama," Michael said, handing the boy over when he lunged for her.

"Da," the boy mumbled around his thumb.

She touched the knot rising on his forehead.

"Jesus, Michael. Did he lose consciousness?" Her protective hackles rising, she yanked one of the boo-boo bags from the freezer and sat at the kitchen table.

"Ow!" Tyler whimpered but let her put the soft, cold pack on his injury before he leaned into her neck, his familiar little-boy scent filling her brain. She kissed his hair and stroked his arm as he attempted to cry again. "Ma," he said, rubbing his nose against her neck.

"Gross. Let's blow your nose, sweetie."

Michael handed her a tissue. He looked appropriately contrite. She attempted not to bite his head off. She put the tissue to Tyler's nose. "Blow, please." He blew, winced then rubbed his head. "Hurt me."

"I can see that. What happened, exactly?" She looked at Michael who was sipping the beer she'd poured for him as Tyler settled himself back against her, soothing her with his familiar scent and the heft of his growing body. Michael licked a bit of foam off his upper lip, which cut a swathe through her rising anger at his irresponsibility. She sighed and cuddled Tyler a few more minutes, while she held the boo-boo bunny to his boo-boo.

When he tried to lift her shirt and get at her boob, she stopped him. "No, Tyler. Not now. Only before bed, remember? We decided that big boys drink from cups during the day."

"Wanna," he insisted, his tiny features screwing into the familiar pre-tantrum expression. "Want Mama," he insisted.

She sighed, ready to give in to it out of sheer exhaustion when Michael plucked the boy off her lap and carried him to the fridge. "You heard Mama, Son. You're a big boy now. Big boys use cups. Want some juice?"

"No," Tyler insisted as he tried to escape Michael's grasp. "Want Mama!" His voice was rising. "Want Mama now!"

She got up and was headed for him, her nipples tingly with the onset of doing their maternal duty. She'd been determined to wean him off her over the next few months and had only introduced the concept of "big boys use cups during the day" twenty-four hours ago. He'd seemed amenable to it then. But he was hurt. And he needed her. She was lifting her shirt and reaching for him with the other hand, but Michael held out his hand.

"No, Amelia." He tightened his grip on Tyler as she watched. "It's time to stop that. We agreed on it." He turned to the fridge, grabbed the organic apple juice, filled half of one of the collection of sippy cups then filled the rest with water, the way she'd told him to do. "Here you go, my man." Tyler took it, but his face was stormy, and she waited for the inevitable heave of the thing across the room. Michael picked up his half-finished glass of beer. "Let's watch some sports and drink out of our big-boy cups, whaddaya say?"

Tyler glanced at her then back at his father, who was taking a sip from his glass by way of example. Tyler put the cup to his lips and took a long pull. "That's the way we big boys do it," Michael said, winking at Amelia when the boy touched his cup to Michael's glass. "Time for some football."

"Foo-ba," Tyler said as he sucked on the cup's top. "Ma," he said, reaching back as if to placate her. She smiled at them.

"Go on, be a big boy with daddy."

"'K." He wiggled out of Michael's arms and stood, staring up into his father's eyes, the hero worship hard to ignore. Michael held out a hand. Tyler took it and together they marched themselves into the family room, parked themselves on the leather couch, and flipped on the giant flat screen.

"I'm gonna go for a walk," Amelia said, thankful for the moment, which felt pretty huge in the scheme of things, weaning-wise.

"Okay, Mama," Michael called.

Tyler was standing on the couch, facing her, clutching his sippy cup. "Okay, Mama!" he parroted.

"Okay, my boys." She walked over and kissed Tyler's chubby cheek. "Gan-gan will be here later, Ty. You're having sleepovers with her at the cabin. How does that sound?"

"Gan! Gan! Gan!" Tyler yelped as he jumped on the couch.

Michael dragged him down to his lap. "No jumping on the furniture, pal. That got us both into trouble once already today."

Amelia walked out into the warm, late-summer afternoon with a sigh of relief. The temperature hovered in the low seventies. The sun skirted in and out of fluffy clouds. The breeze lifted her hair off her neck and cooled her skin as she headed out of the cul-de-sac and onto the street.

She had a set of pleasant hours ahead of her. Her mom was coming to spell her and Michael for a few days, going with Tyler out to their family's lake house nearby. Her father would join them tomorrow. And she and her husband would have their new house to themselves for a solid four-day span. Michael had the day after Labor Day off. He'd probably spend the bulk of Tuesday logged on and working in his office. But when he wasn't...

She shivered and grinned at her dirty thoughts. He'd outfitted a grown-up playroom in the basement and wouldn't let her see what he was doing in it. Up to and including buying and setting up various pieces of furniture and god only knows what else without allowing her to open any of the boxes that had been delivered to the house while he was gone.

Her phone buzzed, interrupting her favorite Spotify playlist. She glanced at the screen. Not recognizing the number, she touched the answer button and turned the volume up on her wireless earbuds. "Hello?"

"Hi! Amelia? This is Emily. Your neighbor."

"Oh hi," Amelia said, trying to recall what Emily looked like. She was easily the most forgettable of the women she'd met these past few weeks. Melissa she knew well, based on the time they'd spent together as Realtor and client. Janice was the attractively preserved older woman at the end of the cul-de-sac. A sort of matriarch for the group who'd hosted the party. Cassie was the gorgeous young woman with the bright-blue eyes who was pregnant and seemingly not too happy about it. Emily...which one was she?

"So, I was wondering if you'd like to come out to brunch with us."

"Oh um..." She was preparing to beg off, not willing to change her plans for the next forty-eight hours. She'd been walking around feeling like a giant exposed horny nerve ever since their little kitchen table interlude. She wanted more. A lot more.

"I mean, um, next weekend. While the boys are golfing?"

Amelia blinked then realized what she was talking about. The "boys" had invited Michael to golf. And she was going to lunch with the ladies. Part of her bristled at this. Why couldn't they be in on the golfing?

But she hated golf.

She forced herself to stop thinking ridiculous thoughts.

"Sure, that sounds like fun. Where?"

"Oh, at the club. I figured you guys had already joined."

"No, not yet." To be honest, she'd avoided it, although she knew they should do it. She'd done her research. And her mother had, too. They'd decided that Forest Hills Golf and Swim Club was the best one to join. And she liked to believe that the fact of her husband's skin color wouldn't matter in this enlightened, Midwest college town. But part of her wasn't certain about that, and she was reluctant to put Michael through it. Perhaps going to a day at golf and lunch would ease their entry a bit. "But we have every intention of it."

"Any of us can sponsor you. They still require that. It's so...colonial, don't you think?"

Amelia hesitated, wondering if Emily would realize the awkwardness of that question. She picked up her pace, nervous and yet somehow pissed off at the same time.

"Well, anyway," the woman went on, not realizing it, apparently. "Why don't you ride with me? The guys usually all carpool to their golf days."

"Sure, sounds good." She didn't want to go now. In fact, all of a sudden, if she never saw or spoke to any of her immediate neighbors ever again, she'd not mind it one bit.

She shook her head at this ridiculous thought. One of the reasons she'd chosen this street was for the social opportunities. She was being paranoid. Her neighbors were just...a little enthusiastic and, well, touchy, when it came down to it.

The memory of the women surrounding Michael, leaning in, hands on his thighs and arms as he sat in the midst of them like some kind of a sultan among his harem wafted through her brain. Even as she recalled the way she'd been the center of the male attention most of the night. How attractive they all were, those men, from brash contractor Ryan to soft-spoken, exotic-looking Sai, to the two older men, Barrett and Allen. All of them were rich, handsome, fit to the point of model-perfect. And they'd been all over her.

She stopped in her tracks, recalling something else from that night she must have been suppressing as a figment of her imagination, or something her drunken brain had conjured. The large bedroom window on the second floor of the Coopers' house. The light, the shadows she'd taken for Janice and Allen at first in an embrace. Then the other shadows that joined them. The other people who'd been in that room and...and...

That is crazy, Amelia Elizabeth. Stop it. You're pent up and horny and are taking care of all of that within hours. Get a damn grip on yourself. These people are inviting you and Michael to a snooty country club that has likely only recently allowed Black people to be members. Keep things in perspective.

"Amelia? You still there?"

"Yes, sorry. I'd be happy to join you all. Looking forward to it."

"Great! Super. We'll...um..." There was a beat of silence that made Amelia uncomfortable again. "Anyway, if you need any tomatoes, you should stop by this week."

"Tomatoes," Amelia said, confused by the shift of topic.

"Yes. Between my garden and Cassie's, we're overflowing with them. There's only that much sauce and salsa I can make. Talk soon!" She hung up before Amelia could say anything else.

• • • •

"BYE, BABY! LOVE YOU! Be a good boy for Gan-gan!"

Tyler hardly glanced back at her as his grandmother led him to his car seat in the back of her SUV. Michael had his arm draped loosely around her shoulders as they stood in the doorway. The tiny tickle of worry that always lit her consciousness whenever she let Tyler out of her direct line of sight for an extended period of time made her suck in a breath.

As if sensing this, Michael tightened his grip and kissed her temple. "He's fine. He's in his happy place now. Ice cream and pancakes for breakfast and all that."

"Bye-bye, Mommy!" her mother called as she got in behind the steering wheel. "See you in a few days!"

Amelia slumped against Michael's torso, waving until the car was well out of sight. Michael turned her to face him, lifted her chin. He kissed her, teasing her lips, pressing her close, and leaving her breathless in the open front door, in view of all the neighbors. Something about that made her pull him toward her as she leaned in the open doorway. Inviting him to do more.

"Mmmm," Michael said as he flipped her bra open, as eager to get at her as Tyler had been but for a much nicer purpose. "Should we go inside?"

"No," she gasped as he lowered his lips to her breast.

She smiled as his talented fingers slid into her shorts. She spread her legs and let him do what he wanted, setting the stage for later, downstairs, in their playroom.

He kissed her again, shoving his tongue into her mouth and jamming his thigh between her legs, putting on a public show for whomever of their neighbors might be watching. It was one thing he'd always wanted for them to try, but she'd been reluctant. Until now.

"That was lovely," he said into her lips as she shivered from her knee jerk orgasm. "But it was only a taste, as you well know." He touched his fingers to her lips, then stepped back, took her hand and led her inside, slamming the front door behind them. "Bath," he said. "I'll draw it. Get us some water, please?"

"Okay," she said. He frowned and crossed his arms. She almost came again, without him touching her. God, she loved this game they played. And she'd missed it, more than she'd realized. She dropped her gaze to the floor. "Yes, Sir," she said. He put a hand on her arm, gentle for now.

"I'll meet you upstairs."

Chapter Eighteen

Peeping Toms

. . . .

"YOU KNOW WHAT I WANT to know?"

Emily poured hot water over the custom sachets of spice and herbs, relishing the aromatic steam rising from both cups for a few seconds before turning to face Cassie. The few seconds she allowed herself not to be aggravated by the girl's presence gave her enough inner strength not to bite her whiny head off.

"Here you go," she said, as she placed the cups on the table between them, along with a dish of grapes she'd purchased that morning. This was her last day of peace before the school year exploded onto her life. It was a twenty-four-hour period she typically spent in solitude, gathering her thoughts and energy. She was going to need it this year. She had two students with varying levels of disability, both of whom she knew personally, and she was uncertain how their integration into a mainstream elementary school classroom would go. This surprised her, since she usually welcomed students of all abilities, thinking it made for a class more reflective of the real world.

But she'd woken this morning with a deep sense of dread, something she'd never experienced in her many years as a teacher. She'd felt lethargic, as if she'd taken a sleeping pill—something she had done before, many times, to get her through long nights facing the fact of her infertility. And, as if karma had been paying attention to her mood, Cassie had materialized at the patio door, clutching a plastic container of vegan brownies and looking like death warmed over. But not as bad as the last time she'd shown up, thank the Lord. Emily couldn't take another pregnancy-inspired trip to the hospital.

She blew on the tea and tried not to fixate on her neighbor's baby bump. A challenge, since Cassie's new favorite thing to do was to stroke it constantly.

If she asks me to feel it kick, I will scream.

Emily shook her head. That was both unkind and unnecessary. She closed her eyes for a second to attempt an attitude reset. When she opened them again, the damn woman had both hands on her stomach and was staring into the middle distance. Emily felt her irritation heat her from the inside out. She was familiar with the sensation. It was the same one she'd get at the end of a long day in, say, early November, or mid-February in the classroom, when the school year felt like it would never end and she'd be stuck managing twenty moderately spoiled children by herself forever.

She took a deep breath through her nose. Blew it out her lips. She repeated this twice more. Her usual coping mechanism for that feeling. By the time she looked at her unwanted company again, she felt a bit more settled.

"Are you all right?" Cassie leaned forward, hiding the pregnancy bump for a few seconds and holding her hands, palms up, on the table between them. When this young woman had decided that they were the hand-holding type of neighbors, Emily wasn't 100 percent certain. She stared at them, Cassie's lined palms, callused from gardening and her art projects. When indeed? *Maybe when you and your calm, cool, collected, moderately handsome husband decided to jump into bed with Cassie and her hotheaded, alpha male, very handsome one?*

Nausea rose in Emily's throat, clouding her vision with tears and forcing her to rise and walk to the sink. This had to stop. It was wrong on too many levels. This was not how normal, healthy couples behaved. She turned, ready to declare this to Cassandra LeBlanc, the silly woman made accidentally pregnant by their dead neighbor to find the woman right up in her personal space. Cassie put her hands on Emily shoulders, the obvious evidence of her stupidity sticking out from her skinny hips, practically brushing Emily's own stomach. Emily tried not to flinch, unwilling to hurt her feelings. But her ears were ringing, and her gut roiled with all the depraved behavior she'd engaged in while this woman—hell, while all her neighbors—watched her.

While she preferred making love with Allen Cooper, with his gentle, soothing, supportive yet sexy talk in her ear the whole time, sex with Barrett was less gentle, less caring, but no less enticing because of it. She'd be the first to admit she enjoyed it, once she got past her disbelief that he would want anything to do with her. She was hardly his type, with her mostly makeup-less face, her under-styled hair, her soft body. But he had. And they had coupled up more than once, an experience that would leave her breathless, slightly ashamed, and eager for more.

She shivered at one particular memory, not many nights before she and Sai had been summoned to the Franks' house to fish Tom's dead body out of the tub. Emily's arms hung limp at her sides until she realized that was rude. She patted Cassie's back a few times, while attempting to end the close contact.

"Should we meditate? You have such a great space for it," Cassie asked once she finally let go of Emily. Her eyes were shining, her face flushed. She put her hand back on her bump. Emily turned away, making fake busywork in the sink. "Em? Seriously? What's wrong?"

"I'm just...anxious about the school year, I guess."

"Oh okay." Cassie moved away from her, thank God, and plopped back in front of her tea. She popped a few grapes into her mouth. "I swear, this medicine they have me on keeps me from throwing everything up, but it makes everything I put into my mouth taste like cardboard."

Emily opened the plastic container of brownies and put it on the table. She bit into one, barely tasting it as she chewed and swallowed. Cassie did the same, putting half of one down, uneaten, on the table next to her mug. "So, back to my original question," she said, picking up the mug in both hands like a child and taking a sip. Emily blinked. Had she asked a question? It felt as if the woman had been in her space, annoying her for hours. She glanced down at her phone's screen when it flashed to life with a news notification. It had only been twenty minutes.

She sighed. "What was the question?" She sipped her tea. Took another bite of the mostly tasteless brownie.

Cassie parroted her sigh. Between that and her self-centered body language, she was more like a teenager than a grown woman. Emily's ire rose again. "I asked if you knew what I wanted to know." She rolled her eyes. Emily tried not to smack her stupid face.

"About what?" She could hear the tension in her voice, constricting it and making her sound strangled. She sipped more tea. Took more bites of brownie.

"About those new people." She jerked her chin toward the front of Emily's house, indicating, Emily supposed, the neighbors across the street, living in the Franks' old house.

"Oh, you mean Amelia and Michael?" She used their names on purpose, to remind both herself and this immature woman at her table that calling them "those people" was inappropriate. Cassie waved a dismissive hand, which made Emily's face burn hot. She needed Cassie to leave before she blew up and called her something she'd later regret. The silly, stupid slut.

Whoa. No, not that word.

But yes, Emily's inner pissy adolescent girl argued with her adult one. *That is exactly what she is.* Laura Franks had told her how she'd acted with Tom. How she'd caught them in broad daylight in her bed, at her house, going at it like a couple of teenagers. Well outside the framework of the group arrangement.

As if that matters, her own inner teenager reminded her. Fucking outside your marriage is exactly that—fucking outside your marriage. What difference did it make who was watching, or who knew about it at the time? It was a goddamned Pandora's box and one that Emily wanted to wrap in yards of duct tape and stuff under her bed, never to be opened again.

"Well?" Cassie tapped her fingers on the tabletop, as if expecting that Emily would actually guess. As if she actually cared.

"I can't imagine. Why don't you tell me what you want to know." It was challenging to keep the blatant sarcasm out of her voice. The "I don't give a shit but you're going to tell me anyway," tone. Something that was likely lost on Cassie.

"I want to know if they were handpicked. By the Allens and Murphys, like we all were."

Emily almost spilled her tea setting it down on the table. Her ears were ringing again. On some level, she had guessed this, right after Cassie and Barrett had moved in next door to her, and she'd gotten the full effect of their shocking combined attractiveness. She'd almost asked Melissa about it. But she'd let it go. The couple had been assimilated into their arrangement quickly, a lot faster than she and Sai had been. And for nearly a year, everyone had been happy with it.

"That's silly, Cassie." Emily rose, taking her empty mug and grabbing Cassie's nearly empty one on her way. She was done with this and with the person in her kitchen. She needed to spend some hours in her customized meditation room. Alone. She had to work tomorrow. All Cassie had to do was get up, eat a few bites of food, and breathe. Nothing more. She dumped the herb sachets into the composting bin, rinsed the mugs, and placed them in the top rack of the dishwasher. Then she turned, ready to politely suggest that Cassie take her theories and go the hell home.

Her neighbor was staring down at the table. As Emily watched, tears plopped onto the table between her hands.

Guilt flooded her consciousness, and she walked across the hardwood floor to sit next to the now-sobbing woman, to pat her shoulder. To endure the sloppy, wet face buried in her neck.

"I swear to God, Emily, the baby isn't Sai's," she heard Cassie mumble into her now-soaking-wet shoulder.

Emily closed her eyes. She knew this was the case. She and Sai had discussed it already. It was how she knew about Cassie's predilection for sex with her male neighbors outside their established rules. How every single one of them—Allen, Ryan, and of course, Tom—had been invited by the skinny, sexy, somehow childlike yoga instructor to partake of her body while their wives weren't aware of it, condoning it. Hell, watching it.

"I never did it, Emily, I promise you that," Sai had proclaimed, a lot. Maybe too many times, she thought. Maybe a bit too stridently, declaring his relative purity when it came to extra-extracurricular activity with Cassie LeBlanc. Emily had chosen to believe him at the time. Her sweet, softspoken, successful husband and his big dick had been the subject of plenty of attention in their group. But it had always been under her close eye, her supervision, as it were.

Ridiculous, Emily. Do you get how ridiculous that sounds? How completely preposterous it is that you've been doing this? With your damn neighbors? What if the school board finds out? The hospital board? Your family, or, worse, Sai's?

She squeezed her eyes shut and pushed a sniveling Cassie off her, keeping a tight grip on her upper arms. They felt like a couple of sticks under her fingers. Sticks covered with a soft sheen of young, healthy flesh. "I need to do some work to get ready for school tomorrow, Cassie."

The woman blinked at her, as if confused by this. Emily handed her a tissue, almost holding it to her streaming nose as if the woman was one of her students, upset by some shift of classroom politics. Aggravated with herself and her innate need to caretake everyone, she got up and grabbed her phone. "I actually need to call Amelia. Invite her to lunch, remember?"

Cassie blew her nose, dabbed her eyes, and nodded. "Yeah, okay. When is that again?"

"Next weekend," Emily said, not sure why she was doing this right now. She'd all but talked herself out of it, girded her loins to tell Janice and Allen that she and Sai would no longer be a part of the activities.

Oh, don't be coy, Emily. You mean the sex.

The damn orgy she'd engaged in not two nights ago, once the inciting couple who'd worked everyone into such a frenzy had made their boozy way home. It had been shocking. And amazing. And horrifying. And perfect.

Her face flushed hot as she searched for Amelia's phone number, keeping her back turned to Cassie, willing her to leave. While another, more sinister part of her, willed her to stay. To talk, to share, to be miserable, giving Emily some small measure of satisfaction at her stupid predicament.

• • • •

ONCE THE DEED WAS DONE, Amelia invited, plans made for riding together to the club, she turned back to see the table abandoned. She took a long breath, blowing it out when she heard the toilet in the powder room flush. Resigned, she put the kettle back on.

"Do you still want to meditate?" she asked Cassie when she emerged from the bathroom, dabbing at her bloodshot eyes. She attempted not to acknowledge the relieved desperation in her neighbor's expression.

They spent about thirty minutes in cool, eucalyptus-scented silence, sitting in lotus pose on separate pillows, letting the sunlight hit their faces from the specially installed skylights in the bedroom that was once-upon-a-time designated for a nonexistent baby. Sai had insisted that they do it, once it was understood that her body would never hang on to a baby longer than a few weeks or months. It had three large skylights, bamboo wood floors, extra insulation, a built-in sound system. Ryan's company had completed the project to her exact specifications in record time. He'd personally supervised it. Melissa had helped her source the materials and the sound system.

At first, she'd accepted their help, understanding that it was pity at her poor, miscarriage-riddled state. Once it was done, and she'd thrown out all the IVF paraphernalia while her embattled body and hormone levels righted themselves, she'd felt semi-normal. It had been the end of a school year, which always made her feel revitalized. Her last messy miscarriage was months in the rearview mirror.

Then Janice and Allen had invited her and Sai to a dinner party.

Emily's eyes flew open at that memory, of her initial shock, of how Sai had stared at her, his mouth hanging open at what was being proposed to them. She glanced over at Cassie who was still deep in her own meditative state. The sound of the subtle chimes floating through the hidden speakers, the odor of the diffusers releasing expensive oils, the very sensation of the air on her skin made her want to scream and rip the drywall down with her bare hands.

She rose quietly and left the room, biting back tears of frustration, anger, and anxiety. This was no way to go into the school year. Not at all. As she descended the stairs, she noted that someone was putting Tyler into a car seat in a large, unfamiliar SUV. The woman was slender, attractive, older but with shoulder-length blonde hair and a smiling mouth. Emily watched as the woman got behind the wheel and pulled away from the house. The absence of the large vehicle revealed the collective subject of the cul-de-sac's obsession: Michael and Amelia Ross.

Emily recalled the jolt she'd experienced when she'd been introduced to the tall, dark-skinned, handsome Michael at the party. Realizing that she and all her fellow female neighbors had been lusting after him earlier in the month when he'd been unloading stuff at the house, along with who she now knew was his brother. Thinking of him as not some hot-as-hell moving guy and her actual neighbor and all that might entail had revved her up, preparing her for the wild free-for-all they'd engaged in later that night.

When the couple kissed in their open doorway, Emily moved back as if worried they would spot her spying on them. When the kiss turned into a full-on groping session right on the porch, Emily's face flushed, and her nipples hardened under her well-worn sports bra.

"Damn," Cassie said from behind her as she took the last few steps and ran over to the window to ogle the show. She turned back and motioned Emily forward. Emily felt her feet move her, partly against her will, in eager cooperation with another part. A part that was now fully inclined to voyeurism. A part that needed to watch. A part that knew full well she and Sai would not be quitting the cul-de-sac sex club anytime soon.

"Wow," Cassie exhaled as the tall, muscular, hot black man fingered his wife to orgasm in the open front door of their house. When he pulled his hand from the front of her shorts and put those fingers to Amelia's lucky, smiling lips, Emily's knees nearly gave out from under her. Cassie was gripping the curtains, her face almost touching the windowpane.

The couple smiled, spoke words only they could hear then shut the front door behind them.

Chapter Nineteen

You Want To Do What?

. . . .

"I'M COMING ALREADY. Hold your water."

Melissa rolled her eyes at her husband's favorite saying. He was truly a font of clichés. Wielded them at every opportunity with her, his kids, his employees, and his clients. It was maddening sometimes. A reminder of his humble background—car mechanic father, mother who took in babysitting for extra money, barely graduated high school, no college—it made her feel like a stuck-up bitch whenever thoughts about his "humble background" crossed her mind. It wasn't like her own background was terribly high-minded. But she had gone to and graduated from college.

She sighed and dug around in her purse for her favorite lipstick. It was subtle, the way she preferred her makeup, but expensive. After applying the purplish-brown color to her lips, she played with her hair a few minutes, touched the deepening line between her eyes that Allen had commented on the other night. A shiver shot down her spine at that particular memory. She shoved it aside and spent a few seconds observing the various ways gravity was weighing on her face.

"There's my gorgeous, super-smoking-hot wife." Ryan gripped her shoulders and put his annoyingly youthful face next to hers.

"You're only saying that so I won't nag you about getting me a facelift," she declared, hip-bumping him to one side. He pretended to stumble before he reached out and grabbed her around the waist and yanked her close.

"I've said it once, I've said it a million times," he declared with a smile she couldn't help but return. "You don't need any work done. You're perfect."

She scoffed, but it was kind of nice to hear him say the words. "Get off me," she said, pretending to struggle. He only tightened his grip. "I mean it, Murphy. Get your damn paws off me. We're going to be late."

Instead of letting her go, he gripped her ass with both hands. In spite of her overall irritation with him, a familiar thrill shot down her spine. She stared into his eyes, the man she'd either seduced or been seduced by while she worked her fresh-out-of-college shit job for the general contractor. Sometimes, she wondered who'd made that first step. Ryan was a natural flirt. He always wanted everyone in the room to like him, pretty women especially, and went out of his way to make sure that happened. He still did it. And could get away with it since the damn man truly was only getting more attractive as he aged.

No, he wasn't the six-foot-four, raven-haired billionaire of her dreams. He was a six-foot, sandy-haired fireplug with a hair-trigger temper and a tendency to drink to excess. But his silver-blue eyes always seemed to light up when he looked at her. He kept himself slim. Although she didn't know how, since he had no time to go to a gym.

"I love you, ya mick," she said, grinning when one of his hands let go of her ass long enough to slide up her skirt. Ryan Murphy was an expert lover, concise and precise in his movements and effort, that much was true. She sighed into his neck, her mind suddenly awash with memories of watching him screwing her neighbors. It was something she insisted upon after some initial missteps. They played as a couple, or at the very least, in the same room. And every single damn time, it very nearly drove her insane with jealousy. When her sweet, amenable, cliché-laden husband would lay one of his patented class-A kisses on Emily, Janice, or his one-time favorite, Laura Franks, it took everything she had not to leap across the room and tear him away.

But they were well matched in this. Their fights after some of those early encounters with the Coopers and Franks still made her wince. They'd learned a lot about themselves, to be certain, and about how they would have to operate if they were going to keep participating in the cul-de-sac's unique social circle. They would not be like the Coopers, Franks, or, later, the LeBlancs who had no qualms about closing the door on each other when they wanted private time with someone else's spouse.

"Love ya back, bitch," he said in his terrible accent before kissing her and making her wonder why, exactly, they were leaving the house right now. As she was reaching for his belt buckle, he stopped and stepped back from her, hands on his hips, his expression a strange, confused mix of lust and frustration. She mirrored him, pondering how much she'd rather dive back into bed with him for the afternoon as opposed to taking the new neighbor lady to a country club lunch.

Maybe they should stop altogether. Maybe it was out of their system.

Then she recalled that the hot and sexy new neighbor lady had a husband. A man she knew the others would be fighting over, and with good reason, should their new neighbors agree to join the cul-de-sac debauchery. She smoothed her hair, pursed her lips, readjusted her panties, and grabbed her purse. "Let's get this over with," she said as she headed for the mudroom.

He followed her in silence. As the two-bay door cranked open, they stood side by side, not discussing the events ahead of them. "So, are you going to come out and tell him about it, or what?" Melissa asked before hitting her key fob. She'd managed to get Danny an appointment with his occupational therapist for the afternoon, and he'd get a ride home with the nanny. They had the entire afternoon ahead of them.

"Let's not go," she said, turning to her husband and trying to pull him back into the house. "I want to go to bed. With you. No one else." Why she was saying this, she had no idea. She'd been more enthusiastic about the whole thing from the get-go. Not that Ryan ever complained, of course. Sex was sex for men. A way to get off, reset, move on with the day. Sex was connection and emotion for women, at least it was for her.

"I leave that up to Allen," he said, draping his arm over her shoulder and kissing her temple. "And you haven't only wanted to go to bed with me for the past, what, three years or so? I doubt that's changed, has it, my love?"

She twisted around to face him, alarmed by the odd tone of his voice. His expression was flat, but she could tell he was pissed about something. Her own fury rose to meet his, as it always did. "Well, at least I didn't break any of the rules."

Ryan sighed and let his arm drop to his side. "Yeah, yeah, I know. Come on. Let's go." He pulled his leather golf bag down from its designated hook on the garage wall.

She glared at him as he shouldered it, conflicting desires knocking around inside her head like hot marbles.

"Jesus Christ in a sidecar, Mel, I know. I broke rules. I'm sorry. Again. Please forgive me. Again. I thought we were past this," he said, not looking at her.

Melissa's fingers curled into fists at her sides. Heat rushed into her face and neck. He stood there, looking the opposite of contrite. "You are the most colossal ass in the known universe."

"Again, I know this. Can we please go now?"

"So, what's going to happen, Ryan, when that kid is born looking like your goddamned grandpa from the goddamned Old Country?" The words hurt her throat. She had to slap a hand over her lips to keep from screaming at him. "Are you going to pony up? Adopt it? Pay for it to go to college?" Tears burned her eyes, but she refused to let them fall.

"I told you already. I used a condom every time."

"You're a liar, Ryan Murphy. I had to drag it out of you that you fucked her outside of our designated parameters: at parties, together in the same room. Why should I believe you used a rubber?"

His shoulders slumped. "You're going to have to, I guess. You know how I am about that. You know me, Mel." He let the leather bag drop to the garage floor and took a few steps toward her. She stayed put, willing him to be right. Because if that brat was Ryan's, she would know it the second she laid eyes on it. And she wasn't a hundred percent sure what she'd do to Cassie LeBlanc when that happened.

"I don't know you," she whispered as tears burned tracks down her cheeks. Ryan wiped them away, the pads of his thumbs as rough as the palms of his workingman's hands. Her man, she thought as he held onto her and let her sob against his shoulder.

"Hush, now, my love," he soothed, stroking her hair. She sniffled and backed away from him, but he held onto her arms and ducked down to meet her gaze. "Okay? Waterworks over?"

"Shut up, you asshole." She dabbed her eyes and cheeks with a tissue. "You made me ruin my makeup."

"I'm sorry." He stood in front of her, hands stuffed into his khaki-trousered pockets. Her man. The man she'd been eager to screw around with all those years ago—forbidden fruit and hot fruit at that. When she'd figured out she was pregnant, a few months after they began their affair, this after six months of nonstop flirting and buildup, she thought she might jump out a window. In the end, she'd decided to have an abortion, but Ryan had talked her out of it. Told her he adored her, that he was all but divorced anyway—which he most definitely was not—and had scooped her up from the clinic waiting room like some sappy, Catholic-guilt-riddled romance hero.

They'd married, once his first wife had agreed to divorce him for a shit ton of money. And she'd come home from her honeymoon in the process of having a miscarriage.

"I hate you, sometimes," she hissed, as she waved her hands in front of her face to help dry the tear tracks.

"Yeah, well, I think we both know that is mutual."

Ears still ringing with anger, she marched out into the hot sunlight and closed her side of the garage behind her. Emily was driving the ladies. Allen was carpooling the guys in his Mercedes SUV. She stood on the sidewalk in front of her beautiful home, her handsome, sexy, infuriating husband making his happy-ass way toward the Coopers' house. At that moment, the front doors of all the other houses opened, their occupants emerging onto front porches at once, as if choreographed.

Melissa slid her Maui Jim sunglasses onto her face, taking it in. Every couple was frozen in place. Sort of like they were staring at each other, as if unsure what was supposed to happen next.

Ryan kept walking toward Allen's driveway where his black SUV was idling, the tailgate up, ready to accept five sets of expensive clubs. He glanced over his shoulder at her at one point, shooting her a look full of anxiety. He always felt like a second-class citizen when they did this kind of social thing with their neighbors. She knew this well. He'd admitted it more than once, when he was feeling emotional and vulnerable, usually after too many glasses of whiskey.

She smiled at him, hoping to dispel the aura of bitchiness she'd concocted. Yeah, he'd cheated with Cassie. She was pretty certain every man in the cul-de-sac had done the same. It was a total crapshoot who'd donated sperm to sprout that kid in Cassie's belly. The general consensus was on Tom, of course. That he'd committed suicide in his bathtub in remorse. But, sometimes, Melissa wondered about that.

"Hi, Melissa!"

She sucked in a breath, slapped on her best professional smile, and headed toward Emily's house. Amelia was right behind her, crossing the road from her house where she'd kissed her way-too-sexy husband goodbye.

"Hey, Amelia," Melissa said. "Glad you could join us today."

Amelia's face was serene. She looked as if she'd emerged from a week-long spa vacation, truth be told, which was weird, since they had a toddler in the house. A bolt of lust shot through Melissa as her gaze fell on Michael Ross who was making his way toward the men gathered around Allen's car.

Unable to stop herself, she licked her upper lip then turned back to her friends, neighbors, fellow swingers. "Okay, ladies, there are some great bottles in my wine locker calling our names. What do you say?"

She air-kissed everyone then got into the backseat of Emily's Volvo, somewhat aggravated that they were doing this ridiculous carpooling thing. At least Cassie was taking her own car, she noted. Barrett was still with her, in their driveway, handing her gently behind the wheel of her Beemer. Which was an interesting turn of events, Melissa thought, watching as the tall, handsome lawyer leaned into the window for what she assumed was a kiss.

Amelia got into the front passenger seat. Janice sat next to Melissa in the back, patting her hand as they backed out into the street. Melissa stared out her window, marveling at herself, at what they were about to propose to the pretty woman chattering away with Emily. She sighed and shut her eyes long enough to conjure him—Tom Frank—the man who died in their midst and with whom she, herself, had broken plenty of rules in the months prior to his untimely death.

* * * *

"I CAN'T IMAGINE WHY you haven't joined yet," Janice said as she smiled her thanks for the pour of expensive white wine into her lead crystal glass. She spent a few seconds smoothing her linen napkin across her lap while the other women got their share of the booze. Amelia picked her glass up when the others did, wondering if her smile looked too fake.

"Cheers," Janice said, gazing with a sort of maternal pride at the women gathered around her. It felt creepy to Amelia, but she touched her glass to the ones raised over the middle of the table, trying to discern why the air felt as if it were simmering, like the heat rising off asphalt on a summer day.

The other women sipped. Well, all of them except for Melissa, who downed half her glass in one graceless gulp.

"Heavens, Melissa," Janice said, as she patted her perfectly red lips with her napkin. "Should we get you a straw?"

The other woman put her glass down with exaggerated care. Amelia watched while she turned it around and around, keeping her gaze fixed down on it as if it might refill itself.

Amelia saw Emily lean slightly closer to Melissa, as if giving strength via body language. She sipped a bit more, enjoying the citrusy, light sauvignon blanc as it coated her tongue and throat on the way down. Before she could stop herself, she realized her glass was as empty as the angry real estate agent's. She pushed the glass away, embarrassed as she recalled her drunken exit from the welcome party.

They all spent a few painfully quiet minutes studying their menus. Melissa made a subtle motion with her head, which brought two waiters with a fresh bottle of wine. Glasses recharged, orders for various forms of salad and one bowl of tomato soup for the pregnant Cassie LeBlanc placed, they all sipped whatever was in front of them. The second helping went down too fast as well, but Amelia figured she needed it to lubricate her nerves.

Why was she here anyway? What did these women want from her and Michael other than to make her feel awkward for not having joined the lily-white country club.

Emily, who was sitting at her left, turned to face her. "How are you settling in, Amelia?" Amelia smiled at the woman who was a tad too heavy for her own good. She was pretty. She'd look even better if she dropped a few pounds. But her expression was kind, as opposed to Melissa's scowl, Janice's aloofness, and Cassie's obvious anxiety.

"Pretty well, thanks," she said, as she toyed with the stem of her wineglass. "I mean, Tyler's having some issues but from what I've read, it's nothing out of the ordinary."

"Oh? Who do you read?"

Emily was a teacher and had a decent handle on child development stages. She picked up her glass and drained it, thankful for the helpful waiter scurrying over with her refill. Maybe she should join up here after all. Screw her tendency to overthink everything. This was the enlightened college town she'd loved for four years as a student. They'd welcome her and Michael here. She knew it.

"Terry Brazelton mostly," she admitted, putting her glass to her lips and taking another sip at the same moment she accepted she should slow it down.

"I was a fan of Dr. Spock myself," Janice interjected.

"No surprise there," Melissa said. Amelia watched the two women shoot eyeball daggers at each other.

"I'm reading Dr. Brazelton's book," Cassie piped up in a voice that Amelia barely remembered from the party. It was soft, almost musical. Amelia turned her full, now-tipsy, attention to the lady with the baby bulge. "It seems like a good way to raise a child."

"It works for us," Amelia admitted. "*What to Expect From your Toddler* is coming in handy."

Silence fell when two baskets of delicious-smelling rolls were set in the middle of the table. Amelia hadn't touched a carb that wasn't from alcohol in over a decade. It was no hardship to watch Cassie and Emily reach for them. Melissa, she knew from their many hours spent together house hunting, avoided carbs as well. Janice looked around, as if she wished she were having lunch with some other group of women.

"How is Michael liking his new job?" Emily again, gamely attempting to draw her into some kind of a discussion.

"He really likes it, I think. It's exactly what he wanted to be doing."

"Really? What sort of law does he practice?" This from Janice, which shocked Amelia based on her behavior the past fifteen minutes.

"Patents, mostly," she said, shocked this time by the empty reality of her wineglass. "He has an engineering degree. He's kind of a genius, really." She winced internally at her silly brag.

The women all nodded as if agreeing with her. As if they knew anything about her Michael. She turned her attention to Cassie. "Are you excited? Have you made your birth plan? Do you know if it's a boy or a girl?" She hiccupped. "Oh sorry." The waiter rushed over with the wine, but Amelia held her hand over her glass. "No, I really shouldn't."

"Well, it's nice that some of us know our limits," Janice said, taking a sip of her second, almost-full glass.

"Should I repeat myself?" Melissa said. But she was smiling now. Thank god for the fermented grape juice, Amelia thought.

When she glanced back at Cassie, the poor woman was blinking fast. Amelia thought she might be about to burst into tears.

"I'm...I..." Her watery blue gaze darted between all the women, who were focused on her with a sort of laser intensity. Amelia immediately felt shitty for making her the center of attention. Likely not everyone felt as happy as she had been when she'd been expecting. She smiled at Cassie, trying to prove her harmlessness.

Janice put a hand over Cassie's, which was plucking at her napkin on the table in front of her. "Cassie had a rough start, didn't you, hon?"

The woman chewed on her lower lip. Amelia wondered what in the hell was happening, since the booze had sharpened her already keen senses when it came to personal interactions in social settings. When a different waiter hovered nearby with the wine bottle, she nodded but kept her focus on the nervous pregnant lady at the table.

"I had terrible morning sickness for about three weeks," Amelia said, trying to prod more info.

"Poor Cassie ended up in the hospital," Emily said, but with a tone that didn't exactly match her words. Shocking again, Amelia thought. Emily was such a mealymouthed fatty. Amelia smiled at Emily then turned back to Cassie, determined to get some answers.

"Oh no! What happened?"

"I have hyperemesis gravidarum," Cassie said. "I got sick and stayed sick. I couldn't eat anything and ended up in the hospital with severe anemia and dehydration." Her voice was flat. But she kept her gaze on Amelia's. "And no, I don't know if it's a boy or girl." She rested her hand on the bump under her tight-fitting sundress. "We...um, think it will be nicer to be surprised."

Amelia wasn't quite sure who let out the snort, but she chose to ignore it. Cassie's eyes shut for a split second before she looked back at Amelia. "And no, I'm not terribly excited. But I guess I might as well be. I mean, *Barrett* is. *Now*. And that's what matters to me."

Amelia caught the way she leaned on her husband's name, and the word "now." Intriguing, she thought as she sipped and studied the dark circles under the woman's eyes and the way her shoulders seemed permanently slumped. *Such a cypher. I need to know more.*

She turned to face Melissa, figuring her for the best source, but later, of course. Melissa was staring blankly into her wineglass again. Before Amelia or Emily could make another attempt at something resembling polite conversation, their food arrived. Five separate waiters were required to place the food in front of the women all at once, which was impressive but required, as she knew. She was used to such treatment, having been a country-club-raised baby in an upscale Chicago suburb.

They all took a moment to eat a few bites and make noises about how delicious the various salad options were. Cassie merely stared at her soup bowl. Janice leaned close to her. "Go on, dear. Your baby needs you to eat." Cassie picked up her spoon and dunked it into the creamy red depths in front of her. She ate like a robot. A robot triggered by Janice Cooper's commands.

Someone nudged her leg under the table. Startled, she glanced at Emily, who gave a tiny frown and shake of her head. Embarrassed to have been caught gawking, she picked up her wineglass and sipped. Then put her glass down and picked up her fork. Her salad—a classic Caesar complete with salty anchovies—occupied her for a few seconds. The other women made some stilted small talk about the start of school, how Melissa's son Danny was doing, all stuff Amelia could give a rip about.

Irritated now, Amelia pushed her plate away and put her wineglass in front of her. After taking a few minutes to ponder the women around her, she let the booze push the words out, willing them back as soon as they escaped her lips. "So, who's going to be the first to tell me what this lunch is about. I mean, other than it being a two a snipe-fest for you two, and making us all feel sorry for Cassie."

Melissa blinked at her. Emily pursed her lips and looked down at her plate. Cassie ate the last of her soup then let the spoon drop into the bowl with a loud clatter. Janice kept eating, putting a bite of her wedge salad into her mouth and chewing slowly, as if counting. Stalling, Amelia figured.

Or proving herself as the ice-queen bitch leader of this particular happy little party.

"Well?" she demanded before draining her glass and motioning for the waiter as he was making his way toward her. "And if you must know, we haven't joined this country club because you might have noticed that my husband is black. I mean, I'm sure we'd be allowed to join, but I'm not sure that I want to subject him to the ongoing strangeness of being the one black guy in the group, you know?"

Jesus, where had that come from? She glared and swallowed the mortification rising in her throat.

"Don't be ridiculous," Janice said, patting her lips once more then covering the remaining sixty percent of her meal with the napkin. "This isn't Alabama or Mississippi or someplace."

"You have no idea what it's like," she said, surprised to feel tears threatening. *Too much wine, Ames.* She could practically hear Michael's deep voice in her ears.

"Well, no, I guess I don't." Janice fixed her gaze on Amelia, making her feel like a specimen under a microscope. But she didn't blink in the face of it. No, sir. This woman would not intimidate her with her passive aggression and fake friendliness. Amelia had been president of a major sorority at a major university. She was an expert at this sort of female status-establishing behavior. She rested one elbow on the table, or at least she tried to but misjudged it in her wine haze.

Damn it.

Janice's lips twitched when her elbow landed on her lap instead.

"Amelia, we...I mean...we have this..."

She whirled to face Emily's wimpy voice. "It's about sex, isn't it?"

The woman flinched as if Amelia had struck her openhanded across the face. Which only aggravated Amelia more. She hated it when women were wimpy.

Ugh. She should shut up, get up, and leave before she embarrassed herself any further.

"Yes, actually, it is." Janice's cool-as-a-cucumber voice made her turn again, which made her a tad dizzy.

"I knew it," she whispered, as an illicit thrill shot up her spine. "You guys are swingers, right?" She bit her lip and looked around the table. All the women except Cassie met her gaze. "Wow."

"We have an arrangement between us," Janice said, looking down her regal, surgically adjusted nose at Amelia. "It's something we worked out, about ago now, I believe. Melissa?"

"Yep," Melissa said, motioning for the waiter. "Bring me that Veuve from my locker, please. And some flutes? We need a real toast at this table."

"I don't think—"

Melissa held up her hand before Amelia could protest. Which was fine. She could already taste the bubbles. And something else. Something she could feel. Someone's hands, someone not her husband's, touching her, stroking her, kissing her. She shivered.

The other women exchanged glances. Emily held out a small brown bag with handles. "Here. You and Michael should read a few things. Make sure you're, um, dialed in, as it were. And you'll need to make some rules for yourself."

Melissa was the one who snorted this time, cutting her gaze to Cassie. Amelia glanced between them, confused, intrigued, and yes, horny in ways that made her want to crawl under the table and die.

"We only participate as couples. That means that you and Michael would be expected to join us together. With both of you willing to participate," Janice said.

Amelia blinked, confounded by this for a split second.

"What she means is, your hot-as-shit man is going to have a lot of sex with us, while you enjoy intercourse with any one of our husbands. One a time, or not, however you prefer," Melissa blurted out.

"Melissa, please. Some decorum?" Janice sniffed, but her face was red, her lips pressed so tight they almost disappeared. A real shame, since she'd obviously spent a lot of money to plump them up.

Melissa shrugged. "She seems like a straight shooter to me. I sort of guessed that about you, you know, all that time we spent together." She smiled at Amelia, but it was sharp, practically predatorial. Amelia frowned, processing what the woman had said about Michael.

The champagne arrived, was opened, and poured. All of the women lifted their glasses. The bubbles tickled Amelia's nose and made her splutter and cough when she swallowed.

Images were dashing around in her mind. Images of her "hot-as-shit husband," as Melissa had dubbed him, kissing, touching, pleasing, being pleasured by, the women at this table. She pressed a hand to her chest. "I don't...know."

"Of course you don't. Not yet," Janice said, patting her hand, which made Amelia want to smack her. "Why don't you and Michael talk it over. Read some of the books we've given you. And reach out to me if you have questions."

"Or me," Emily said.

"Or better yet, me," Melissa said, eyes bright with some kind of unexpressed emotion.

"Okay," Amelia said. She downed her champagne. Her head was now officially pounding from too much booze and too little food too early in the day. For some reason, she fixated on Cassie again. "Do you...um, still...you know..." Her neck flamed hot with embarrassment.

Cassie's head jerked up. Her expression was resolute. "Yes. We do."

"Oh. Okay." Amelia reached for her water glass about two glasses of booze too late. Her vision was swimming, her chest tight, her stomach roiling. And yet, still, that tiny tickle of something deep in her belly, in that place where she always felt her deepest orgasms. She wondered for a hot second how Michael would react to this.

He'd hate it. He'd refuse to share her with anyone.

At that, though, her chin lifted. "I'm not sure what I'm supposed to say right now," she admitted. "I mean, I guess, thanks for asking? Or for considering us. Or inviting us."

She tried to parse the various odd expressions that met her eyes. These women seemed simultaneously pissed at each other yet bonded in a way only they could be. It didn't exactly bode well for making them closer as a group.

She shivered again, as imaginary images of orgies and whatnot filled her woozy brain again. She shook her head, drank more water, and pushed her chair back. "I know the men won't be done with their game, but I...I think I need to go home." She met Emily's sympathetic gaze.

"Of course. This is a lot to take in over lunch," Melissa said as she stood up, listing alarmingly to one side. Emily gripped her arm. "Get off me, god damn it, I'm fine. I'm staying. Ryan and I can get an Uber home or something. I need something stronger than wine."

Janice rose majestically, gracefully, like a dancer. "I think I may join Melissa." She reached down to take Cassie's elbow. The woman let her help her to her feet then pulled her arm away. "Emily, do you mind terribly getting Amelia and Cassie home? I'll sign for the meal."

"Of course not." The women made their way to the door, to the car, and all the way home in total silence. But it didn't seem awkward. It seemed natural. Emily parked in her drive and shut off the engine. "Amelia, please, if you want to talk to someone other than Melissa or Janice...or Cassie, of course, please feel free to reach out to me. I'm happy to discuss it—the good and the bad."

Amelia nodded and slid out of the backseat, made her way across the street to her lovely dream home and opened the front door without a backward glance or a word to either woman. Rude, she knew. But she was confused.

And drunk. She needed to sleep then she and Michael would have to talk.

She assumed the men told him about it at the golf game. Introducing him to the concept that the men with him on the eighteenth hole were proposing that they be allowed to have sex with his wife.

Chapter Twenty

Four Years Ago

"Allen! Will you please hurry up?" Janice jammed her twenty-year anniversary diamond earrings into her ears. She stared at her reflection a few seconds, noting the lines breaking through despite the expensive efforts of her husband's colleagues and paraprofessionals. Frowning, she stretched the skin between her eyes, pulling the stubborn divot flat.

"Coming, dear heart," her husband said. He appeared behind her in the mirror, smiling like a fool. "There's my beautiful wife." He gripped her hips.

"Get off me. We're going to be late. You know how the boys get if they have to wait." She slipped past him, irritated by his presence, aggravated at herself for being irritated. She was eager to take her grandsons for the weekend. But something about A.J. worried her. The last few times they'd been together, he'd been distant, distracted. She blamed that bitch of an ex-wife of his. Allen blamed the stress of owning three successful car wash locations around the county.

"Did you set up the playroom?"

"Of course," Allen said. He brushed his teeth, ran fingers through his hair. Janice tapped her foot on the imported walnut floorboards, waiting for him to stop admiring himself. When he turned to face her, she was shocked to see anxiety in his expression. Allen was never anxious. Or, at least, if he was, he rarely showed it. It was one of the secrets to his success as a plastic surgeon.

Feeling guilty, she sidled up behind him and put her arms around his waist. She pressed her nose between his shoulder blades and sucked in a breath of him, her twanging nerves soothed by his familiar odor and the press of his strong body against hers. Under normal circumstances, they'd decamp to the bed for a quickie right now. It was a testament to the seriousness of shared worry about their son that they didn't.

Allen pulled her hands up to his lips, kissed them then turned to face her. "Don't worry about him," he said, cradling her face in his hands. "He's fine."

Janice closed her eyes and let him hold her a moment. "He's not fine, Allen. We both know that." Tears burned her eyes. She wanted to scream, to shove him down onto his perfectly toned ass, to cry. But instead, she kissed her husband, tolerated him gripping her ass for a few seconds. "We need to go pick the boys up, honey. Come on. Let's go."

After they had the kids fed, they sat with A.J. in the kitchen, nursing bottles of local craft stout. "So," Allen said, beating around the bush in a way that bugged the shit out of her. "You need some money, Son?"

A.J. winced, finished his beer, and plunked the empty on the table. "No, Dad, I don't need any damn money." He got up and marched over to the fridge to grab another beer. Janice stared at him, pondering his body language. She used to pride herself on her ability to gauge her children's needs before they acknowledged them. To anticipate what they were thinking before they knew they were thinking it.

Of course, that had all been shot to shit once her own ungrateful daughter had proven her wrong. Lately, she felt like a sick joke as a mother—the one thing she put everything she had into for years only to be thwarted by a girl who hated her. Janice took a long drag of her beer, dispelling all thoughts of the daughter she hadn't spoken to in nearly two years, from her mind.

"I need..." A.J. began. He closed his eyes. Janice's heart pounded in her ears. When he opened his eyes, he reserved his dark-blue gaze for her. "I need someone to manage the money, you know? Cynthia did that, and now..." He shrugged and looked pitiful, making her want to simultaneously hug and smack him. She opted for staying seated.

"What about Tom Franks?" she asked Allen. "He left the big firm a couple of years ago and set himself up in a little office downtown. Seems to be doing really well." The understatement of the century, she mused as she sipped her beer and let her husband mull this over before claiming the idea as his own.

Laura Franks had been flaunting a new wardrobe, a fancy imported SUV, and had spent at least twelve grand on her face and tits at Allen's practice. A sudden turn for the family, which had spent the first six years of their lives in the cul-de-sac in a nice house but without spending any real money on it. Melissa had told her Tom had signed a contract with Ryan's company for a sixty-thousand-dollar renovation of kitchen and bathrooms last week.

"You know, I think you should contact Tom Franks," Allen declared after a few more seconds. She smiled at him then shot her son a significant look. One she hoped said more than any words she might utter.

His broad shoulders slumped. The light had gone out of his eyes ever since his bitch of an ex-wife had demanded a divorce and full custody of Janice's beloved grandsons. She'd gotten her divorce but not her way with the boys. They were hollering and rolling around in the family room right now. A.J. always brought them over for quality time with their grandparents whenever they were with him. Something she valued, but understood as his excuse to continue not parenting them himself.

Her son glanced at his Rolex. "So, um, I've got this thing…" He ran a hand through this thick, dark-blond hair. "Would you mind keeping the hellions overnight?"

Janice's jaw tightened and her shoulders stiffened. She really had not done her children any favors, raising them to be such spoiled brats, assuming the entire world revolved around them and their whims.

Ah well. Too late to do much about that now. "Of course," she said, getting up and taking the empty beer bottles out to the recycling container in the garage. She hesitated, hand full of empties hovering over the big blue bin. The cool air hit her face and arms, calming her.

Why wouldn't she want to keep the boys overnight? It was warm enough for them to swim. She kept a closet and chest of drawers full of extra clothes for them and their father. She and Allen had no real plans for the evening. But that wasn't the point. A.J. was dumping them here more and more on the weekend nights he was supposed to be spending time with them himself. She figured it was some woman. Some gold-digging slut had her fake nails in him. He was such a sucker for a pretty face and tight ass. Not unlike his father. Probably why Cynthia had offloaded him in the first place.

She sighed and took a few moments to refasten her ponytail. She'd been doing some needed deep cleaning when A.J. had called, asking if she and Allen could pick the boys up from soccer practice. But now, she'd adjust her plans to suit her son. It was what she always did for the men in her life.

When she wandered back into the kitchen, Allen was slapping A.J. on the shoulder, grinning like a fool. They must have been having man-talk about A.J.'s new bedmate. She wondered for about a half a second if she should ask about the woman. Knowing A.J., she'd be foisted on them for the holidays without any warning or fanfare, like Cynthia had been. Hopefully her grown son had learned his lesson and would manage not to get this new one pregnant.

She smiled at them. "I have Tom's business card around here somewhere," she said, going right for the small stack of cream-colored cards in an upper drawer where she kept such things. Laura had given them to her, flouncing in with her Lululemon workout gear and expensively preserved face a few weeks ago. *"Just in case you know anyone who could use a great accountant or business consultant,"* she'd said, blowing air-kisses and trailing a slight whiff of fabric softener on her way out the door.

Janice frowned at the memory, clutching the card hard in one hand, crumpling it into a fancy paper ball. That had been two nights after one of their gatherings. A gathering at which she'd been suspicious, on edge about something directly related to the way Allen and Laura acted around each other—like a married couple or something, a couple with secret, knowing glances and shorthand communication.

Sometimes she honestly wished she weren't as tuned in to her husband's many foibles as she'd forced herself to be.

She fixed a smile on her face, turned, and handed a non-mangled card to A.J. He glanced down at it then back up at her, his eyes no different than those of the little boy who'd stare at her adoringly across the kitchen while she fixed dinner to suit his picky leanings. All the while, Alicia would be glaring at them both from the family room. She'd been born angry, that girl.

Janice shook her head again, unwilling to visit the fact of her ungrateful daughter's existence.

"So, this guy is good?" he asked her, while pretending to ask his father. It was the method of family communication they'd worked out years before. Letting Allen think he was in charge of everything, while managing it all herself.

Allen clapped his shoulder again. "Tom's the best, Son. And based on the amount of money he and his wife are tossing around lately, leaving that firm and going out on his own was the best idea she ever had."

"She?" Janice heard the sharp edge in her tone. A.J. glanced from her to his father.

Allen grinned at her, ignorant or possibly simply impervious to her angry tone. "Yes. Laura told me she was the one who convinced Tom to hang out his own shingle, as it were." His eyes widened and got a little dreamy, which sent Janice's mood spiraling further downward.

She'd suspected he was getting with Laura Franks on the side—the very activity they were ostensibly guarding against with their mutually pleasurable neighborly arrangements. But her husband was the world's biggest horn dog. His ego's need for constant positive, female input would not be stifled, not even with her careful machinations of their sex life.

She sighed. What did she care, really? She'd watched him go down on every woman in the cul-de-sac. Seen them all give him blow jobs. Participated in three-way sex with them all herself. What did it matter that he snuck off to screw his favorite swinger partner while pretending to be on the golf course?

She glared at him, about to spill her suspicions in front of A.J. if only to figure out why he felt like he needed to lie to her about it, to hide it. It was ludicrous, really, all that sneaking around, considering what they all did in the big bedroom upstairs together. But Allen had to be hiding something sexual from her, she supposed, in order to keep up his charade of being forever young.

The realization that she really didn't care, other than the way it made her look foolish to the woman in question, hit her like a pillow to the face. That Laura Franks honestly believed she had something over Janice, engaging in illicit hookups with Janice's constantly horny husband was nothing but amusing as far as she was concerned. She clenched her jaw, bit her own tongue, and smiled wider.

"Yes, I'm sure it was her best idea ever." Allen beamed at her. A.J. tucked the card into his wallet.

"Okay, spawn, Dad's got to go. You're gonna hang out with Nana and Gramps for tonight, that okay?" he called out as he headed into the family room.

General sounds of glee ensued. Suddenly exhausted, Janice sank into a bar seat. Allen put his arm around her shoulders, but she jerked away from him, worried she might scratch his ignorant cheating eyeballs out if he kept touching her.

"Take them out to the pool, will you please? I'll...pat out some hamburgers."

"Sounds great, baby," Allen said, pressing his lips to her temple. She shut her eyes, shuddering at his touch, furious at him, at her spoiled son, her distant daughter, her own weakness, but most of all that slut, Laura Franks.

Later, she lay in Allen's arms, sweaty and spent from an angry, satisfying quickie. The boys were installed in their own room in the basement, adjacent to the obnoxiously finished room that had seen plenty of action, she figured, between her own children, not to mention their many parties. "That was...nice," Allen said, his voice uncertain. She rolled away from him in lieu of an answer, body languorous, her mind spinning with unhappiness.

Six months later

"Wow, Mom," A.J. said as they sat around the Easter dinner table. "You weren't kidding about Tom." He poured more French Chardonnay into his date's glass. She—Tiffany or something equally stripper-like—had indeed shown up at a holiday table, sans warning or real introduction.

Typical A.J. And, of course, her own husband couldn't take his eyeballs off her. Janice would admit she was extremely attractive. Better looking than Cynthia, which was saying something. But there was something predatory in her eyes that bothered Janice more than it should. Her son was technically a grown man who could make his own grown-man choices about girlfriends after all.

"I told you," Allen said from the other end of the carefully laid table. "Here, my dear, you must try Janice's..."

But she shut him out, unwilling to watch or listen to him fawn over the woman. She picked up her fork—real silver, which she polished herself and reserved for use three times a year—and speared a small bite of roast pork loin.

"I'm glad to hear that he's helping you," she said, before putting the bite into her mouth, chewing carefully, while observing how much the new woman was observing the niceness all around her.

Trailer park trash. No doubt about it.

"Yep," A.J. said, as he helped the boys cut up their meat. "He's worked all sorts of magic with my books. Way better than...um...it used to be." The girl—Jesus, what was her name?—shot him a harsh look. A jealous one. Janice sighed and focused back on her meal.

After the usual rounds of her admonishing her grandsons for bad manners, which Allen and A.J. completely ignored, and everyone exclaiming over the lemon torte, plus the coffee, the boys leapt from the table and ran to the basement where Allen had installed the latest, greatest, enormous TV with gaming system for them. Noise from computerized gunshots and other random violence burst up from the stairwell.

A.J. got up and shut the basement door. When he sat back down, he took the girl's hand in his, kissed it, and looked at Janice. She braced herself, ready to bear witness to a sappy proposal. God knows he'd done it before.

"Tom thinks I should open another LLC," he said, making her blink in surprise. "What do you think...Dad?" A.J. turned to face his father, leaving her gaping into the subtly made-up face of his date.

"Why?" Allen asked, in an uncharacteristic fit of parental responsibility. "Don't you already have one?"

"Yeah," A.J. said as he dragged fingers through his hair. "But something about sheltering more tax money, I don't know. I'm leaving it up to him. He's the expert, right?"

"He is," Allen acknowledged. She watched as he set his mother's bone china cup into its delicate plate without a rattle. Mama Cooper had raised her sons on God, manners, and corporal punishment. Janice had tried to do the same, sans the spankings. "I guess I'm curious why you need two. They're not free."

"Yeah, but in the scheme of things, it's chump change. What he says makes sense to me. And he's really cleaned everything up for me, especially with my payroll. I never understood that shit. My previous bookkeeper never really explained it to me...I mean...um..." He glanced at his date, whose brown eyes narrowed at him. Janice attempted not to roll her eyes at them both. Cynthia, his ex-wife, had been that bookkeeper. Cynthia, the pregnant daughter-in-law foisted on Janice, but whom she'd come to love or at least appreciate, who was now no longer in her life, thanks to A.J.'s inability to keep it in his pants.

"Anyway, I'm gonna take his advice. He helped me refinance two of my mortgages down to realistic payments, which gives me enough wiggle room to buy that small self-storage place I've been eyeballing."

"I'm curious," Janice said, taking a last sip of her coffee. "How did he make all that money right off the bat, you know, after leaving his corporate job?"

A.J. frowned at her. "What difference does that make, Mom?"

She shrugged. "I don't know. It seems a little too good to be true. Especially considering all the money they're throwing around lately."

"He figured out how to bring some of the midsized clients from the big company with him," Allen declared. "Laura said—"

Janice pushed her chair back, dragging the feet across the floor behind her with a loud, wince-worthy screech. "I don't care what Laura says, Allen."

She started picking up plates, ignoring how everyone stared at her apparent rudeness as she started removing plates from the table.

"I can help," Tiffany-the-stripper declared. "Thank you for such a lovely dinner."

"You're most welcome," Allen said, beaming and not moving from his spot at the head of the table.

Janice blew out a breath of frustration. Something about Tom Franks working on "fixing" A.J.'s books was making her nervous. But she'd suggested it, of course. She had no reason to be anxious about it, did she?

She and the new girl worked in near silence to hand-wash the china and crystal. The woman made valiant attempts at various conversational gambits, but Janice was not feeling chatty. By the time she was putting the silverware into their individual flannel blankets before placing them into the mahogany chest, the girl had given up and was parked on A.J.'s lap in the family room, enjoying a glass of expensive whiskey with the men. Janice stood at the kitchen bar, pondering their little tableau before deciding she'd had enough holiday family togetherness.

"I'm going for a walk," she said, as she marched across the family room toward the back patio, ignoring them all, discouraging any questions.

Chapter Twenty-One

P *layroom*

• • • •

WHEN SHE FELT MICHAEL'S cool, familiar lips on her cheek, Amelia smiled. "I love you, baby," he whispered into her ear. "I'll always love you."

They lay entangled in each other's arms and the silky, zillion-thread-count sheets on the custom mattress Michael had special ordered for their playroom. Amelia was waking from a light doze post-subspace sex and met his dark eyes staring down at her. He smiled. "That was pretty special," he whispered, running his finger down her face. "I hope I didn't hurt you."

She shook her head and propped up on her elbow. "I didn't use my safe word." She'd only had to use that word twice in their relationship, both times when she realized that hot wax was simply not going to be her thing. She pressed her hand to his chest, loving the sensation of his racing heartbeat beneath it.

He was amazing, her man. She'd fallen hard for him, once she'd gotten past the whole "I'm screwing a Black guy," moment and realized Michael Ross was the best thing to ever happen to her, for a lot of reasons.

"You are on fire tonight," Michael said as he leaned in to kiss her temple. "What's got you worked up? Not that I'm complaining."

She almost laughed, but she choked it back. He looked sincerely innocent, which made her second-guess what the purpose of separating them for lunch earlier had been. "Regaining my mojo, I guess." She kissed his chest, neck, and finally his lips.

"No, there's something else. I can tell." He lifted her off him and moved to sit on the side of the bed. "You can't keep secrets from me, Amelia, remember?"

She clambered over to him and draped her arms over his shoulders. He gripped her hands before she could touch him anywhere. She could sense his sudden tension, pending anger. She slid down to the floor and knelt at his feet, hands on his knees, head bent. He thumbed her chin, lifting her face up.

All she ever wanted was to please this man, her man. And he was angry with her now for some reason.

He rose, bringing her with him, their still-naked bodies pressed close, sweat drying, making her shiver. "What is going on, Amelia?" He let go of her arms but didn't move away from her. "Talk to me."

She met his gaze, understanding that this wasn't about play, this was about communication, something they'd decided early on was the key to their marital success. Open, honest discussions about everything, including things that were uncomfortable. "The neighbors..." she began. "The women. They asked me if..." She paused, unsure how exactly to broach this despite their heretofore useful honesty with each other.

Michael took two long steps back from her, leaving her cold and shivering. He went into the custom-designed bathroom and took her robe off a hook. He wrapped her up in it in silence, poured her a glass of her favorite pinot noir that he kept in a small bar in the far corner of this special suite since alcohol was only allowed after play.

He guided her down onto her favorite chaise, tender, loving, always looking out for her post-subspace, although she felt the opposite of vulnerable and afraid right now. She felt tingly. She felt excited. She was still horny, truth be told. She sipped the velvety liquid and watched as he pulled on a pair of jeans then sat in the cushy leather chair across from her. He smiled. She smiled.

"Our neighbors want us to join them...having sex."

He blinked. His jaw dropped open. His eyes—ever his tell when it came to emotion—brightened then darkened then widened. "Our neighbors want to..."

"Have sex with us, Michael." She sipped again, watching his reaction evolve. "Our lovely, friendly, attractive new neighbors want us to join their swinger club."

He shook his head. Got up to pace. Sat back down again, glared at her for a few seconds then slumped back, his legs sprawled out in front of him.

"Don't tell me you didn't get a weird, like, sexual sort of vibe from them at that barbecue party," she said. "Those women were practically humping your leg right in front of me."

"I...they weren't...I mean..." He leaned forward, head in his hands.

"Yes, they were. And the men...well..." She shrugged, recalling their laser focus on her, how they seemed to be eating her up with their eyes. How much she loved that feeling. Odd, considering how fabulous her sex life already was. But she was enlightened enough to understand that all humans were hardwired to crave attention. Not to mention genetically programmed to do exactly what her neighbors were proposing—to have sex, and a lot of it, with as many different people as possible.

Michael's beautiful eyes filled with fury then went scarily blank. He rose, took her glass, pulled her to her feet, and kissed her hard, making her see stars behind her closed eyelids. He maneuvered them back to the messy bed, threw her down on it. Without a word, he plowed into her, hurting her a little. But she liked it, which made it okay.

He was propped over her, his well-exercised biceps bulging as she gripped them, keeping her ankles locked behind his back. "Jesus," he whispered. "What...is happening to us?"

She slid her hand up his neck, cradled his stubbly cheek. "Something tells me you're into it. That the thought of watching me...with someone else turned you on. Huh, baby? That it?" She grinned, exerted her pelvic floor Kegel power, making him groan again. "I think it is."

• • • •

A FEW HOURS LATER, they sat at the kitchen table, eating directly from Chinese take-out cartons and sipping water, reading out loud from the books Emily had given her at lunch. They laughed at some of it, but a lot made perfect sense. Making rules and holding to them. Honing their communication skills to encompass how they'd let each other know, in the middle of a potential sex party, who they wanted to play with and if that was okay with the other one.

By the time she was in the shower, relishing the various parts of her that stung from their earlier vigorous play, she was convinced they should at least try it, once. To see if it suited them. She felt rather smug about their ability to handle it without drama—something the books said were almost a guaranteed bit of fallout after the first few times you watched your spouse enjoying sex with someone else. She and her spouse already had a unique sexual relationship. They were more than equipped to handle anything. Given their honesty and excellent communication skills they were especially perfect for such an adventure.

They'd set their initial parameters. They would only play as a couple, in the same room, and only with one other couple. No orgies. She already knew who she wanted first. Shouldn't be a problem, since any one of those women would gladly take on her Michael. Suppressing a slight twinge of jealousy, something that was 100 percent normal, she dried off and applied lotion to every inch of her skin.

Tyler was due back tonight. She needed to do some laundry. She wanted to take a nap.

But something had been nagging at her, something she'd noticed in the original closet of the basement room they'd designated as their private playroom. It had once been an office, Melissa had said. Tom's office, she thought, which was weird, since there was a perfectly nice study on the main floor that Michael now used when he worked from home.

After tossing in a load of whites, she unlocked the playroom door, smiling around at the mess they'd left earlier. She stripped the bed, tossed the bedclothes out into the hall then headed for the closet. They used it to store their many toys, but the last time she'd cleaned in here and tried to move one of the locked chests back into place, it got hung up on something, which meant she couldn't get the closet door to shut properly. Which was the exact sort of thing that drove her mad.

She pulled all the wooden boxes back out and found the culprit. A cutout square of drywall was sticking out, blocking the proper stacking of her containers full of dildoes, butt plugs, floggers, ropes, and nipple clamps. She giggled at her own thoughts as she tried to get the bit of sheetrock back into its place.

"Dang it," she said, when it refused to submit to her desire. "Why is this here anyway?" She pulled on it, surprised when it came free, the effort she'd put behind pulling it making her land on her butt on the floor. She set the piece of drywall aside, used the flashlight app on her phone, and crawled toward the four-foot hole in the wall.

The space was mostly empty, but for two boxes that once held copy paper and now held file folders stuffed full of papers. She recalled Melissa telling her that Tom Franks had been an accountant and worked from home when he'd died. His family must not have known about this space, and whatever all this crap was had been left behind.

She dragged both boxes out and tried to make sense of what they contained. It was mostly LLC filings, a few tax returns, what looked like mortgage papers, all stuffed without any kind of organization into random folders. How an accountant could be this sloppy and still able to support his family mystified her.

She shoved everything back in the boxes and carried them up to the kitchen, figuring she'd show it all to Melissa. Right after she told her that they would like to join in on the fun at the next cul-de-sac party.

She grinned to herself. Then got back to work on cleaning her house, making it perfect for her family while her husband worked in his office with the door closed, loud, old-school rap music blaring from his Bluetooth speaker.

* * * *

THE FOLLOWING AFTERNOON, she got Tyler down for nap and opened the door to let her one-time real estate agent, now neighbor, about-to-be fellow swinger Melissa into her home. She smiled.

Melissa smiled.

"I need to show you something," she said, leading the woman into the kitchen where the two boxes were on the table. "Tea?" she asked, as she turned on the kettle.

"Sure. Do you have Earl Grey?" Melissa pulled one of the files out and opened it.

"Of course," Amelia said, taking out the loose blend of custom Earl Grey she always bought and placing enough for two cups in the steeper. "What is all that anyway?"

"Not sure, but some of this looks like it could be A.J.'s car washes."

"Who?" Amelia busied herself with the tea, nervous all of a sudden about the real reason she'd invited Melissa over.

"Janice and Allen's son. He owns three or four car washes and a self-storage company. Ryan's convinced he's laundering money through them."

"Really? Is he cooking meth, too?" She set the cups down on the table and moved the box to one side.

"Nah, he's not smart enough."

"Ah, okay, then. I mean, keeping his records hidden in the wall is kind of a clue, I guess."

"Hidden? Seriously? Where?"

Amelia sipped and pondered her answer. "I'll show you," she said, rising to her feet after making a snap decision. "Come on. It's downstairs."

She led the way after grabbing the key to the playroom. Michael normally kept it with him, but she'd told him she needed to do more cleaning today. She wanted Melissa to get a true picture of how healthy and alternative her sex life was already. They weren't rookies or pearl clutchers when it came to sex. But given the nature of their particular kink, the fact that her husband was willing to consider a proposed adventure down swinger lane was actually a pretty big goddamned deal.

She unlocked and opened the door. The familiar odors of leather and mild lavender filled her nose. Melissa looked around, taking in the bed, the spanking bench, the St. Andrew's cross, the hook in the ceiling from which dangled a pair of velvet-lined handcuffs.

Melissa ran her hand along the cross, touched the handcuffs then turned to face her with a wicked smile. "Amelia Ross, you are one big surprise after another." She held on to the handcuffs as she spoke. "This is the bathroom Ryan's company did for you guys?"

Amelia smiled. The tub was huge, the shower big enough for six people, with the same number of showerheads from above and the sides. The tile was Italian. The fixtures top drawer Kohler. The art was expensive, tasteful nudes. Melissa whistled. "This is where you found Tom's old files?"

"Over there," Amelia said, pointing to the closet doors that now shut properly. She watched Melissa wander over slowly, letting her fingers trail along the spanking bench on the way. The woman opened the door, eyes widening at the sight of a shelf loaded down with all manner of sex toys. Amelia had decided she didn't want to keep them put away, hiding them in chests and boxes. She was proud of her desires and her husband's ability to meet them.

"Damn," Melissa said.

"The boxes were behind the wall. I didn't put the piece of drywall back. There." She pointed to the obvious hole behind one of the chests. Melissa leaned over the chest and peered into the space. Amelia took a moment to study the other woman's rear view. By the time she stood back up and faced her, Amelia had decided that she'd have sex with Melissa. But only for Michael, if he wanted her to.

What a difference a few months made, she mused as she stepped back to allow Melissa to exit the closet. "So," she said, crossing her arms. "We want to join you."

Melissa frowned, glanced around the well-equipped playroom then back at Amelia. "What?" She seemed honestly confused for a second. "Oh right. That." She waved an arm around, encompassing the room's contents. "Seems like you guys are pretty set. You sure you want to add the rest of us into that mix."

Amelia took a step forward. Melissa didn't budge. "We're sure. When's the next party?"

* * * *

"MICHAEL, WOULD YOU please get Tyler out of the bath?"

Amelia wrapped a towel around her damp body, freshly shaven and waxed, hair washed, teeth whitened. Their nanny had taken a half day off, but had promised to be back in plenty of time for their date. Their party. The party where they'd be having sex with their neighbors.

She giggled as she slathered on her favorite lotion. She was nervous. Big-time nervous. Not just about herself, either. Ever since she and Michael had had their long conversation about the prospect of engaging in this fresh kink, he'd been on edge.

He pretended not to be. But he was. She could tell.

It was the first time in their marriage that she felt unsure about what to do or say to him. She'd tried not to sound overly eager about the whole thing. But maybe she'd come across as a bit too into the whole thing. But she was most definitely into it. Why that was, she hadn't bothered to analyze. What was the point? It was worth a try at least once and if she knew her husband—and she believed that she did—he wanted it as much as she did.

He'd said he did, at that first long talk, and several subsequent ones, once she'd read all those books, back to front, doing her homework as it were. After one of their talks, they'd engaged in a bit of mild bondage play that had ended strangely, to be sure. As in, he didn't finish at all. Claimed he wanted to hold back. Which was unlike him. She'd immediately said they shouldn't do it. Shouldn't go. Claimed she didn't want to go. Not if it affected him like that.

His response had been to untie her wrists and ankles, carry her up to their bedroom, and make tender love to her. This time, allowing himself to come inside her. Something she permitted now that she'd promised never again to abandon her birth control without telling him.

"I don't want to do it, Michael," she'd insisted afterward while he held her close to his sweaty chest.

But that night, she'd not felt her usual combination of vulnerable, sated, and shaky. That night she'd felt empowered, strong in a way she enjoyed and wanted to feel again. Michael had drawn back from her, kissed her forehead, swiped his thumb across her full lips.

"I want to do it, Ames. We will do it. Together. Like we discussed. And if we don't like it, we won't do it again. Deal?"

She'd nodded, something about his words made her want to crawl on top of him, to come again, and again. She'd kissed him instead, holding him close. "I love you, Michael."

"I love you, Amelia. And I'm willing to give this a try. As long as we keep to our rules."

"Of course," she said, as she climbed out of the bed to pee and clean up.

But, ever since that night, two weeks ago, he'd been weird. She knew why, but every time she asked, he insisted that he was "fine." That they'd "try this thing." That it would be "fun" and if not, they'd leave.

By the time they'd made it to the Big Night, he'd barely been talking to her beyond the logistics of their day-to-day existence. She'd decided to let him stew. If he wasn't willing to damn well talk to her, then screw him.

She could hear him now, hollering and cutting up with Tyler. She focused on her reflection in the mirror and spent the next forty-five minutes letting her husband be in charge of their child. It was easier said than done, considering all the yelling, ripping, and running she could hear coming from outside her bedroom.

She distracted herself by blowing out her hair and straightening it then applying a careful layer of makeup designed to look like she didn't actually have any on, participating in the ultimate artifice that she simply looked this good on an everyday basis. It was an art form but one she'd spent years perfecting.

By the time she was satisfied with her efforts, Tyler and Michael had moved downstairs. She heard the sounds of a random Disney movie, and a higher-pitched voice indicating that the nanny had arrived. Relieved, Amelia slipped into a silky robe and sat a few minutes to relax, or at least trying to.

"Hey," Michael said from the doorway. She kept her back to him, feet up on an ottoman, relaxing in the leather chair by the window. He'd been acting like some kind of a jealous teenager all week, and he knew it. She'd offered to stay home. To skip the whole stupid thing. But he'd kept insisting otherwise. At least when he was talking to her about something other than what time he'd be home for dinner.

She waited. He made his slow way across the room to her and sat next to her feet on the ottoman. She felt his warm hand on her calf but kept her eyes shut. It was going to take a bit more effort than that as far as she was concerned. She realized and fully accepted her own high-maintenance reality. In her soul she was a spoiled only child of super-wealthy and overly indulgent parents. She knew that. And when she needed to channel her inner brat, she was aces at it.

"Ames," he said, sending a pleasant chill down her spine at the sound of his deep, gravelly, voice. "Open your eyes."

She turned her face away from him despite her long-ingrained desire to do exactly what he said. Their dynamic demanded clear roles be played and she played hers well. But the past couple of weeks had been challenging to say the least. She felt unsure, uncertain about pretty much everything. Especially their decision to engage in this crazy endeavor with their new neighbors.

Michael's grip on her leg tightened. She shifted in her seat, eager to please him, wanting to make this whole thing go away by saying she no longer wanted to go to the stupid party tonight.

But she'd be lying. She did want to go.

"Open your eyes, Amelia," he repeated.

Using every bit of her willpower, she pretended not to hear him for a few more seconds. Then she opened her eyes.

"That's more like it." He slid his hand up the inside of her thigh, hovering over her lips before kissing her gently. "I'm sorry."

She pouted a little longer. He deserved it. When he reached down to untie her robe, she let him.

• • • •

"WOW," SHE SAID, SMILING down at him when she opened her eyes after he'd indulged himself with her. "Nice fluffing."

He grinned as she clambered off him and grabbed the towel next to the chair.

"So, to review," he said, as he walked past her toward the shower. "We only go forward with this if we both feel 100 percent comfortable with it. And then, we're only playing with another couple, alone, in a room. No orgies."

"No orgies," she agreed as she reapplied her blusher and ran fingers through her hair. She was tingling all over from the quickie and in anticipation of what was to come later. She knew what couple she hoped wanted to play with them. But, given the existing group's history, she wasn't quite sure how the whole thing would proceed.

Michael emerged from the shower. Water beaded up on his beautiful, ebony skin. She rose and went to him, ran her hands across his firm chest, down his six-pack abs, around to his sweet ass. "I don't know if I want to share you," she whispered into his shoulder. And at that moment, she honestly didn't know.

He kissed her hair, then tilted her chin up. "Well, that makes two of us." They stared at each other a few seconds. "Ames, I...I mean, I want...let's see how it goes. Okay?"

"Okay." Her voice broke. "Okay," she repeated. "Let's see how it goes."

They got dressed in silence. Her in a clingy black dress and heels. Him in a pair of dark jeans and a soft oxford cloth shirt that clung to his body like a glove. As he was sliding his feet into a pair of brown lace-ups, she dropped onto the floor in front of him, her hands on his knees. She kept her face down.

"Sir, please. Tell me what I should do. I'm not sure I want to go anymore."

He put a hand on her head. "Amelia, get up. Look at me." She rose and he pulled her onto his lap, holding her close. "This thing we're considering. It isn't part of what we do. We keep that separate, understand? I'm not your Sir, tonight." She thought she heard his voice break. "I can't be that tonight, okay? That won't work for me. Not if we're...really going through with it."

"I understand," she said, pressing her face into his neck. "I'm sorry."

"No sorry. We're married adults, and we've consented to try this particular activity together. But if we don't want to engage with these people, we won't. We'll come home. And I'll be your Sir or whatever it is you need me to be then."

"We shouldn't. Let's not."

He got up and set her on her feet. In her five-inch stilettos, she was almost at eye level with him. But she loved looking up to him. Always had. Call her a feminist traitor, but she wanted to look up through her eyelashes to her man.

"We should, and we are." His voice was firm, almost stern. She did a double take. His chestnut-brown eyes were hard, without the pleasant, humor-filled light that usually made them sparkle. He took her hands in his. "They asked. We talked. We agreed. And we're not going to back out now."

"But...Michael..." Alarm bells were clanging in her brain. He was pissed. No, he was furious. She'd only seen him this way a few times, and she was determined never to go there again. That sort of fury messed with her perfect life concept and she had no time for it.

"No buts, Amelia," He let go of her hands and stared down at her, fists clenched at his sides. "Stop waffling. Let's go. Get this over with already."

He stomped toward the door. She stayed where she was. When he realized she wasn't following him, he turned to face her, anger in every line of his face. She felt her own fury rising to meet it. He was humoring her, reminding her that this was her idea, not his. That he was going along with it to appease her. And that would never work, at least not according to the books they'd read together.

"No," she said, folding her arms. "No. I'm not going. Not like this."

His shoulders slumped. "You are killing me here, woman. Do you know that?"

She stomped into the bathroom, ears ringing. Slamming the door felt great. She barely contained her scream of frustrated satisfaction behind it. But she didn't want to scare Tyler.

She was sitting on the edge of the big tub when Michael shoved the door open, putting a divot in the drywall behind it. He stood over her, hands on his hips. She glared up at him.

"I am not going if all you're doing is humoring me. We both have to want it or it won't work. You read those books with me." She slipped her shoes off and was about to toss them into the closet when Michael grabbed her wrist. "Let go of me."

"Amelia, can I be honest with you? Completely, totally honest?"

"That is what we agreed to in the beginning if I remember correctly."

They stood staring at each other, her shoes in her hand, his hand holding her wrist. He let go. Her arm dropped to her side. "Talk to me. Right now. Tell me what you want to do, please," she said.

He slumped. She stood watching him, taking in his perfection and changing her mind for the millionth time about this whole sex-with-the-neighbors thing. He leaned forward, elbows on his knees, keeping his gaze downward.

"I don't know if I can watch you have sex with another man. I just...don't know if it's in me."

She opened her mouth. He held up a hand to stop her, keeping his gaze trained downward. "However, on the other hand, the thought of me with another woman while you watch turns me on and I...shit, I'm getting hard right now, thinking about it." He glanced up at her, his eyes full of emotion. She took a step toward him, but he held up the hand again. "Wait. Let me finish." He took a deep breath.

"I figure that if you're feeling the same way as I do, we owe it to ourselves to do this once. And possibly only once. Does that make me bad? A bad husband? An awful human being?"

She knelt in front of him and put her hand alongside his cheek. "I love you, Michael." She rose up and kissed him, gripping onto his shirt hard, likely wrinkling it under her hands. "I don't want to share you, either, but if we can get this out of our systems, then maybe that's all we need. To get it out of our system. Nothing more or less."

He got up, bringing her with him. They held onto each other a few seconds, listening to their son giggle from downstairs as the strains of that random Disney movie rose with it. "Just this once, Ames, okay? Let's see if we can do it. Being honest with ourselves and each other the whole night."

"What do you think... I mean who... I mean...shit. I don't know what I mean." A nervous giggle escaped her lips.

"I don't know. But there's really only one way to find out." He checked his watch. "And if I'm not mistaken, we're already an hour late. That's rude. Let's go check it out." He kissed her nose then both her cheeks. "Okay?"

She nodded. "Okay. I'll meet you at the front door. I need a few minutes."

He cupped her chin. "I love you, Amelia. With everything I have and will ever be."

"I know, baby. I love you that much and more. See you downstairs."

Amelia sat a few minutes, trying to get her spinning and roiling, churning emotions under control. She applied lipstick, brushed a bit of sparkly powder across her cheeks, put her shoes back on, and headed downstairs. Tyler was drinking from his cup, sitting in the nanny's lap, mesmerized to the point of sleepiness by the movie. She leaned down and kissed her son's cheek. He grinned at her. "Mama! Pretty!"

"Yes, son. Your mother is beautiful. Be good. Get to bed soon." He kissed Tyler, took Amelia's hand, and led her to the front door. "We might be kind of late, Sheila," he called to the nanny.

"No problem, guys. Have fun!"

Amelia tried not to read anything into that, not fully convinced that there wasn't a sign over her head that read *I'm a Swinger!* Flashing neon over and over. Which was ridiculous, of course. She leaned into Michael as they made the short walk over to the Coopers' front porch.

"Wait," she said, freezing in panic as he reached for the doorbell. "I can't."

He kissed her softly, like the brush of feathers fluttering at her lips. "Okay. Let's get this out of our systems."

"Right. You're right." She clung to his arm. The door swung open, revealing four couples, all dressed nicely, holding glasses of what looked like water. All were smiling. Amelia caught a whiff of candles, and possibly weed.

Amelia and Michael stepped inside, letting the door swing shut behind them.

Chapter Twenty-Two

O*ne Month Later*

. . . .

"MICHAEL, WILL YOU ANSWER that?"

Amelia continued hanging his dress shirts on the line that hung from the basement ceiling. She hummed to herself as she shook out each one and made sure they were properly draped. She knew she was a total throwback on this, but nothing pleased her OCD-inclined soul more than to take a basket full of wrinkly shirts on Sunday night and transform them with her starch and iron into something no other shirt laundry could do.

It was the least she could do, really, considering what an amazing husband she had. Handsome, a great provider for her and their son, indulgent when he needed to be, yet stern when the situation demanded it. He was her everything. She smiled as she passed a hand across the front of one of the damp swaths of 100 percent pima cotton now dangling from the laundry room ceiling.

By the time she made it back upstairs with a basket of clean and dry clothing to put away, she'd forgotten the doorbell altogether.

"Oh hello," she said, when she saw the stranger leaning against her kitchen island. The woman was tall, and super thin, almost painfully so. Her huge dark eyes were watery. Her long brown hair scraped back into a messy ponytail.

She set the basket of perfect-smelling clothes down and brushed her hair back, seeking some kind of an explanation. Michael emerged from behind the open fridge door, holding a couple of a cans of LaCroix—grapefruit, her favorite.

"Ames, this is Laura. She lived here. You know. Before us."

Amelia blinked, her brain taking on the fact that her smooth-talking spouse was a little tongue-tied at the moment. "Right," she said, holding out her hand and hoping her smile didn't betray the creepy feeling slithering down her spine.

Laura Franks. She of the dead husband. The husband who'd offed himself in Amelia's master bathroom. But not in the same tub she used, of course.

"It's nice to meet you." Laura's hand felt limp in hers. She dropped it fast, flashed a wide smile to Michael, willing him to join the awkwardness. She had less than zero idea of what to say to this woman. And was getting the beginnings of a headache over the sheer audacity of her, waltzing in here like she still owned the place.

She took his outstretched can of fizzy water and handed it to Laura. The woman stared at it as if it were something Amelia had scraped off her shoe. A tear escaped her left eye and slipped down her cheek. Amelia watched, fascinated, horrified, and suddenly sympathetic.

"I'm sorry," Laura Franks said, her voice choked. Her words barely discernable. "I shouldn't have come here. I...I don't know why I came here."

Michael stepped around the island and caught the woman's arm before she hit the floor. Amelia put the unopened can on the counter and took her other elbow. "Come on, Laura. Let's get you sitting before you fall."

"I'm sorry," the woman declared again. Her voice stronger now. "I was meeting my lawyer downtown and when I left, I automatically drove here, like some kind of an idiot. Like someone who had her life back."

"There, there," Amelia said, feeling foolish for saying such an old-fashioned, useless thing. But Laura slumped against her as they led her into the formal living room and eased her onto the couch. Michael met her gaze. She shrugged and sat next to the obviously distraught woman, her arm around Laura's thin, shaking shoulders. Even as she did it, something pinged in her brain, declaring this whole scene felt off. Forced. Fake.

But she kept sitting and patting the now-openly sobbing woman's shoulder. Michael hovered. She waved him off, as the lingering feeling of "this is bullshit" filled her brain.

Once Laura had herself under some semblance of control, Amelia plucked a tissue from the box on the table next to her and handed it over. Laura took it and dabbed her eyes, face, and nose before taking a deep breath and fixing her watery gaze on Amelia. Amelia leaned away from her, startled by the sudden scrutiny.

"Are you doing it?" she asked.

Amelia's mouth dropped open, a response along the lines of "am I doing what?" on her lips. But she knew what the woman meant. Oh yes, she did.

"We are," she said, smoothing her leggings over her thighs. "Is there anything else I can get you? Someone I can call to come…collect you?" She winced at the snippy, old-lady sound of her words.

When Laura's hand shot out and grabbed her forearm, Amelia let out an involuntary squeak of surprise. The woman's apparent frailness didn't include her grip, Amelia noted as she gazed down at the thin fingers digging into her flesh.

"You should let go of me now," she said, surprising herself with her calm tone. But, if anything, Laura Franks dug her fingers in deeper, making Amelia blow out a puff of air at the not terribly small amount of pain.

"You have to stop. They're like vultures, flapping around, sucking everybody into their…their…sickness." A distinct blob of spit landed on Amelia's cheek. "Don't do it. Don't let them do it to you." The woman's dark eyes were wide, wild, crazy-looking.

"We can take of ourselves, thank you," Amelia said, her anger flaring up at the nerve of this crazy bitch, coming into her house and pawing her, spitting on her, like some kind of psycho. "I'm sorry for your loss. But I really do insist that you let go of me now." She pried the woman's skeleton-like fingers off her arm, one by one then stood, staring down at the poor excuse for a human, huddled on her ten-thousand-dollar suede couch.

Michael made a well-timed reappearance. Amelia backed away from Laura, honestly afraid to take her eyes off her lest she pick up the crystal vase on the mantel and heave it across the room. When she bumped against his firm body, she relaxed and slipped her arm around his waist. "Laura, really, there must be someone here in town with you we can call. Your mother, maybe? A friend?"

"I don't have any friends," the woman said with a shocking bite behind her words. "Well, I don't know. I thought I did. Here." She waved her hand around, indicating her former home. "But I know now what a naive idiot I was to think that. To think that any one of those evil bitches and their pussy-whipped, horny husbands were my actual friends."

A tremor ran down Amelia's spine and hit her knees, making them wobbly. She leaned against Michael for strength. Ever since they'd been partaking in the cul-de-sac's more intimate gatherings, she'd developed a strange sort of mistrust about some of them despite enjoying their company, naked, on three separate occasions.

She'd figured things would be super awkward after their first time—the one they'd both declared to be their "one and only time." That the whole dropping-by-on-Sunday-morning-after-wild-and-crazy-couples-sex with a basket of homemade blueberry muffins just to chat would be way more than she was prepared to handle.

It had been. Weird. Awkward.

And yet, somehow, surprisingly normal after the second time.

And even more after the third.

And what a time that third one had been. Amelia pressed her hand to her burning face, embarrassed at herself for reliving it at this particular moment. Michael tightened his grip around her, as if sensing her discomfort and distress. Bless him.

But something about that third, semi-casual muffins-and-coffee moment with Janice and Melissa in her kitchen, her ass still stinging from the crazy thing she'd done with Michael's permission the night before while the others had watched them—watched them like they'd been doing a porn or something—had left an odd taste in her mouth.

The women had been their usual, chatty, gossipy, relaxed selves. Talking about nothing and everything all at once, in that way they had. She'd caught Janice glaring at her at one point, which had startled her. She'd ignored it, but when she intercepted a pointed look the two other women gave each other, she'd declared herself "tired, needing a nap and an Advil, sorry to cut it short, but I'm sure you understand."

They'd left, swearing that if she needed any old thing, she should call them and they'd come running to help with Tyler or whatever. But of course, not before they'd both undressed Michael with their greedy eyes as he stood, sipping his coffee and staring at his iPad at the tall kitchen counter.

Greedy. That was it. That's what bugged her. The way that, despite having both been the more-than-willing recipients of his many talents not eight hours prior, they wanted more. Now. Right here in her pristine kitchen.

She'd pondered this awhile in her new bathtub, as she ran her hands along the skim of bubbles over her body, considering her new reality.

Watching her husband go down on all four of her female neighbors over the course of the past three neighborhood gatherings had turned her on more than she'd ever imagined it might. Observing his bare, muscular ass as he fucked first one then another one of them—she forgot which ones, and it didn't really matter—during those erotically charged evenings together had almost made her come on the spot. Of course, she'd been on the receiving end of some incredible attention her own self.

She'd ducked under the water, amazed at how sexy she felt. How full and powerful, how ripe and ready for more she was, almost twenty-four seven.

Michael was no better. They spent an inordinate amount of time together in the playroom, taking full advantage of a nanny they'd send out with Tyler to the park, the library, anywhere to give them an hour alone. But even that wasn't enough. She wanted him touching her, kissing her, licking her, taking her, nonstop, and he was happy to oblige.

Right this minute, with the sad-sack widow sniveling on her couch across the room, Amelia honestly believed she could march upstairs with Michael and screw the man silly. She sighed, attempting to corral her newly rambunctious libido.

"I'm telling you, you have to stop. They'll ruin you with their catty lies and gossipy bullshit. It's all bullshit. All of it." The woman laced her bony fingers together on her lap, her already pale skin whitening. She'd heard all the theories. The most popular one was that Tom had knocked Cassie up and had been planning to run off with her until Laura had figured it out and told him she wanted a divorce. Which had led to the pills and the bathtub ending for him.

But she suspected something else. Something that the women wouldn't cop to, even if she got up her nerve to ask them. Something that involved a lot more "extra" in the extra-curricular activity they engaged in together. It wasn't exactly rocket science, since Allen Cooper had come right out and told her that if she ever wanted company while Michael was at work, to give him a wave. Like some kind of a booty-call high sign across their backyards.

That was definitely something she wasn't about to do. There were rules. And she and Michael understood rules when it came to their preferred kink.

She sighed. She had no use for this and wanted the woman the hell out of her house. She'd definitely touched a nerve. Melissa and Janice were catty and gossipy, and downright mean when they'd giggle about fat Emily and vacuous Cassie. Janice, of course, couched her derision in terms of fake endearment, and worry about the "poor dears." Melissa pulled no punches. Amelia had been shocked at her capacity for nastiness and what sounded like jealousy on many levels, although she knew the woman would deny it.

This whole thing was sick. And having Laura Franks in her house, reminding her of that fact, was pissing her the hell off. She shook off Michael's arm and took her phone out of her tunic pocket.

"Here. Call someone. You need to leave." She held the phone out to Laura, hearing and choosing to ignore Michael's loud inhale behind her. She waved the phone in the other woman's face. "I'm serious, Laura. I think you should go."

When Laura took the phone from her, she turned and marched past Michael. "I'm going to put away the laundry," she declared. "Michael will see you out."

Her husband grabbed her arm as she breezed past him, sending a near-blinding shock of lust up her spine to her brain. "Amelia," he said, his voice low and full of meaning. "I think you should..."

She jerked herself out of his grip, glanced back over her shoulder at Laura who was staring at them, her eyes narrowed now, taking in their exchange. Something in her gaze ramped Amelia's anger up by a thousand-fold. "Don't stare," she snapped at the woman. "And get out of my house."

She snagged the clothes basket, made it up to her room, shut the door then slid to her butt, sobs barely contained behind her hands. Why she was crying, she had no idea. But it seemed to go hand in hand with her level of horny. If she wasn't pawing her husband, trying to get at his body, she was sniveling and whiny.

This whole thing had to stop. She was inhabiting a fantasy world of illicit sexual encounters, and it wasn't normal. No matter how fun it was. Especially that three-way she'd had the weekend before, sandwiched between Michael and Ryan Murphy.

No orgies, they'd said. But it hadn't been an orgy per se. It was voyeurism. And she'd agreed to it. It had been Michael's idea, after all.

After a few minutes, or maybe it was an hour, a soft knock on the door behind her jolted her out of her half-napping reverie. She got up and opened it, took her husband's hand, and led him to their bed.

Chapter Twenty-Three

N *osy Parker*

· · · ·

"EMILY!"

Emily slid the blinds closed fast, smacking them into the lower sill, making her flinch. She closed her eyes then turned to face the woman who'd half whispered her name. The sight of Melissa standing there in her full-on-real-estate-selling regalia complete with high heels and perfect pencil skirt made her want to scream. Tears prickled her eyes.

"What? Were we supposed to get together?" It wasn't in her to be rude, but the woman's distinctly uninvited presence in her home irritated her. She'd had a long day, pondering exactly why she'd allowed herself to be convinced to participate in the weekend's cul-de-sac party. A party she hadn't really enjoyed that much.

But, at the moment, that was secondary. The sight of her old across-the-street neighbor, the one who'd screamed at her door that horrible night and dragged them to her house to confirm what she already knew about her husband—that he was naked and dead in their bathtub— had turned her inside out. Pretending Laura Franks and her family's drama had never existed had become her reality. The sight of her, in the flesh, exiting her old house and standing there, staring across the street at Emily's, had made her guts clench.

She pressed a hand to her lips, not missing the look of disgust that passed across Melissa's perfectly made-up face. A burst of anger hit her brain, at almost the same moment as a surge of pity for poor little Danny Murphy. She was thrilled to have him in her class. He was a total sweetheart, and she was an expert with kids on the spectrum, if she did say so herself.

She stared at the woman glaring at her from across the dining room and wondered, not for the first time, how the poor kid managed in that house. It was well-known how many times Melissa and Ryan had separated, and how much of their time they spent fighting. It was the worst possible environment for Danny and a wonder he was as well-adjusted as he seemed to be.

"Did I see what I thought I saw?" Melissa said, her voice pinched, the deep groove between her eyes suddenly more pronounced than ever. Emily bit back a catty comment about how she might be better served to get some face work done and leave her tits alone.

"I don't know," she said, crossing her arms. "What did you see?"

"Laura Franks is what." Melissa stomped over to the window and parted the wooden blinds slightly before letting them close with a muttered curse. "What in the hell is she doing here?"

"It's a free country," Emily declared, unwilling to get into her own misgivings about the whole thing. Her knees shook, and her pulse raced, the blood whoosh-whooshed in her ears.

"I know that," Melissa whispered at her before leaning in to peer out the window again. "Christ. She's just...standing there. Staring at my house."

"I'm pretty sure she's staring at my house," Emily said, unable to understand why she'd said such a thing.

"Oh, who cares whose house she's staring at. She needs to leave. Go back to Grand Rapids and live her life. Leave us alone."

"Well, Janice did say that she was trying to open up the case or something."

Melissa blew out a breath and rolled her eyes before peeking through the blinds once more. "Ridiculous." She glanced at Emily. "Don't you think?"

Emily shrugged. "I don't know. I mean, it was her husband."

"He was a loser, and you know it. He couldn't handle that he fucked that girl without a rubber and knocked her up. Lame."

Emily rubbed her arm, wishing Melissa would leave. She was tired. She needed a nap. She wanted to be alone, to think about Tom and how much she missed him.

"Don't give me that look," Melissa said before brushing past Emily on her way back to the kitchen. "Do you have any wine?"

"I...yes. I mean, what look?" She followed her neighbor, hating herself for being weak. "It's there. We don't keep a lot of it."

"This works." Melissa pulled a small glass from the cabinet, stared at the lack of a cork on the bottle then twisted it open and sloshed a healthy portion into the glass. "Want any?"

"Sure," Emily said, as she slid into a seat at her kitchen table. She was almost completely numb. Might as well drink something.

Melissa plunked both glasses down and sat. Emily stared at hers a few seconds before taking a sip. Melissa took two huge drinks then stood up and snagged the bottle from the counter. "What look?" Emily repeated after swallowing a big gulp of the fruity white wine.

"Huh?" Melissa helped herself to more.

"What did you mean, don't give me that look?" She knew. But wanted Melissa to say it—to admit it.

"Oh." Melissa rotated her glass on the table, staring down at it, her face flushed. Melissa's temper was legendary. It was no wonder she and Ryan fought as much as they did. She was shocked to note the watery condition of Melissa's eyes when she met Emily's gaze. "You think Ryan did it. That it's his kid, don't you?"

"I don't have any idea whose it is, Melissa. And I don't care." She finished her wine and set the empty glass on the table. Melissa refilled it and pushed it back to her.

"It could be any of them, you know," Melissa said.

"I guess. I mean, we were sort of...always...I don't know."

"Fucking?"

"Yeah. That."

"I know." She leaned back and swiped at her eyes. "Am I the only one who actually enjoyed taking that break?"

"I know what you mean." Emily turned her glass around.

Melissa frowned, leaned forward, her elbows on the table. "Jesus. We should stop this before something else bad happens. It feels sort of inevitable, you know?"

"Sometimes, yes, I do." Emily sipped. "We've decided not to join you next month."

"Oh?" Melissa's carefully shaped eyebrow arched higher. "Really?"

Emily sighed and got up to pour the rest of her wine down the drain. "Really. I'm sorry. I know you enjoy Sai."

Melissa shrugged. Emily slumped against the sink. This had to be the dumbest conversation she'd ever had. They were about to say how much they enjoyed having sex with each other's husbands. For real. A surge of nausea at the thought of the ridiculous thing she'd been about to say to her neighbor brought her up short.

"You should go," she said. Melissa turned to her, surprise on her face. Emily never pushed anyone out. But she was over this. She was done with this, with all of these people. She and Sai had talked the night before about selling this house and moving away. They didn't know where. But anywhere not here would do at this point.

As Melissa was getting up, the doorbell rang, making both women jump.

"Holy crap, it's her. It has to be." Emily pressed her hand to her throat. "I can't deal with this right now."

"Let me handle it."

Before Emily could react, Melissa was heading for the front door, her glass in hand. She wanted to walk past her, to answer her own door. But she was frozen in place; her feet refused to budge. Her head pounded. Her throat was closing up. At the sound of Laura's voice, she was thrust straight back to that night. Flashes of memory rushed at her, making her want to scream, cry, hide.

"Is Emily here?"

"Yes. But she's not feeling well," Melissa said. "Is there something I can help you with?"

"God, Mel, don't be a bitch. Let me in."

"Sorry, Laura, it's not my house. I'm here to help poor Emily. She has the flu or something. I don't recommend coming in right now."

While part of her was grateful for the help, another part, the part of her that was more normal Emily and less *Emily who lets her neighbors screw her six ways to Sunday and regrets it for days* made her straighten up, tug her shapeless sweatshirt down, and walk across the dining room to let Laura get a glimpse of her.

"Oh my god, Em," Laura said, her eyes full of tears. "Can I..."

Emily nodded. Melissa blew out her breath again. Laura launched herself into the room and threw her arms around Emily's neck. "I'm glad to see you. I've missed you," she sobbed. Emily patted her back and resigned herself to this whole thing. Whatever it was.

"Can I get you some tea?"

"Yes. Please." Laura cut an ugly glance at Melissa who stood by the still-open front door. "Thanks."

"Well, you gals probably have a ton of catching up to do," Melissa said, breezing past them into the kitchen. "I should go. Houses to sell. You know. Busy. Busy."

"I think you should stay," Laura said, her voice suddenly stronger as she disentangled from Emily's embrace. "You need to hear what I have to say."

"Oh, I doubt that very much." Melissa swept her hair back.

"Okay. But please know that I've hired new attorneys and they're filing to get the case opened."

"Opened? What's to open, hon?"

"A murder case, Melissa, that's what. I am done pretending that my husband committed suicide."

Chapter Twenty-Four

D*ead Neighbor*

. . . .

"DON'T BE RIDICULOUS," Janice said. She plunked the mugs of tea down hard on the burled walnut surface of her table, making them slop over. Emily stared at the mess, her mind awash in confusion, unhappiness, and straight-up fear.

Fear of what, she had no clue. It wasn't like she killed the guy. She'd seen him, of course, his face mottled, his skin somehow weirdly luminescent under the gone-cold tub water. Sai had insisted that she leave the bathroom and be with Laura and the kids while he pulled the poor man's lifeless body up from under the water to confirm that he was, indeed, dead.

Emily had done her part, keeping all of Tom's loved ones away from the gruesome scene while they waited for the ambulance. She'd gotten Laura's parents' numbers and made that call. All while Sai sat upstairs in the bathroom with Tom, or what was left of him. Laura had screeched and tried to drag Tom's bagged-up body off the stretcher out in the driveway, which had only added to the horrific chaos. Sai had told the ambulance guys to give her a shot of something, which had turned her into a zombie, a state she held on to for weeks after.

Emily herself had suffered from nightmares for weeks afterward, forever waking up in a cold sweat, a scream barely held back at the memories. Sai had suggested a mild sedative for her, too. But she didn't trust big pharma after her brief and ugly foray into the infertility scene. She'd increased her melatonin doses and practiced meditation before bed. After about a month and a half post-ambulance lights, police questions, and hysterical neighbors, she was able to sleep through the night again.

And by then, Laura had moved herself and her kids out to Grand Rapids to her parents' home. The house had sat empty for a week before a moving company showed up and emptied it out, where it sat while Ryan and his crew took over, demolishing the upstairs and reconfiguring it.

Melissa grabbed her mug and held it to her lips, ignoring the splatter of tea water on the table. Emily got up and pulled a paper towel off the roll in the kitchen, returned, and swiped the mess away before folding the towel and placing it under her as-yet untouched cup. Janice stared into the depths of hers, her lips pressed together, her normally smooth brow furrowed.

"There's a box of papers you might want to know about in that house," Melissa said, seemingly out of the blue.

Janice raised an eyebrow at her. Emily picked up her cup and sipped, waiting for the explanation.

"It's A.J.'s books, it would appear. Amelia found it in a closet in the basement. In the room they use for their S&M playtime or whatever it is."

Emily had always read books where some character would be so surprised, they'd spit out what they'd been drinking. She never bought it. Until now. She wiped her lips. "Sorry," she muttered as she used the already damp towel to clean up again.

Janice sighed and put her mug down. "Why didn't you tell me?"

"Tell you what? About the box of papers from A.J.'s car washes or about their preexisting kink?"

Emily watched Janice's face turn an alarming shade of pink. Janice put her mug down carefully. Emily knew she was seething, ready to lash out. But knowing better because if anyone was her match in the temperamental bitch department, it was Melissa Murphy. Melissa continued to sip, her face serene, enjoying her neighbor's extreme discomfort across the expanse of the dining room table.

"About the papers, of course," Janice said after several long, quiet moments. "A.J. mentioned something about them, actually. That there was something missing from what they found in Tom's records. He'd been handling the books for a few years when… Well." She ran her fingers through her expensively balayaged, shoulder-length hair. Emily couldn't take her eyes off the woman. It was fascinating, the play of emotions that danced across her face in quick succession.

"I'm sure it's nothing important," Melissa said, her tone making it clear that it probably was, somehow, crucial.

"I'm sure you're right," Janice said, standing up fast, grabbing the back of her chair to keep it from toppling backward. Emily and Melissa stayed seated, staring up at her.

"What's wrong, Janice?" Melissa asked. Emily was flabbergasted by the woman's nerve. She resumed sipping her tea, her gaze shifting from one woman to the other, as if she were watching a slow-moving tennis match. *Your serve, Janice.*

The woman heaved a sigh and picked up her cup. "Not a single thing, Melissa, but thank you for asking." She paused then went into her kitchen to pour herself a glass of water. Melissa winked at Emily. Emily had no idea how to respond.

These women were the main reason she wanted to ease herself and Sai out of their complicated entanglement. They were intimidating as all get out. Bitchy, really. But they kept her sucked in, and she let them. She fully understood that she was the nice-schoolteacher-lady foil they required for an audience.

At that moment, she wanted nothing more than to be at home, with Sai, snuggled into his side watching one of his interminable History Channel war shows. She didn't want to spend another minute in the presence of these...harpies. She put her mug down and patted her lips with the much-used paper towel. "Well, I should get going."

Melissa put a firm hand on her arm. "Hang on a second. Aren't we going to chat about this a little?"

"Chat about what?" Janice had returned to the dining room and looked less fraught, or, at least, less pink-in-the-face pissed off.

Melissa rolled her eyes but kept her hand on Emily's arm, pinning her in place. "I have to tell you about the Rosses'...erm...playroom. Those two are full-on into it. He had one of those, whaddaya call 'ems...the cross thing? And I saw an amazing collection of dildoes, not to mention a rack of what I swear were whips."

Emily swallowed hard. "I don't really think..." Her face got hot. She and Sai were the couple the Rosses had chosen for their first interaction. It had been unexpected to them both. But it had easily been one of the most amazing nights she'd spent in a while.

"Do tell, Em," Melissa demanded, turning the full force of her gaze on Emily, making her blink and lean away from the woman. "I mean, seriously. You guys were all door-shut that first time. Did he tie you up? Spank you? Did you like it? What did Sai—"

"Melissa." Janice's sharp voice made both women flinch. "That will be quite enough. You know our rules. What goes on behind a closed door at our gatherings stays that way. Stop needling poor Emily." Janice put a hand on Emily's shoulder, effectively trapping her between the alpha females. Sweat gathered under her bra as she stared at Melissa's hand on her arm and sensed the pressure of Janice's on her shoulder.

She squirmed, a fog of anger rising in her as she realized how these women were using her to get at each other. It took a few seconds to gather her backbone, but she took it and wrenched herself free. She stood, staring at her neighbors, women she'd seen in all manner of undress, engaging in the sort of sexual behaviors she'd only read about in books before letting herself get caught up in their world. They both looked at her, their expressions a combination of innocence and malice.

"I need to go," she said, turning and heading into the kitchen with her half-empty mug. When she returned to the dining room on her way toward the back door, the women hadn't moved a muscle. They were glaring at each other across the table, the shootout-at-the-OK-corral atmosphere never stronger. Emily eased behind Melissa's chair and made for the French doors.

"Thanks for the tea," she said, her hand on the cool metal of the handle.

"Wait," Janice said. Emily closed her eyes then opened them and turned to face the room again.

"What?" She crossed her arms. She had zero intention of sharing anything about her and Sai's time spent with Michael and Amelia Ross. Not one blessed detail.

"Melissa owes you an apology," Janice said.

"No, she doesn't. I'm fine."

Melissa rose and stretched, giving Emily a brief glimpse of the tanned firmness of her abs between her yoga pants and tight-fitting top. Fury rose in her again. She tugged her own loose tunic down and sucked in her gut.

"Well, anyway, we thought you should know what Laura said." She handed the empty mug across the table. Janice stared at it a few seconds too long. Finally, Melissa gave a little sigh and took it into the kitchen herself.

Emily was frozen in place, unable to rip herself away from this power play but at the same time so disgusted by it, she thought she might puke. She hated these women. But she couldn't divest herself of them. The way they acted like her friend during the days, helping her through her messy infertile life, only to drag her and her sweet husband into their web of filth.

At that moment, she decided to go home, take Sai to bed, make love to him then tell him she wanted to move. Where to, she didn't care as long as she could be away from these people and their never-ending need to top each other.

"I'll...talk to you later," she said, slipping out the door before Melissa returned from the kitchen.

Sai was sitting at their kitchen table, scrolling through something on his computer tablet. She kissed his cheek then took his hand. "Let's go back to bed," she said as she pulled him to his feet. He looked surprised but not displeased.

Later, after a solid hour of the sort of sex that her husband truly excelled at, as all her neighbor women now knew, she lay on his chest, listening to his heart beat. She took his hand and twined her fingers in his, startling him from his light nap. "I want to move," she whispered.

He kissed her hair and rolled to face her. "Anything you want, my love," he said, his deep-brown gaze making her shiver with happiness. "But why? I thought you liked it here." He brushed a lock of her hair off her face.

Emily bit her lip. "Laura's in town. She's...she's going around insisting that Tom was murdered. That his...whaddaya call it, the coroner's report was somehow tampered with. That he drowned." A tear slipped down her cheek. "I thought you...I mean, weren't you there, for the autopsy?"

Sai sat up, an expression she didn't recognize marring his handsome face. "I was there. Laura asked me to be. And I can assure you nothing was tampered with in any way. He overdosed and was dead before he could drown."

"I want away from here, Sai. I mean it." Something about the way he'd half smiled at her, and the way his features were getting all scrunched up and unhappy looking was leaching away her happy, post-sex feelings.

"That's fine. You manage it. I need to..." He rolled away from her and got up, heading for the bathroom.

She sat, gathering the sheets around her, shocked at his abrupt departure from their warm, postcoital nest. He never did that. He'd lie here and hold her all day if she wanted it. She heard the shower water hit the tiles. "Sai," she called out.

He appeared in the bathroom doorway, his firm, dark-skinned body familiar and well-loved. She bit her lip, suddenly, inexplicably horny again. She let the sheets drop away and slid out of bed. He smiled and put his hands on her hips when she wrapped her arms around his neck, loving the firm press of his skin to hers. But his kiss was perfunctory. He wasn't going to humor her with another tumble today.

"What's wrong?" she asked, dropping her arms and staring into his eyes. He glanced away.

"Nothing. I mean, I've got a tough case and I'm...I think I need to go check on his post-op progress. You know me."

She smiled. Her Sai, ever the worrier, about everyone but himself.

"Okay," she said, giving his ass a smack and shivering with the distinct memory of their time with the Rosses in the Coopers' spare bedroom. As if reading her mind, he grabbed her wrist and tugged her to him, kissing her as if his life depended on it.

• • • •

FORTY MINUTES LATER, she sat on the couch, curled under a blanket, her iPad in her lap. a most pleasant soreness between her legs. She looked up and smiled when Sai approached, kissed her cheek, and headed for the garage door. "How late?" she asked to his retreating back.

"Not sure. I'll text you. But by dinnertime anyway."

"I love you," she said.

He turned and pinned her with the oddest look, it made her face hot. But then his features relaxed, and he smiled. Her Sai. "I adore you, my Emily."

Chapter Twenty-Five

The Contract

. . . .

"RYAN! CAN YOU PLEASE hurry up?" Melissa shouldered the leather messenger bag she used as a briefcase and caught a quick glance of herself in the mirror in the front hallway.

"Mom!" Danny hollered from upstairs. "Where're my jeans? I can't go to school without my jeans!"

"Seriously?" She grabbed her Yeti cup full of coffee. "Danny, honey, your dad's taking you to school today, remember? Mom has an early meeting."

"Mom! Where're my jeans?"

"Christ," she muttered under her breath. "Ryan!"

"What?" The man in question wandered down the back stairs into the kitchen, yawning and scratching his balls. She watched, flabbergasted, as he poured himself a cup of coffee then turned to face her, a shit-eating grin on his face. She sucked in a breath.

"You are in charge of our son this morning," she reminded him, proud of herself for keeping her voice calm. "Or have you forgotten."

"Nope." He sipped his coffee and kept his gaze on hers. She spent seven seconds trying to calm down, or better yet, trying not to launch herself across the kitchen and claw his stupid, ever-roaming eyes out. "Hey, Dan," he hollered, never breaking their eye lock. "You about ready, buddy? I'll make some eggs."

"There's no time for eggs, Ryan," she said, her jaw clenched tight.

"Sure there is. You leave this to me." He brushed her cheek with a light kiss. "Go on, hot stuff. Make some money for us." He smacked her ass. She glared at him.

"Mom!"

She rolled her eyes. "Go upstairs and help him. His jeans are in the closet where they always are. He's stalling."

"I got it. I told you."

"Oh, by the way," she said as she re-shouldered her bag and took her keys off the hook by the garage door. "The accountant called."

"Oh?" Ryan drained his coffee and refilled the cup. "What did she want?"

"Something about a discrepancy on one of the Detroit jobs? I don't know. Call her."

"Yeah, yeah, fine." She chose to ignore the look of worry that passed across his face. She sometimes wished she didn't know him as well as she did, that she couldn't see it. He'd managed their money pretty well, with Tom's help at first of course. Tom had been a total lifesaver, getting them out of hock with the IRS for a song then using his contacts to get Ryan's company some killer contracts on some of the revival construction work going on in Detroit.

Truth be told, one of her first thoughts when she'd learned about Tom's suicide, or whatever the hell happened, was that they'd never find anyone as creative as he was to handle their money.

They hadn't.

This particular accountant was the second one they'd hired, and she wasn't too thrilled with the woman's prissiness. Her insistence that both of them record every single expenditure they incurred in some kind of a bookkeeping app. Not to mention the fact that she was starting to question Ryan's most recent Detroit contract. It was a big one. A massive demolition and renovation on a row of buildings and empty parking lots along the river.

It figured that something was screwed up about it. She made a mental note to ask around at work for a new accountant. "Get him fed and to school in one piece, please. You can manage that?"

He shot her a jaunty salute. She flipped him off in reply and headed into the garage, hitting the door open button on the way down the steps.

The day was a long one, more stressful than most. It was almost six thirty before she managed to break away from it all and head home. Her phone rang as she was pulling out of the parking lot, and the calls didn't stop until she drove into the garage. And even then, she had to sit for fifteen minutes to wrap things up, calming down her latest high-maintenance seller while managing another deal that was falling apart via text messages.

Finally, she ended the call and pressed her forehead to the steering wheel for a few seconds, reminding herself this was the career she chose for herself. And, for the most part, she didn't regret it.

Until she had a day like today. She always claimed real estate was a karmic business. You'd have a run of crappy luck then a spate of wins. The past two quarters had been gangbusters for her business. She was due for a few crappy days. But oh, how she hated them.

Ryan tapped on the car window, making her leap out of her skin. "You coming in or what?"

She sighed, took his hand to climb out of her SUV, and headed into the kitchen. Ryan took her bag and handed her a glass of wine. The place smelled great, like garlic and tomatoes.

"You cooked?" She sat and sipped, wanting a shower but without the energy to attempt it. Her phone buzzed. She glanced at it. Ryan took it from her hand and put it on top of the fridge. "Hey!"

"Work time is over, lovely wife." He put a plate in front of her. Spaghetti and homemade meatballs, freshly shaved parmesan, and a dark-green salad. "Bon appétit."

"Wow. Impressive. Where's Danny?" She took a bite.

"In the tub. I fed him already."

She shot him a look. He smiled and sat across from her, his own plate in front of him. "Made him his chicken nuggets and mac and cheese. No sweat. Cheers." He held up his wineglass. She lifted hers, wondering what had happened to turn him into such a suck-up. But she was too tired to worry about it.

"You call the accountant?" she asked about halfway through her dinner.

"Yeah," he said looking up when their son appeared beside the table. "Hey, Danny boy, you want some ice cream?"

"Maybe. Hi, Mom."

"Hey, honey. Give your mom a kiss." He pecked her cheek, then sat, his iPad propped in front of him. She watched him eating the ice cream in silence, noting that his face looked a little puffy from the combination of medication they had him on.

"Did you clean up the bathroom the way I showed you?" Ryan asked as he rinsed dishes and put them in the washer.

"Maybe," he said. Danny-speak for yes. She smiled, resisting the urge to brush the hair off his forehead. Even as a baby, Danny wasn't soothed by close contact. He cried more when you held him than when he was alone, self-soothing with his thumb then later with his blanket. And now with the damn iPad. His total aversion to being touched by anyone, including his own mother many times, made her want to cry.

Ryan rubbed her shoulders. She leaned back against him as they watched the boy together. "Why don't you get a bath, honey?" He kissed her temple. She turned her head.

"Why are you being so damn nice?"

"A man's not allowed to treat his wife the way she deserves? Come on. Up you go." He held out his hand. She put hers in it, her suspicion ramping up as exhaustion wrapped her in a warm blanket.

"Here," he said, handing her a refreshed glass of wine. "Take this with you."

She sipped as she dragged a finger through the water filling the bathtub. Her favorite playlist was dialed up on the built-in bathroom speakers, candles were lit, and Danny was handled for a change by Ryan and not her—a minor miracle worth celebrating. She slid into the extra-hot water with a sigh of relief. Honest to God, it was better than sex sometimes.

She touched the button, and the small jets at the bottom of the tub whooshed to life. "Oh hell yes," she said with a smile as she stretched her legs out in front of her, never more grateful for a husband who understood a woman's needs when it came to her bathroom sanctuary.

She let her mind drift, thinking of nothing at all for a solid twenty minutes. The door opened and Ryan stepped in, fresh wine bottle in hand. She closed her eyes, not quite ready to come out of her happy place and talk to anyone. She heard the wine splashing into her glass, sensed him sit on the edge of the tub, and felt his hand on her foot.

She kept her eyes closed. His hand moved up her calf to her knee then her thigh. She shifted, sending a splash of water out onto the floor. "Look at my hot wife," he said as his hand moved higher. She kept her eyes shut, letting the smells, sounds, and sensations of the water on her skin keep her in a state of suspension.

She sighed, opened her eyes and met Ryan's gaze. "What is up with you tonight?" He kissed her, sending her world spinning into orbit the way he always did with those kisses of his. Damn the man.

"I love you," he muttered into her lips.

"I love you, too," she said. Because she did, god help her. "Give me a hand out?" He did, wrapping her in a soft towel and putting tiny kisses up and down her neck. "Ryan," she said at one point, not willing to give in to him but at the same time wanting nothing more. They'd spent a lot of their pre- and post-married lives screwing their way out of having actual discussions. Why stop now?

Why did she even need to have sex with anyone else, when she had Ryan, the man who knew her better than anyone and who could bring her the sort of pleasure in bed she'd always read about in magazines.

Why indeed...

* * * *

LATER, SHE LAY ON HIS chest, listening to his heartbeat thud under her ear. "Baby," he said, stroking her arm. "You're amazing."

She rose on her elbow, meeting his gaze. "What's going on, Murphy?" He shrugged and looked away. She pinched his cheeks between her fingers and forced him to look at her. "Talk to me."

He sighed and put his hands behind his head. "It's nothing."

"You're lying."

He sighed again. She rolled her eyes and climbed out of bed, wrapping herself in the towel she'd abandoned earlier. "Get up and talk to me, god damn it. I know there's something going on with you. Something you're not telling me. Spill it."

Ryan rolled to his side and sat, facing away from her. "It's the Detroit contract. It's...fucked-up, I don't know. This new accountant, she doesn't know how to handle it."

"What do you mean, handle it? It's a contract. It's black and white. She can't read?" But she knew what the problem was. She knew damn good and well the sort of "contacts" Tom had with the Detroit officials. Pretending it wasn't what it was did neither of them any good.

"How much, Ryan?" she asked, keeping her arms crossed tight over her chest. "How much are we talking about here?"

His shoulders slumped. He got up and faced her, the perfection of his naked body mocking her mounting fury at his weakness when it came to this, their livelihood, their family's well-being. God damn Tom Franks. If he weren't dead, she'd kill him herself.

"It's just that, without Tom as the intermediary on this one, things are getting a little...wonky."

"Wonky," she repeated. "Can I get a better definition than that?" She was shaking all over, her earlier peace and orgasmic relaxation lost.

He held up his arms then let them drop to his sides. "Shit, I don't know. These guys are...I mean..."

"'They' are the goddamned mob, Ryan. You do get that, right? You understand that Tom Franks gave your company jobs that were being 'managed' by the goddamned Midwest Mafia or something equivalent, don't you? Who else do you think handles 'big jobs' like that in cities, huh? Jesus H. Christ. You're such a child."

His pale complexion betrayed him, flushing beet red at her words. "Yeah, Melissa, I get that. I knew it from the start."

"Did you? Then why pray tell are things all of a sudden 'wonky'? What exactly does that mean? Did you piss somebody off? Tread on territory that's not yours? Not pay the fake supervisors or inspectors?"

He scratched his head and looked honestly perplexed. She almost burst out laughing. "Oh my god, Ryan." Tears rolled down her cheeks. "What have you done to us?"

"Nothing, baby. I swear it. I'll get it sorted out, I promise."

"Damn right you will. You're in this up to your neck now. You'd better figure out how to get us out of it. Tom's not here to help anymore. It's on you."

He headed toward her, reaching for her, but she held out her hand. "No, I can't figure it out, okay? Please?"

He nodded as she brushed past him. She dropped the towel, put on a pair of her favorite silky pj's, and headed for the kitchen, her head pounding with renewed stress and anxiety.

Chapter Twenty-Six

I *t's a Boy*

• • • •

BARRETT STARED DOWN at the golf ball, blinked to clear his vision, took one more look at the green where he was aiming, then swung. He watched the ball arc high then shift slightly to the left when the wind took it in the exact direction he'd anticipated when he'd hit it at a slight angle.

He dropped the iron into his customized bag, got behind the wheel of the cart, and started it up. But, for some reason, he couldn't do anything more. The early hour had been his choice. He needed some time alone, doing something he truly loved, in the cool fall air before the course closed for the season.

He had to think about a few things and determine the correct course of action, and the best way he knew how to do this was here, on the links at his club. He'd done this before, of course, plenty of times. He was part of two regular foursomes that met weekly during the spring and summer, but usually he preferred to be alone.

Being out here, thinking about nothing but getting that tiny, dimpled ball into that elusive hole always allowed his mind to clear, leaving it open to solutions to tough cases. Or his personal life. Which lately was proving tougher than any of his actual paid work.

As he squared up on the hole after placing the ball in a near-perfect position on the green, thoughts of his current situation—Cassie's condition and his recent acceptance of it—attempted to invade and distract him. He blinked it away, tapped the ball, and watched it roll to, around, and then into the hole.

"Yes," he muttered under his breath before plucking the ball out and heading for the next one.

He was on the final and toughest hole when he allowed himself to ponder the current predicament. The return of Laura Franks, the late Tom's wife, the woman he would admit to considering the hottest of the women not his wife whom he'd fucked at those damn parties. Which was appropriate, considering his beloved Cassie's seeming obsession with Tom.

He blew out a breath, dispelling all the memories that crashed in on him. No. He simply wouldn't allow it. Barrett was a master of both compartmentalization and discipline. He never consumed too much alcohol. He only ate a certain number of calories per day. He exercised with religious regularity. And he worked his ever-loving tail off to be the successful, wealthy, sought-after attorney that he was. A partner in a huge Detroit firm, ex-husband to two, husband to one—the only one he'd actually really loved. And about to be a father to a kid who wasn't his.

He licked his finger. Held it up to the air. The wind had more or less died down, letting his final swing be more direct. This hole had a par five, and he'd birdied it enough in his years playing here he was determined to hit the damn thing in one stroke. He paused, stared at the ball at his feet next to his custom-made driver, inhaled, and swung.

The sun was still low, hugging the horizon as he watched the ball make its initial arc. The green was on the far side of a copse of trees. He couldn't see where it landed, but he had a sense of it. This was the day he would hole-in-one that son of a bitch. He jumped into the cart and hightailed it around and over a hill. Sure enough, the ball wasn't anywhere on the green because he'd aced the hell out of it.

He pulled it out, smiled at it, and tucked it into the compartment on his bag where he kept them. A successful morning, he thought as he zoomed back to the clubhouse, anticipating a hot shower and breakfast, his mind a pleasant blank. That's why he did this, almost every day that he could manage it and why he planned vacations in the winter around where he might find the best courses. Golf gave him a few hours of mindless bliss—free of work, home, or other concerns. And the sensation would usually last him another hour or two afterward. A rarity, given his stressful job.

He whistled his way through the shower in the club's luxurious locker room, emerged, dried off, and redressed in a pair of jeans and a structured yet casual blue-and-white striped shirt. As he was sliding his feet into his favorite leather driving shoes, he marveled at how calm he felt. Especially given the news about Laura Franks.

At that thought, everything came rushing back at him, drowning his pleasant golf-induced, blank-minded happy place in a wave of ugliness and reality. He rose, frowning at himself in the full-length mirror at the end of the row of mahogany lockers. He touched his neck, his hair, the lines around his eyes, and tried to quell them, but the memories would not be squelched, not this time.

He muttered multiple curses disparaging his once beloved neighbor under his breath as he dropped his golf clothes into a hamper, knowing they'd be cleaned, pressed, and ready for him if he returned this evening for another round. He stomped out of the locker room, nodded to a few guys who were showing up for their tee times, but avoided any attempts at actual conversation. He was not in the mood.

He sat at his favorite spot at the bar, one where he had a decent view of the room and the large flat screen mounted over the rows of top shelf liquor. "Hi, Terry," the woman behind the bar greeted him. "Coffee?"

"Uh, yeah. No. Wait." He ran a hand down his face and cursed himself all over again. "Make it a Bloody Mary, good and spicy. And water."

Like any well-trained private club bartender, she made no comment and gave no reason for him to think his request odd at nine in the morning. He paid a huge membership fee to belong here, had not one but two wine lockers, sponsored at least one hole in their annual charity fundraiser scramble. She knew the drill.

"Here you go," she said, after a few minutes spent preparing his drink with top-shelf vodka and a Bloody Mary mix she made herself. They went through gallons of the stuff on weekends, he knew. He sipped, made appreciative noises then focused on the football gossip playing out post-Saturday college and pre-Sunday NFL games on the television. The bartender took her cue and left him alone.

He sent a quick text to Cassie, letting her know he'd run into a few of the guys and was going to hit another round. That she should not count on him until at least two, probably later. That he was sorry he'd miss their scheduled morning walk and breakfast at her favorite vegan place. That he'd make it up to her.

He stared at the words then hit send. He wasn't in the mood for her, her walks, her vegan breakfast. None of it.

He had to think.

He nodded his thanks when the bartender put his usual breakfast in front of him—a poached egg, a slice of wheat toast, and two pieces of bacon. He bit into the meat, relishing the crunch between his teeth and the fattiness coating his tongue. He missed meat, regardless of his protestations when Cassie would ask him that very question. She'd smell it on him later and ask but was in no real position to complain.

The fact that he loved his wife as much as he did overwhelmed him at times. He'd entered into the relationship with nothing but younger woman sex on his mind. And she hadn't been a disappointment once they got to that stage after weeks of wining, dining, rejected expensive presents, and other briberies, none of which he begrudged her.

During those early dating stages, prior to her letting him go where he wanted with her, he realized she was not only an interesting human being, she was funny, charming, sincerely nice to pretty much everyone around her, a natural caretaker. He'd fallen for her, hard, in a way he'd never anticipated. Which helped when he faced yet another dinner of grilled tempeh with Moroccan lentil sauce and a spinach salad on the side.

He'd say one thing—his bowels had never been more enthusiastically regular in his life since he'd married her and embarked on the almost-vegan life. He would never give up eggs or cheese and had convinced her to eat both of them again, if only once or twice a month.

Then they'd bought the house on Connolly Court at her urging, spent the total value of the house updating and renovating it, and moved in, next to the real estate agent who sold it to them. Then came the welcoming barbecue at the Coopers' where they'd met the Franks. Then came the private dinner invitation with Janice and Allen.

The rest, as they say, is history.

And a sordid one at that.

He dropped his fork to his plate with a clatter and drained the Bloody Mary before signaling the bartender for another.

"I'm done with this," he said, pushing the half-eaten breakfast away from him without touching the second slice of bacon. She whisked the offending plate away without comment and returned with his second drink and a refill for his water glass.

He'd been pleasantly shocked by how quickly Cassie had agreed to jump into the fray with the neighbors. The year had been one long, incredible, erotic journey for them both. One that enhanced their own sex life to a point he almost had to turn her down because he'd be raw from all the activity.

When she'd determined that Tom and Laura Franks were their go-to couple of choice, he'd been all for it—letting the women lead was the rule in their group. Then, when she'd decided Janice Cooper was her favorite play buddy, he'd encouraged it and enjoyed the shows they put on as much as the next guy, availing himself of Laura's eager body afterward.

He shifted in his seat, pissed off at himself that he was actually getting hard, sitting here at this stupid, stuck-up country club bar on a Sunday morning, a second Bloody Mary in hand. But here he was. Popping a teenager-worthy boner at the memory of his wife making out with his neighbor's wife in the middle of the room while everyone around them got so worked up they had to turn to whoever was next to them to relieve the pent-up pressure. Laura had, somehow, always been next to him. And he'd enjoyed the ever-loving hell out of it.

When he realized that he'd never enjoyed the company of any of the other women in the room—the brittle but hot-as-shit Melissa or the soft, comfortable, beautiful Emily—he'd told Cassie he needed to change things up. The fact that Laura Franks was getting more than a bit territorial when it came to him hadn't escaped him. He'd read the books, too. He knew women tended to assign emotion to their sexual partners, whether they were married to them or not.

What he hadn't anticipated was how much Cassie did not want to have sex with either Ryan or Sai. They'd fought. Taken a month-long break from the whole scene to clear their heads at her insistence. He'd flown them to St. Bart's for two weeks of sun and relaxation, not to mention plenty of golf for him, during which they reconnected, spending long lazy afternoons and evenings in bed, making love slowly as opposed to the frantic, lusty screwing they'd been doing for the past months.

When they returned, they'd jumped back into the group fun and enjoyed themselves thoroughly with all the couples, one by one. Things had been great. He was killing it a work, making money hand over fist. Cassie was happy teaching her yoga classes and almost had him convinced to stake her opening her own studio. Then, one day, he'd had a judge cancel an entire afternoon's worth of hearings over some asinine procedural, and he'd decided to head home early.

It had been a gorgeous, early spring day. Typical Michigan with a few splotches of snow hanging around but temps in the high fifties and the sky a stunning shade of pure blue. He'd put the top down on the car, cranked the tunes and the heat, and sped home, anticipating a lovely surprise for his wife when he gave her the diamond tennis bracelet he'd picked up earlier in the week and had been saving for a special occasion, like him coming home from work early on a random Friday in March.

He'd been pleased to see her car in the garage when he pulled his in and shut the door. He headed through the immaculately tidy mud-and-laundry-room combination and hung his keys on their designated hook. After grabbing one of the high-protein oatmeal and banana muffins she had cooling on the counter, he drank some orange juice straight from the carton and shucked out of his suit coat.

She was probably meditating or something, he'd thought as he'd headed up the steps, loosening his tie as he went, the concept of having sex with her on a pile of her yoga mats bringing on a tidal wave of lust. He didn't think twice about the fact of their closed bedroom doors. He pushed them both open, even as he was unbuttoning his shirt and grinning in anticipated pleasure.

He'd frozen, his brain unable to compute what he was seeing for a split second. But, sure enough, it was exactly as he was seeing it. Tom Franks, with his wife, on his bed. They were positioned in an odd way that registered with him on some level. Cassie didn't like it doggie-style. Didn't like it from behind, he'd been led to believe.

Either way, all he knew after that thought flickered through his brain and back out on the heels of a fresh surge of rage, was that he couldn't see his wife's face. Which was probably for the best. There were reasons they rarely partook of their neighbors together in the same room. He knew himself well enough to accept that it would be beyond his ability to bear. Since he'd never actually seen any other man fuck his wife, he supposed he was able to pretend that Cassie was sitting downstairs having tea and meditating while he was boinking Laura, Melissa, Janice, even Emily.

Yeah. This is why we never do this together, in the same room, he thought, unable to take his gaze off the fact of the man putting it to his wife in front of him. Because right now, all he wanted to do was walk to his bedside table, take out his handgun, and put a bullet between Tom Franks' beta male eyes. At that thought, he hated himself for suggesting any of this crap to Cassie.

What an idiot he was.

And now, here it was for him to watch in all its glory. And best he could tell, they were enough into it, they didn't even hear him. In that second moment, as he realized Cassie's face was pressed into the duvet cover on their bed which was why it remained hidden from his view.

Regardless, this wasn't how their arrangement was supposed to work. Fury had coated his brain and all his nerve endings like molten, hot lava. He'd backed away from them, images of them etched onto his retinas, unwilling to let on that he'd seen anything. Forcing him to own up to something he'd managed to compartmentalize for the past three months.

He'd steered clear of her, staying in a condo he owned downtown and had kept after his first marriage had dissolved. They hadn't talked for a week. But by the end of that week, he was miserable, missing her, hating himself for getting them involved with their neighbors in the first place, hoping she was okay. Owning up to his own off-the-books dalliances with Laura was the hardest thing he'd had to admit, but it made the fact of her letting Laura's husband into his house, his bedroom, and doing him, doggie-style in full daylight without the benefit or excuse of it being at a party slightly less difficult to take.

Weak-ass shit, without a doubt. But when she'd shown up that Friday, greeting him at the door of his condo because he'd forgotten to tell the security guy not to let her in, he'd caved. And he'd spilled it all—told her about the three times Laura had visited him at his office, and once at this very condo. It was, in a word, refreshing, even if it took a solid hour or arguing to work through it. Cassie finally ended it by telling him she didn't want any part of the neighborhood sex parties anymore. She only wanted him.

He'd agreed, and they'd made excuses, begging off when the next party night invitation arrived.

Two months later, she told him she was pregnant, and that it might be Tom's but it could be Ryan's since she'd confessed that she'd let him go bareback on her at one of the Coopers' more frenzied gatherings. He'd moved out of their house with little fanfare and even less conversation, hating her, hating himself for letting it get this far, only to return when he'd been informed she was in the hospital.

He stared into his drink as the dining room picked up business, getting noisier around him. He heard nothing but the sound of Cassie crying, begging him to come back.

Then the second sound, that of Laura's voice, begging him to leave Cassie and run away with her and the kids. That she hated Tom. That she knew he was in with some low level organized crime types, helping A.J. launder money through those stupid car washes to hide his drug business That Ryan Murphy was half-assing important commercial construction jobs and getting kickbacks from questionable sources.

Barrett groaned and put his head down on his hands, not caring who saw him. That was the thing about places like this, he knew. Everyone saw everything. He'd already heard rumors that pretty much every member of this place knew exactly what Janice and Allen Cooper did at their house, with their neighbors.

And now? Laura Franks was back.

He had to figure out if she was going to reveal everything they'd done, that he'd done, their plans for leaving together that he'd agreed to simply to get back at Tom Franks. Because he simply couldn't endure watching Cassie's belly get bigger with a child that wasn't his. Why not run off with the man's wife?

Why not indeed.

The night Tom's body had been discovered in the tub was supposed to be the night he told Cassie that he and Laura were in love and were going to be together. He'd be lying the whole time to get back at that asshole Tom for screwing *his* wife outside the parameters of their arrangement. Never mind that.

He'd backed away from the flashing lights surrounding the Franks' house and pulled Cassie into theirs, shutting the door and pulling the blinds closed.

Because if the cops ever found out the truth of his involvement in the whole mess, he'd be finished.

He'd had zero intention whatsoever of running away with Laura. He'd only told her that to get at her husband. Anything to make Tom Franks experience the utter devastation of knowing his wife had betrayed him in the most basic of ways.

Because he knew Cassie didn't love Tom Franks or Ryan Murphy. She loved him. He wasn't a hundred percent sure he'd stay married to her. But he knew without a shadow of a doubt that she loved him, Barrett, her hotshot, handsome, successful, rich-as-God husband. *Not* the smarmy little bookkeeper who was busy getting everyone else in trouble and knocking up his neighbor's wife.

He'd been at the Franks' house that night, when Laura had told Tom about their plans to "run away together." He done it with the express intention of seeing the look on the shithead's face. Tom hadn't said a word. He'd gone upstairs and slammed the bedroom door. Barrett then turned to Laura and told her, calmly, that he wouldn't be going anywhere with her anytime soon.

She'd lost her mind, of course. But he'd gone to his downtown condo where he'd been staying until Cassie had called him later, hysterical and sobbing and saying he had to come home. That someone was dead in the Franks' house.

"Any more?" the bartender asked, interrupting his stream-of-consciousness nightmare reliving of the past year and a half.

"Tempting," he said with a wide smile that made her smile in return. Barrett wasn't an idiot. He knew his own charms and how to wield them. He'd done it to Laura Franks, after all, convincing her he loved her, that he'd leave his wife and his life and go with her wherever she wanted. "But no. I should get home."

"Tell Cassie I said hi," the woman said, again a credit to her training to know when to bring up a member's spouse and when not to do so.

"I will, thank you." He signed for the tab, his heart light all of a sudden, as if forcing himself to relive all of that awfulness had purged it from him.

And now, Laura was back. What could she possibly have to say that would affect him in any way whatsoever now?

All was well. Cassie was at home, waiting for him. The baby was healthy and due soon enough. And he was ready to be a father. Because he did love Cassie. He wanted nothing more than her complete happiness. Having this baby would make her happy, she'd claimed. So, he was going to support it.

But he'd already identified some places with promise in the northern Detroit suburbs, away from the craziness they'd endured in the tidy, sweet little college town she'd chosen. It was time to move on, and he couldn't wait to tell her they had some houses to look at.

He got into his Jag and stuck his phone in the holder, noting he'd missed a text from Cassie. Worried, he swiped it open and stared at the words on the screen. He blinked and read them again, unbelieving.

Hands shaking, he touched the phone icon and put the device to his ear.

"Barrett?"

"Yeah, babe."

"I knew it," she said, her voice breaking. "I knew it had to be this way."

"Okay. I'm...get ready. I'll be home in a few, and I want to show you some new houses."

"I will be. Oh, Barrett...I'm so..."

"I know. Me, too."

"I love you," she said, sniffling.

"I love you, too."

He was halfway home, a short trip across town, when he had to pull over, lest he run off the road, his eyes blinded by tears.

Chapter Twenty-Seven

A *Regular Day*

• • • •

JANICE WENT ABOUT HER day in the usual fashion. She woke up, kissed her husband's shoulder, got up, made coffee, drank two cups then changed to go to the gym. She belonged to a couple of them, but her new favorite was a combination spinning and Pilates studio downtown. Many times, she'd go back-to-back from one class to the other, returning home by noon exhausted yet satisfied with her extra effort.

Today promised to be one of those. She needed the outlet. Her nerves were on fire with anxiety, and the fact she had Laura Franks to thank for that made her madder than hell. An actual hell she'd been inhabiting for the past few days since Laura had shown up at Emily's house.

She sat, sipping her first cup, and let her gaze wander out to the patio. It was in perfect shape, as she'd left it. They only had another week or two to keep the pool open, but it had been warm enough for the boys to swim as much as they liked. And she liked making them happy. Although, lately, there'd been a smart-ass undercurrent to their interactions with her that she didn't care for one bit. They were always respectful to Allen. But with her and their own father they were getting pretty mouthy. She blamed their mother for it.

She scrolled through some gossipy celebrity news on her iPad. Losing herself in the fantasy lives of others had always been an escape mechanism for her. She adored romance novels—the less realistic, the better as far as she was concerned. Who wanted more ugly realism when being entertained when the world was ugly enough already?

Her favorite TV shows were about to come back on. Her taste tended toward *The Bachelor*, and audition-style shows with weepy backstories like *The Voice*. But she also adored *Grey's Anatomy*—hadn't missed an episode in years—and *Bridgerton*.

She froze at that thought then her finger resumed its motion. Allowing her to take in micro-snippets of pseudo-news she loved because no one's feelings got hurt by it and no politics were involved. She poured her second cup and sat again, taking a moment to assess her lovely surroundings. She was lucky, she knew, to have found and latched onto Allen Cooper when she had. Not that being married to him had been easy. But they'd worked through that of course, coming up with their own unique way of coping.

Her kitchen was exactly the way she'd always wanted, thanks to Allen's money and Ryan's talents. She blushed, thinking of Ryan Murphy's many talents and how much she was looking forward to being the recipient of them tonight at the monthly neighborhood gathering.

Frowning, she got up and wiped a miniscule smudge from the otherwise-pristine cooktop surface. While she was at it, she gave the stainless fridge door a spritz of special cleaner, taking pride and comfort in wiping it down. She was one of those oddballs who actually enjoyed the act of cleaning.

Unlike Melissa Murphy, who took pride in nothing but herself, or poor, fat Emily Arya whose house always smelled of curry.

Busywork complete, she picked up her cup and headed back to the table to finish her ritual. She was halfway through it, enjoying her dose of non-news, when the front door opened without preamble, releasing a stampede of little boy noises into her quiet home. She put her cup on the table and watched as her grandsons spilled into the great room, already fighting over the remote.

"Go downstairs," she told them. "That's where all your games and stuff are."

They rolled and tumbled in their pre-adolescent boy way past her and down the steps to the basement while she waited for an explanation from her son, who had his phone stuck to his ear out on the front lawn. She stood in the open doorway, aggravation twanging her nerves yet again, while he paced, talked, made wild gesticulations with his hand then finally slumped against the side of his overpriced, gas-guzzling Range Rover. She hated that car. It was too showy and unnecessary.

Finally, he ended his call and trudged toward her, head down, shoulders slumped in a way that used to rev all her mama-bear instincts. What was it? What could she fix for him?

She let him push past her and into the house without saying anything. She shut the door behind him and saw Allen coming down the stairs in his robe and boxer shorts, his thick hair disheveled, his eyes bleary. "What's with all the noise?" He shut the basement door, which cut off some of the loud gun blasts and tire squealing from the boys' games.

Janice glared at him as he joined A.J. in the kitchen where her son had proceeded to empty the coffeepot into his cup. "Got any more, Mom?" he asked.

She brushed past him, snatched the thing out of his hand, and made a fresh pot. She remained quiet, afraid that if she spoke, she'd yell at him which wouldn't help anything.

"I'm sorry but I need to leave the spawn here for the day," A.J. said. She turned to look at him.

"We have plans for tonight. You'll need to pick them up by five."

Both men stared at her. Normally she was all in for time with the grandboys. But she'd had them more than what she considered to be her fair share these past couple of weeks. A.J. would drop them without warning, something she'd flat out told him he couldn't do.

"Where are their other grandparents? Don't they live nearby, too?"

A.J. sighed and filled his father's cup once the machine gave the all-clear beep. "They're in Europe all month. I'm sorry, Mom," he said, walking over to give her a one-armed hug and kiss on the temple. "You're a real saint. I'll pick them up around four. Thanks for the coffee." He set his empty on the counter.

"Wait, A.J. What's going on? Who was on the phone with you earlier?"

He paused on his way to the front door. The expression on his face when he looked at her was one she couldn't quite place at first. She'd gotten used to the various forms of exasperation, tolerance, smugness, and anger she'd seen there. Most of them were mirror images of the ones his father had given her before, and therefore she'd considered herself immune. But once she identified it as frustration that quickly morphed into something more alarming—abject panic—she felt a thrill of the same.

"It's nothing, Mom."

"Bullshit," she said, walking over and planting herself between him and front door. "Tell me...us...what it is."

Allen seemed to have caught on that something not good was going on with his only son and joined them in foyer, coffee in hand. A.J. sighed and looked up at the ceiling, glanced at his father then back at her. She pressed her lips together, determined not to ask another question until he spilled it.

"It's this new accountant. Your neighbor Ryan Murphy recommended her after Tom Franks…um, well, anyway. She's kind of, I don't know, nosy or something. It's getting on my nerves."

"Nosy," Janice said, her heart doing a tiny dance in her chest.

"Yeah, I guess some of Tom's records were never recovered after he…ah…well, you know. And mine were among them. She's giving me all this crap about inconsistencies and things not 'adding up.'" He hooked his fingers around the words. Janice resisted the urge to slap him. "So, now I have to go over to her office, on a Saturday morning I might add, to sit and discuss all of it. I don't know. Tom never did this."

"It'll be fine, Son," Allen said, patting his shoulder. "You want your accountant to be on top of things. Good standing with the IRS is not a bad place to be."

A.J. rolled his eyes then met her gaze. She frowned at him then slipped her feet into a pair of Birks she kept by the front door. "Hon, would you ask the boys what they want for breakfast and get that going? I'll walk A.J. out." She smiled her best go-away-and-let-me-handle-this smile. He returned it. Such an innocent.

Such an idiot.

"Come on," she said to her son. "Let's talk outside."

"But…" he protested, obviously not interested in any more motherly chat.

"Come on, Allen Jr.," she said through clenched teeth. "I need to get to my exercise class."

He followed her out into the cool, sunny morning. When they reached his obnoxious vehicle, she whirled to face him. "I know what Tom was doing for you, A.J."

He blinked at her, looking as handsome and dumb as his father for a split second. Then his eyes narrowed. "What are you talking about?"

"You know what I'm talking about. Now, you listen to me. If you've put those boys—or me and your father—in any direct danger, thanks to your stupidity, I'll turn you in myself."

"Turn me in," he spluttered, his face going beet red. "What kind of danger? Jesus, Mother, what do think I am?"

She leaned into his ear, unwilling to voice what she was about to say to him, something that had needed saying for far too long, too loudly.

"I know what you're up to, A.J. Stop acting like I'm a fool, please."

He leaned away from her, his eyes wide.

"Those stupid car washes we helped you finance that you paid off inside of six months? Then asking your father and not me about helping you buy a self-storage business? Seriously? I know money laundering when I see it. Tom Franks told me about it himself, but he didn't have to."

He scoffed, but she knew her boy well enough to know he was caught, red-handed. She grabbed his arm and yanked him closer. "Your father has no clue, of course. And you'd better keep it that way. Tom Franks was up to his armpits helping other people hide their illegal activities. That's the only reason he could've left that lucrative job at a top accounting firm and been able to throw around all that money the first year he was on his own. I figured that out, and I'm the one who recommended you use him, unless you've forgotten."

A.J. swallowed hard then met her gaze. "I'm sorry, Mom."

"Don't apologize to me. Save it for your sons when you get hauled off to prison."

There, she'd said it. Spoken the words that had been tumbling around in her brain for far too long. She sucked in a breath and tried to calm her racing pulse. He blinked fast then slumped back against the car, head in his hands.

"What the hell am I going to do?"

"Go to the police or the FBI or whoever and turn yourself in. If you get caught outright, you're going to jail anyway. If you don't, you might get killed by the people who don't like what you're doing." She put a hand on his shoulder, wondering where in the hell she'd gone wrong raising this man.

"I can't do that. I gotta go. I have to figure out a way to work with this accountant to show her what her real job is."

"Fire her," Janice said. "Give her a decent bit of cash to go away and not talk. Then, go to the police. A.J., it's your only way out of this now."

"If I could get my damn hands on those records Tom had, that would help," he said, as if he hadn't heard a word she'd said. "They were so...clean. I swear the guy was a miracle worker."

"Yes, well he had a lot of experience working with criminals...not unlike you, I'm afraid."

"Listen, Mom. Let me explain. It's not what you..."

She held up a hand, amazed to note it didn't shake. "No, I don't want to know anything more." But her mind was turning over something Melissa had said. Something about a box of paperwork Amelia found in her basement. She glanced over her shoulder at the Ross house, pondering her next move. "Go on now, Son. Fire the accountant before she figures anything else out."

"I don't know..."

"I do. Now, go on. Do what I'm telling you. I'll figure out a way to break this to your father."

"No, Mom. Don't do that."

She turned to face him, arms crossed, anger pounding through her veins. "Why not? You're the one who made this mess. It's high time you own up to it before anyone gets hurt. I'm sick of it, A.J. Sick of pretending you're some kind of a legit businessman when you simply aren't. That what you're doing isn't hurting more people. That what you're doing isn't the worst possible thing a man with children could possibly do." Tears were running down her face. She'd had such high hopes for him. He'd never know how badly he'd disappointed her.

He started toward her, his own eyes shining.

She stepped back. "No. Don't try to do or say anything more to me right now. I've done what I can to...to help you. Now you have to own this. Man up, god damn you. It's gone too far."

He paused in mid stride, his expression puzzled. "What have you done to help me, Mom?"

She waved a hand then pressed it to her lips to stifle a sob. She was tired of all of this.

"Tom Franks was about to rat you out," she said. "You and Ryan Murphy both. He was ready to toss you both under the bus."

"What is Murphy doing?"

"Cutting corners to get a low-bid contract on some work in Detroit. He's made a ton of money doing it that way but is tucked right into the front pocket of some organized crime types in order to do it."

"How in the hell do you know all of this?"

"Tom Franks told me."

Her son's mouth dropped open. She wanted to tell him to close it. That he looked like the village idiot. But she was trying not to make ugly statements about poor unfortunate retarded people anymore. She took a breath. "It was a few days before...before he took his own life."

"Mother, you can spare me your 'close relationship' with your neighbors BS." He waved an arm, apparently indicating the cul-de-sac around them. "I know what you do with him." His lip turned up in a distinct and unpleasant sneer. "You and dad and your...your orgies."

She took two steps toward him and slapped him so hard her palm stung for hours afterward. He stared at her, as the mark on his face turned white then flamed red as the blood rushed to his vessels. She wanted to do it again. And would have, if Allen hadn't grabbed her arm.

She jerked out of his grip. "I hope you're happy," she snarled at him. "I'm going to miss my exercise class now." She turned and walked away from them both, headed for the Ross home, intent on getting A.J.'s business papers from Amelia before things got any worse.

Chapter Twenty-Eight

P apers

• • • •

AMELIA SLIPPED OUT of bed and tiptoed down the hall to check on Tyler before she headed to the kitchen to make coffee. Her head was pounding. They'd gone out with some of Michael's co-workers, saving their knock-down-drag-out for the trip home from Detroit and continued it into the house. The volume of his voice as he yelled at her—granted after she'd shrieked at him—made Tyler wake up and freak out which was a total cherry on top of that cake.

As she rinsed the carafe and ground the beans, she tried to erase all the ugly things they'd said to each other. She'd started it, and she damn well knew it. She'd had way too much to drink piling expensive red wine in on top of her martini cocktail. But things had been strained between them these past few weeks and he wouldn't confess to anything. She'd decided to drag it out of him.

Which she had. And she wished like hell he could take it back, now. Leave her in blissful ignorance of the viper's den they'd managed to step into by living here and agreeing to be a part of their biweekly gathering with the neighbors.

She sighed and poured reverse osmosis filtered water into the reservoir then turned the thing on. Doing these little tasks always soothed her. She and Janice Cooper had chatted last weekend about how they both really enjoyed housework—everything from laundry and ironing to meal planning and tidying up. Having a clean and orderly home gave them pride.

She flushed hot at the memory of how the rest of that day had progressed. A nice swim with Tyler in the pool, followed by lunch and some wine, putting Tyler down for a nap in Janice's grandsons' room. And then, the hot tub, relaxing while her boy slept upstairs by letting Janice touch her under the bubbly water.

She cursed as she slammed the cabinet closed in an effort to shut the door on the memories of that day.

They were back at the kitchen table polishing off the wine by the time Allen got home from his golf game.

"Well would you check out my luck," he'd said, giving them both kisses on the cheek, his hand lingering on Amelia's plenty long enough for her to get all shivery. "Two gorgeous women here to greet me when I get home."

She'd studied him as he washed his hands and poured himself a glass of water at the sink. He had to be the handsomest older man she'd ever encountered. Her gaze lingered on his long, talented fingers as he dragged them through his still-sweaty hair. His body was simply amazing for his age.

She was licking her lips when Janice put a hand on her arm at the table and said, "Allen, why don't you take a shower?"

"Great idea, my love," he'd said, bussing her on the cheek once more as he passed them.

They drank and chatted a bit more and then Janice had said, "Go on, hon. He's ready for you." She nodded at the steps. She'd protested, but Janice leaned over and kissed her softly on the lips. "I'm the fluffer, Amelia. Go on to the main course. I want to watch."

She had. And Janice had joined them on the floor of the bathroom, which was covered with soft, fluffy rugs Amelia meant to ask about.

"Oh shit," she said, putting a hand to her burning face. She'd learned that the "rules" the neighborhood group operated under were loose guidelines at best. While she'd done her best to ignore some of the more overt invitations during the day from Ryan Murphy—something about him made her nervous and choose not to risk a one-on-one encounter—she'd thoroughly enjoyed the Coopers' and the LeBlancs' company during the warm afternoons while Michael was at work and Tyler napped.

Hands on her bare shoulders made her flinch and curse. "Michael," she said, loving the feel of his lips on her neck, the eager press of his body against her ass. "You scared me."

"How much longer?" he asked. She knew the shorthand.

"He'll sleep another hour probably." She closed her eyes and pressed back into her husband's torso, loving the warm familiarity of his hands on her.

"Mmmm," he said as he slid a hand into her pjs. "Is this all about me?"

"Of course it is," she lied.

"I don't know yet," he said, between kissing her shoulders and neck. "I'm still mad about last night." He angled his hips in a familiar way. "You were very bad last night."

The smack landed on her ass with the exact correct amount of sting without too much actual pain. She muffled her own cry of pain and pleasure, willing her son not to wake up.

"Very, very bad," he whispered into her ear before pulling her up and turning her around to face him. His eyes were dark with intent, but not the sort of intent she'd hoped to see there. "Do you think I don't know why you were defending the Coopers last night?" He kept his distance from her, just enough to make it clear he would not welcome her touching him.

"What? What are you talking about?"

"Laura Franks," he said, which snapped her right back to herself. She straightened and tried to turn away from him to collect her racing thoughts. She didn't want to talk about Laura Franks. But once Michael was on a topic, he wouldn't be diverted by anything. It was the lawyer in him, she supposed.

She moved over to in the chair nearest him and sat, slowly, sexily, at least she hoped. "Why do you think I was defending them?"

"Because, I think...no, I actually know, what you've been doing with them during the day."

This alarmed her but only a little. She'd fully planned to tell him about it, eventually. Her face flushed, but her body was still on high horny alert. She kept her expression neutral. "How do you know this?"

"Laura Franks. She came by my office and told me all about Tom and what he was up to working for our neighbors, cooking books, hiding money, all of it. All the things you refused to believe when I told them to your drunk ass last night."

He moved fast, making her gasp as he pulled her to her feet, his strong fingers wrapped around her wrist. "Downstairs," he hissed in her ear. "Now."

"No, Michael. Tyler might..."

"He'll be fine. I won't need long. But we are going to talk more first, on my terms."

He pointed her to the basement door. The sight of it made her shiver, as she'd been fully programmed to do. She looked back at him, nervous for the first time. He seemed calm, but she knew how he was—how he seethed under the surface until he'd explode with rage.

He'd never hurt her in any way she didn't want. She'd only used her safe word a few times. But, for some reason, right now, this morning, since he'd found out what she'd done without him, she was scared.

As if reading her mind, he pulled her into his arms and kissed her. No one compared, not one of the men or women she'd been messing around with for the past two months. Only this man, the one kissing her so damn hard she wanted to cry at the perfection of it. When he broke the kiss, he stepped back, chest heaving, nostrils flaring.

"Go downstairs," he repeated. She went.

He locked the door of their private room behind them and turned on the one-way intercom they kept between this room and Tyler's. She hesitated, unsure of what he wanted from her. He kept his back to her for a few seconds then turned, his face a mask of frustrated anger.

"I'm sorry, Michael. I didn't mean...it wasn't...I was going to tell you."

His shoulders slumped. She bit her lip. This wasn't like him. Not at all the way they played. He put his hands on the ebony-colored dresser where they kept all manner of costumes and paraphernalia and looked at her for a solid two, maybe three minutes in complete silence.

She waited it out, accepting that this was his space, where he was one hundred percent in charge of her. She loved it and could feel her need ramping up again, smothering the tiny flame of fear she'd felt earlier. She trusted him implicitly with her body and her soul. Her future and her well-being. And he'd not disappointed her yet.

She trained her gaze on the floor in front of her, waiting for him to tell her what to do. Finally, she sensed him approaching her, smelling his lust as if it were a live thing between them. She shuddered when he put a hand on her shoulder and pushed her down until she was on her knees on the soft rug.

He stayed enough out of her reach for it to feel awkward, her on her knees, looking at the rug and waiting for him to say something, anything. Finally, he tilted her chin up, and she found him on his knees, right in front of her, his dark eyes shining with an emotion she couldn't name.

"I'm sorry," she said again.

He rubbed a finger across her lips, down her neck to her shoulder and to her breast. "We have to stop, Amelia. These people are...they're not good people. I don't want you going near them again, do you understand me? I'm serious. As a heart attack."

She sucked in a breath and tried to reach for him, to kiss him, to connect with him. But, all the while, a part of her protested. She was having way too much fun with her neighbors. What in the world could Tom Franks have been doing to cause this level of concern?

"Amelia," he snapped, using the tone of voice she craved. Except this time, it blew oxygen on the cinder of fear she'd been nurturing, sending the flame high into her chest.

"Yes, S-s-s-sir?"

He blew out a breath and got to his feet. She stayed down, as he hadn't told her she could get back up yet.

"Come here and sit." She heard a drawer opening. When she rose, he handed her a soft robe, and he put on a pair of freshly laundered boxer shorts. His erection hadn't abated one iota and made an impressive tent, but she fixed her eyes on his face.

He pulled her over to a leather love seat they'd picked out together at an expensive furniture store, bouncing around on it like naughty kids, making sure it was wide enough to accommodate them in almost any position they chose.

She sat, pressed close to him, his arm around her shoulders. "Are you mad at me?"

He sighed. "The thing is, I'd be a total hypocrite if I got mad at you for a little extracurricular action with the neighbors. I've not exactly been forthcoming about my own activities in that department, either."

She gasped and pushed herself off and away from him. Jealousy hit her brain hard, causing a funny taste in the back of her throat. It was metallic and gross and made her want to puke to get it out of her mouth. He raised one eyebrow at her as if to say, *"Really? You're gonna be all righteously mad about this? Now?"*

She slumped and fell against him, her hand on his firm chest. His lips touched her hair as she draped a leg over his and reached for him. But he held her off. "This is what I mean, Ames. I don't like myself right now because I feel like I'm sneaking around on you but that it's somehow okay. That's it's all justified. But it's not."

She nodded and used her fingertip to trace the outline of his abs under his skin. "I feel the same way. Like I'm doing something illicit and keeping it from you instead of sharing it with you, like we do at the parties."

He tightened his grip on her. "I don't want to do it anymore. The parties or any of it. And if it becomes some kind of a problem with the neighbors, we'll have to move, I guess."

She sat up again. "I am not moving again. This one was stressful enough. Dear God, the thought of house shopping again and all of that shit makes me want to die." A tear slipped down her cheek. He caught it on his finger and put it to his lips.

"All right, fine. We won't move. But we are done playing with these people. Or, at least, I am." His face got a distinct look to it she didn't care for much.

"What's that supposed to mean? Like you think I'm not done if you are? If one of us wants to stop, we stop. That's the agreement." A flicker of resentment flared in her. She'd had fun with the Coopers last weekend. And she'd been looking forward to tonight's full gathering. She wanted to try things out with the Murphys, with Michael in the room, of course.

"Who did you fuck?" she demanded, getting up and crossing her arms. "Tell me. And I'll tell you about mine."

He looked up at the ceiling, his long legs stretched out in front of him, his boxer tent getting bigger by the minute. "Are you sure you want to know? Because if you don't, you really shouldn't ask me."

"I asked you, didn't I?"

"This is precisely what Laura told me would happen," he said, shocking her a little. "That this was how things devolved before and would again. She told me she didn't want anything bad to happen to you, to us."

"Was this before or after she told you about the drugs and the Mafia and whatever the hell else she was babbling about?"

Damn that Laura Franks. Amelia had known she'd cause nothing but trouble.

He leaned forward, wincing a little as he readjusted himself. "Before," he said. "We had a long talk. She told me that Barrett LeBlanc pretended he was in love with her, promising he would leave Cassie and run off with her. That he only did it to get back at Tom for..."

"For knocking Cassie up?" Amelia's defenses crumbled. He was right. This was a such a weird-sex mess, and they needed to extricate themselves, the sooner the better.

"Yes, for that." Michael stared at her. "You know that Laura believes someone—one of our neighbors—killed Tom. We are talking about murder, Amelia."

"I know, Michael. Janice told me."

His eyes narrowed. "Was that before or after you guys got off in the hot tub until Allen got home so he could fuck you?"

Amelia's mouth dropped open. She clapped it shut with an audible pop. Her face flushed. Tears formed again. "How did you..."

"Laura said that's their favorite thing to do. Janice likes making her husband happy by giving him some woman that she's spent a few hours fluffing. God. This is...sick."

Amelia nodded, knowing he was right. "But...what about Tom? Who does she think killed him?"

"She doesn't know. But she's asked the judge to reopen the case, and she asked me to help her. One of the partners at my firm is pretty pissed off at me about it."

"Who...oh." Amelia sat on the bed, all the energy gone from her at that realization. "You aren't going to, are you?"

"No, I can't. I'm not senior enough, and I told her that. Besides, criminal stuff isn't my area." He flopped back and put an arm over his eyes. She flew to his side, cuddled into him, and kissed his neck. "Don't," he said, but his voice was weak. She kissed her way down his torso then dropped to the floor in front of him. "I love you, Amelia," he said, his voice breathy.

"I love you, Michael. You're right. We'll stop."

She used all her skills with lips, tongue, and fingers to bring him to a loud, enthusiastic climax then rose and swiped the back of her hand across her lips as she swallowed.

"My turn," she whispered. He grinned, eased her down to her back, and gave her the same courtesy.

• • • •

AN HOUR LATER, MICHAEL was in his study, and she was trying to get Tyler to stop throwing bits of homemade, whole-wheat waffle on the floor. "Yuck!" he kept yelling at the sticky mess he was making.

She sighed and picked it all up, gave him a sippy cup of milk when he kept reaching for her breasts, and put him on the floor. Exhaustion stole over her, forcing her to sit and take in the messy kitchen, when the doorbell rang. She glanced at the stove clock. Who would be by at this hour on a Saturday morning.

"I'll get it," Michael called, which was followed by a squeal of delight from the boy. She smiled, knowing he must have scooped the kid up and had him on his shoulders. "Oh hi, Janice."

Amelia froze in her tracks. Memories and random images swirling in her head from the past few days when she heard her neighbor's voice. "Hi, Michael. And hello there, young man. How are you this morning? Did you eat your breakfast?"

"Yuck!" Tyler yelped. Michael must have put him down. He scurried into the kitchen and clung to her legs. She picked him up and held on tight. Mostly for defensive purposes. As if holding her son would prove she was a good person. Not someone who'd let her neighbors both within and outside the sight of her husband.

"I'm glad you stopped by, actually," Michael said. "Amelia and I need to talk with you about something."

Amelia pressed her nose into the little boy's neck while he fumbled around with her shirt front. "Ma! Milk!" She grabbed the cup he'd tossed the floor and gave it to him.

"Big boy milk," she muttered, straining her ears to hear the conversation from the next room.

He wriggled his way out of her arms and ran into the great room, muttering, "Big boy milk," around the nipple of the cup before he flopped onto the couch and curled in a corner. She watched him, wondering if there were any way in the world she could love another human being as much as she did him. But she knew that she would.

She pressed a hand to her flat stomach. She wanted another baby. She'd decided this over the course of the past few weeks. And she knew she could convince Michael, now that they'd decided to extract themselves from the cul-de-sac sex club.

She smiled when Janice and Michael walked into the kitchen.

"I'm sorry. It's a wreck in here." She tossed dishes into the washer and wiped down the surfaces, using all her nervous energy to keep from looking at Janice.

"Michael said you wanted to talk," the woman said. "What about?" Her tone was light, but Amelia had been around her and the other women in the group long enough to know when she was pissed.

Michael moved to stand next to her, his arm around her shoulders, which helped some. Janice cut her eyes to him then focused on Amelia. Her smile, while some would consider angelic and friendly, was cold and a tiny bit intimidating. "We—" Michael began. Janice held up her hand.

"Michael, you know the rules. The women call the shots. I would like to hear this from Amelia."

He nodded. Amelia looked from him to Janice and back again. "We aren't going to participate anymore," she blurted out fast, running it together like one long word. She cleared her throat. "In parties. Or any...other things."

Janice's smile got wider. "Oh gosh, is this about the other day? Did you not tell him, Amelia, honey? Is he mad at you because he thinks you're cheating on him?" Her eyes narrowed, and Amelia felt as though an ice cube had dropped down her back at the other woman's expression. Before either of them could speak, Janice rose and walked toward them. "Because you really ought to ask him about his own afternoons sometime. I hear he and Melissa have a lot of fun downtown, you know, 'looking at condos.'"

Amelia sucked in a breath. Michael tightened his arm around her. She corralled her anger. She had no right to it, after all, and she knew it. "I already know about that," she said, although she now had way more details that she wanted. He'd been right about that, too.

"Ah well," Janice said. "That's fine. I understand. Really, I do. This can be tough on newly married folks like yourselves. It's for the best. I do hope you won't be strangers though. You know we'll have plenty of opportunities to socialize, outside our usual fun ways."

Amelia suddenly did want to move. As far away from this sick circle of dysfunction as she could get. Like, this week if she could manage it.

"I'm actually here for a favor," she said, sitting back down. Tyler wandered in and over to her, patting her leg. She pulled him into her lap, and he snuggled in close. It took all Amelia had not to snatch him away. She sensed Michael tensing and knew he wanted to do the same thing.

"Okay, what can we do for you?" he said, in his formal, lawyer, we-are-officially-no-longer-friends voice.

"My son, A.J., was a client of Tom Franks'," she said, looking down and making silly faces at Tyler, which made him giggle and pat her well-preserved cheek. "I understand you found some of Tom's old files. And that A.J.'s car washes and other businesses were in them. I'm here to request that you give them to me. I need to give them to his new accountant."

"That's not possible, Janice, I'm sorry," Michael said in his legal, not-sorry-at-all voice.

"Oh?" The woman's ire was rising almost visibly in a fog around her head.

"No."

"Well, why not? I mean, they're A.J.'s property. You of all people should know—"

"Laura Franks has them. If you want them, you'll have to talk to her. Now, if you'll excuse us, we have plans for the day." He picked Tyler off Janice's lap and held out a hand, indicating she should head for the front door.

She did but turned at the last minute. "I know what you think," she said. "And I want you to know I wouldn't do anything to hurt anyone. Tom was weak. Weak-willed, weak-minded, a slave to his booze really. I know Laura wanted to leave him. She told me so."

The woman lifted her chin. "Everyone talks to me. Which is why I know all about you and Melissa Murphy, going after each other every day for weeks in empty condos." Her gaze landed on Amelia's, full of fake sympathy. "It's why I initiated a visit with us, for you, my dear. And encouraged the LeBlancs to do the same. I know you enjoyed it. All of it."

She looked at Michael who was moving Tyler from one arm to the other while he glared down at her. Amelia shut her eyes then opened them again.

"Get out of my house, Janice." She barely recognized the chill in her own voice as she spoke.

"Now, now, don't be angry with me, young lady. You didn't have to come over the other day, you know."

"You're a sick, psycho...a vampire," she spit out, embarrassed by the silliness of what she'd said but unable to come up with any better description. "You suck the life out of everyone around you. You and your husband both love watching people fall all over you, worship you, fight to have you as their best friend. Well, you know what?" She took a step forward until she was within inches of the other woman's face. "You can fuck right off and out of our life. We're done. We had some fun, but we know it's wrong. It's sick. And we are finished with it and with you. Do you hear me you stupid, face-lifted bitch?"

The woman smiled at them while looking over their heads then turned and left without responding.

Chapter Twenty-Nine

C ounting Down From Four...

• • • •

SAI STARED AT THE COMPUTER screen in his office, seeing nothing, his brain spinning in too many directions to focus.

Laura Franks.

Holy mother of all that was unholy.

He leaned back in his leather desk chair, pressing the pads of his thumbs against his eyes as if he could press her out of his consciousness. Her and that damned in-over-his-head husband of hers. He'd never be shed of them.

It was a lot of his own fault, of course. His own stupid tendency to want to help people in distress. And the Franks had been the epitome of that, to be sure.

"Dr. Arya?"

"Yes," he said, leaning forward and pretending to be engrossed in whatever was on the screen on his desk.

"Can you come see a patient with me?"

"Of course." He got up and pulled on his white coat, grateful for the distraction.

A couple of hours later, he was on his way home, windows down, the pleasant fall evening air clearing his mind. He parked in the garage and headed indoors, feeling a thousand times lighter than when he'd left.

Emily had parent-teacher conferences and wouldn't be home until late. He pulled a container of leftovers from the fridge, filled a plate then heated it in the microwave. Still operating under a pleasant haze of medical success—he'd helped catch a rare congenital disease in a colleague's patient—he poured himself a huge glass of water and decided to eat out on the patio. He put his plate and glass on the table and lit the tiki torches. After taking a few deep breaths, he tucked into the meal—a lovely mix of roasted fall vegetables and wild rice—one of his favorites.

But, for some reason, every bite he took tasted like oversalted cardboard. "Shit," he said under his breath, getting up and heading inside, seeking alcohol. That was another argument to move from this damn place, he thought as he poured the last of a bottle of Malbec on the counter. But that tasted like vinegar. He poured the rest of it down the drain.

He put his hands on the cool granite counter and leaned forward, head dropping between his shoulders. He hated himself at that moment, but he hated his inability to disentangle from these people. He was a nice guy—a good Indian boy who didn't eat meat, barely drank, rarely cursed. He was loyal to the wife who'd never give him the biological children he'd always wanted. He'd worked his ever-loving tail off to be the successful, sought-after, wealthy cardiothoracic surgeon he now was.

He was not the type of man who'd join in the sort of behavior that he and Emily had been engaging in. He couldn't recall how it had started, other than the triple seduction they'd endured at the hands of the Coopers, Murphys, and the Franks. He'd be the first to admit that Laura Franks had captivated him from the start. But he'd only agreed to participate if Emily felt comfortable. Which she had, surprisingly.

He sighed. He needed Emily. Her cool, calm, motherly demeanor, her soft, pliant body, her soothing words. His fingers curled into fists as irritation and fury rose from the base of his spine to heat his face to the point he thought it would shoot out his damn eyeballs. He headed upstairs, leaving his unfinished plate of food in the sink.

A shower. That would at least help. He turned on all six of the heads, letting the steam fill the large room while he did push-ups then sit-ups then planked until his body shook, and he fell over onto his side. The shower felt great as he stood and let the hot water hit from all sides. Of course, despite his efforts, she came rambling back into his thoughts, reminding him what a total fool he'd been to try and help.

Pressing his hands against the tiled wall, he let it happen. Let the rush of memory he'd been suppressing ever since Emily had told him Laura was back, poking around, causing trouble, making everyone upset all over again.

The afternoons she'd shown up at his office, looking lovely and eager, ready for anything, he should have told her no. Should've told her to leave. That what they were doing as a group was bad enough. That he had no desire for anymore.

But he had, apparently, plenty of desire for screwing the woman six ways to Sunday in his office, and in several expensive hotel rooms. When she'd come to him claiming that she and Tom needed his help, that Tom was in big trouble and needed a way out, he'd agreed to help.

He groaned and slid down the wall, coming to rest on his heels, as the hot water kept beating against his skin. This was, of course, post Cassie's little news flash about her pregnancy that had put all the men in the spotlight and brought out a whole pack of true confessions.

"God, god, god," he moaned, bumping the back of his head against the shower wall over and over again. He never should have listened to their stupid plan. Never let himself get drawn into such a ridiculous arrangement.

But he had. And he'd never get past it now.

What was she thinking of? Reopening the case? Seriously?

The sensation of being hollowed out, raked clean of everything good he'd ever done in his entire life was consuming him all over again, exactly the way it had after the group had been told that Cassie was pregnant, but her husband Barrett was incapable of making her that way. He tried to get up, but his legs wouldn't cooperate. He wanted to make things right, but he had no idea how.

Finally, he pulled himself up and turned off the water, stumbled out of the shower, and grabbed one of the thick towels. Avoiding his reflection, since he was afraid that he'd punch his own face in the glass, he headed out into the bedroom, checking the time against when he figured Emily would be home. He sat on the edge of the bed, frozen in place from the sheer weight of his cumulative bad decisions.

"Honey?" Emily put a hand on his bare shoulder. He shut his eyes and leaned into her arm. "Sai? What's wrong?"

"I'm...we have to leave here." He got up, letting the towel drop to the floor. "I can't live here anymore, Emily." His voice was tight with anxiety. His head pounded in time with his heart.

"Okay, hon," she said, kicking off her medium heels and taking off her skirt. "Whew. I'm beat."

He watched her, his vision narrowing, his mind racing. "I love you, Emily."

She glanced up at him as she was unhooking her bra. "I love you, too, Sai. Oh Lordy, that feels good." She headed into the bathroom. He followed her, needing to keep her in his sights, feeling if he couldn't see her, he'd fall apart completely.

"I'm going to start looking for a new house," he said, leaning against the shower door while she rinsed off.

"Okay," she said.

Aggravated that she wasn't as enthusiastic about it as he was, he handed her a towel when she stepped out, her skin pink and glowing from the soap and water. "Let me," he said, wrapping her up and patting her dry, kissing her neck, her shoulder, her arms. "I need you, Emily," he said, tugging her over to their bed. "I need you," he repeated, as he laid her back, kissing his way up her legs.

• • • •

HE LEFT HER DROWSING in the rumpled sheets and headed downstairs for water. Restless in a way that wasn't his usual, post-sex state. Using that energy, he cleaned up the mess he'd left in the kitchen then took his iPad from his briefcase. Time to initiate a house search. For real.

Two hours later, he was still wide awake, staring out onto the darkened backyard. Despite everything he'd tried to stop it, memories of that final, disastrous week with Laura filled his mind, overflowing it, making him have to sit in his leather recliner before he fell over. She'd been unbelievably sexy, in a sort of girl-next-door way, not unlike his sweet Emily but much more confident of her own beauty and worth. Long dark hair, deep-brown eyes, somewhat up-tilted nose, full hips and breasts, her abdomen silvery with stretch marks from her pregnancies. She'd hooked him hard from the start, and he knew it.

He leaned forward, elbows on his knees, fingers entwined, thumbs pressed against his forehead. But the march of memories wasn't letting up. If anything, it was getting worse.

As if the mere mention of Laura Franks' name had unlocked the steel box with the padlock where he'd stuffed her and all the stupid things he'd done with and for her, and now they were finding fresh, free rental space in his brain, Pandora-style.

"We need your help, Sai," she'd said the last time she'd met him off premises, as it were. It had become one of their habits, a Thursday late-afternoon hookup in a different hotel room each time. He always had a two-hour window of downtime, unless there was an emergency surgery. He took full advantage of it and, by the time Laura made her outlandish request, he was able to self-justify the blatant cheating he was doing on his wife. Oh yes, he was damn good at convincing himself that because she had initially agreed to participating in the "neighborhood gatherings," he had every right to go outside the strict realm of those, straight between the welcoming thighs of a fellow participant without letting Emily know he was doing it.

He groaned and clutched his stomach, sick of himself and his ongoing inexcusable behavior. That had landed him square in the middle of Tom Franks' dilemma, at least as his wife represented it.

"He's about to do something...rash. Something I keep telling him not to do. But he's letting his inner puritan get the best of him, I guess."

Sai had stared at her, slack-jawed and woozy, as they lay naked for a few more minutes in the hotel bed and she explained her plan. Then he'd agreed to help her. Like the complete fool he'd been.

A simple plan, on the face of it. And he could get all the necessary materials to make it happen. Timing was important, of course, but they'd manage that between them.

Sleep finally stole over his fevered consciousness, and he sat back on the recliner, his feet up, his dreams a dark, foggy tangle of sex, bathwater, and syringes.

Chapter Thirty

T*hree...*

• • • •

ALLEN PUSHED THROUGH the chlorinated water, churning with his arms and legs before executing a perfect somersault to continue his laps going the other way. He'd been at this for almost an hour, but he had to keep moving. Otherwise, he'd shatter into a zillion tiny pieces, each piece guilty of bad behavior, up to and including...

He increased his speed, blocking out the rest of that thought. Long gone into his exercise white space, he had a vague realization that his body was still moving, but that it was starting to put up a fuss. Muscles were crying out for rest or hydration, cramping and tightening in his shoulders and hips. When he couldn't push himself another inch, he gripped the side of the pool and hauled himself up and out.

Limping his way toward the lounge chair and a towel, he cursed under his breath at every step. He needed to close the pool this weekend, but something about that—about ending the summer—made him depressed and pissed off in equal measure. He swiped at his hair and draped the towel around his shoulders, taking deep breaths until he had it back under control.

He could hear Janice humming and puttering around inside, cleaning, as usual. It was her go-to activity whether she was happy, sad, content, or anxious. He should consider himself lucky, he knew, about pretty much every aspect of his wife's demeanor, including her willingness to allow him to play outside the technical boundaries of their marriage, as long as she got to do the same thing. He knew that, times about a million. But, sometimes, he wondered how much of her willingness was setting him up to fail—to be the bad guy, the horn dog, the ever-cheating spouse to her martyr.

He sighed and rubbed his eyes. Not that it mattered one bit anymore. Now that Laura Franks had decided to bust back into their lives and scatter all the puzzle pieces they'd been slowly putting back together. She always did know how to ruin things. She'd outed him to Janice, for some reason, risking her own position in the carefully structured female pecking order. He had been doing her on the side, but she'd made some kind of weird confession to his wife, getting him in extra-special hot water in the process.

"I tolerate all of it, Allen," Janice had said, her eyes dry, her sculpted chin lifted in the face of his legitimately contrite guilt. "I know I instigate a lot of it. But if you can't manage to keep your dick in your pants after everything I've orchestrated for you, then I think I may be done. For good."

And that, he knew, was no idle threat. But he'd be lost without her. Ergo, he'd spent his requisite time in the doghouse, letting her roam around and screw whomever she wanted on the cul-de-sac while he stayed home, minding his manners. Finally, he'd been let out, set free to join her in some of the better sideline activities. Which had thrown him headlong into the mess with Tom and Laura Franks.

Of course, if his own son weren't such a dumbass...

Allen sat back and closed his eyes, letting the early fall afternoon sun warm and dry his skin. Why in God's name the woman hadn't asked him to do something simple, like get her a good deal on a nose job, he had no clue. But, of course, there was that whole thing about the Franks being investigated by the feds. Tom claimed that he was going to turn A.J.—and that little shitweasel Murphy—in to the authorities. She had him by the balls, as it were, which forced him to help her. All while keeping it from Janice.

"Allen?"

"Yes, dear," he said, his eyes still closed.

"Would you like something to drink?"

"Some iced tea, if you don't mind."

"I'll be right out."

He drifted, noting the slight coolness in the breeze, reminding him swimming pool season was over. On the heels of that innocuous thought, Laura Franks blazed in, searing his brain with memory of her tight body, her dirty mouth, her not terribly subtle neediness for a man who'd be in charge for a while. Tom was the quintessential beta, ever deferring to her and her opinions and ideas about everything from child-rearing to his career. She'd been the one to push him to leave corporate life and strike out on his own. She'd rounded up clients for him, including A.J., Ryan Murphy, and whoever else was needing someone creative to cook their dirty books.

Turned out, she'd been the one to push Ryan into business with a certain group of individuals who did not take it lightly when someone became unwilling to play their game their way. He didn't know much about organized crime other than what he watched on TV but it would appear that his neighbor, Tom, was, as they say, "connected."

Allen tried to keep her out of his head, but she was stuck fast, like burrs on his trouser leg. Her and her "You have to help us, Allen, or we'll be forced to tell the feds about A.J."

"What about A.J.?" he'd asked.

"About the drugs, Allen. Please. Are you really that clueless?"

He hadn't been. Of course he hadn't been. But some part of him wished it not to be true. He'd managed to pretend that it wasn't. Until it hit him upside the head with the force of a two-by-four. His son, his only male progeny had not only barely passed high school, dropped out of two different expensive colleges, been dumped by his first wife, and still went around acting like some kind of entitled brat. He'd now managed to get caught up in money laundering for a couple of prescription drug dealers—as in he was helping fuel the opioid mess right under their noses. The fact of that matter made him want to go breathe into a paper bag.

Sometimes he wished he could leave like his daughter had, to move to the farthest reaches of the U.S., somewhere on the West Coast, and never acknowledge any of this ever again. But, of course, he couldn't. So, he'd agreed to help her and Tom, to assist with her plan that sounded somewhere between a bad episode of television and a mediocre thriller movie. They'd never get away with it, he'd figured.

He'd been wrong.

"Here you go," Janice said, startling him from out of a half sleep, almost knocking the full glass from her hand. "Goodness, Allen. Are you all right?" She wiped her fingers on her jeans and took the seat next to him.

"Yes, sorry, Janny," he said. He wasn't—all right that is. But he had to play this thing cool.

"I hear our new neighbors are unhappy with us," he said, keeping his gaze on the pool's smooth blue surface.

"That would seem to be the case," she said, equally neutral in tone and manner.

He paused. "What happened?"

She moved ever slightly, turning her face toward his. It took him almost a full minute to realize she was livid, with a razor's edge of panic.

"Laura Franks happened," she said, not taking her gaze off his.

"Ah, I see."

"And what, exactly, do you *see* about it, Allen?"

He closed his eyes. *Here we go. Into the brink.*

He shifted, putting his legs on the side of the chair between them, his feet on the patio. He put his still-full glass on a short, glass-topped table. "Janice, you know I had to do it."

"I'm sure I don't know what you're talking about." She looked away from him, her jaw clenched in a way that would only make her skin sag more. He kept that little truth nugget to himself.

"I had to help them. I had to make sure he didn't get A.J. into trouble."

"Well, it didn't work, Allen. Tom is dead. Laura's back. And A.J. is still in trouble."

"That's because he's an idiot."

"I can't argue that point. But still." She looked at him, her eyes now hidden by the sunglasses she'd slipped on. "I told him he had to turn himself in. That it was his only hope of salvaging anything, of not putting our grandbabies in danger." Her voice broke. He put a hand on her arm.

"I told him the same thing," he said. "Hell, I offered to go with him to the...wherever you go for such things. But that won't alleviate the other problem."

She sucked in a breath and pulled her arm away from his touch. "No. It doesn't," she said, her voice low. "But I need you to know something." She spun around and sat facing him, her knees next to his. He observed their hands as she took his in hers—the one thing he couldn't nip, tuck, lift, or otherwise enhance to hide the fact of their age. "I didn't do it."

He stared at her. "Janice, I know you were there. I saw you leave the..." He paused, his throat clicking with anxiety. "The bathroom. I know you gave him...the stuff."

She sighed and put her forehead on their joined hands then looked back up at him, her eyes filled with tears. "I couldn't do it, Allen. Not for A.J., or you, or anyone else."

"But he was...he was dead when I checked later."

"He was alive when I left him. Alive and ranting about Cassie and Barrett and... heavens, I don't remember what all."

"So, what did you do in there?"

"Well, I..." She flushed and pursed her lips. "I comforted him. He was distraught about Cassie and for some reason thought Barrett was about to run off with Laura, of all things." She blew out a breath.

"You comforted him," Allen said, numb with the realization of what that actually meant with regard to the man's ultimate end that night. "But how did he get the stuff? I mean, the dope to take, you know."

"I have no idea."

"Oh," he said, feeling suddenly boneless with relief. "We didn't...I mean, he didn't take..."

"No, my love. Tom Franks didn't take the drugs A.J. gave me to give him. He died, but some other way. Drowning, is what Laura is going around telling everybody, I guess..." She swiped at her eyes.

"But the coroner's report..."

"She told Emily it was forged."

"And how would she know this?"

"I don't have any idea, and since he was cremated..." She shrugged.

He grabbed her hands again, holding them tight. "You swear to me, Janice Cooper, that you didn't..."

"Drown him? Please, Allen."

"Then who did?"

"I don't know or care. I think Laura Franks is chasing her own tail and to what end? To get more money? To get her hands on his life insurance?"

Allen sat back, the adrenaline and air whooshing out of him all at once. It hadn't been her, or them, rather. They hadn't given Tom the tiny packet of powdered poison that would have easily killed him, at least according to their drug-money-laundering son.

"I need you to make it look like an accident," Laura had said. "Like he was trying some of the, you know, the drugs or whatever, and overdosed."

"You don't get life insurance if it's a suicide."

"Don't worry about me," she'd said, clinging to him, the sweat from their recent close contact drying on their skin.

He hadn't, but, then again, he was a simple man. Give him an expensive steak, a good glass of bourbon, and a hot woman to bang, and he was happy as a pig in...well, anyway. It had been declared a suicide, at least as far as he was aware, and she'd left town. He didn't know anything about any life insurance payouts.

And she'd put on quite a show—screaming and wailing and clawing her eyes—considering she'd been the one to set the whole ridiculous thing in motion. He rubbed his forehead, as the tight knot of stress he'd been lugging around since hearing that Laura was back and causing trouble on the cul-de-sac loosened a bit.

Janice slid in next to him, draping her leg over his and letting her fingertips trail down his bare chest. He grabbed her hand and kissed her knuckles. "But we still have a problem," she said.

"I told you I'd handle that," he said, meaning it. "I'll take A.J. to the police or FBI or wherever the hell I have to. He'll probably have to go into hiding or something, right?"

"And Cynthia will get full custody of the boys. But we can't let him go on like this, can we?" She looked up at him, her expression full of fear and remorse.

"We can't." They lay together a while as the fall evening fell, making them shiver. "I'm kinda bummed about the Rosses."

She sighed and got up, pulling him to his feet. "You're such a simpleton, sometimes, but I love you."

He got up and followed her inside, upstairs, and into their bed. When he woke, hours later, he thought he heard a noise but chalked it up to the dream he'd been having. When he woke for real the next morning and went downstairs, the sight of his son's body, hanging from the ceiling fan that was making slow circles in the middle of the cathedral ceiling made him cry out in a voice he'd never heard coming from his own lips.

"Allen Junior," he croaked, making his stumbling way down the flight of steps and into the high-ceilinged room. "Oh God, my boy, Allen..."

A ladder was on the floor, kicked over. One of A.J.'s shoes was next to it. He looked up, sure he'd dreamed the whole thing. But there it was, A.J.'s body, with the fan was running on slow gear, turning him around and around and around.

"What is it?" he heard Janice call.

"Stay upstairs, Janice. I mean it," he said, using his deepest, most serious physician voice. "Stay where you are and call nine-one-one," he said, staring up at his son's denim-covered legs. He'd pissed himself, which happened. But the sight of that would likely do his mother completely in. "Stay, Janny. Please. Stay upstairs."

He sat on the couch, and waited for the proper officials to show up and cut his son down to confirm what Allen already knew.

Chapter Thirty-One

T*wo...*

• • • •

RYAN MURPHY'S MOTHER hadn't raised any fools. He'd known damn good and well what he'd been getting himself into once he'd opened up to the concept of working on some of the bigger projects in Detroit. He'd been feeling a little desperate, truth be told. The local work was drying up. While his company had a solid rep, it only took one or maybe two clients to put a kink in the works, references-wise. Never mind they might be the type of people it was impossible to please.

He sat on his back deck, glass of brown liquor in hand, glaring into the middle distance. The words of the new, goody-two-shoes accountant bounced around in his head, a few of the more alarming ones flashing red and green and blue neon behind his eyes.

"Hey," Melissa said, taking the seat next to him and putting her bare feet up on the ottoman between them.

He grunted and sipped, not anywhere near in a mood for chat, especially given what a total bitch she'd been the night before. She was pretty much spot-on correct about the whole thing anyway. He set the half-empty glass on the table at his elbow. Getting shitfaced wasn't the answer, and it would play to type, straight into her opinion of him. He had no inclination to give her that satisfaction.

He had to fix this, somehow. He stared down at his hands, finger pads calloused, nails wavy, most of them having grown back after losing the originals. Turning them over, he rubbed the back of his left one, which had a lump where he'd broken it and not been able to afford to get it set correctly, back when he'd been humping drywall and concrete, post high school. Back in the good old days when he'd been free to screw any chick he wanted.

He put his head in his hands. "Why did you do it?" he said, staring down at the deck surface. It needed to be power washed, he noted with a sort of distance.

"Why did I do what?"

He heard wine splashing into a glass. Heard her sip. Set the glass down.

"Why did you tell Tom we would help them?"

"Oh, I don't know. Something about him throwing your sorry ass under the bus unless we did," she said with a slight sneer in her voice.

"You should have told me."

"You were too busy sticking your dick in Cassie LeBlanc to pay attention to me, remember?"

He glanced over at her, opened his mouth to defend himself then stopped. She spoke the truth after all.

"This is the part where you start denying things, Murphy," she said, her eyes bright. But not with tears. Not his wife. Not in a million years.

"Melissa, you have to tell me the truth. Did you have anything to do with Tom's death?"

"For fuck's sake," she said, getting up and walking to the railing. "As long as we're being all truthful in our marriage tonight, I'll tell you. No. I didn't. I was letting him go down on me with semi-regularity though. But I don't think you can die from that."

"Why did we get into this with these people?" he asked, more of himself than anything.

His ears rang, pulse raced. She turned to face him. She looked amazing, as usual. Perfectly put together in her slim skirt, silky sleeveless shirt she'd had on under the jacket that matched the skirt, although she'd kicked off her high heels and was standing there barefoot. She looked like the killer negotiator who'd made over a million dollars the year before and was on track to make more this year. And given all of that, what was his problem? Why had he sought out Cassie, Laura, or Janice once or twice outside the agreed-upon parameters of their arrangement?

"We got seduced by a couple of experts, I guess. We were horny, bored with each other, seeking something different. Name your poison," she said, sticking one of her illicit cigs between her red lips.

He got up and walked over to her, waited until she'd had a drag then took it from her. "I'm going to ask one more time," he said, blowing out a puff of smoke then handing it back to her. "Did you have anything at all whatsoever to do with Tom Franks' death?"

She sucked on the death stick, held in the smoke, and let it curl out of her nostrils. "No. But I told them I'd be the one to 'discover' his body, to go run for Sai in time. I guess he was supposed to revive him or something, but in such a way he could be spirited out of the house as if he were dead."

"As if...he were...what the actual fuck? And you kept this from me because..."

"Because it was just this side of harebrained, but she said I had to help them, to play my part, or she'd..." A tear slipped out of one of her bright-green eyes. He watched it track through her makeup before he reached out and touched her jaw where it hung. "She said they were going to turn you in, in order to save Tom's ass, unless I did this stupid thing, covered for them, whatever, letting him go into hiding." She turned and tossed the spent butt onto the ground below them.

"But that's not how it went down, apparently," he said, blown away by this. But, of course, she'd been protecting her own interests, and their son. It wasn't about helping him.

"Nope," she said, heading back for her glass of wine.

"What did happen?" All he'd known was the chaos that night, the cops and ambulance, the crying women.

"Whatever it was, it happened before my part came into play. Whatever it was, it was a fuck-up."

"I guess so," he said. "So, now what?"

She sipped her wine, uncrossed and recrossed her legs. "I have no idea what Laura thinks she's doing. The whole thing was supposed to be a distraction, a red herring or whatever. Fake his death with Sai's help. Get him out of town. That's all I knew or wanted to know. Since they both told me that's all I needed to know. But"—she shrugged—"he died for real. Laura's running around scaring the new people, claiming Tom was murdered, drowned, or whatever. It's a complete mess."

"That it is."

"What are you going to do about those contracts?"

He ran a hand down his face then wiped his lips. "I don't have a choice. I have to go through with the ones I'm locked into. These aren't guys I can say, 'Oh hey, I discovered that you're super-bad dudes, and I don't want to be a part of it anymore, so, later.' You know what I mean?"

She nodded. "Finish them up, and let's move."

"Move? Where? What about my company?"

"I make enough money for us to live on and then some. I can pick up my license somewhere else. Or maybe I'll open a bookstore, or a dog daycare, I don't care as long as I don't have to live here anymore."

As surprised as he was by this outburst, he was even more so when she jumped up and ran over to him, wrapping her arms around his neck, her face wet with tears. "I don't like it here anymore. Please. Can we leave?"

"I'm...I don't..." He held onto her, his mind whirling with this new concept. "I still don't get what happened."

"Someone killed Tom, Ryan. Someone not me and not you, I'm assuming. And Laura has decided she's going to figure out who it is. Never mind the giant scam they'd set up to escape from their own entanglements with the IRS or the FBI. Who the hell knows?" She grabbed the front of his shirt in one fist and glared into his eyes. "Take me and your son away from this freak show of a neighborhood."

He nodded, kissed her absently. "I have to finish those contracts first, which means I gotta hold off the new accountant lady."

"Fire her," she said.

"What if she reports me?"

"We'll find a good lawyer and threaten to sue her if she does."

"God, Melissa. That'll make everything worse."

She reached down and tugged at his belt buckle. "No, it's the solution. We'll work the problem together. And then we'll get the hell out of this place. Okay? Baby?"

"Okay, but what you're doing right now is going to lead us somewhere else."

She grinned and pulled him by his belt loop back into the house.

· · · ·

THAT NIGHT, HE SAT in his home office, turning slowly, around and around in the overpriced desk chair. He'd sent the email, telling the new accountant her services were no longer required. He'd need someone new to handle everything. And had no earthly idea where to begin to look. But he felt lighter than he had since they'd resumed their group sex thing with the neighbors. That had been a capital B Bad plan. Thankfully, he and Melissa agreed they wouldn't be participating anymore.

He fired up the computer and started doing a search for businesses in Manistee. They'd decided they'd move into the lake house first, leave this damn place behind lock, stock, and barrel. Melissa had already researched the schools, found the best teacher for Dan. That was the thing about her, he mused as he dug into his research about businesses he might pick up on the cheap. She never went into a anything unprepared.

It was well past midnight by the time he shut everything down, drank a couple of glasses of water, and headed to bed. After checking in Dan's room to make sure he was still asleep—the kid had been getting up and wandering around some lately, which Ryan realized meant he was picking up on the general stress level in the house.

A change would be good for all of them, he decided as he shut the boy's door. The big window at the end of their upper landing gave him a view of the end of the cul-de-sac, where the Coopers' house stood. A car was sitting in front of it, idling. Ryan watched it a few minutes, wondering what was up. When he saw someone get out of the car and head for the house, he ran down the steps, grabbed the baseball bat he kept in the hall closet—leaving behind the pistol he kept in a locked box next to his bed—and opened his front door. It was too late for company and, as much as he currently hated this damn place, he wasn't about to tolerate creepers or break-ins.

"Hey," he hollered, shouldering the bat. "What're you doing?"

"It's me," the man-shaped shadow said. "A.J."

"Oh okay, sorry, man." He waved. The shadow waved. Ryan went back inside, put the bat away, and headed upstairs, thinking he'd wake Little Miss Super Prepared up for another round.

Chapter Thirty-Two

O*ne...*

. . . .

CASSIE SAT WITH HER feet in Barrett's lap, sipping decaf tea and snacking on popcorn. The TV was on, some random football game. She was scrolling through her Instagram feed, noting all the lovely likes and comments on her most recent posts—she'd been showing off her baby bump now that she didn't look or feel like warmed-over death. Barrett was doing something on his iPad, checking his stocks, or looking at porn, more likely. It was cozy, she thought as she wiggled her toes, smiling when he put his warm hand on the top of her feet.

They'd picked out and made an offer on a new house, and she hadn't told a single soul on this street about it. That felt better than almost anything.

Almost.

The doorbell rang, startling her. She moved her feet, allowing Barrett to get up and answer it, then rose to follow him. She peeked around his torso, her heart jumping up into her throat at the sight of Laura Franks, backlit by the cheerful string of orange Halloween lights she and Barrett had strung around the doorway. They'd decided to make it look like they were A-OK. That nothing was amiss. That they weren't within a few weeks of moving the hell away from here.

"She needs to leave," she said before turning away and walking into the kitchen. "Make her leave, Barrett."

Barrett stood, hand on the door, staring at the woman he'd been obsessed with. Then he turned to look at Cassie, who stood in the kitchen, gnawing on her lip, running her hand over the top of her belly.

It didn't matter now. None of this crap mattered.

"Did you tell her?" Cassie said, stomping back to the entry. "Well?"

"Tell her what?" Barrett looked tired.

"About our baby," she said, barely resisting the urge to stomp her foot. "Tell her."

"The baby is mine," he said, his voice a tad stronger when he turned back to Laura. "We had a DNA test."

Laura frowned at him. "I thought..."

"Yeah, well, that one-in-a-thousand thing?" He shrugged. "It worked." Cassie wished he'd put his arm around her or something. She glared at Laura.

"So. You can go now. Tom's...thing wasn't my fault." Her face was burning.

"Cassie," Barrett said, reaching for her as if to shut her up.

"No. We don't need to talk to her anymore. I want her to leave."

He turned to the woman who still stood there, staring at them both.

"Someone killed him," she said, her voice whispery. "He...I...we had this thing we'd planned. To keep him safe. And...and..." She broke down then, sobbing, leaning against the doorjamb.

"Oh, for heaven's sake," Cassie said. "Get inside before anyone else sees you."

She tugged the hysterical women into the entryway and shut the door. "Barrett, get her some water. Come on, already." She didn't want or need this. They were about to make their clean getaway. The second she'd found out the baby was actually Barrett's, and he'd come home and held her all night, made love to her twice, held her some more then taken her house shopping the hell away from this place all day the next day, she knew everything was going to be fine.

All she had to do was get Laura Franks the hell out of her house, but she wasn't about to let the neighbors see her having some kind of fit in her doorway. They sat around her kitchen table, glasses of water in front of them. She gave Laura a box of tissues. "Now, what is all this about a plan to keep him safe?" She shot Barrett a glance. He had on his lawyer face, serious but neutral.

Laura blew her nose, drank some water then took a deep breath. "He was about to get busted by the IRS. He was trying to work a deal. He was going to...t-t-t-to turn in some of his clients. But I figured out something better. We'd pretend he died, then set it up so he could escape, you know, by ambulance."

"Set it up?" Barrett said, leaning forward. "Set what up?"

"He was going to... Take the drugs, you know. The oxi or whatever A.J. was getting for us. Then Sai was going to come over to revive him with Narcan, but pretend he was dead." She wiped her eyes, which were streaming again. "But it didn't work. I mean, he ran upstairs, you know, about the time you said you were coming over to tell him you were leaving with me." She glared at Barrett then shot Cassie an apologetic look. "Sai was going to come over then, after Janice."

"What did Janice have to do with it?"

Laura sighed. "I was covering my bases, okay? Her boy launders money for dealers. He gave her the drugs to bring to us." She sucked in a shuddery breath. "Melissa was going to find him, run over and get Sai."

"Wow. Everyone was in on this little plan." Barrett's brow creased. "I'm pretty sure we don't need to hear any more. Cassie, honey, let's get you upstairs." He got up and practically yanked Cassie to her feet.

"Wait," she said, brushing him off. "I want to know more."

"No, you don't. Trust me. We already know too much."

Laura sat looking pitiful. "No, god damn it, I want to hear all of this," Cassie insisted.

Barrett let go of her arm. "Laura, you need to leave," he said, not taking his gaze off Cassie. "Now."

"But..." Cassie said, her need to know how Laura was spinning it greater than her desire to get the woman out of her house.

"Now!" Barrett's deep voice boomed through the kitchen, making her flinch.

Laura got up and headed for the door. She turned at the last minute. "Someone murdered him, Barrett. Held him under the water, drowned him sometime after he went upstairs when you were there, and before I could get Sai over. I think Janice did it."

"God damn it, Laura," Barrett yelled, marching over to her. "I told you to get the hell out of here."

She ran out, slamming the door behind her. Cassie was shaking when Barrett came back to her. "You have to forget everything she told us, do you understand me?"

She nodded.

"Tell me, Cassie. It's important."

"I understand you. I didn't hear her say anything."

"Jesus humped-up Christ," he said, running a hand down his face. "This has gone beyond fucked."

Cassie watched him pace a few minutes. "Let's go to bed," she said, touching his arm.

He smiled and followed her to the bedroom.

"I need you to hold me, okay?"

He nodded and held her until she could tell by his breathing he was asleep. The carpet was soft under her feet as she padded barefoot into the living room with the wall of windows. She curled up on the large leather couch, looking out into the dark, memories crowding in on her.

Tom Franks had been a kind and generous lover when they were together as a group. Sought after by all the women. A nice guy to everyone around him on top of that, including his bitchy, overbearing wife. But when he'd come over that one time, wanting to mess around while Laura and their kids were at her parents' and Barrett was on a business trip, she'd been tempted, but it hadn't felt right, and she'd told him no.

He'd apologized afterward because he was such a nice guy.

Tears burned her eyes, slid down her face. She stared at her hands, turning them over and over, pondering the strength in them that had surprised her on more than one occasion.

As she was walking back to the bedrooms, she saw a car drive down the cul-de-sac. Curious, since she knew way more about her neighbors' business than she should, she went to the front window, parted the blinds, and watched it park and idle in front of the Coopers'. Then the headlamps went off. Someone got out. The door to the Murphys' house opened, showing Ryan in silhouette. She heard him holler. The guy in front of the Coopers' hollered back. Ryan went back inside. She let the blinds close again.

This whole Tom thing was going to cause trouble. Laura was already stirring it up. Cassie shuddered as tears began to fall at the memory of him, of Tom, leaning in her doorway, wheedling his way into her house, then grabbing her arm, hurting her, forcing her upstairs into her and Barret's bedroom. Then he'd...he'd forced himself on her, he'd hurt her. The son of a bitch had raped her, fucked her like some kind of an animal on her bed, pretending the whole time she wanted it that way.

She bit her lip. She'd been furious with him. And yet somehow, Laura was the one who was wronged?

Yes, it was time to leave this terrible place.

She headed into her bedroom. It would all be over soon enough. She crawled into bed and kissed her husband awake, already looking forward to the day they'd move away from here.

Chapter Thirty-Three

Veritas
Earlier that evening...

Amelia sat and observed Michael as he questioned Laura. The woman had reason to believe any one of their immediate neighbors could've snuck in and held her husband under the water in the bathtub until he drowned, which was more than a tiny bit alarming. But after about an hour of it, she was starting get suspicious. It was too neat and tidy, too well-thought-out. Too much like the plot of a television series that had jumped the shark but was grasping at plot straws in the interest of staying relevant.

Granted, she'd had a while to contemplate it all, leading her to the multiple scenarios she'd spelled out to Michael, Amelia thought as she got up to refill teacups. She checked the time, yawned, and motioned over Laura's head that Michael should consider ending the conversation. It was getting silly, all these wild accusations. All the stories about faking a death, then being surprised he was actually dead. It made no sense whatsoever.

Michael nodded to indicate he'd seen her but kept his focus on the woman in front of him. He was pacifying her, at best. It wasn't like he was a criminal defense lawyer. Why was he wasting all this time on her? She needed to leave.

"Okay, I'm going to recommend you contact a guy I went to law school with. He practices out of Detroit." Michael wrote something on a page of his ubiquitous yellow legal pad, ripped it off, and pushed it across the table toward her. Laura took it but didn't move, other than to put a shaking hand on Michael's arm. That simple motion did a real number on Amelia's rattled nerves. Realizing he'd chastise her later for acting immaturely, she plucked the other woman's hand off her husband's arm and put it back on the table.

"Time for you to go," she said, not bothering to keep the irritation out of her voice. Laura glanced up at her, her expression an odd combination of angry and smug. Amelia gave herself a mental shake. The woman was distraught, she reminded her inner, jealous cynic. She didn't know what she was doing.

Michael frowned at Amelia and got up from his chair, giving her a slight hip bump out of the way. She moved but stayed close in case Laura got handsy again, watching Michael take her elbow and guide her toward the front door, making noises about "hiring the right lawyer" and "it will be expensive but worth it for her peace of mind" or some such nonsense.

Finally, the door shut, leaving them alone. Amelia waited, hands on the back of one of her favorite leather living room chairs. Michael stood a minute, keeping his back to her. Something about the set of his shoulders made her anxious. Finally, he turned around, rubbing the back of his neck.

"This is..." He sighed and looked up at the ceiling of her dream home—or at least that's how she'd thought of it up until about a week ago.

"Completely sick? Wrong in more ways than I can count?"

"Yeah." He crossed his arms and glared at her. "All of that and a little more."

"Do you believe any of that?" She waved a hand at the closed door. "Seriously?"

"I did, at first. But I don't know what I believe now. All those people we...we..." He leaned against the wall, closed his eyes, and slid down to his heels, face in his hands.

Amelia gnawed the inside of her cheek, already ragged from the past weeks' worth of stress. She watched, her feet frozen in place, unable to go to him and comfort him, her fingertips dug into the leather back of the chair that at that moment seemed ridiculously overpriced and showy. The sound of Tyler crying out from his room upstairs was the only thing that forced her to move, and then she felt stiff, as if she'd been standing in one position for way too long.

Her baby boy was sitting up and sobbing his head off, fists smashed into his eye sockets. Another bad dream, she figured as she scooped him up and sat on the side of his bed, cooing and calming him. While her mind was still downstairs with Michael, agonizing over the fact of the awful choices they'd both made in the past six weeks. She pressed her lips to Tyler's sweaty hair, trying to get him to stop crying.

There was so much wrong in the world—from climate change and homelessness to animal abuse and food deserts—all of which she'd believed she would be doing something about, right here in her newly adopted town with her successful husband and growing family. But, instead of doing anything remotely good, she'd done what? She'd jumped into some kind of sick sex club, with a group of people she'd completely misjudged. Because as much as she doubted Laura's wild accusations for some of them, for others, she could see it happening. Some of them were, to put it mildly, narcissistic whack jobs who might commit a murder to keep anything negative about them from emerging.

At that thought, she began to shake all over. Tyler pulled away from her and stared up at her. "Mama?" He touched her face, which was when she realized she'd started to cry. "Mama," he said, before sticking his thumb into his mouth and snuggling against her neck. When he reached up to pat her cheek, as if he were the one whose job it was to comfort her, it solidified her resolve. She sat and rocked her boy a few more minutes until he dropped back to sleep. Once he was tucked back into his bed, she sat a few seconds, gathering her thoughts.

She rose slowly, still stiff, her mind awash with images of her most recent encounter with the Coopers. A blush rose, along with a wave of nausea that forced her to run from Tyler's room into the guest bathroom instead of going to her own suite. The wave passed, but she stayed in the bathroom, staring into the toilet bowl.

"Ames?" A soft knock at the half-open door made her flinch and stand up, wiping her lips. "You all right in there?"

"No," she said, launching herself at him. "No, Michael. I'm not. We're not. We have to get out of this house." She had her face jammed into his chest, needing to hear—to feel—his heartbeat, his arms around her, more than she needed anything at the moment. "I'm s-s-s-sorry."

He hugged her close then led her out of the bathroom and into their bedroom. "Sit," he said, guiding her to one of the chairs in front of the large window. "Let's talk." He dropped into the one across from her, leaned forward, and took her hands in his. "I'm going to come clean about something. I want you to do the same, okay?" He ducked his head, making her meet his gaze. She nodded. He took a deep breath.

"Okay, so..." He paused. She stayed quiet, already tamping down the jealousy flames threatening to choke her. "I did hook up with Melissa, three times, all in empty condos, like Janice said." He blew out a breath. "I spent a few hours messing around with Janice while Allen watched, too. And, let me tell you, that gave me a serious slave-and-overseer vibe." He shuddered then smiled at her, squeezing her hands. "Now, you."

"When?" she asked, her voice small, but steady.

Michael sighed. "I've met Melissa for the last three weeks, on Thursday afternoons. The Janice-and-Allen thing was the weekend you took Ty to your parents.'"

Her throat clicked when she tried to swallow.

Jesus, woman, you were no better. Arguably worse. Stop applying a double standard and tell him what he thinks he wants to know. She let anger feed her, which, in hindsight, was a perfectly terrible plan.

"Fine," she said, pulling her hands out of his and sitting back, legs crossed. "I let Janice fluff me in the hot tub then let Allen fuck me while she watched." She paused, feeling the tiny, mean-spirited smile play around her lips while Michael tried to keep his cool. "Oh, and yeah, I went over to Cassie and Barrett's one afternoon for a threesome." She touched her fingertips as if counting. "Right, and there was that time Emily and Sai invited me over for a glass of wine..." She shrugged and settled her hands on her lap.

"I assume you did more than drink their wine," he said, his voice distorted from clenching his teeth.

"I did," she said. "And how."

"Amelia, this isn't a joke."

"I'm not joking, Michael," she said, leaning on his name. "Don't lecture me."

He took a deep breath.

She waited, the jealous fire still flaring, burning her eyes and throat.

"You've had sex without me with everyone on this cul-de-sac." He didn't frame it as a question.

"No. I've never had sex with Ryan Murphy outside of that one time at one of the Coopers' parties when we...I mean you and he...." She felt the blush spread up her neck. "Ironic, isn't it?"

"I wouldn't use that word for it." He got up and started pacing. "God damn it, what were we thinking? It's like, they drew us into the whole party thing so they could, I don't know, separate us, pit us against each other like this."

She sucked in a breath, the now-slightly sputtering flickers of remaining anger going out as if he'd poured a bucket of water over them. Tears sprang to her eyes. She let them fall as she watched him pace, running his hands over his close-cropped hair, in between the fist clenching and the jaw grinding. "Yes," she said. "You're right."

"Hell yes I'm right. Jesus, Amelia. What...why...I mean, are you not happy with us? With how we are? Why all the...the..."

"Cheating?" she spat out, her voice breaking. "I don't know. It's a weird, accepting mindset. I'm sure you can relate to it."

He shot her a look full of dark, seething rage. She shrank back into the cushy chair in the face of it. Then his expression seemed to crack in half, and he dropped back into the chair across from her. "I don't know why I did it, either. And I'm...it's..." He blew out a breath. "I'm having a tough time with this. I'm not gonna lie."

She could tell that much. Amelia wasn't sure she'd ever seen the man as flat-out furious as he was right now. But she felt the same way, if not more. They glared at each other in silence, the sounds of the house carrying on around them. A ticking grandfather clock. The dishwasher changing cycles in the kitchen. Late-season crickets outside.

"I'm perfectly happy with you," she said, getting up slowly and pushing him back into the chair. He let his arms flop over the sides as he stared up at her. "I'll never not be happy with you. You make me who I am. Who we are is who I am, now. And I'm never going to do a damn thing to risk that." She straddled his lap, her need for him like a living, breathing animal inside her, pushing her forward, urging her to do the familiar things.

He felt the same way, she could tell. All this talk about sex with their neighbors, watching or not watching, had made her want him so badly her bones ached. He let her kiss him, parted his lips when she pressed her tongue between them. Didn't say anything one way or another when she slid his shorts and underwear down, but he kept his hands off her, making her do the work. The entire time, he stared at her, his deep-brown eyes barely blinking until she stopped and lifted her shirt up and off.

"Oh...God," he groaned low and loud, his face jammed against her neck. "Mine," he said, his voice low.

"Yes, Michael. I am." She pushed away from his chest, meeting his gaze. "We have to move."

"I know we do. But can I not think about that for a couple more days?"

She lifted up and off him and headed into the bathroom to clean up. "Let's have another baby," she said, returning with a water they kept in a small glass-fronted fridge in the closet.

"Fine, great, yeah, whatever you want." He downed half the bottle in one gulp.

"I think Cassie might have done it," he said, staring out into the darkness beyond their windows.

Amelia took the bottle from him and finished it. "Really? She's so...tiny. Like a pregnant baby bird."

"I get that, but Laura kept coming back to her, as if the least obvious person should be the one. Considering what happened with her and Tom and the bun in her oven."

"I don't think so," Amelia said, as exhaustion stole over her in a rush. "I think it was Laura. She seems like the type to me."

"I gotta sleep," he said, lurching up off the chair and onto the bed, his face down in the pillow.

"Okay, but, Michael?" She sat and pulled covers up over him, her love for him strong. And at that moment she acknowledged that she might kill him if he'd knocked up some other woman, regardless of their "arrangement" about sex.

"Hmmm?"

"Don't let that woman back into my house, okay? Promise?"

He rolled onto his back. "I won't."

"Good." She pulled the duvet up to his neck with a smile. "She kind of scares me."

"She's harmless," he said, shifting over to his right side. "I love you, Ames. And I am sorry."

"I am, too, but as long as you're telling me everything..."

"Mm-hmm," he mumbled. "Gotta sleep now."

She patted his hip a few seconds, as if he were a child who needed soothing into slumber, pondering the possibility that little Cassie LeBlanc might be a murderer. Still pondering, she headed downstairs, figuring she'd do some more laundry or something. But she'd been super-efficient the day before. The laundry hamper was empty. The counters clean. Rugs vacuumed. She waited for the dishwasher to finish then put dishes away, her mind a pleasant, post-orgasmic blank.

After sitting almost forty-five minutes in the window seat next to the kitchen table, a glass of red wine in her hand, she realized it was well past midnight. As she was passing by the living room window to shut the blinds, she saw headlights from a car turning onto the street. Intrigued in a halfhearted way, she watched it head down to the Coopers' house and stop, idling with the headlamps off.

No longer interested, she flipped the blinds closed and headed for the stairs. She added a hot bath to her usual pre-bed ritual, which went a long way toward easing her still-twanging nerves.

It was that damn Laura and her wild stories. It had invaded her very bloodstream. Chaos on the part of other people always threw off her carefully regimented life. Sighing as the heat and fragrant bubbles loosened her tight muscles, she eased farther down until only her eyes and nose were above the water's surface.

She let her fingertips climb up the sides of the deep tub, trying to come to terms with what her marriage had been through the last couple of months. Which brought her to the same conclusion she'd already formulated. These people were poison, toxic vampires, like she'd said to Janice—which, she now realized were Laura's words, used to describe this very group of people.

It was too confusing. One minute, she was convinced that Michael was right, that Cassie had drowned Tom somehow, probably with Barrett's help. Hadn't Barrett and Laura been screwing around on the side, too? She'd said Barrett had told her he'd run off with her and her kids. Which was ridiculous. Amelia felt sorry for Laura for believing it. Barrett LeBlanc was one of the biggest egos in the group, but he was smooth, polished in a way that none of the others were, and he got away with being a giant shithead.

What about Ryan Murphy? She'd avoided him at first. Not that he wasn't attractive. He was, in a short, handsome handyman kind of way. She understood his appeal. He'd been amazingly in tune with her body and its triggers the one time she and Michael had... She squeezed her eyes shut. She should not know this much about her damn neighbors. It wasn't right.

But could he have done it? Killed Tom Franks by holding him underwater until he died? It would've taken someone pretty strong, or really mad. But she'd listened to enough true crime podcasts to know, in heat of the moment, most humans because strong enough to do what needed to be done.

She shivered and pulled herself up and out of the warm water. Her limbs were heavy and languorous, her body fully sated by the one and only man she'd ever need. They needed to decide where they were going. As far as she was concerned, this damn town could stay in her rearview mirror. She'd been wrong. So, maybe Michael should choose this time.

Lotion applied, teeth brushed, vitamins taken, she slid in behind Michael, wrapping her body around his, her arm over his waist. Dreams were filling her subconscious, dragging her toward sleep when she heard a siren. Michael mumbled something and flipped over onto his back. She tried to ignore it, figuring something was going on over near campus.

But a loud burst of the thing pierced her dreaming brain, making her sit straight up. "Michael," she said, poking his abs. "Michael, wake up."

"Huh?" He sat up, rubbing his eyes at the same time a second siren blasted, sounding like it was on their front lawn, hell, in their living room. They scrambled out of bed and grabbed sweatshirts and shorts. She stopped outside Tyler's room, her heart racing, praying he wouldn't wake up while Michael took the stairs three at a time, hitting the front door and opening it in one quick jerk. The front room filled with red-and-blue strobing lights. Amelia came down the steps slower, her entire body one tight band of terror. She made her way to the open front door, hand to her throat, her mind taking in the scene.

A fire truck, an ambulance, and a police car were gathered around the Coopers' house. She could hear something odd, out of place, now that the sirens had stopped. A consistent kind of sound, familiar and yet not at the same time. Michael was standing at the foot of their driveway, hands on his hips. She looked around, willing that sound out of her head because she knew damn well what it was.

Sai and Emily were on their front lawn, arms around each other. Their festively lit pumpkins making a mockery of the current scene. Ryan was walking quickly toward the Coopers', carrying...she squinted, of all things, a baseball bat. There was no sign of Melissa, but she was likely trying to calm down their poor, autistic boy.

The LeBlancs' house was pitch-black, no sign of life anywhere other than the silly orange lights around their doorway. They must be out of town, she thought as she made her way to Michael's side. The ambulance crew rolled in a stretcher while they watched. Each couple stayed in their space, which suited her.

But the more she heard that sound, the more she knew she had to get down there. "I need to go," she said to Michael. He tightened his grip on her waist.

"No. It's their mess."

"Don't you hear that?"

Michael closed his eyes and nodded his head.

"I'm going." She started toward the Coopers' house, following the horrific sound of Janice Cooper's wails of distress. Her screams, Amelia thought as she kept going, shoving her way past the cops into the house with an "I'm family," kind of a confidence.

"Allen," she said, trying to figure out what was going on if he were fine, sitting upright and perfectly healthy, if a bit zombie-like. She headed toward him, looking for Janice, still following the sound of her voice.

He looked at her, his head moving in slow motion. His face was haggard, his expression horrified. "What is it?" She grabbed his arm.

She followed his gaze, as he stared into the large, cathedral-ceilinged family room. There was a flurry of activity, concentrated in the middle, under a slowly turning ceiling fan. When she located Janice, curled up on the floor, holding onto something that looked like... Amelia put her hand over her mouth.

"Oh...Allen," she said.

Janice kept screaming.

Chapter Thirty-Four

O*mnia*

• • • •

CASSIE WOKE FROM A near-dead sleep, convinced she'd heard something. She did that a lot. It irritated Barrett since he was such a light sleeper. But he still lay snoozing away, oblivious. Sleepiness draped over her, dragging her back down into the warm cocoon of covers and Barrett's body.

The same sound she'd first heard hit her brain, jerking her awake again, this time on full alert, ears ringing, pulse racing. It was the French doors out onto the deck. There was a distinct scrape and squeak when they were opened or closed—something Barrett bitched about every time they used the doors, but they'd both forget about it until the next time they opened them. And she'd heard that sound twice, she was certain of it.

She slid out from under the covers. "Barrett," she said in a whisper yell. "God damn it," she said, sliding her hand under the swell of her stomach.

She yanked the covers off him and onto the floor. He snorted and sat up straight. "What? What is it? What's wrong?"

"Shh," she said. "Listen."

He rubbed his face then got up and walked to the half-closed bedroom door, naked, his usual sleeping state. "I don't hear any—"

She froze at the distinct sound of a glass being set on their granite countertop. "What the ever-loving fuck?" Barrett reached for the door handle, but she grabbed his arm.

"No. Wait."

She pointed to the side table drawer where she knew he kept a handgun in a small locked safe. He frowned at her. "It's some kid, probably."

"I don't care. Take that damn gun." She pointed to the drawer again.

He grabbed a pair of shorts and T-shirt, put them on then took the gun from the safe.

"Is it loaded?" she asked.

"Jesus, Cassie, what's gotten into you?"

"This," she said, pointing to her belly. "Our baby, Barrett. I want him protected."

"Okay, calm down." He checked the chamber. "It's loaded. Stay here."

She crouched behind the door, watching him head down the hallway.

"Laura," she heard him say. "What the hell are you…"

A gunshot shattered the air like a broken mirror, making her scream and slap her hands over her ears. In the silence that followed, she stumbled out into the hallway, headed for the kitchen. "Barrett," she was shrieking. For some reason, there were ambulances, a fire truck, police cars already in the cul-de-sac.

Who'd called them? How could they have known?

She skidded to a stop. It was dark—too dark. What had happened to her nightlights? She hated the dark. "Barrett? Honey?"

"He's here," a female voice said. Cassie's face got hot.

"What do you want, Laura? Where's my husband?"

"He's right here, Cass. Relax."

"I need to turn on a light."

"Do that, and I'll put another bullet in him, this time in a spot that will kill him a lot faster."

"What? What are you talking about?"

"Jesus, stop your mewling already."

Cassie smelled something coppery, metallic. She put her hands around her belly protectively. "Where is Barrett?" Her voice broke at the end.

"I told you, he's right here."

"Cassie, go," Barrett said from somewhere inside the large kitchen. She squinted, her eyes adjusting enough that she could make out shapes, distinct from the appliances and countertops. His voice sounded watery, pinched.

"Barrett," she said, moving into the dark room.

"I said go, god damn it," he said with a grunt of pain.

"Cassie, sweetie," Laura said, her voice as sharp as a blade. "Come on in here. We need to have a little chat."

"I'm not…" She backed up, her hands on her belly as if shielding it.

"Come in here, or I'm going to shoot your precious Barrett right between his lying eyeballs, or maybe I'll blow his dick off. What would you prefer?"

Cassie took a step forward, her breathing ragged, tears rolling down her face. "Laura, please don't..."

"Shut up, silly bitch." Her tone was light, conversational. Crazy, Cassie thought. She always had been great at pretending to be normal, that she'd be a friend, a confidant. But she'd used every single female member of their group to get at their husbands, like some kind of a succubus. Between that, and attempting to one-up Janice at every turn, she'd definitely worn out her welcome by the time Tom... Cassie shook her head, forcing thoughts of him out of her head. She didn't need any of that distraction. She and Barrett were leaving, soon. She just needed to get Laura Franks out of her life.

The red-and-blue flashing lights filled the front entry as she passed through it on her way into the large, open kitchen, which remained dark. "What do you want?"

"Well, let's see," Laura said, her voice eerily disembodied. "You let my husband fuck you way too many times. He liked it too much. But, you know, Barrett here and I...we had our moments, didn't we, lover."

Cassie heard Barrett grunt, as if he were being poked by a stick.

"How did you get in here?" She wondered if she ran out the front door toward the cops or whoever was out there would shoot first and ask questions after or if they'd actually help her.

"You didn't know? Barrett, you're a bad boy."

"Know what?" Cassie reached out and grabbed her phone from the hall table, where she'd left it the night before, wondering if she could finagle a text.

"If you use that phone, I will kill you both."

She froze. "Sorry. I'm putting it down." She swallowed hard and stepped all the way into the kitchen. "Listen, Laura, the baby is Barrett's. We had a DNA test."

"I heard."

"And now you can...not be mad at me, or whatever."

"Oh, yes I can. My husband fell for you, you granola-crunching cow. He loved you. He told me."

"I...didn't know."

"The hell you didn't."

"I swear it."

"It doesn't matter. Barrett and I were running away together anyway. He loved me. Didn't he tell you? He gave me a key. You know, to your house?"

"He told me about that, Laura. He only did that to hurt Tom. I'm sorry that he did that to you though. That's ... mean."

"That's mean," Laura said, her voice a high, little kid's mocking tone. "Oooo. Barrett's a big ol' meanie. Jesus, man, how do you stand this one?"

"Laura," Barrett, said, his voice croaky and hoarse. "Please, let her go."

"Shut up," Laura said. "I'm not done with either of you yet."

"We all know what happened to Tom," Cassie said, her voice soft. She remembered something about talking to crazy people in high-stress situations. Treat them like rabid animals. Don't trap them. Don't be confrontational.

As if reading her mind, Laura laughed, cackled, more like. "Oh my Lord. Really?"

"Yes, really." Cassie moved toward the counter to lean against it, still in the room but able to run out if she needed to.

"He was such a sap. All you ladies loved him sooo much. Ugh. It was sickening."

"Was he not the same with you?"

"He was a pussy, a...a loser. If it weren't for me, he'd still be counting beans at that stupid firm, working all hours, making nothing."

"I'm sorry that he..." She paused, at a loss for words for more reasons than she could name at the moment.

"Laura," Barrett said, his voice slightly stronger. "Let Cassie go. We can...take off, you know, like we planned?"

"You must think I'm a total idiot." Laura's voice broke on the last word.

"No one thinks that, Laura," Cassie said, trying to figure out how to talk the woman out of whatever it was she was intent on doing. She glanced behind her at the front door. The flashing lights had moved down to the end of the cul-de-sac.

Her heartbeat had calmed. Odd, considering the situation. It was as if reaching the somehow unavoidable end of this whole mess, right here, in her too-dark house with Laura Franks pointing a gun at her and Barrett was somehow the ending they all deserved.

The baby gave a fluttery kick, reminding her of her prime directive. "We don't think that, do we, Barrett?"

She moved closer to where their voices seemed to be coming from, the corner of the kitchen near the garage door. "Don't," Barrett said. "Cassie, please stay back."

"I'm calling the shots here, lover boy," Laura said. "Come on in, dear. Join us."

Cassie wondered for a split second if anyone would notice that they weren't out in their driveway, checking on whatever was going on at the Coopers'. If that would matter, in the scheme of things.

"We made a mistake," she said, keeping her voice low and slow again. "We shouldn't have done the things we did. We should've kept it inside the parties. But we didn't. None of us did."

She took another step closer to their voices, desperate to see Barrett, to make sure he was okay, but at the same time ready to bolt to protect her baby.

"We did, indeed," Laura said. "And I couldn't leave well enough alone, could I?"

"I don't know what you mean," Cassie said, her entire body shaking.

"I accused Tom of knocking you up. Not unlike all our women friends on the street did, I guess. You were totally slutting it up there for a while, weren't you, Cassie-girl?"

Cassie clenched her jaw, knowing that saying something about pots and kettles and black would not help the situation.

"I thought Tom's death would be the end of it. I could leave. Get the hell away from you sex-crazed assholes. But I couldn't do it—I can't seem to stay away."

"He hurt me," Cassie blurted, before slapping her hand over her mouth. She'd made a promise to herself to never reveal that to anyone, much less the two people in front of her, somewhere in the dark. "He hurt me," she repeated, louder this time.

"Who did?" Laura asked, sounding closer. "This one?" She flapped her empty hand behind her where Barrett sat, bleeding, probably dying. "I don't doubt it. He's kind of a selfish asshole. I mean, he won't even go down on me. Told me he never did that. What man doesn't do that?"

Cassie swallowed, feeling the dryness of her throat and mouth. "He...Tom did. He came over here one afternoon you all were gone." She heard Laura's sucked-in breath. But plowed forward. If not now, when? "He wanted to...you know."

"For fuck's sake, you little twit. You can say the words."

"He wanted to have sex with me, just the two of us, in my house. I didn't want to. I wanted to stop all of it. But he..." A single tear slid down her cheek. "He didn't care. He hurt me, Laura."

"No. That's not possible. Tom would never. He didn't have the balls for that kind of thing."

"Well, he did." Cassie put her arms around her belly, the memories filling all her senses, including her nose. The smell of the silky duvet cover under her nose, the sensation of being...taken, like some kind of cat in heat as she gasped for breath, afraid he was going to suffocate her by making her keep her face pressed into the bed. The way he'd slapped her ass too hard. Ripped off her clothes. Jammed himself into her while she was dry. "And it hurt, Laura. Your husband r-r-raped me." She bit her lip and closed her eyes.

Cassie gasped when Laura loomed up into her direct line of vision. She had a gun pointed straight at her head. She looked godawful, Cassie thought, as if that mattered right now.

"You are a lying whore. My Tom would never do that." She sucked in a breath. "I need to finish this. You were all way too malleable, you know? And weak. Every single one of the oversexed, horny men wanted to have me every chance they got. It was sickening. But I didn't count on little miss fertile turtle over here." She moved the gun down, pointing it at Cassie's belly. "And stupid, this one. Such a disappointment." She sighed. Cassie could make out her expression—somewhere between fury and disgust.

"I told you. The baby, it's Barrett's. I had the test." Cassie's voice cracked in terror. "But I was sick because I couldn't get the smell of...the feel of...of Tom off me."

"Yeah, yeah, whatever. Nice try, Cass. You wanted to take my husband away from me. He was weak enough to think he could leave. But hot-stuff Barrett over here wanted to take off with me. You're all so...stupid!" She screamed this last word, making Cassie flinch. "Such assholes!" Her voice got louder. She was moving forward, forcing Cassie backward into the foyer, toward the front door.

The next few seconds had the aura of a silent movie, slow motion, which allowed Cassie to follow every single moment of it. Someone rang her doorbell, which made her turn her head toward the door.

"Cassie? Barrett?" a voice said, followed by loud banging on the door. "Are you in there?"

It took her a half a second to place the voice. Ryan Murphy.

"Ryan!" she shrieked at the top of her lungs. "Help!" She lunged for the door, unlocked it, and yanked it open.

Ryan and Sai stood in the doorway. Her mind registered that Ryan was holding a baseball bat for some reason. Both were in shorts and sweatshirts.

"What the fu—" Ryan began. She turned to face him, knowing she shouldn't put Laura behind her, but needing someone to take control of this scene. Someone not her.

"It's Laura. She's hurt Barrett," she said. "She has a gun. Sh-sh-she...she...she..."

Sai grabbed her arm and yanked her, hard, out the door and onto the front lawn. Off-balance, she landed on her hip. She watched Ryan run into the house, yelling for Barrett. Sai and Emily helped her up and tugged her down the driveway. She could barely see for the tears. Couldn't hear for the ringing in her ears.

"Barrett," she managed, as they pulled her toward a police car.

What's wrong at the Coopers?" she asked someone standing next to her. "Oh, Amelia," she said, stupidly relieved. Amelia was nice and smart. She could help. But her world was going dark, her vision dimming from the outside of her vision inward. "I think...I'm going to..."

Another gunshot split the night. This time, everyone heard. The police ran toward her house. The firemen following behind them.

The blackness felt way better than the insane, blue-and-red strobing reality. So, Cassie slipped into it, Barrett's name on her lips.

Chapter Thirty-Five

V*incit*

. . . .

EIGHT MONTHS LATER...

The snow must have been falling steadily for hours by the time Amelia woke on the second Monday in January. It had turned her street into a wonderland, as it was a heavy, wet snow. The kind that sticks to anything not moving too fast and piles up, transforming the ugly, winter-bare trees into something out of a Disney movie. She moved slowly down the steps into the kitchen, looking out of every single window she passed, her smile widening.

Tyler was going to lose his mind over this. Thank goodness, Michael had been working from home and would continue to do that for a few more months. She no longer had the sort of energy required to railroad her son into layers of snow play clothes, boots, hat, gloves. The very thought of it forced her to sit down and rest before she got to the coffee maker. She stayed seated a few minutes, enjoying the music of the falling snow—it was quiet, yet, somehow, had a sound she'd always loved.

When she heard the boy jump down from his bed in his room over the kitchen, she sighed and hauled herself to her feet. "Time to make the donuts," she said under her breath as she ground fresh Kona blend coffee beans, poured them into the basket, and added a pot of reverse-osmosis filtered water. That done, she had to rest again, leaning against the tall kitchen counter she'd had renovated to her specifications.

It had been a pitched battle, but in the end, both she and Michael had compromised regarding their new home. He'd put up an admirable argument in favor of one of the gentrifying neighborhoods near downtown Detroit. She'd humored him, and the over-eager real estate agent for a few afternoon tours.

In the end, she'd stuck by her resolve, and they'd landed more or less in between the rich, white, college town and the rapidly gentrifying areas he'd wanted. After she'd presented well thought-out data supporting her thesis that they had no business poking their new money into areas that were already priced well out of reach of the original inhabitants.

A couple of years ago, she'd never in a million zillion years considered Ferndale, Michigan as her dream town, where she and Michael would raise their family, make new friends, do good for the community. But it emerged as a leading contender and ultimately where they chose to live. That had been Michael's compromise. Hers had been on the house itself.

This time, they went with a twenty-three-hundred-square-foot, 1940s-built bungalow with a large front porch and a decent fenced yard, that was in need of many dollars' worth of upgrades. She loved the precious, tree-lined street, never busy but full of families and older couples. She could walk to a small grocery store if she wanted, to the downtown area that was reviving in such a way that she pictured herself there, opening a little bookstore, maybe one with a bar that served coffee and tea until happy hour, and then local beer and Michigan-made wines.

Maybe someday.

The two-and-half months of extensive updates and renovations had taxed everyone's nerves, especially since she and Tyler had to extend their time living at her parents' house past the sale of the Connelly Court house, while Michael continued to work at his law firm in Detroit, living in one of those extended-stay places.

It had been a solid seven months of complete hell, really. But she stood by her decision to decamp from that damned cul-de-sac the day after all that shit went down. They'd spent Halloween, Thanksgiving, Christmas, New Year's, and Valentine's Day at her parents' house on Lake Michigan in Chicago. She'd had no issues with that, per se. But, of course, it had chafed Michael and with good reason. Her parents were the sort who were constantly saying things they thought were supportive and woke but were actually stupidly racist.

It had been exhausting on many levels. Plus, it had been all she could do to not imagine Michael taking off on a Thursday and hooking up with Melissa Murphy. But that was something she was dealing with, while he dealt with his own version of jealousy.

They saw a couples' therapist twice a month—someone her mother had found for them. Tyler was attending the local Montessori preschool where she volunteered once a week, or had been until recently. The house was an absolutely perfect blend of forties décor and arts-and-crafts touches combined with modern finishes and appliances and a lot more livable now that she'd increased it to almost three thousand square feet. She adored it. Even more now that they'd managed to escape from that horror show with their relationship—not to mention their lives—intact.

They liked to joke that he'd knocked her up their first night in their nice new house. But Amelia knew better. She always had a plan and knew she wanted to have a baby during the winter this time around. And that's exactly how it was going to happen.

"Mama!" Tyler rushed into the kitchen wearing only his Black Panther undies. He insisted on sleeping "like a big boy" the same way his father did. Who was she to argue about pj's vs. naked skin? "I'm hungry."

"Of course you are, my sweet. Come and give me a kiss, and I'll make you some breakfast." Tyler wrapped his arms around her neck, gave her two sloppy kisses on each cheek then ran toward the family room couch. She watched him, never more aware of the strength of her emotions toward him—her handsome, smart, loving little boy.

"Hot mama," Michael said from behind her. She grinned when he slipped his arms around her. "Looking good this morning. How're you feeling?"

"Like crap, but it'll pass. Coffee?"

"Please."

She poured him a cup then herself a half, topping it off with organic, whole milk. She'd do a lot in the name of healthy offspring, but giving up her one cup of coffee in the morning was not on that list.

"Cassie and little Henry are coming over," she said, using his shoulder as a support when she handed him his cup.

"Okay. Cool. Guess we can make snowmen or something."

"That would be nice, Michael. Thanks."

"Anything for my baby mama," he said, grabbing her hand and kissing it before letting go and running his hand around and under her protruding belly. He leaned over and kissed the taut skin on her stomach.

"Get off me, unless you have a plan to occupy him while you take me upstairs and treat me properly."

He chuckled and picked up the TV remote.

"Disney?" he asked their son.

"Disney," the boy confirmed before curling into his father's side.

• • • •

BREAKFAST DONE AND cleared away, Amelia sat sipping bland, decaf tea while Michael wrestled Tyler into the many layers required for an outdoor play session. The temperature hovered around the thirty-two mark and she wanted him in full gear, including gloves and hat and snowsuit. Thankfully she had a hall pass on the whole dressing-him-for-snow-time thing.

As they were finishing up, Cassie arrived, baby Henry in her arms, a canvas bag slung over one shoulder. "Ty!" the kid yelped, struggling to get down and race over to his buddy.

Michael laughed at them and pulled out Tyler's outgrown snow regalia then repeated the struggle with Cassie's boy.

"I've really got to stop thinking of him as baby Henry," she said, giving Cassie a quick hug and taking the containers of gluten-free snacks she'd brought.

"I know. He's huge," she said, taking one of the tall bar-height chairs. "Thanks, Michael."

"My pleasure," he said, looking up from attempting to put on Henry's snow boots. This done, he stood up, put on his boots, coat, hat, and gloves. "Let's go, guys. Snowmen wait for no man."

"Mama, we need carrots and stuff, for his face," Tyler yelled as he followed his father out onto the deck.

"I'll bring that in a minute. You guys start making one first." She sat next to Cassie with a long exhale. "Jesus. I'm beat."

"You definitely look like a woman about to pop," Cassie said with a smile. She'd filled out after Henry's somewhat-premature birth and was back to teaching yoga in her own studio now. Henry had accompanied her in his babyhood, allowing her to nurse him in between holding posture clinics and training her new group of teachers. Now, he had a nanny and stayed home more, but Amelia had convinced her to try the Montessori school's new daycare section starting in the spring.

They never talked about Janice or Allen. She felt awful about it but after that last bizarre, deadly night in the old neighborhood, Amelia had made a personal vow that she'd kept to never see or speak to either one of them again. Melissa had told her that they sold their house and moved to one of the coasts, but she honestly didn't want to know any more about them once she'd seen their grown son, dead from hanging himself, and tried to comfort Janice, to no avail.

Emily and Sai had rented their house out and headed overseas where Sai was giving lectures and teaching surgeons in India and Pakistan while Emily gave English lessons. She communicated with them via text photos Emily would send or sometimes on a Whats App call.

Melissa had sold her own house and left for her Lake Michigan house with Danny. Amelia saw her posts on Facebook and Instagram occasionally—shots of sunsets, their small strip of sandy beach, Danny with his step-sisters fishing, swimming, skiing.

Amelia and Michael had used a different Realtor from a different brokerage to sell their place, which had taken longer than they'd hoped, no surprise there, considering. But she kept up with Melissa, out of both guilt and a sense of relief.

Ryan Murphy had been cremated, after taking the full force of a bullet from Laura's illegal handgun in the chest, dying in the ambulance on the way to the hospital. Amelia had held Michael back from rushing over to Cassie and Barrett's house, thank god, otherwise he would be the dead one right now. She thought about that a lot, the many nights she lay awake, wondering about her part in all of that ridiculous and more-than-a-little-bit-embarrassing tragedy.

"Laura's got another hearing," Cassie said, picking through a bowl of trail mix Amelia had set out for them to share.

"Oh?" The thought of that woman free and walking the streets made Amelia woozy. "And what are her chances this time?"

"Pretty much nil," Cassie said, watching as Michael had a snowball battle with the little boys in the yard. "Now that her connection to A.J.'s death has been established."

"Oh right." Amelia shivered and rested her hands on top of her belly.

"She told him that week she was going to turn him in, which meant he had to then either turn on his own drug buddies or get killed by them. He decided on a different path, I guess," Cassie said, between bites of her gluten-free chocolate zucchini bread.

"Ugh. She was so..."

"Now that I think back on it, I realize that she was the instigator of most of the unnecessary bullshit on the street. She constantly pushed Janice's buttons, trying to out-alpha-female her. She had Sai and Ryan wrapped around her little finger. Barrett, too, I suppose." Cassie's expression darkened for a moment then cleared, as it usually did. The woman was relentlessly optimistic, Amelia thought. Part of why they'd become such good friends.

"There was a point that they'd do anything she wanted," Cassie said. "And then I got knocked up, and she was convinced it was Tom's—I was, too, of course. He was the only one it could've been, regardless of what Melissa or Emily thought." She reached out and grabbed Amelia's hands, gripping them tight. "Thank you for sticking by me, Ames. I needed a friend, even if I don't deserve you."

"That's half your problem right there," Amelia said, smiling at her then wincing when the baby gave her bladder a whack. "You never believe you deserve anything nice or good."

"True." They sat in silence awhile, watching the boys cavort around the yard and make zero progress on anything resembling a snowman. Amelia's heart broke for the woman, but she didn't know what she could say to make it better. She'd been raped, and kept that from everyone, including her own husband. Had almost died from being pregnant, spent months as the butt of snide commentary and slut shaming, and then Laura had broken into her house that night, sending everyone's lives into a tailspin.

The doorbell rang. "Come in," Amelia called out, too tired to think about getting back on her feet.

"Hey, guys." Barrett shook the snow off his hat and stomped it off his boots. "I'm taking a snow day, and I brought hot chocolate."

"Hey, honey," Cassie said, jumping off her barstool and taking the cup holder from him.

"Hi, Barrett," Amelia said, still running her hand absently across her belly.

"I think you're needed out in boy-land," Cassie said, pecking his cheek and pushing him toward the sliding glass door onto the deck.

"Okay, okay," he said, laughing. "Sorry for all the snow on your floor." He paused, his hand on the French door handle, his expression pained. "I have some news for you both."

"Oh?" The baby was rolling around hard now, doing somersaults and backflips and god knows what else, but it hurt. She got up to alleviate the discomfort then gasped.

"You okay, Ames?" Cassie said, her hand on Amelia's arm.

"Actually, no," she said. "I mean, I'm fine but you'd better get Michael in here. You guys still good keeping Ty for a few days? My mom's coming as soon as I call her...oh...ow!"

"Shit," Cassie said. "Barrett, go get Michael. Tell him Amelia's water broke."

Amelia stared down at her feet, feeling sluggish and stupid but unable to move or speak at the sight of the splash of fluid on the floor. "Crap," she said, when the contraction gripped her. "Yeah. Get Michael."

"On it," Barrett said, heading to the backyard while Amelia began her breathing exercises, a crucial piece of her birth plan.

• • • •

LATER, AS SHE HELD the newborn baby Zara June Ross in her arms she couldn't stop smiling. She was exhausted, but jubilant. The little girl had come into the world in line with all of Amelia's plans. They were going to have an amazing mother-daughter bond.

Michael sat next to her, his hand cradling the back of the baby's head. "I love you so hard, Ames." He kissed the baby's forehead then Amelia's cracked lips. She sighed.

"Tyler okay?" she asked, realizing with relief that a mother's love could indeed contain multitudes. It had been one of her worries in the early days of her pregnancy.

"Of course. He's in boy heaven over at Henry's place. I should go," he said when she yawned. "You get some rest and do some bonding. I'll be back in the morning. Your parents are on their way. Mine want to come by tomorrow."

She nodded, her eyes already closing as she nestled the baby against her nipple, unwilling to engage in any mine-vs-yours when it came to parental appropriateness—especially considering that she'd grown close enough to Michael's mother to realize that her mother had serious attachment issues.

Zara latched on like a champ and started tugging. "Oh wait, Michael?"

He turned at the door of the birthing suite. "Yeah?"

"What was the news Barrett had? Before all baby hell broke loose?"

"I don't want to upset you," he said, his forehead creased with a frown.

"You won't. Tell me. I need to know." She didn't. But she wanted to know, and that was more or less the same thing in her book.

He ran a hand over his lips, sighed then stuck his hands in his jeans pockets. "It's Laura Franks," he said, his voice low.

Amelia's scalp prickled, and she squeezed baby Zara too hard, making the girl squawk in protest. "What about her? I'll move out of this state if they're letting her out."

Michael held up a hand. "No need. She's dead."

"Dead." She said it in a flat voice, trying to picture that reality.

"Yes. Not sure how, but they quote-unquote *found* her that way. Probably killed herself."

"Oh." Amelia stared down into her baby girl's deep-brown eyes that were studying her with such focus it took her breath away. "Okay, then."

"I'll be back tomorrow, baby mama. You sure you're all right?"

"Yes. Hand me my phone."

He did, kissing her cheek one more time. "You did good, Ames."

"We did. But yeah, I did the heavy lifting. That's for sure."

She blew him a kiss then sent a quick, one-handed text to Cassie.

"Hey. I heard about Laura."

She got a reply in a few minutes. *"You good? Can I come see you?"* Nothing to acknowledge the fact of Laura Franks' suicide in a prison cell.

When the baby drifted to sleep, Amelia shifted in the bed to lie on her side, Zara's tiny form nestled against her. She stared at her phone's screen, contemplating her friendship with Cassie. It was complicated to say the least, since the woman had clung to her like a leech for the first few weeks post-Connelly Court's night of disaster. She'd even come out to stay at Amelia's parents' house for a while, needing a break the gunshot injury to Barrett's foot had healed and baby Henry had been released after a few days in the NICU to ensure that he was healthy despite being born four weeks early.

During that fraught time, one night they'd been sitting in front of a roaring fire, Tyler asleep on her lap, Henry asleep nearby, Michael playing chess in the other room with her father, when Cassie had blurted the truth. Amelia had guessed as much already. *I should probably write mystery novels,* she'd thought at the same time she'd given herself a mental high five for figuring it out. *How hard could it be?*

"He'd taken some of the drugs, I guess. He was woozy and out of it. I don't know. I was so...angry. I felt like I was going to die every single damn day from what he did to me. I was convinced I got pregnant that night he attacked me. The dates lined up. He was out of it, talking crazy shit about Laura wanting to kill him, thinking he'd be better off dead. And I...I just...pushed him under. He only fought me for a few seconds." She'd chewed on her lower lip, not meeting Amelia's gaze. "I killed him."

She'd said this without tears or her usual multiple apologies. And honestly, at that moment, Amelia didn't blame her a bit. Personally, she thought Cassie should've told Barrett about their neighbor attacking her. But she didn't ask for any more details, like how she'd gotten into the house without Laura or Melissa or Sai seeing her.

She wanted Cassie to be believed. Any woman who'd been raped deserved that. She planned to teach her son that no meant no this very year, before he went full time to preschool and would be tempted to put his hands on anyone who didn't want him to. It was all part of her plan for raising the sort of non-toxic man her future daughter-in-law would appreciate.

"You're safe," she'd finally said to Cassie, her body moving quickly toward sleep. "And your story is always safe with me."

She fell asleep with her perfect new baby daughter next to her, before she got Cassie's reply. It didn't matter anyway. Amelia knew that someone like innocently and naïve like Cassie needed to hear words like that. Besides, it gave her a tiny bit of an advantage, something she always sought in most relationships. She pitied women who didn't have firm plans, like she had. But she liked having them as friends. The combination of superiority and pity was a total rush.

"I love you," she whispered to her baby, who was snoozing away like an angel. "I have so much to teach you," she said, before dropping into a light doze.

. . . .

THE END.

About the author.

Liz Crowe is a Kentucky native and graduate of the University of Louisville living in South Carolina. She's spent her time as a three-continent expat trailing spouse, mom of three, real estate agent, brewery owner and bar manager, and is currently a digital marketing and fundraising consultant, in addition to being an award-winning author.

The Liz Crowe backlist has something for any reader seeking complex storylines with humor and complete casts of characters that will delight and linger in the imagination long after the book is finished.

Her favorite things to do when she's not scrolling social media for cute animal videos is walk her dogs, cuddle her cats, and watch her favorite sports teams while scrolling social media for cute animal videos.

• • • •

FOLLOW ALONG WITH LIZ online:
WEBSITE: lizcrowe.com
TIK TOK, FACEBOOK, INSTA, TWITTER/X: @lizcroweauthor

Don't miss out!

Visit the website below and you can sign up to receive emails whenever Liz Crowe publishes a new book. There's no charge and no obligation.

https://books2read.com/r/B-A-ZHTD-RHOYC

BOOKS2READ

Connecting independent readers to independent writers.